Praise for Victor McGlothin and His Novels

SINFUL TOO

"Steamy...McGlothin unravels at a relentless pace a sexy story...a shocker of a conclusion...Eric Jerome Dickey, watch out."

—*Publishers Weekly*

"A page-turner...McGlothin should be applauded for writing a sequel that stands on its own."

—*RAWSISTAZ Reviewers*

"A fast-paced novel that takes readers through twists, turns, and mouth-hanging events...I recommend this book to everyone."

—ApoooBooks.com

AUTUMN LEAVES

"Unforgettable...McGlothin has given *Autumn Leaves* a life of its own, with a compelling story line and a strong depiction of the trials and triumphs of interesting and appealing characters...He immediately draws the readers into the depths of his characters' emotions."

—*QBR*

"Credible, honest."

—*Kirkus Reviews*

more...

"An absolute page-turner...intriguing and thought-provoking."

—Kimberla Lawson Roby, bestselling author of *Too Much of a Good Thing*

"A very moving story with plenty of drama, heart-pounding action, and seriously emotional scenes."

—*RT Book Reviews*

WHAT'S A WOMAN TO DO?

"Engrossing and entertaining."

—*Booklist*

"A fast-paced, soulful, dramatic story."

—*Sunday Oklahoman*

"A talented storyteller with a knack for telling a convincing story, McGlothin manages to weave an entertaining story that may indeed ring true to many readers...[a] new and refreshing voice in the world of contemporary African-American fiction."

—*QBR*

"Four stars...a superb, true-to-life book. With a masterfully created plot, it explores the turbulent lives of three courageous women...offers a gripping emotional glimpse into the dark world of the unknown."

—*RT Book Reviews*

The *Secrets* of NEWBERRY

Also available from Victor McGlothin

Sinful Too

The *Secrets* of NEWBERRY

VICTOR McGLOTHIN

NEW YORK BOSTON

This book is a work of fiction. Names, characters, places, and incidents are the product of the author's imagination or are used fictitiously. Any resemblance to actual events, locales, or persons, living or dead, is coincidental.

Copyright © 2010 by Victor McGlothin
All rights reserved. Except as permitted under the U.S. Copyright Act of 1976, no part of this publication may be reproduced, distributed, or transmitted in any form or by any means, or stored in a database or retrieval system, without the prior written permission of the publisher.

Grand Central Publishing
Hachette Book Group
237 Park Avenue
New York, NY 10017

www.HachetteBookGroup.com

Printed in the United States of America

First Edition: June 2010
10 9 8 7 6 5 4 3 2 1

Grand Central Publishing is a division of Hachette Book Group, Inc.
The Grand Central Publishing name and logo is a trademark of Hachette Book Group, Inc.

Library of Congress Cataloging-in-Publication Data
McGlothin, Victor.
The secrets of Newberry / Victor McGlothin.—1st ed.
p. cm.
ISBN 978-0-446-17813-6
1. African Americans—Fiction. 2. Domestic fiction. 3. Family secrets—Fiction. 4. Murder—Fiction. 5. Louisiana—Fiction. 6. Nineteen fifties—Fiction. I. Title.
PS3613.C484S43 2010
813'.6—dc22

2009027124

A special thanks to Karen Thomas, Latoya C. Smith, and Carol Mackey—Three queens of New York.

1

Gin and Gamblin'

In the early spring of 1955, money sprang up from the ground for those who knew where to dig. Lively music commingled with cheerful chatter and cigarette smoke in the sprawling antebellum plantation home called Twin Cedars. The tables were hot and the beer was cold at Rudolf's illegal gambling house, which was reeling in more money than his family's cotton crops ever did. Six nights a week, the eight-bedroom gaming station in St. Bernard Parish, Louisiana, was open for business. Locals fluttered in, most of them from New Orleans. The allure of chance and fast times attracted blue bloods steeped in old money and pretenders who didn't belong. Odds were always with the house. Only fools bet otherwise.

It was nearly half past midnight when Ivory "Bones" Arcineaux's winning streak turned on him like a woman he'd done wrong. He'd had his heart set on breaking the bank when he stepped through the door in a dapper white tuxedo jacket and a fistful of money. Before Bones knew it, the wheels of misfortune relieved him of his wishful wad along with any chance of draining the bank. Nearly empty pockets relieved him of any hope to break even.

"Blackjack dammit!" Bones cursed, saliva gathering at the corners of his mouth. He tossed his fifth shot of gin down the back of his throat then wiped his sweaty forehead with a silk handkerchief from his breast pocket. "I'm goddamned due for a goddamned blackjack! Dealer, you ain't worth a two-bit hooker and a dry hump!" Bones yelped, shaking his finger at the card shuffler. Despite how badly the gambler wanted to believe he was entitled to the Twin Cedars brand of entertainment, he wasn't.

"Hey, pal," a man's voice whispered sternly. "Take it down a notch."

"Get lost!" Bones snarled before discovering the bouncer with the soft voice was twice his size.

Two hundred and fifty pounds of muscle grimaced irritably. "That's it, pal, I warned you!"

"Oh, oh...hold on now," Bones grunted repentantly. He stumbled from the table with both hands raised then scooted out onto the broad cement veranda fearing a sound thumping. At age twenty-three, Bones didn't appreciate the thought of getting reprimanded like an unruly child. Embarrassed to the point of making a stupid move, he clenched his teeth. "You wouldn't be doing this if I had a silver spoon hanging out of my ass," he griped. The bouncer looked through him as if his words didn't warrant a response.

After a fleeting thought to pick a fight sailed past, Bones sneered at the gargantuan man as he casually strolled back inside the mansion. "If you wasn't such a big hairy ape, I'd give you a run for your money," Bones ranted hastily, once his adversary was gone. "And if you wasn't..." he began to say, until something odd beckoned him to take notice. Bones witnessed a black man in a red valet jacket, the same man who'd been casing the joint through the window, sliding in and out of parked cars on the side lawn. While he didn't consider a black valet with unlimited access to the white customers' automobiles all that unusual, the way he went about it was. Bones studied him, rambling through one glove box after the next. He didn't seem to be taking anything. Instead, the valet appeared to be jotting notes on a small tablet. "Hey, you! Hey! What gives, Slick?" Bones inquired with a healthy dose of suspicion. He was surprised when the black man, about his age, looked up nervously then gazed back with a blank expression. "Hey, come over here," Bones ordered. "Come on, I ain't gonna make trouble for you."

The lanky, dark skinned man huffed as if bothered by Bones's demand as much as by his presence. "Yessuh," the valet answered, obviously annoyed by the interruption. Reluctantly, he sauntered closer to the elevated cement porch, pushing the small tablet he'd been scribbling on into his back pocket. After sizing up the dapper fellow on the veranda, the valet was sure of a few things right off. One, the bossy white man swaying on that porch was drunk. Two, he didn't try to conceal his suspicions of foul play. And three, his attempt at bullying the Negro failed miserably. While staring at Bones without trepidation, the car attendant's eyes wandered over him vigilantly. Bones's pasty skin and rusty red hair had the valet pondering a thought he dared not voice, just in case his assumptions were wrong. The gambler's outfit was stylishly tailored and his two-tone shoes appeared to be handmade. However, in the pale moonlight, the valet couldn't conclude with any degree of certainty whether the man who'd stopped him from carrying on with his business at hand was colored and passing for white or a white man with the worst head of cantankerous hair in Louisiana. Before he could mull it over any further, the wind seemed to howl out loud.

Suddenly, the nearby bushes rustled. The white man on the veranda staggered to the edge of it and peered out into the distance. His bloodshot eyes widened when he couldn't believe what they saw. "Oh, man, it's a raid!" he griped, then dove into the back of a brand-new turquoise Chevrolet convertible. "Grab baits, the jig is up!" Bones shouted. When a swarm of dark-suited federal agents ascended on the mansion like ants at a church picnic, he slouched down on the bench seat to hide. "Are you lame in the head, man? Git to gittin' so we don't get pinched with the rest of these suckers."

"Sounds good to me," the valet answered back. He swiftly leapt into the driver's seat, snatched a set of keys from the sun visor, and nervously started up the engine. As the government agents cast a dragnet to snare the houseguests, the colored man mashed down the gas pedal. The fancy car kicked gravel in every direction. Clouds of thick dust rose into the night air as the whitewall tires spun furiously. Within seconds, that flashy convertible glided across the neatly manicured lawn like it was skating on ice. Agents hollered and sputtered when the car fishtailed, heading toward the back of the estate.

"Git gone, boy! Git gone!" Bones cheered. "Whoo-hoo!"

Bones's getaway driver dodged a bevy of police cars moving in to surround the parking lot. He sped through the back pasture and onto a farm road, praying the lawmen were too busy rounding up Rudolph's high-toned crowd to chase down a nobody Negro and his liquored-up passenger. When it appeared the coast was clear, the rattled wheelman flicked a wicked glance over his right shoulder. His heart pounded like a deep bass drum while the man in the backseat cackled riotously.

"Hey!" the driver yelled. "I'm glad one of us thinks almost getting nabbed is a hoot. Seeing as how this here was your idea, you mind telling me where we going?"

Bones eased back against the leather upholstery to catch his breath. "Huh? Oh, home, James," he replied with a hearty yawn. "Make a left at the next fork and then keep on the back roads for about six miles. When you come to the bayou, take the bridge toward town. Wake me up when we hit Canal Street."

Studying the rearview mirror, the valet frowned angrily. "That rusty-headed skinflint sure do bark out orders like a white man," he said under his breath. "I'll grant him that."

For three miles, the brand-new convertible floated along the dusty unpaved pathway. Dense fog began to rise from the marsh as the Chevrolet rounded the bend. The colored man stopped the automobile to survey a crusty patch of southern Louisiana he hadn't set eyes on before. He raised himself up to sit on the top of the front bench seat. Herds of mossy trees cast a canopy over the road, stifling their path. Other than the high-beam lights shining straight ahead, pitch-blackness seemed to be closing in. Bullfrogs bellowed in the distance. Crickets chirped insistently. The scene was eerily unnerving, even for a backwoods country boy. When the driver considered turning the automobile around, he glanced at the passenger, who was asleep, stretched out, and snoring like a three-hundred-pound baritone. "I can't see up ahead through this swamp gas, mistah," he admitted wearily. "This can't be the way you told me and I can't hardly make out the road or nothing."

"Stop bothering me now," Bones mumbled slovenly. "Just keep straight and make a left. Hurry up. Be quick about it. I'm hungry and..." he added before falling off to sleep again.

The valet shook his head. His eyes darted back and forth across the field of uncertainty stretched out in front of him. "This some bullshit," he smarted back, "got me out here in the middle of nowhere. I'd be a might better off going to jail." He grunted and huffed, easing his skinny butt back down into the front seat. "Hell, I might as well go on up yonder another mile or so, but you got to wake up, mistah. Mistah?" he called out again, only to be answered by another chorus of snores and snorts.

Against his better judgment, the colored driver followed Bones's instructions to the letter. He kept on up the road then took the first left he came to. It wasn't long before he realized that was his second mistake; agreeing to go along with the irritating gambler was the first. "Ohhh, mistah? Missstaaah!" he yelled, clutching the steering wheel with both hands as the shiny convertible sailed off a wooden embankment. The Chevrolet splashed nosefirst into a shallow pond.

Bones slammed against the floorboard with a powerful thud. His eyes flew open wildly. He craned his neck to peek over the rise of the back passenger-side door. "What's the matter with you?" he complained irritably. "You done wrecked this fine classy car, and we ain't even close to Canal Street."

"Sorry I tore up your car, mistah," the driver apologized half-heartedly.

"This wasn't none of my car," Bones quickly informed him.

"Good, 'cause I wasn't really sorry."

Bones panned the area cautiously. "You could've kept it dry, though."

The black man casually untied his shoes then began to roll up his pant legs. "Oomph, tell me something I don't know. *You* was the one who talked us both right into the middle of the damned swamp. It was *you* who got us dumped waist-deep in gator piss."

"Yeah, but it was me who got us both out of those feds' mitts, too, remember that?" Bones fussed.

"Yep, I do, and that's why I'm willing to let it pass. Seeing as how I ain't locked up in no parish jail tonight coupled with the simple fact that this here ain't none of my damned expensive anchor parked in the water, I'm in a frame of mind to call it even."

Bones shot a stinging glare at him before the man's audacity forced a smile onto his thin lips. "Huh! Call it even?" he bellowed. "You're some kind of different pal, some kind of different, indeed."

"We'd better get out of this tuna can," the valet reasoned as he balled up his red jacket and flung it farther out into the water. He sighed when he heard it splash.

Finding it a peculiar way to shed his uniform, Bones questioned, "What'd you do that for?"

"To distract the alligators whilst I make a run for it," he answered, dipping one leg into the pond. "They's out there and they's onto us by now."

After Bones watched his chauffeur's quick jaunt toward the shore, he gulped then pulled a black long-barreled pistol from his belt. "Hey, fella, wait up!" Bones pleaded anxiously. "I'm allergic to alligators."

Both men tramped down the dirt farm road en route to New Orleans and away from the stalled Chevy. Bones didn't happen to see any bayou wildlife to speak of, but that didn't stop him from following closely behind this headstrong Negro he was growing fond of. "Hey, fella, what's your handle?"

"My which?"

"What's your name?" Bones cackled.

"Name's Hampton Bynote," he answered rapidly with a tinge of French dripping from his tongue when he said it.

"A tough guy like you must have a street handle," Bones concluded. "So, what do they call you?"

"They call me who I am. Hampton Bynote," he answered

again, failing to understand why he had been asked the same question twice.

"Okay, Hampton. That last name of yours, how you spell it, case I want to look you up later?"

"B-y-n-o-t-e. They say that there *t* near the end is silent."

"They're right," the white man agreed. "That there *t* don't say nothing at all. Where you from, Hampton Bynote? Wait, let me guess. Tremé, Backatown, Marigny?" Bones mentioned three of the four major neighborhoods where most blacks had settled in New Orleans.

Confused by his companion's compulsion to chitchat, Hampton cut his eyes sharply. "'Round about Newberry," he offered cautiously.

Bones's smile returned when he heard that. He was familiar with the small farming community about fifteen miles west of town. "Yeah, I knew they grew tall cane in Newberry, but now I see they raise high-minded jigs with a keen sense of swagger, too." He hadn't noticed that Hampton was carrying two fists then. "Ahh, that's it. *Swagger*, that suits you down to that *t* that don't make a peep," Bones announced with a great deal of pride. "My friend Swagger. How'd that sound to you?"

Hampton continued his lengthy stride in damp trousers, broken-in leather shoes, and squishy cotton socks. "How'd you feel about this jig thumping you down to the dirt?" he answered sharply.

"I'm sorry, I meant no offense. I thought we're friends or at least on the mend," Bones said, smooth and regretfullike. "What you say we forget it and let bygones be bygones?"

"Don't matter to me. I don't plan on setting eyes on you no more after tonight. I'm done with you, mistah. Ever since you called on me, feels like I stepped in quicksand."

"No, no, don't say that, Swagger. No way," Bones fussed. "I found you and I'm keeping you, as a friend, I mean. There's a ton of money to be made in Nawlins. I'm all but certain that my know-how put together with the tablet in your back pocket can help fetch us a pile of it."

"All but certain, huh?" Hampton questioned. "I ain't been all but certain about a damned thing since you dove into the back of that Chevy and started sparking loud for me to burn out of that lot. Only thing I do know is *some kind of different* fits you like a pair of broke-in shoes."

"Who, me?" said Bones, shrugging his narrow shoulders. "No, I'm as regular as rain. Ivory's the name, Ivory Arcineaux."

Hampton eyed the man curiously then smirked. "I knew a fella once with the same name. What, a tough guy like you got no street handle?" he chided, using the same reasoning thrown at him earlier.

"Bones," he said quickly, as if being quizzed. "People who know me best call me Bones."

"Bones, now that suits you right fine." Hampton nodded assuredly because of the man's fair complexion. "Answer this for me, Bones. See, something I've been figuring on hadn't added up since the minute you hollered down at me from that veranda back at Twin Cedars."

Bones grinned knowingly. "Go ahead, shoot."

Hampton stopped on a dime. "Like I was saying, I've been stuck on it so I hope you don't take no offense. Can't say I ever seen many men quite such as yourself. My question being... is you colored or is you white, 'cause I can't rightly factor out either account."

With a thorough appreciation for Hampton's unabridged candor, Bones laughed before answering. "Swagger, the honest truth is, I've always found myself caught somewhere between the two."

Considering the man's answer carefully, Hampton nodded again, only slower than before. "Well, ain't that something, you and me got the same problem," he replied, guessing how the man's unusual complexion must have drawn considerable unwarranted attention his way as well. Hampton extended his hand to seal their acquaintance. "I don't like people trying to tie me down to what they think I ought to be, neither. Glad to know you, Bones. Glad to know you."

Bones gripped Hampton's palm then quickly dipped into a moneymaking proposition. "All right then, it's like this. We hit a few of those spots you have written down in that book of yours before they get sprung from the clink in the morning. We split everything down the middle, minus my expenses, of course."

Hampton had no idea what expenses were, but it sounded close enough to even so he agreed with a heavy disclaimer. "It's a deal, but just in case you all breath and britches I'ma need you to hear me clear. If you ever crawfish on a caper we pull together, white man or not, it's gonna get real gritty between us."

Bones swallowed hard. He understood how deadly serious the Negro was so he took him at his word. "All right, and you can expect the same in return. Agreed?"

"Yeah, agreed."

2

Bayou Blues

The morning sun peeked over the Mississippi River when Bones pulled his car onto the soft shoulder of the dirt road leading back to the Twin Cedars Casino. He didn't have to explain why it wouldn't bode well to be seen giving a black man a lift in his car that early in the morning. Besides, Bones was aptly concerned about being publicly connected to his new protégé in the presence of other white people, on general principle, not to mention their unlawful business association. After he and Hampton had robbed three of the homes on the list using the car registrations he'd gathered the night before, Bones yearned for a familiar bed to crawl into with his share of their score, plus expenses, of course. Hampton agreed to take his cut in loose cash and silk handkerchiefs he'd stumbled on during the second heist. Bones had no problem with fencing the lion's share of their loot with a number of shady pawnshop owners near the French Quarter. Since Hampton wasn't allowed to transact that sort of business with the unscrupulous white men dealing in fencing stolen goods, he didn't care how much money his new partner received for his bag of diamond rings and assorted fancy jewelry. Cash in hand was his perfect idea of a sure thing. He waved good-bye to Bones with a wad of folding money. In one night, Hampton came into enough of it for two months' rent if he had half a mind to sit on it awhile. However, a swollen knot of greenbacks had a way of burning a hole in his pocket.

Hampton climbed into his secondhand jalopy parked at the rear of the mansion. He stretched his long arms then yawned toward the sky. Bones left a trail of dust down the winding road toward the city. Hampton frowned, wishing he was headed that way as well. The one thing stopping him was the phone call he'd received from his sister, Pearl Lee, demanding he make his way out to see her as soon as he was able. There was something she had to tell him, something that needed to be said in person. Hampton pulled onto the same road Bones traveled along, only he was driving off in the opposite direction to a place he despised almost as much as he cherished it, the Delacroix Plantation he once called home.

During the fifteen-mile drive along the scenic Terrebonne Bayou road, Hampton's mind traveled back in time to an era when his entire family shared a one-room shack and his life was in an incomparable and continual state of bliss. He felt good about seeing his folks when racing along the bayou. Hordes of mighty oak and moss trees lined the waterway where he'd spent countless hours swimming as a rambunctious child. Before learning that his father had been crushed to death in a sugar mill accident, Hampton imagined running just as wild as the Terrebonne. As a twelve-year-old youth, suddenly fatherless and alarmingly fearless, he couldn't manage to sit still for the time it took to catch his breath. In the midst of a difficult time deep in the tumultuous South, his mother's unrivaled love kept a roof over his head. A brutal attack at the hands of the only white man he ever truly respected kept Hampton's chest swelled with hate. Like a moth drawn to a flame, he often returned to visit his family and to a constant reminder why he had to leave them when he did.

Hampton maneuvered his rusty old blue clunker down a farm road separating mountainous two-story homes with monumental columns, extending from the ground upward of forty feet, supporting vast sprawling roofs and broad piazzas surrounding the entire second floor. He hadn't once taken the time to notice the magnificent splendor along the corridor of mansions because, although a mere stone's throw from the former slave village where he'd lived for most of his life, they weren't ever a part of his world. Palatial homes, black servants, and wealthy white landowners lording over them wasn't nearly as picturesque from the inside looking out. The Delacroix estate wasn't any exception.

Hampton always got a knot in the pit of his stomach when he soared over the wooden bayou bridge leading to the five-hundred-acre plantation where Spanish moss draped over trees nearest the water, flowers bloomed in the gardens of the eight-room mansion, and calm winds sighed ever so gently. The scenery changed severely as Hampton traveled a quarter mile past the main house. Rows of old one-room shacks in poor condition greeted him. Then unrelenting poverty turned a blind eye.

Hampton pulled behind a large cargo truck with an assortment of household furnishings tied onto it. Suddenly, the truck began to roll back toward him. Hampton leaned on the horn. "Hey, man, watch it!" he yelled from the driver's-side window. He wiped his brow when the truck jerked forward, then he squinted at the dust-covered license plate. "South Carolina?" Hampton mouthed quietly. "Oomph, they must be lost." Hampton drove onto the grass beside the monstrous vehicle loaded with stained mattresses, bed frames, end tables, and chairs stacked nearly one story high. The driver was a colored man who appeared to have fallen asleep at the controls. A small child sat on his lap wrestling with the steering wheel. He didn't pay any attention to the man parked on the lawn. The boy was too busy pretending. "Hey, mistah!" Hampton yelled, hoping to wake the older man too tired to keep his eyes open. "Hey! You lost? Hey!"

Eventually, the truck driver shook off the sleep he'd longed for in order to investigate what all the noise was about. "Yeah, what is it?" he shouted back.

Hampton crawled out of his car then walked to the front of the truck. A closer look revealed that the narrow-faced man had not only packed everything his family owned, he'd loaded up the family, too. It appeared that the man had uprooted his wife and four children, all the shade of coffee beans and flat worn-out from their journey. "Seems to me you's lost," Hampton told him. "You's a might far from South Carolina, too. Take a wrong turn?"

The fellow shot a cautious stare at the young man standing near everything he held dear. He noted Hampton seemed to have an easy way about him, but his clothes were meant to be worn within the city limits. "What makes you think I'm misguided?"

"Well, most folk who pick up and haul down here from the Carolinas are usually bound for Nawlins. That's another dozen miles or so." Hampton almost smiled when the little boy on his papa's lap sneered at him with his tongue poking out. "Nice youngun you got there."

"Don't mind him, he don't cotton to strangers much," answered the father.

After considering how he might have felt after being on the road for days on end, a bright smile burst through Hampton's lips. "Can't say I blame him," he admitted. "I'd be glad to point you back to the main road if you like."

The older man's face softened for the first time following a bit of Louisiana hospitality. "Much obliged, but this here is where we's headed. We come down to work the sugarcane crops. We heard tell there was free room and board at that. I got this letter from a man named Trotter Delacroix saying we's welcome to sharecrop as long as we want." He flashed a wrinkled handbill to authenticate his claims.

Because of what Hampton knew about the sharecropping institution, he took pity on the man whose luck had obviously forsaken him. "Well, I'd debate you over the free room and board, but as you can see, there's a heap of work to be had. I'm Hampton Bynote. My people stay on the back row nearest the big house. When you get settled, ask around for Toussaint Baptiste, he'll give the lowdown. You can trust his word." Hampton deliberated over coming right out and telling him that he'd probably be better off heading the other way. A truck overloaded with desperation and six mouths to feed convinced Hampton to keep his two cents to himself. He couldn't know the things that family had left behind, but it was obvious that hope wasn't one of them.

"Much obliged, Hampton," the family man told him. "It'll be good seeing you around. Name's Buck Ravenell." Before he'd given Hampton a chance to tell him how unlikely that would be, Buck cranked the motor and rubbed his boy on the crown of his head, then he casually started on his way.

Moments later, Hampton pulled off the dirt road in front of his mother's cottage and tried to relate to Buck's handful of responsibilities. The knot in his belly tightened when he realized it was despair he saw on the man's face. He was resolved never to wear the same expression on his. Hampton kept that in mind while dealing with his own immediate concern, an urgent summons from his older sister, Pearl Lee.

Before climbing the wooden steps to the front door, Hampton rubbed his stomach. The anxious knot was still there, only now surrounded by a powerful hunger for the grits and pork sausage he knew would be awaiting him. The bowed planks creaked as he landed on the raised porch sitting atop a wooden frame hammered into the ground. "Come on in, Hamp," his sister's voice beckoned from the inside.

Hampton turned the rusty metal knob then pushed the door open. "How'd you know it was me?" he asked with a labored smile.

"It couldn't be nobody but you driving that loud jalopy out there," she answered. Her beautiful eleven-month-old daughter squirmed restlessly to be put down.

"See what you done?" Pearl Lee snickered. "Odessa loves your dirty drawers. Go on to him then, ungrateful child." Pearl Lee, twenty-four years old and married for more than three of them, was taller than the average woman with a rich complexion the color of molasses. Thick wild hair ran halfway down her back. She wasn't all that particular about styling it because of the work she did in the plantation's washhouse. Heat, sweat, and humidity fought mightily against any hairdo she did manage. Ultimately, it proved futile to fight back, so Pearl Lee quit trying altogether. Her eyes were big, brown, and set close together. Her lips were full and perfectly shaped. There was nothing pretty about Pearl Lee independently but everything came together nicely, making her an oddly attractive woman. "See if you can get her to eat, Hamp," she said, gesturing at him with a carefree flip of her hand.

"Sure, I'll give it a try." Hampton held out his arms when the baby took one calculated step and then another. "Heyyy, Odessa. Come on over here with Uncle Hamp. How long she been wobbling around like this, Pearl Lee?"

"Near about two weeks, but you'd know better if you was to come by more often," she quipped.

"I come by enough to know who this child's favorite uncle is."

"Because you're her only one. Now hold her a spell. She's been fussy since..." she started to say then held her tongue. "Just try to put something in her mouth that don't get spat out." Pearl Lee wrung her hands together nervously.

Hampton caught the tip of her thought but waited until she was ready to come out with the rest of it. "That sounds good to me. Is there enough grub for the feeder, too?" he asked, sniffing the air.

Pearl Lee glided to the right side of the front room where the wood-burning stove, sink, and kitchen table were situated in a cramped space. She reached above the stovetop to get a plate covered with wax paper. "Now tell me, have you ever come around not expecting to shove your face in some of my good cooking? If this don't get it, I made groceries so there's plenty to be put on."

The plate she slid on the table was stacked high with scrambled eggs, grits, and sausage patties. Hampton grinned. Odessa grabbed a handful of eggs, stuffed them in his mouth then did likewise to her own. "Pearl Lee, this child is a mind reader. She must have picked it up from Toussaint's side of the family." Hampton's brother-in-law came from a long line of fortune-tellers, voodoo priests, and charmisses. Although he never claimed to possess spiritual powers himself, it was widely believed that Toussaint's gift was charming the ladies. "To speak of, where is that slick husband of yours?"

"Trotter Delacroix come by this morning asking all the men over to the sugar mill. Said something about fixing a new filter or strainer or something 'nother he bought."

"Hmmm, fixing it? I thought you said it was new."

"Uh-uh, those was Trotter's words."

Hampton forked sausage into his mouth then chewed on it awhile. "Maybe it's just new to him," he reasoned. "He's the one man I know who'll spend a thousand dollars on a fine automobile and less on secondhand tools that put his workers in harm's way." Hampton didn't care for the plantation owner's son. He despised the fact that Trotter tried to bed Pearl Lee when they were younger. He actually meant to beat every ounce of the lust out of the white boy once. Hampton figured the sound trouncing must've taken hold because he hadn't seen Trotter making eyes at his sister since. But it was like Pearl Lee said, Hampton would have known better had he come by more often.

Pearl Lee thought it necessary to share what she'd been holding back and the reason she'd begged him to make the trip. "Hamp, I thought you ought to know that Mama's been sickly lately. She hadn't rested enough to serve this morning. I didn't know how to tell you, but it's awful bad." Rayletta, Hampton's mother, had served breakfast to the Delacroix household just about every day since she was sixteen. She was very proud of it and often made a fuss when anyone suggested she take a day off.

"She ain't at the big house?" Hampton asked as his chest swelled with anxiety. Since wild horses couldn't keep Rayletta from looking after the head family's meals, he reasoned she had something stronger than wild horses holding her down. "Where is she?"

"Still at home in bed, I expect." Hampton sat the baby on the floor then leapt from his chair. "Don't get riled up," Pearl Lee said to calm him down. "I checked already. She was asleep." Watching her brother deal with their mother's unexpected illness was just as painful as it was for her. Because Hampton had no wife or children, Rayletta was the most important thing on earth.

Hampton fought off several nasty accusations all crowding his throat. Panicked flames of emotion danced in his eyes. "How long you known?"

"Hamp, I didn't stumble on it until the other day when I found a pill bottle from one of those colored city doctors in her stocking drawer. I called and talked to this lady over there who told me that sort of medicine was for soothing terrible pains. I saw Mama hunched over a few days before that, but she told me it was just something she ate." Pearl Lee didn't know what cancer was or how to explain that it was eating at her mother's intestines.

Hampton paced the worn and uneven floor with his head bowed. "Why didn't she just call on Toussaint's great-aunt, Madame Baptiste? She took care of our ailings since I can remember."

What Pearl Lee had to offer next took the most to say. "Uh-uh. Can't no medicine woman voodoo priestess revile Mama's sickness. It's deep down in her gut. Mr. Delacroix carried her over to Nawlins hisself. He sat in the colored waiting room half the day until the test came in."

"Delacroix? That devil did what?" Hampton couldn't believe his ears. "I can't see him sitting in no doctor's wait room, much less a colored one."

"You know how him and Mama was close when they come up together. Grandpapa was friends with the Mister's daddy just like you and Trotter used to be. Our families have been together since the beginning of Broussard Parish."

"Yeah, them in that big house and us in these matchboxes," he argued.

"Matters not what you think about my home. I'm happy here. I was born here and I'm gonna die here like our daddy did and his before him."

"Well, that might suit you, but it ain't near about good enough for me." Hampton was breathing fire. His mother was prescribed pills to curb her pain. He had just been reminded that his family was still living the slightest cut above slavery. Fire within his chest stoked when someone knocked at the door. "If that's Trotter Delacroix doubling back to catch you alone, so help me I'll kill him on the spot!" Hampton raced to the door and flung it open. There was a teenage girl standing there with an armful of books. He eyed her long plaid skirt and two-tone saddle shoes.

"Sorry to bother y'all," the shaken girl said, rocking back on her heels. "I'm here to study with Pearl Lee."

Hampton stepped aside to let the young lady pass. He shrugged his shoulders at Pearl Lee as if to ask for an explanation. His sister marched over to welcome her pupil inside. "This is Magnolia. She's down here to work from Virginia, a place called Prince Edward County, what's like a parish." His peculiar leer begged for additional information as he focused on the girl's books. "They decided to close school up there for a while, so Magnolia's catching up on her learning."

"She look a touch too old for book studying," Hampton challenged. "How long they close them schools up there, anyhow?"

Pearl Lee looked at Magnolia for an answer. "Shoot, girl, I don't know everything."

"Since 1953," Magnolia replied in a timid voice. "They ain't, I mean they *haven't*, had schooling for colored children going on two years now. When I heard Pearl Lee taught others to read, I figured she could help me do better, too."

Hampton didn't know what to believe then. "You saying a whole parish cut out learning for colored children all that time?" Magnolia nodded shamefully that it was true.

"Yes, sir." She reasoned that the national news about her hometown had somehow skipped the *Newberry Gazette*.

"Don't waste your sirs on him," said Pearl Lee. "That's just my li'l brother, Hampton."

"Pleased to meet you, Hampton," Magnolia offered in a coy schoolgirl manner that had something else lurking behind it. That embarrassed Hampton. She didn't have the wherewithal to be carrying on like she knew what she was doing.

"Yeah, nice meeting you, uhhh...?" Just that quickly he'd forgotten her name.

"Magnolia," she replied cheerfully. "Holiday, like the famous singer."

Hampton cut his eyes at Pearl Lee then back at her youthful pupil. "Like *Billie* Holiday? I don't see no resemblance. Y'all do whatever. Pearl Lee, I'ma be over at Mama's. I've got to try and sort this out."

3

Secrets to Keep

Unwittingly, Hampton slammed the door behind him. He was frustrated and unsettled. Other than an occasional head cold, his mother was as healthy as a horse. The mere thought of her being ill to the point of seeking conventional health care from an authentic doctor floored him. Roots, herbs, voodoo charms, and prayers from the local Catholic priest had served as sufficient remedies up until then. As if that wasn't enough to cast credible fears, Mr. Ransom Delacroix having taken the day off to personally drive Rayletta into town suggested she was near death or worse.

Hampton opened the door and called out for his mother. When she didn't answer, concern devoured him. "Mama! You here, Mama?" he hollered again, his heart racing. Hampton was beginning to feel light-headed until he saw a new pantyhose wrapper sitting on top of the trash pile in the metal pail by the old wooden table in the kitchen. Immediately, he rushed to the large washtub sitting beside the stove and looked into it. There was a single drinking glass and a small saucer with crumbs from a piece of pound cake. Hampton didn't have to speculate on what all of it meant. He was sure as the sun was shining, his mother had gotten dressed, drunk her customary glass of milk, and eaten a slice of cake before climbing the grassy hill to serve someone else their breakfast.

Suddenly, the door flew open. Pearl Lee stood there with her hand over her heart. "I heard you shouting," she bellowed, scared to ask what all of his fussing was about but feeling compelled to nonetheless. "Where's Mama?" she whispered, much softer now. Pearl Lee barely heard the words she'd given life. Hampton didn't reply. Instead, he stared right through her before heading out the door. "Where you going, Hamp?" Pearl Lee begged, recognizing that hauntingly blank expression saddled on his face.

"Move now," he barked, shoving his sister aside. "That man's got my mama working in that house of his and you saying she's been sick as all get out."

"What you gonna do, Hampton?" she squealed desperately.

Magnolia eased behind her tutor after watching their awkward exchange. She watched Hampton's powerful strides as he marched up the hill toward the enormous plantation house. "Where's he off to?" she asked quietly.

Pearl Lee folded her arms across her full breasts and sighed heartily. "More than likely to get all of us into some big trouble," Pearl Lee answered. "Come on. We got to find Toussaint." The ladies skirted up the dirt road leading to the main warehouses used for housing a commissary and heavy machinery.

Hampton was huffing mad by the time he reached the top of the hill. As he approached the rear of the mansion, his brother-in-law came running through the tall grass a few hundred yards off. Toussaint's voice was so faint in the distance that it had little effect on Hampton, who barreled through the back door. He stomped past several female servants catching a snack between chores in a room no bigger than a closet.

"Hey, boy, where you think you goin'?" fired one of the older women from the house staff. Mrs. Kittleston was over seventy years old. Her duties had dwindled to pouring coffee and juice in the main dining hall. However, she felt it her responsibility to save the young colored man from himself. Black men were never allowed in the big house, under any circumstances. The Mister didn't want to be concerned with having colored men near his wife and daughters.

"Don't go getting in my way, Mrs. Kittleston," Hampton replied harshly. He searched the rooms frantically until overhearing familiar chatter emanating deeper within the vast dwelling. Hampton found Rayletta in her full working attire, doubled over in the dishwashing nook off the main kitchen. He noted her white stockings and black serving skirt, blouse, and apron. He paused to catch his breath when nothing he saw made a lick of sense. "Mama, what's going on?"

Rayletta was so shocked to hear her son's voice in that house, she popped straight up in the middle of the biggest laugh she'd had all month. "Hampton? Boy, what's gotten into you? Ain't no colored men supposed to be in here. You knowed that since—well, since forever." Her wide eyes darted back and forth to Mr. Delacroix and her foolish man-child. Rayletta was only forty-five and usually very fit, but she had begun packing on pounds lately. There were also flickers of gray sprouting at her temples.

Hampton measured her sudden changes as if he hadn't seen her in years. He had also heard what she said and the tone she'd used, but none of it registered. "Mama, I heard you was carried all the way to Nawlins to see a doctor, then I find you putting on for," Hampton ranted before Rayletta's pleading eyes warned him to stop talking altogether.

"Sorry M-m-missstaaah Ransom," she stammered nervously, using the man's first name as she did on occasion. "The boy's just scared for me is all. He'll be going now."

"Hampton," Ransom Delacroix said in a manner void of emotion. The Mister was a farmer, tall with spindly legs and a thickening trunk. For a man in his early fifties, he was still as tough as nails and twice as rigid when he felt the need to be. He stood three feet from Hampton in his faded blue jeans and cowboy boots, waiting on him to heed his mother's advice. "She's right, son, ain't no colored men nor any other have a right to be in my house unless I say so."

"See there, Hampton, all is forgiven," said Rayletta. "I'm not as sick as I thought. I'm fine, really. Let's talk about this outside." The woman smiled sorely then began pushing her son toward the direction he came in, through the back door. "In all my life," she screeched, "I ain't never seen such a willful child."

"I made twenty-two last year. I ain't been a child in a long while, Mama," argued Hampton as they passed by the colored cooks and dishwashers. Rayletta wasn't in the mood to continue their argument. She drew back her hand and slapped the taste out of Hampton's mouth.

"Don't you ever disrespect me or Mistah Ransom like that again! You hear me?" she growled. "He's been good to us, you and me. Don't you forget that. You owe him at least the respect of not barging in his home uninvited."

"I don't owe the *Mister* a damned thing, Ma." Before Hampton managed to finish his thought, Rayletta had gone across his face again with the back of the same hand as before.

"Lawd, please help me before I hurt this boy," she cried,

viewing Hampton's actions as incorrigible and ungrateful. "Son, you got to learn."

"She's right about that, Hampton," Toussaint agreed. He cut his eyes at Mr. Delacroix's on the other side of the kitchen window. Toussaint had sprinted the distance of two football fields after getting word from his wife that Hampton was liable to start an uprising.

"Hell, naw, man. Let me be!" Hampton barked furiously. "I got to know what business my mama got bowing and shuffling with a doctor's drugs running through her."

Trotter Delacroix roared up in his pickup truck then slammed on the brakes. He hopped out and strutted to the rear entrance with a rifle in hand. He hadn't seen black men that close to his house unless they were repairing it. The scene was extremely unnerving to him. "What's going on?" he yapped, like a small dog pretending to be a much larger one. True to form, Trotter was playing the big shot. Next to his father, the spoiled young man couldn't cast his own shadow.

Hampton forced Toussaint out of his way like he'd done to Pearl Lee. Her husband was stronger but she had him on the stubborn end by a long shot. "I know you'd better get that goddamned rifle out of my face if you don't want it broke over your head," Hampton grunted at Trotter. "I come to see about my ma, but now that I'm here, we can pick up that game of uncle we never got around to finishing." Hampton grinned when it appeared that Trotter took the bait. He was prepared to hand his weapon to Toussaint. It had been four years since Hampton goaded the white boy his age into a bare-knuckled street fight then commenced to beat him to a pulp.

"Trotter!" his father yelled from the now raised window. "Get in here, and I mean right this minute!" Mr. Delacroix's son was a handsome young man. At twenty-four, thin and fair-haired, he had become engulfed by the privileges provided by his family's wealth. The Mister loved his son and once held a special place in his heart for Hampton as well. That lopsided game of uncle, and the excessive cuts and bruises Trotter endured, changed all that. "Hampton!" Mr. Delacroix yelled from the rear doorway. "You're no longer welcome here. Rayletta, Toussaint, and Pearl Lee, they's all abiding and can stay as long as they like, but you got to go!" Mr. Delacroix grabbed the gun from his son's hands. His nostrils flared like an angry bull's. "Don't make me have to say it again or we'll all be sorry."

Hampton didn't back up. The elder Delacroix was different from his son. He had the look of cold-blooded murder in his eyes. To save face alone, that white man would pull the trigger if the staunch Negro didn't back down. Hampton was a lot of things but not the kind of man who'd suffer to have his own mother watch him get splattered all over the back porch.

"Go on now," Rayletta said in a subdued tone. "You heard Mistah Ransom. This is his land. We all got to abide by what he say." As Hampton passed her, Rayletta grabbed his arm. "What's gotten into you? You just like your papa."

"I remember when that used to mean something to you." Hampton jerked his shirtsleeve away from her grasp. He was certainly out of line, but he'd concluded the way Rayletta stuck up for her boss was inexcusable. "And I can do without you choosing another man's side over mine," Hampton added bitterly. He took one step toward the cottages where his car was parked when a gunshot sounded off behind him. He glared at a puff of dust rising near his shoes. Having hunted with the Mister, Hampton was sure that the bullet didn't miss him accidentally. He kept his feet planted while peering over his shoulder.

"If you ever treat your mama like that again, I'll put one through that black heart of yours," Delacroix promised him. "She's too good for that, even from her own son."

"Ransom!" a woman's voice shouted in a way that gave him pause. It was the Mister's wife, a pleasant woman with light-colored hair and attractive features. She was rarely seen outside the house unless she was entertaining on the veranda or going to town for department store shopping. She valued her alabaster complexion above most everything else, except for tall glasses of mint juleps on ice, spiked with an extra shot of brandy. The Louisiana sun had proven to be hell on both. The Missus gathered herself then stepped over the doorway threshold. "Enough, Ransom. That's enough for today." Like a trained puppy, he returned to the house without voicing a single utterance in opposition to her demand.

Hampton didn't have to witness it to be assured that his mother's eyes were cast toward the ground when Mrs. Jennifer Ann Delacroix was addressing her husband. He'd seen it countless times as a child. *Some things would never change*, Hampton thought, speeding from the plantation.

With that in mind, a strange idea picked at him. For just how long he couldn't tell, but something stood between Mrs. Jennifer Ann, her husband, and Rayletta; something deeper than an occasional laugh in the dining hutch. Perhaps it was Mr. Delacroix's personal interest in Rayletta's health. Whatever the case, a disturbing predicament had reeled each of them in and hadn't begun to let go. All three were snagged on the same fishhook, pretending not to notice the other two.

Toussaint paced furiously around the small living room area of his cottage. He'd seen his share of men fighting over everything from dirty looks to borrowed money and he didn't care two ways about either. The episode he witnessed behind the big house had him stirring on the inside. He was at odds with the man he was and the one he knew he'd never amount to. Angry and envious, Toussaint understood why Hampton put his life at risk by standing up for the only woman worth turning his whole world upside down. Toussaint was admittedly jealous because of his own lack of selfless admonition. Hampton was made in his father's image, Toussaint was cut from a thinner cloth altogether.

Pearl Lee sat at the table with Magnolia. They attempted to continue with the young woman's studies of state capitals, but Toussaint's excessive stomping made that impossible. "Toussaint!" Pearl Lee shouted finally. "We can't get nothing done over here as long as you keep striding a path in the floor."

"What else can I do, Pearl Lee? Your brother stood up to them Delacroix like we all should have been doing for years. He's got some kind of fire, that Hampton. Maybe I shouldn't have held him off of Trotter's ass."

"Toussaint Baptiste, if you don't watch your mouth in front of this girl..." Pearl Lee protested.

"I'm eighteen," Magnolia quickly asserted, her eyes locked onto Toussaint's mouth. Pearl Lee's husband was twenty-six, had an average build, a tanned complexion, soft Creole features with thick black wavy hair. He was easy to look at, all of him. "What Toussaint's saying ain't of no offense to me. I've heard a heap worse."

Pearl Lee snapped back with her hands raised. "Well, that ain't no excuse. You get back to your lesson."

"I already know the capitals of mostly all the states in this book," said Magnolia, like a child who wanted further into an adult conversation. "What I don't know is why Hampton jumped up against a white man with a gun. Isn't he scared of dying or nothing?"

"Hush, girl," Pearl Lee warned. "Toussaint's just making a racket over nothing when he ought to let it pass."

The steam building up in his throat came hissing out. "You only saying that because I won't go up against that jackleg agreement they been holding over us, if I had to."

Magnolia's mouth watered then. "Was it because of some agreement? Is that what got Hampton so mad?"

"I thought I told you to hush," Pearl Lee insisted. She was wringing her hands again but had no idea how disturbing it looked. Magnolia knew that whatever agreement Toussaint complained of caused his wife just as much bother. "Hampton is just mule-headed. Ain't no old plantation law got anything to do with it. Anyways, Magnolia ain't from around here, Toussaint. She wouldn't understand how things is done in Newberry." She glared at her husband, strongly suggesting he shut his mouth about family business.

Toussaint grabbed his hat and hit the door when his chest tightened all by itself. He had to force his lips to do likewise. There was so much he wanted to say but thought better of it when faced with his wife's pleading expression not to divulge a major strain affecting the life of everyone on the Delacroix Plantation and many other sharecroppers on surrounding farms. The wealthy landowners called it a gentleman's agreement, an unwritten understanding instituted during slavery. Poor black servants called it an abomination before God and a declaration of hell on earth.

4

Whiskey and Women

Later that day, Hampton sat on the iron-frame bed in the room he rented on LaSalle Street. The apartment building was situated in Tremé, which was the oldest colored neighborhood in the country. A thriving black community north of the French Quarter, it was inhabited by skilled laborers with good jobs, teachers, physicians, and the like. There were other sections of town available to Hampton, but he liked the idea of being around Negro men and women who'd dreamt of being somebody and also had the kind of grit it took to chase down those dreams and nab them. Hampton often dreamt of buying a home and paying it off before the bank could come up with an excuse to take it back. It was just a dream but it was his.

After sleeping off a hard night of criminal activity with Bones and the subsequent physical reprimands from his mother, Hampton glanced at the circular windup alarm clock resting on the nightstand near the bedpost. It read 4:17 in the afternoon, and he couldn't remember if he told Bones he'd meet up with him at half past four or at five o'clock. Too tired to think straight, he crawled back beneath the sheets. In what seemed like the blink of an eye, someone was banging on his door at five-thirty.

"Hey, wake the hell up in there!" a man's deep voice bellowed from the hallway. "Someone's on the phone for you. Sounds like a white fella."

Hampton went to the door in his boxer shorts and not much else. "What?" he asked, opening the door. While rubbing one eye and focusing on the dark hallway with the other, Hampton didn't see hide nor hair of the man with the heavy fists and the boom in his voice. His eyes found a small circular table in the alcove across from his room and a phone with the receiver off the hook. "Hello. Yeah, Bones, I just woke up. I'm dragging kinda slow. Uh-huh, that the place on North Peters Street and Canal? Okay, give me another hour. I got to get cleaned up. All right, I'll meet you outside."

Bones wanted to meet with Hampton to check his oil. Having recently formed an alliance, Bones needed to feel more comfortable with Hampton's state of mind before cashing in on a few dreams he'd been carrying around in his pocket. Where Bones wanted to meet was a whites-only establishment in the toughest part of the Quarter near the Jax Brewery and the riverfront. Thugs often hung out by the park where the trees provided natural cover for shady deals they'd rather not make out in the open. On the sidewalk in front of the Montrose Moon Bar, Hampton looked over his teal blue sharkskin suit, one of two he'd purchased for special occasions. Saturday evening in the Crescent City was as good a time as any. Now that he expected money to blow in like a storm, he decided to dress like a man who didn't mind that kind of rain falling down on his head.

"Now, that's a suit," Bones hailed. He exited the social club with a long unlit cigar hanging from his mouth. He wore a very stylish jacket, hand tailored in a soft shade of blue. His black lace-up pointed-toe shoes shined like glass. "You're late as hell, Swagger, and right on time. Good to see you."

"What's so damned good about it?" Hampton growled. He hadn't completely gotten over the trip he made to Newberry. The odds were stacked against him shaking it off anytime soon.

Bones cocked his head suspiciously. "Hold on a minute. Let me knot my laces. Damned things won't keep hold. Too much wax is my guess." Hampton frowned while the white man put his right shoe on a raised step next to an alleyway.

"What's eating you?" Bones asked. "Where's that Newberry grit and country wit from last night?"

Hampton didn't answer right away. He had a bit of oil checking to do on his end, too. Sure, breaking into homes and taking what valuables they could make off with was one thing. Trusting Bones with his personal issues, that was something altogether different.

"All right, Swagger, go on ahead and keep it to yourself, then," Bones teased. "I'll bet there's a girl involved. When a man gets that big of a crook in his face, it's always behind a woman." The surprised expression Hampton put on confirmed Bones's theory. "Is there anything else you don't want to talk about?"

"Naw, I'm open for pret' near anything else, like where I can get some grub close by. And I don't want to shuffle to nobody's back door for it, neither." Hampton made that proclamation to inform his partner of his disinterest in second-class citizenship, as long as he could help it.

Initially, Bones stared at the black man like he was trying to figure out something, then he burst out laughing. "I don't blame you, Swagger. Not at all. Back doors are meant for breaking into and sneaking out of." When Bones walked past his sporty Cadillac parked at the curb, Hampton hesitated.

"What's wrong with taking your wheels? I took a cab hurrying to get here."

"I thought we'd see some sights, plus I don't like everyone I deal with to know what I drive." While that was partly true, Bones still had reservations about white people seeing him chauffeuring around a black man. Friendships worthwhile came hard, but challenging old traditions and prejudices was even harder.

They walked in a westward direction along North Peters Street, looking at the pretty girls while rehashing the jobs they'd pulled the night before. Hampton was appreciative of the additional two hundred dollars Bones gave him after fencing some of the fancy items they'd snatched. Bones kicked in the extra money for another reason he wouldn't readily share with his partner in crime, not unless he had to. Until all of their cards were on the table and nothing but the truth stood between them, lies and secrets remained. Each one had plenty of both.

After traveling a few blocks, Bones pulled on Hampton's jacket at the Canal Street streetcar stop. Hampton was confused. "What we stalling here for?"

"The next lady in red." Hampton hadn't heard the term before so he peered to the left then to the right for women dressed in varying shades of crimson. When the streetcar pulled up and then idled for them to step on, Bones chuckled. "And here she is now, on time and fine as wine. Get on her, Swagger, before she leaves us standing here holding our tally whackers." Again, Hampton missed the metaphor entirely. Bones laughed. He took a seat near the streetcar conductor, two rows from the front, in the white section. His black companion held the leather strap, feeling awkward about bucking Jim Crow laws forbidding him to sit there. "Rest easy and take a load off, Swagger," Bones suggested. "Ain't nothing gonna happen whilst you're with me." His words came out even and steadily, like a dare he knew Hampton would gnaw on.

The burly conductor pulled the hand brake then sneered at the black passenger, who seemed more confused than defiant. "What in Sam Hill?" the white conductor questioned. His face was red and flushed. "Maybe you're not from around here, but the colored section is that away. So get on back there or get off." The haunting look on Hampton's face gave the bigger man pause. The pistol grip sticking out of his waistband gave the conductor a reason to get the car moving while he still had the chance. "Oh, I didn't know you had a special pass," the conductor reconsidered. He stumbled tentatively back to his seat. "Sorry to make a fuss. I'll get her moving right away."

"See there, some people got to be motivated to do the right thing," Bones said. His smile beamed brightly.

Hampton stared at Bones peculiarly, just like every other black passenger stuffed like sardines behind the color line, despite several rows of open benches in front of it. "Man, you is some kind of unpredictable," Hampton heckled harshly.

"Thank you," said Bones to all who must have felt the same as his friend. "It really wasn't a bother."

When the streetcar reached the next stop, Hampton jumped off hurriedly. He started out with a steady pace, not interested in concerning himself whether Bones had gotten off with him. "Hold on now," Bones called out, several paces behind. "What gives?"

"You's crazy, Bones, too crazy!" Hampton argued. "Plum crazy! My problem is you playing with fire for the sake of it. You can go against Jim Crow all you want, only I'm the one they gonna haul off when that conductor gets sick of being pushed around by you." Bones hadn't contemplated that or how he could have potentially brought the law down on the other blacks on the streetcar. From then on, he was determined to work at seeing things from Hampton's standpoint before showing off. That was his first authentic lesson from the opposite side of the tracks.

Bones kept pace with Hampton's quick strides despite having shorter legs. "You're right. Swagger, I'm sorry. I should have known better." He was winded and starting to perspire. Suddenly, Hampton stopped in front of a mirror factory with oversize samples in the window.

"What you should do is see how silly you look with that stogie weighing you down." Hampton laughed as Bones peered into a carnival fun-house mirror that distorted his figure. His frame appeared ten feet tall and ridiculously skinny. Bones gawked at his reflection, then at the giant cigar perched between his thin lips.

"You think I look a sight, who's that runt looking back at you?"

Hampton's mirror created the opposite effect on his appearance. The squat image staring back at him was barely three feet tall. He and Bones shared a long laugh like a couple of kids with nothing but time on their hands and a lasting friendship brewing in the midst of it. Before long, their laughs would prove bigger liars than the fun-house mirror reflections. Bones knew it couldn't turn out any other way, not if his schemes worked out as planned.

Once Hampton caught his breath, he explained why he'd ridden Bones harder than he'd meant to in regard to the streetcar incident. "I was just giving you the business, Bones. I could have played it out a little longer, but I saw you was already starting to sweat."

"Glad you noticed. We've got some corners to turn." Bones chuckled. "We'd be there by now if you hadn't ditched that lady in red."

"You's forgetting something, Bones. That lady was being led around by the nose by a white man. I'm gonna stay away from her until he gets over your infatuation." Bones agreed wholeheartedly.

The Grizzly Bear Lounge was a neighborhood nightspot where locals fell in to load up on stiff cocktails before taking their money and good times somewhere else. The dust-colored brick building was long and extremely narrow. Constructed between two larger structures on either side, the lounge provided a level of intimacy appreciated by patrons with a taste for mingling cheek to cheek. When Hampton followed Bones into the shotgun-shaped joint on Saratoga Street, his eyes lit up. From the outside, the Grizzly Bear didn't appear to have much to offer. Dazzling neon signs and shapely women decorated the privately owned establishment. While Hampton had seen his share of neon, he hadn't grown tired of tight-fitted dresses and five-dollar hairdos.

"Bones," he whispered. "How'd you know about this saucy spot?"

Bones smiled agreeably. He shook hands with the stout colored man guarding the door. "He's with me, Sty," he said before turning his attention toward Hampton. "Oh, this is just one of the out-of-the-way places I like to slide by every now and again. Let's grab a table by the bar so we can kick back." Hampton was up for it. After three cold beers and a shot of whiskey on an empty stomach, he was up for just about anything.

"I got to tell you, there's a freight car full of girls in here. How is it most of them know you already?" Hampton didn't take his eyes from a hot dish standing in the corner. The moment his gaze landed on her tangerine chiffon dress, tailored natural waistline, and padded shoulders, an old memory resurfaced like a sharp pain in his side. Seeing her again reminded him of the trouble he'd had picking up his self-respect once she'd finished with him.

"You didn't hear a word I said, did you, Swagger?" Bones asked. His eyes were locked on Hampton's heartache as well. "Hey, now, that's one I don't know. She's as pretty as a picture and appears kinda high-class at that. Maybe we ought to meet her. Come on. Let's take her down a peg by starting at different ends and tying a bow around her at the middle." He stood up to introduce himself. Hampton stuck out his arm to block the impending disaster.

"Uh-uh, you'd be going it alone. She likes a downtown man. A gussied-up field hand like me don't stand a ghost of a chance at getting another whiff of that. I know my place and it wasn't betwixt her legs."

"Wait a minute," he whispered across the tiny table. "Swagger, you saying you've been there already?"

"Yep, I'm embarrassed to say. Marie Joliet, that's the name she give me, but she'll let you call her anything you want if the price is right."

Bones turned his head to get another long glimpse of chocolate in a tight orange wrapper. "She don't strike me as the street-cruising type."

"Nope, Marie is what you call the department-store cruising type. Now don't get me wrong, it's good work if you can get it, but the job don't pay nearly as well as you'd expect." Bones leaned in to listen as Hampton laid it out for him. "See, that filly set my soul on fire about six months ago. I carried her out to eat and took her shopping a couple of times. After the bill was paid, she hurried up and put the fire out."

Disbelief was sprinkled throughout Bones's pale face. He'd been drinking one for one with Hampton so his reaction time was beginning to wane. "Nooo," he said in a booing manner. "Man, that ain't right."

"Tell me about it, Bones. She used me down to the nub."

Bones noticed the woman glancing their way while trying to be inconspicuous. "She's quite a looker. You shouldn't kick yourself too hard for it. What's done is done."

Hampton sniffled like a small child holding a grudge. "What's still picking at me is the unfortunate circumstance of my money running out before she could use me a little while longer." His wide-lipped grin confirmed what Bones had already concluded. "I wasn't ever so happy going broke in my whole entire life."

Bones couldn't help but do all he could to examine what the fuss was about up close. When Hampton left for the men's room, Bones winked at Marie. In short order, Bones was rounding second base and slipping money into her brassiere. Hampton didn't get bent out of shape when he stumbled onto their quiet introduction. His money was safely hidden back at his apartment. By the looks of it, Bones had already cast his lot on some fast times with a down payment despite having been warned about the gold digger's charms. Hampton refused to be the same fool twice.

5

Washhouse Woes

Early on Friday morning, Pearl Lee wiped the perspiration mounting on her forehead. She hated the washhouse, a noisy work shed where five women sorted, soaked, and scrubbed bundles of laundry carted down from the big house. There was a row of forty-gallon tubs, folding tables, a stove used to heat the water, and five clotheslines for hanging out clean garments. Pearl Lee slaved for ten hours a day in that heated tinderbox, handling the Delacroix linens and other unmentionables. As a supervisor, she delegated the soiled work clothes to other girls whose families also shared duties throughout the plantation. The faded headscarf tied at the nape of her neck had several holes in it, but she couldn't get herself to throw it out. It had belonged to her father, a poor sharecropper until death. Although he didn't leave much behind, Pearl Lee cherished the paisley scarf immensely.

Magnolia labored alongside her tutor in the washhouse, mending rips in shirts and patching pant legs worn out at the knees. Magnolia didn't mind the heat nearly as much as she did the way her wash mates bit their tongues when she tried to listen in on juicy plantation gossip. If Magnolia didn't know better, women were going out of their way to exclude her from their discussions. Women abruptly cut their chatter short when she approached the tight-knit circles. Magnolia wanted to know why.

"Pearl Lee, I was wondering about something. That brother of yours, Hampton, does he have a special woman he likes to keep around?"

"Does he?" she replied, chuckling. "Hampton ain't what you call the steady type. He's the kind to keep a line of women on a string. He says that string is tied to his zipper." Magnolia's eyes bucked wildly. She'd begun processing what the flippant comment implied and then laughed at how crudely inviting it sounded.

"You saying a man that handy corralling women hasn't kept one for hisself? Don't seem likely," she added, to stir the pot. "Since I've seen that determination of his in action, I guess I can take your word on the other."

Pearl Lee continued pressing and folding clothes until Magnolia's words scratched at her like a kitten pondering for milk. "If I was you, I'd forget about Hampton and that determination you seem to fancy."

"Ain't no shame to say I've been thinking about him," Magnolia admitted. "I'm not attached, and you say he's not claiming to be, either. I didn't say nothing about it for days now because I know how y'all so close to them Delacroixes." Magnolia was inching nearer a pensive line of questioning, but Pearl Lee saw it coming. She dove right in to snip that idea into a million little pieces.

"Look, Magnolia!" she said, in a harsh but hushed manner. "I like you, but don't push it. In two months you'll be headed back north to get on with your life. They's lots of things go on here that don't have nothing to do with you. Them's the things we live with every day. Why don't you busy yourself with needling them torn shirts like I showed you?" Pearl Lee stared longingly at the pile of washables on the table in front of her as if that should have ended the conversation. Conversely, Magnolia had grown weary of being told what to do from dawn to dusk.

"I'll see to the work all right," she whispered, leaning in closer to Pearl Lee's ear. "I'll see to it just like I seen that rascal Trotter Delacroix easing out your back door this morning."

Pearl Lee couldn't deny it. Surprise overcame her. She snatched the scarf from her head and balled it in her fist. "You was snoopin'?"

Standing her ground, Magnolia crooked her neck in opposition. "Didn't have to snoop. I was bringing down a pound of bacon, aiming to help with breakfast. That's when I saw him."

"Hush your mouth!" shouted Pearl Lee. "Hush!" Her gaze floated past Magnolia to find the other women snickering.

"You think they blind to what you're up to?" Magnolia asked matter-of-factly.

"Of course they know. That don't mean you got to be blabbing about it." A sympathetic storm of silence settled in the washhouse. There was something hidden behind the clouds, even bigger than a colored girl mixing it up with the rich white man's son hanging over Pearl Lee's head. She understood how sharing it could have upset their welfare in an instant. On the other hand, if Magnolia stayed on the outside looking in, there'd be no reason for her to remain silent about what else she might see. Pearl Lee decided to call an unscheduled break period. She ran the other women out of the washhouse then closed the doors and latched them tightly. "What I'ma tell you can't be repeated to nobody, and I mean nobody. If you do, I'll find out and have to kill you behind it." Magnolia laughed when Pearl Lee hastily cleared the shed, figuring what her tutor had to tell couldn't have necessitated all the commotion she'd caused. After the stern warning, Magnolia didn't find a single thing to giggle about. "Like I said, I like you fine, but that won't stop me from pouring poison down your throat to slam your mouth shut. You remember that big heifer, Sadie, who used to rake out the barn? Well, she didn't run off like we said. She's planted under my bedroom floor. That's so I can keep an eye on her."

"She's dead?" Magnolia yelped.

"Good, then you do understand how serious this is," answered Pearl Lee. "That gal was out to make trouble by telling Toussaint on me. She can't say boo now. What you saw this morning was nothing but Trotter and me keeping an old bargain, keeping matters peaceful-like."

"One of those plantation laws?" Magnolia asked cautiously, not nearly as interested in knowing now.

"The oldest and the worst," she answered honestly.

Magnolia glanced at the doors, securely latched. "Maybe I should go, too."

"Uh-uh, too late," Pearl Lee hissed. "You can either be trusted with plantation history or you can sprout roots like Sadie." Left with no choice, Magnolia swallowed hard then nodded slowly. "We got a tradition here in Newberry. It's hard to stomach, but there ain't a thing we can do about it. Long before any of us were born, including the Mister, something wicked happened. A murdering pack of coloreds from up the road in Glory, slaves, most of them, killed the sheriff then shot up the town square. Then they came here and hung some real important white folks. I suppose they had the right to do what they done in Glory, but not the Newberry lynchings." Pearl Lee was wringing her hands again, this time for atrocities of the past and present. "That band of rogues burned Glory to the ground because the masters took their women and had at them whenever they got good and ready. Didn't even make no difference that some of the gals carried in the womb at the time. Wouldn't you know it, some of the babes came here whiter than Christmas snow."

Magnolia's mouth was sandpaper dry. Her mind worked feverishly. She tried to envision a horde of black men with guns and torches. Even though the "Road from Glory" occurred during the slavery era, the thought of hate-filled men storming the town, regardless of color, was terrifying. "Those Glory men, they get shot up in the end?" Magnolia asked in a voice so tender that it barely eased past her lips.

"They was going from one plantation to the next burning crops. They even had the gall to take up living in the main houses like a bunch of kings. It must have been a sight, I swear. I heard, too, that they got too full of themselves after chasing a crowd of filthy Klan back into the woods." Suddenly, Pearl Lee's eyes fell dim. "Guess fighting off the state militia wasn't so easy."

"*All* of the colored men died?"

"Yep, every last one. Before they went, they took a slate of white soldier boys down first. Since then there's been this what you might call a kind of association made up of rich white folk here in Newberry. Uh-huh, they got together and came up with a plan so that what set the town of Glory ablaze wouldn't happen here. Everybody benefits from it. We's good Negroes here and don't want no trouble."

True enough, the story Pearl Lee told was clearly the most troubling conclusion Magnolia could have imagined, other than being buried beneath her tutor's bedroom floor. Altogether, she still hadn't heard anything she thought worth killing a big-mouthed busybody over. "This thing, this plan, how does it keep matters peaceful?" Magnolia queried eventually.

Pearl Lee turned her eyes away then sighed heartily before continuing with the history lesson never found in any books. "Well, there was over seventy plantations and large farms in Broussard Parish. Fifteen was tied in with the association. Wise men like Mr. Delacroix's granddaddy built this agreement, a set of rules for taking young Negro girls and laying up with them."

"Seem to me a thing like that wouldn't do nothing but keep trouble stirred," Magnolia smirked. "I don't see no benefit in it for colored folk at all."

"They called it a gentleman's agreement, rules that all of 'em was supposed to abide by. Wicked as it must sound to you, it has saved Newberry for one hundred and fifty years. White men agreed they wouldn't mix blood so that colored men wouldn't rise up behind it. A proud man raising children favoring the master is bound to go crazy soon enough."

Magnolia was extremely confused then. The way she saw it, Pearl Lee had even less of an inclination to kill Sadie. "What is it, Pearl Lee? If white men ain't still climbing into bed with colored girls and ain't no bastard children being made, what are you pressing so hard to keep in?"

"Nobody said they stopped climbing into bed with us," Pearl Lee answered, her eyes glaring brightly now. "Like our mothers' mothers and their mothers did, too, we still bend over and raise our skirt to keep matters calm. You saw Trotter coming out the rear of my house, didn't you? Well, can't hatch no bastard children through the back door. And don't go getting ideas about judging me. At least this way, my husband won't get strung up or shot down if he don't know Trotter's... been sliding his little red pecker where it don't bother nothing that's worth a damn. Listen to me good, I don't figure on giving the undertaker reason to powder up my sweet Toussaint for no pine box funeral."

The original gentleman's agreement called for wealthy landowners to abstain from vaginal intercourse with female slaves, not excluding anal and oral activity, at the risk of inciting another slave revolt and forfeiting portions of their land with each infraction. After the abolition of slavery, rich farmers with vast numbers of sharecroppers continued to force poor, black, unwed females into a similar predicament by using scare tactics via threats of bodily injury to them and their families. It had been widely rumored that free black men began to disappear when they learned the ancient practice continued. Pearl Lee's explanation was a warning as to why Toussaint must never know and what would happen if he did. She could have knocked Magnolia over with a weak sigh then.

"I'm sorry, Pearl Lee," she replied sorrowfully. "But you said that old agreement was for unwed colored women. White boys in Virginia don't need any agreement to take what they want."

"When Trotter started coming around my back door, I didn't know Toussaint. After I got married to him, I thought things was over with Trotter and me until he started leaving notes in my washtub. Toussaint can't read two words put together much less notes wrote in longhand."

"I know, you can uproot and go away," Magnolia suggested. "Take Toussaint and the baby and just go."

"Where to, Mag? Huh? Where is a poor Negro woman, her husband who can't spell his own name, and a new baby gonna run to? I hate it, but this is what the Lawd set aside then dropped me into. I'm gonna make the best of what I have, and that's it. Now you know all of what the whispering between the others has been about." Smoke from the unattended wood-burning stove began to fill the room. "Dammit, gal, look at what you made me do!" Pearl Lee screamed.

Magnolia darted toward the door amid billowing clouds of dense black smoke. She unlatched it then immediately headed for the other one. The washhouse women pushed past her, yelling and dousing the stove with water from the giant tubs until the fire was completely squelched. Magnolia coughed violently as she staggered outside. While gathering her wits, she sat on a broad tree stump reflecting on what could have meant total annihilation for the washhouse. Considering what she'd discovered about the Delacroix family's way of holding on to salacious customs, she wouldn't have cared if every acre of the plantation burned to a crispy cinder.

6

Gumbo

Friday afternoon, Hampton dialed the phone number but couldn't reach Bones at the place where he was staying in the French Quarter. Hampton wanted to explain why he needed time off to spin his wheels. Plotting robberies and late-night creeping had taken its toll after a hard week of professional prowling. He valued his relationship with the white man on many levels. In addition to making money and chasing women, Bones went out of his way to explain life on the other side of the color line. Because he'd grown up with the poor Negroes of New Orleans, tap dancing in streets and plucking guitar strings for nickels, he had ample stories to share and a knack for making each one end with him convincing some unsuspecting female to take her clothes off. Hampton laughed hysterically every time "and that's when she got naked" rolled off Bones's tongue. Hampton didn't see the evil in Bones no more than he did in his own wicked ways.

The Funky Butt Dance Hall spilled over with pretty girls and well-heeled slicksters during the week but never as deep as it did on Friday nights. Hampton was itching to shake, rattle, and roll with everything that caught his eye, except for Marie Joliet.

Bones had readily confessed to spending a wad of money, splurging on shopping sprees with the attractive bombshell in addition to meals in high-toned dinner joints. Hampton remembered how Bones wailed overdramatically when telling him about Marie's habit of guzzling champagne by the bottle and his money right along with it. That memory was stuck in Hampton's head when he saw her sauntering sweetly in his direction. Although he chose to ignore her by chugging a bottle of beer, Marie stood poised and patient, awaiting a warm salutation and a cold drink. After the failed attempt to shoo her away, Hampton rudely struck up a conversation with a friend he hadn't seen in months. "Damned if it ain't Willie Pope," he yelled above the music. "Man, you sure is a sight for sore eyes. How yo' mama 'nem? Yeah, yeah, I've been meaning to look you up. You still pitching mudbug traps down on the Terrebonne? Willie? Willie?"

The craw fisher was the color of a buttered biscuit, and he fancied women who shared his light complexion. He grinned cunningly at Marie because she more than fit the bill. When she noticed his tongue wagging, she leaned forward to introduce her best assets. Willie, close enough to reach out and touch her boastful resources, turned an odd shade of red. From that moment on, he saw Hampton's mouth moving but didn't hear nary a syllable coming out. Willie licked his fingers, slicked back his processed hairdo, then did his best to locate the composure he'd somehow misplaced. Like most men who crossed Marie's path, he was falling like rain. Hampton noticed his old pal gawking at the bait so he started talking faster about old times, new cars, and anything else that entered his mind. He brushed his long fingers against Willie's shoulder to get his attention, all the while brushing off Marie and her propensity for getting both of her hands deep in a man's pockets.

"You just gon' stand there jabbering or can a lady get a drink?" she prodded, while leering seductively at Hampton. Her tight polka-dot sweater with three-quarter sleeves was singing a siren's song, but he refused to listen.

Willie, however, was mesmerized by it. "I'll get you whatever you want," he interjected foolishly. "You want me to reach up, lasso the moon, and put it in a mason jar? I'll do that, too." The country boy loved Creole women. It wouldn't have mattered what package one came wrapped in as long as the color was right. Willie had spent countless days sniffing behind high yellow schoolgirls when he and Hampton were coming of age on the Delacroix Plantation. Now Hampton was looking at yet another of his friends who couldn't get out of their own way.

"No thanks, Marie," Hampton told her finally. "Me and Willie here, we's old friends and got a lot to catch up on. Ain't that so, Willie?" Hampton nudged his pal, expecting him to stand united. Willie stared him down like a stranger on a dark street corner. He shrugged disagreeably then winked at Hampton on the sly.

"Miss, I don't know this man. You, I'd love to get acquainted with. That means I'm buying." Marie smiled at Hampton. She blew him a kiss when Willie made room for her on his lap.

"I'ma tell Bones," Hampton mouthed when there wasn't anything left to say. He felt three times the fool when he caught himself wishing it was his hand caressing Marie's voluptuous curves instead of Willie's. His headache intensified when she slid her tongue between her painted lips in a sensual manner then waggled it at him. *I can't stand that woman*, Hampton thought, turning his back on the entire situation. *I can't stand her. And I wish she wasn't so fine.*

Hampton hit the dance floor to loosen the thought of Marie,

what she'd more than likely be doing later, and the price tag associated with the privilege and pleasure alike. Minutes later, Hampton bumped into an older flame named Thelma Shiloh with whom he'd spent a long weekend some months before. She was a buxom beauty he'd passed time with after meeting her at an ice-cream and baptism social sponsored by the local church. Hampton went solely for the free ice cream. He took home a full weekend of sinful treats to boot. Just when he'd gotten around to liking the company, another man showed up at her love nest and busted in the front door. Hampton took one look at Thelma's brute of a husband and didn't stop running until he'd locked himself into the attic of the same church where they met. Hampton didn't ask the Lord for forgiveness after sleeping with the professional wrestler's wife, he asked the preacher to hide him. He figured that God was already wise to what he'd been involved in, so wasn't any point in bringing it up again.

As quickly as it entered his mind, bothersome thoughts of wayward wives and menacing maniacs dissipated. The Funky Butt was ripe with a collection of women Hampton managed to keep on his string. He openly flirted with most of them. Although he kept his options open, Thelma didn't make the cut. She had something to say about it in the women's room.

Wearing a blue satin dress gripping her curves in all the right places, Thelma dabbed feverishly at her face with a soft sponge from her makeup compact. A rich shade of bronze with a hint of red, she remained transfixed by her reflection in the mirror. "I don't care what she say. That big-boned heifer is greedy as hell. I saw her trying to ease up on him at the bar," she whined. "Marie Joliet got her behind stomped once before when I caught her sniffing around Brutus. She tried to take my husband, now she's after my pride, too."

Thelma's girlfriend Sarah, three shades darker and a whole lot better-looking, stopped primping her cold wave hairdo when she noticed steam spouting from Thelma's nostrils. "Girl, take it easy. Marie learned her lesson after that whooping you laid on her a while back," Sarah said, both hands resting on her size ten hips. She turned her nose up then huffed dramatically, "That skank won't come around your Brutus no more."

"Brutus?" Thelma chuckled. "Honey, please. She can have my husband, but that witch better leave Hampton alone."

"Now you're getting beside yourself. You told me Hampton Bynote won't even let you near him. I know he's a sweet lover man and all, but—" Sarah began to argue until she was cut off by a mean watch-your-mouth stare down.

"It might sound peculiar to you, but I ain't never stopped wishing for Hampton to love me back. I can't let go of what he did to my heart and how he set my body to simmering. No how! No way!" Thelma grunted adamantly. "I'm not of a mind to cease or give up on wishing, neither, not about Hampton and certainly not to Marie."

Sarah must have realized she was fighting an uphill battle that wasn't worth the climb because she let it go without so much as another word. "Let's get back in the ring," said Thelma, giving herself a once-over in the mirror. "You don't have to go along with me but stand back if I decide to charge." When they marched out of the ladies' room, Thelma was still spouting steam.

Magnolia dried her hands with a cloth towel. She'd been washing up in the restroom, listening to two grown women raving about Hampton. All made up with borrowed rouge and lipstick, she held a long gaze at her reflection. Decked out in one of Pearl Lee's dresses taken in here and there, Magnolia tossed a hopeful expression toward the mirror. The woman smiling back could have passed for twenty-two and appeared a great deal more experienced than she actually was. "Like the lady said, let's get back in the ring," she exclaimed, talking her nerve up as best she could. She sidestepped a flock of young women on her way out, all of them cackling about somebody famous who had rolled up in a Cadillac limousine minutes ago.

"Where you been hiding?" Pearl Lee questioned after she found Magnolia lurking near a row of crowded tables, each of them two couples deep. "You done missed Fats Domino strutting in. Me and Toussaint thought somebody got at you."

Toussaint ran his thumbs under the lapels of his best suit, a wide-striped three-button beige number. "Uh-huh, the way Magnolia's skirting about, she just might go for that," he joked. There was no misunderstanding it, that wide-eyed girl from Virginia was hell-bent on getting herself into some adult situations. "Pearl Lee, it'd serve yourself well to keep an eye on her. I'ma get us some drinks."

"You go ahead, Toussaint," she told her husband. "And I'll keep my other eye on you." Pearl Lee was no fool. Every time they drove his old truck into New Orleans for a night out on the town, she'd have to put at least five women in their place before hitting the road for home. Toussaint was exceedingly handsome, fun to look at, and slow to tell interested parties he was taken.

No sooner had he walked away than Magnolia snatched at Pearl Lee's arm. "Wait till you hear what happened. I was washing up and these two women started talking about Hampton this and Hampton that. One of them was married and willing to scrap with somebody named Marie over your brother." She was surprised when Pearl Lee dismissed it easily enough.

"Don't ask me to explain it. Hampton's always had a way with women, although I ain't known him to buzz around nobody's wife before."

"This Thelma, that's the one doing most of the talking, said big as day how she loved him. It was the dangdest thing. She didn't have no shame about it, either."

A wide grin spread across Pearl Lee's lips. "Ain't no way you gonna understand married folks' predicaments until you got some of your own, Mag. That's the way it is. If Hampton is fooling with another man's honeypot, that's news to me. Come on, let's see what's taking my sugar dipper so long."

Magnolia lagged behind, filling out her tutor's classic white cotton dress with miniature black bows on the shoulders. She giggled to herself when several men ogled at Pearl Lee like hungry wolves. Before she knew it, Magnolia had accumulated her share of canine types howling after her, too. "What am I supposed to do, Pearl Lee?" she asked excitedly. "The tall one offered to flip me drinks, and the other wanted to teach me something called the sideways mambo. I can't even imagine what kind of dance that is."

"Oh, no? Give it a little more thought. It'll come to you," Pearl Lee assured her. "Toussaint was right about you, child. Don't catch nothing you don't intend on keeping." She laughed when the younger woman's jaw dropped. "On second thought, don't catch nothing at all."

Magnolia frowned over a half glass of RC Cola. She didn't have anyone on her mind but Hampton. Watching others mingling and matchmaking provided enough excitement to feed her curiosity. How quickly things changed when she spotted him across the dance floor. Hampton was doing his best to keep Thelma away from another woman who looked like a white girl through the smoky den. Moving in from opposite directions, two beefy fellows parted the dance floor like the Red Sea. Magnolia couldn't see exactly what was coming down the line, but it seemed that Hampton was sure to get sucked into the middle of it and spit out onto the sidewalk. She wasn't about to stand idly by after getting all dolled up on the chance of dancing with him. "Pearl Lee, mind my cola. I'm about to catch hold of something I intend on keeping nailed down."

Pearl Lee started after her but gave it a second thought. Babysit Magnolia or let a slew of hussies get next to her own baby? It was remarkable how immediately she came to the right decision. *Sometimes you gotta let 'em learn to fly on their own*, she reasoned, *especially if it means some other hens is gonna be trying to roost with my husband.*

"I told you we was a mistake, Thelma," Hampton shouted furiously. "You ain't got no cause to be at Marie like this over me. Besides, she only wants what's resting in my pockets."

Marie sucked on her bottom lip angrily, having put Willie on the shelf when Thelma confronted her about Hampton. "You don't have to explain anything to that cow. She's hitched but good."

"And both of y'alls fighting over the man I'm about to marry," Magnolia whooped loudly. She stuck her face within inches of Hampton's then threw her shoulders back. "Hampton, darling, tell these women to leave us be." He gawked at her peculiarly while noticing the same thing she had earlier, two of the biggest dance hall bouncers in the city skulking his way. After lunging into his arms, she whispered ever so gently, "It's me, Hampton, Magnolia. Kiss me real hard or get hauled off."

He had no idea who Magnolia was, but even so it sounded better than getting ushered out by the seat of his pants. Hampton placed his lips on hers, wondering where she came from and happy that she had turned up when she did.

"What the hell is all the fracas about?" shouted the first goon to arrive. "Y'all can argue outside. We don't allow no fighting in the Funky Butt." Thelma and Marie began pointing their fingers at each other and yelling obscenities about man stealing and home wrecking. Hampton held Magnolia close to him, stayed out of it, and escaped without drawing further attention. They quickly disappeared into a sea of slow-grooving couples on the dance floor. Neither of them bothered to notice Marie and Thelma's rambunctious departure at the hands of the heavy-handed thugs. Hampton and Magnolia were too busy getting reacquainted.

"So you're Pearl Lee's pupil?" Hampton marveled. "Hot damn, if you didn't grow up three years in a week."

"Yeah, it's just a smidge of polish and paint to make a few things appear what they ain't."

"What did you say your name was again?" Hampton asked, really wanting to know.

"Magnolia *Holiday*," she answered, her fingers casually clasped behind his neck. "You remember, like the blues singer."

Hampton leaned away to better examine her claim. "Yeah, only you's a lot prettier."

7

Manhandling

At half past one, the earlier fast-paced mood of the Funky Butt Dance Hall now coasted like a tired man dragging his feet. Scores of couples stepped lightly, embracing the moment and each other. While the night marched on, soft whispers drifted past the harmless belly rubbing and sweet-talking varieties. The witching hours were at hand. Hampton was surprised when Magnolia started up the kind of conversation he doubted she'd had previously. He laughed at her suggestion to sneak outside for a private dance in a dark, quiet place.

"So, how long are you going to treat me like I'm a child?" Magnolia asked, her feet following Hampton's slow, methodical two-step groove. "Just because you treat me that way don't make it so. I'm a woman, a grown woman."

"You's a grown woman, huh?" Hampton heckled quietly so as not to upset the mood. "Says who?" Magnolia moaned in a sensual manner as if she knew what it was supposed to sound like, then she slid her tongue into his mouth. There was something in the way she went about it that sent Hampton down a different path. After pulling his lips a few inches from hers, he wrinkled his brow. "Girl, you did that like you been practicing."

"You think so? Well, you'd be surprised what all I rehearsed. We grow up pretty fast where I come from."

"You keep talking that way, I might be inclined to believe you."

Magnolia was bubbling on the inside. On her face, she wore a lusty leer to entice the man whose zipper she intended to be tied to. "Hampton, I've been meaning to ask you something. Those women fighting over you, what did you do to make both of them act out so?"

"Wasn't nothing to it," he answered modestly. "They's just spouting off about something that happened between them. It likely didn't concern me at all."

"That one with thick hips, I overheard her in the restroom going on about you. She said how you made her simmer. How does that work, exactly?"

Hampton almost choked. "Why, uh . . . I didn't do nothing but talk to her a few times."

"Talked to her is all?" Magnolia asked with a yeah, right smirk. "If talking is what you call it, I might be persuaded to hear what you got to say firsthand."

Hampton peeked at his wristwatch. It took him three seconds to map out the quickest route back to his apartment and another three before he saw Pearl Lee staring a hole in him from the fringes of the dance floor. Toussaint tried to pitch for Hampton, but his wife felt duty bound to look after her young protégée. Pearl Lee read her brother's expression. Then she read his mind. The minute she saw horns poking out of Hampton's head, she began to eyeball him disapprovingly.

"Come on, Magnolia. I need to take a breather," Hampton

sighed. "Wouldn't be such a bad idea to have a few words with Pearl Lee while I'm at it." He escorted her off the floor, avoiding his sister's evil leer. She was responsible for Magnolia's well-being, after all. He considered that before making an offer that might have put him crossways with his overbearing sibling. "Look here, Magnolia. What if I was to invite you back to my room to do some of that *talking* we hinted around earlier? Well, I was wondering—"

"You don't have to wonder with me, Hampton," she replied quickly, "I was ready to go from jump. Let me tell Pearl Lee."

"Whoa! Unh-unh," Hampton sputtered hurriedly. "I don't think that's the best way to go about it. Why don't you hit the powder room? I'll take care of things with Pearl Lee." Magnolia batted her big round eyes at him. Whatever he said was fine with her. He was up to no good and she was all in.

In the darkened den, Hampton searched through tight-knit pressed flesh to locate Pearl Lee and Toussaint. In doing so, he became a nuisance to several men after mistaking them for his brother-in-law. "Hey. Hey, Toussaint?" Hampton whispered in the ear of a fair-skinned man wearing a similar suit to the one he'd seen often enough. "Toussaint, is that you?"

"Hell, naw, I ain't no damned Toussaint!" the slight man grunted angrily. His breath reeked of stale beer and poor dental hygiene. As Hampton fanned at his nose, the disgruntled man's date glanced at him a tick longer than she should have. "What the hell is going on here, Bessie? Huh? Is this the wretch you been tipping out with? Or maybe his name is Toussaint." When he turned back to argue the point further, Hampton had up and vanished. During his hasty departure, he heard a woman screech above the music. "I done told you once, Larry, I don't know no Toussaint."

It seemed as if trouble was already brewing and he hadn't even had the chance to bring up to Pearl Lee the likelihood of kidnapping Magnolia. When Hampton began to follow his first mind, the one doing the thinking from his pants, he stumbled over Toussaint at the end of a long watering hole. To be sure, Hampton looked him over twice. "Toussaint, that is you," he howled gleefully. He hadn't noticed the man's broken-down demeanor or bloodshot eyes. "Looky here, I'ma take that girl Magnolia with me. Tell Pearl Lee I got her and that I'll get her home safe sometime tomorrow." Toussaint could barely hold up his head. Hampton had the distinct feeling he wouldn't make a reliable go-between on his behalf or a respectable mouthpiece. "Shit, Toussaint, what's got into you? That King Kong holding you down again?" Hampton had seen what effect two quarts of malt liquor had on his friend before. If that was the case, then he'd be useless.

"Naw, man, ain't had too much of nothing but a half-dozen bottles of suds. It's what's on my heart that's pulling me down by my dick."

Hampton did not look forward to hearing the ins and outs regarding Pearl Lee's personal affairs but he was in dire straits, which necessitated a disappearing act without hearing what Pearl Lee had to say. He figured it was more prudent to ask forgiveness than permission. At least, he'd have tons more fun that way. "Hurry up and spit out what's got you bent so's I can tell you what I'm scheming." Hampton kept an eye out for Pearl Lee, while her husband acknowledged his angst.

"I wasn't gonna harp on it none, not on my wedding anniversary, no, sir," whined Toussaint.

"Yeah, yeah, so what's eating you?" Hampton urged him along.

"You's a man so's I bet you can understand my woe. This

morning, I woke up and my whole left side jumped, then my whole flesh began to crawl. You know what that mean." Hampton had heard the old saying and he believed in it from top to bottom.

"It means another man's been kicking in your stall," he replied painstakingly. "But Pearl Lee's crazy for you. She's always going on about having the prettiest man in all of Newberry. She got you and the bragging rights, too."

"That don't seem to amount to a hill of beans from where I sit."

"Don't sell yourself short. To a vain woman like Pearl that means a hell of a lot. You really think she's cattin' about behind your back?"

Toussaint raised his head briefly, then he let it fall again. "Yep, I expect that's the case. It might sound crazy but I can feel it. You know I care for her something powerful, Hampton. If she's taking up with another man, it'd just kill me dead, I swear," he added before tears cascaded down his cheeks. "Oh, I love her so much," he blubbered helplessly. Hampton took one look at those crocodile tears and had only one thing to say.

"Damn!"

"What's wrong, Hampton?" questioned Magnolia after sauntering up behind him with Pearl Lee at her side.

"Toussaint's probably got ahold of that King Kong again," Pearl Lee asserted. Her guess wasn't far off. The gorilla on his back was just as hard to shake off.

"Naw," Hampton offered solemnly. "This time, he's drunk off misery." It was his turn to shoot disapproving eye daggers at Pearl Lee. "Seems like your house could use a bit of dusting," Hampton told her flatly. "Sweep under your bed and set things right with your man. I'ma take Magnolia off your hands so you can get it straight with Toussaint."

Against Magnolia's wishes, Pearl Lee declined on both suggestions. "I'm already right with what goes on in my house, and you ain't taking Magnolia no place tonight. She'll be just dandy with us, all the way to Newberry."

"It's okay with me, Pearl Lee," Magnolia debated, when she should have stood pat. "I can handle myself, really I can." She sounded like a lamb ready to shove her head inside a lion's mouth for an ill-advised tour. Pearl Lee refused to let Magnolia overcommit herself.

"It ain't you I'm concerned about," she answered harshly. "Handling a man like Hampton is another kind of chore you ain't accustomed to. It can be real tricky if you're not too careful." The rivalry between Hampton and his sister was interesting to watch from the sidelines. Pearl Lee loved and adored him, Magnolia was sure of it. Why she worked so hard at keeping him at arm's length from someone who wanted to be held by him was puzzling. It appeared as if Pearl Lee was purposely coming between them out of pure spite.

"What, is you her mama now?" Hampton fired back. Pearl Lee was giving it to him but good for the comment he'd made regarding Toussaint's pitiful conduct.

"No, I ain't, but I'm not letting you have your way with this girl so's you can add her to your chain of fools, either." When it occurred to her Magnolia was in love with that idea, she raised her hand to squash it all around. "Don't even... hush!"

"It's gonna be like that, huh?" Hampton said. His tone was filled with disappointment.

Pearl Lee scoffed heatedly, again with displaced hostility. "Yep, just like that. You ain't gonna keep Magnolia out all night and have folks wondering what you doing with her."

Magnolia raised her hand slowly, asking permission to speak

like a schoolgirl uncertain of the harm her answer could cause. "We done already covered the *what*, so there's no need for wondering." Magnolia's sordid wit put an impish grin on Hampton's lips. Magnolia was growing up by the second, and he was pleased with her progress under his tutelage as well.

"It's clear Hampton done dug a hole in your head, and I say that's deep enough for one night," Pearl Lee hissed at her detractors, still failing to give her husband's dismal state the attention it deserved. "Let's get out of here. Magnolia, sit and watch Toussaint for me whilst I fetch the truck. Hampton's gonna walk me out to the lot to see that don't nothing happen to me."

All of the fight had been whooped out of Hampton and the wind let out of Magnolia's sails. As he headed for the door, Magnolia made one last plea for reconsideration. "Come on, Pearl Lee. I trust Hampton to treat me respectful."

"Child, please! If you respected yourself, I might think it over at that."

"I know what you's thinking. I'm rushing it a bit because I really do think highly of Hampton. What if he moves on to somebody else? What if he don't come around?"

"You'd be more concerned if you let him hop between your legs, then soon after he moved to somebody else. What if he didn't come around then?" Pearl Lee cradled her purse like an important textbook as she stared down at it. "It's like this, Magnolia, answer to me tonight and don't waste your time studyin' no what-ifs. I've known Hampton since he was born. Put him off awhile and he'll come strutting around soon enough."

Magnolia didn't appear to understand how avoidance served her best interest. "I'll do what you say, but I don't follow."

"Listen to me. He's a man. That means he's built with a contrary way of thinking. They all want what they can't have. Child, that's how they's made. Trust in that." Pearl Lee shook her husband's shoulder to wake him. "You got to get up, baby. Magnolia can't wrestle you all the way outside."

"Okay, I'll be on in a minute," Toussaint muttered. He rubbed his eyes, yawned, and then nodded off again as urine began to pour from his barstool.

"Lawd, have mercy," Pearl Lee complained. "He done peed his pants. Go run and get Hampton before we get tossed out." Magnolia darted toward the exit. Pearl Lee threw Toussaint's arm over her shoulder then stumbled with him in that direction. She disregarded the ugly sneers that other patrons flashed at them. "Don't worry, baby, I'll get you home safe." She choked back the tears caused by her own misdeeds.

Toussaint had no idea why his mental health had begun declining overnight. It started with oversleeping and forgetting to do simple things around the house. Unbeknownst to everyone except his wife, Toussaint was falling apart at the seams. Since his rapid debilitation was due to her transgressions, indirectly, there wasn't a soul she could tell.

Before the truck rambled down the block, Pearl Lee told Hampton that she cared for him like always but she couldn't sit idly by as he introduced Magnolia to the types of things she wasn't prepared for. "She's still tender yet, take it slow or she'll bruise real easy," Pearl Lee advised after the others were seated in the cab of the truck. "You got to court her like she means something to you. Mama's taken to this girl and I like her, too. Can't see letting you mess that up. Leastways not before she gets to know you better. Put some time in, then y'all can do whatever you both agree on."

8

Bunches of Mess

The following Tuesday morning, Magnolia scurried into the washhouse, which had been fully restored. She was surprised that Toussaint and two other field hands had repaired the stove hitch, timbers supporting the structure beneath it, and a few bricks that had needed to be replaced long before the fire. Pearl Lee and her crew of three were already hard at work before eight o'clock. The moment she grabbed an apron from the makeshift cupboard where rags were stored, the other women put their tasks aside to tease her. She noticed how their conversation died a sudden death like it had before Pearl Lee's heart-to-heart. "Sorry I'm running behind," Magnolia sighed. "I guess you can't give a girl the day off and expect her to get back on schedule right away." When no one answered, she knotted the apron strings then parked both hands on her narrow hips. "What are y'all gawking at, and why isn't anybody carrying on about what they did on their day off?" Pearl Lee brushed flakes of washing powder from her chin with the back of her right hand, all the time looking at Magnolia with a sideways sneer.

"Because we all hung around here, catching up on raising our younguns and seeing to meals and such," Pearl Lee answered for herself as well as for the rest of them. "Truth be told, we's mighty interested in what you did on *your* day off." Finally, Magnolia had been invited into their exclusive "local girls only" club, on the tail of Pearl Lee's endorsement, of course. Magnolia knew her rendezvous with Hampton was to be kept hidden from the Delacroixes, but she wasn't clear on what was acceptable for washhouse chitchat. The hungry wide-eyed stares in the room begged for answers, in full detail. Pearl Lee's go-ahead nod strongly suggested that it was acceptable to blab all of her business. "If you haven't figured it out by now, we ain't discovered a way to keep secrets among us. It's only matters that we keep some of our own from *them*." Magnolia didn't have to figure out who *them* were. Keeping in mind what Pearl Lee had confided in her about Sadie's sudden absence, there had to be a mountain of secrets she'd kept from everyone, for obviously differing reasons. It wasn't long before Magnolia learned how keeping secrets made the world go around, on and off the Delacroix Plantation.

"Well, it was heavenly," she said eventually, in a light and mellow tone that brought gleaming smiles from each of the older women.

"Come on, Mag," Lillie chided from the other side of the room. "We got bunches to do after the mess you made of this place, and none of us are concerning ourselves with a lick of it until you spill on about your day in town with Hampton." Lillie was darker than soot and as thin as a rail. She had the prettiest head of hair Magnolia had seen on a colored woman and two missing teeth in the bottom front of her mouth, each drawing attention away from the other. "I could use some juicy tidbits to think over today and sleep on tonight."

"Okay, okay," Magnolia said, her hands raised like an actress preparing to act out a scene from someone else's life. "It all started Sunday evening when Pearl Lee come to me with a snitch of paper folded over. She said she found it lying in the washtub on her back stump. I couldn't get a handle on it because she was looking at me all serious-like. Well, on that little piece of paper was an invite for a special lady to dinner in New Orleans. I was about to ask Pearl Lee how she was 'specting to get away from here without Toussaint knowing about it." Pearl Lee laughed the loudest when she heard that. "Yeah, I was set to do a whole slew of questioning and babysitting on top of it until she pushed Hampton's name out all sly and easy. I don't know how he worked it out, but there it was, the chance he took on coming here and the chance he took on me." Lillie wasn't the first to swoon over a clandestine-style hand-delivered declaration of courtship. The room was quiet and still, awaiting more of what sounded like romance from a dime novel. "The note also said if I was interested in meeting with Hampton, I had to be ready an hour after sundown," Magnolia continued. "I was ready, all right; ready to see how that man planned on sneaking me out of here without the Mister shooting holes in him. Oomph, I'm a might bigger than a scrap of paper. As sure as the sun went down, Hampton showed up at Pearl Lee's door with a handful of wilted flowers and a box of melted chocolates. I was afraid he had walked all the way from the city and was threatening to take me back down the same road."

"How'd he get you off the plantation?" asked another member of the washhouse crew.

"He said he was sorry for the condition of the flowers and candy and that he'd been waiting downstream at a crawfish farm for the sun to drift off to sleep. Uh-huh, he motored this little boat up the bayou till he come close, then he paddled the rest of the way so's nobody could hear him." Magnolia went on to share how they later sat down to a reserved table in a mixed dinner joint with cloth napkins, fancy plates, and crystal glasses. When it seemed that she was leaving out the good parts, someone heckled crassly that she should skirt on past the cheek-to-cheek foreplay and break out with the heavy breathing.

"I for one ain't interested in hearing what my kid brother had up his sleeve after dinner," Pearl Lee argued.

Lillie snickered and hissed. "And we ain't, neither. I'll speak where the others are quiet and say how interested we are in knowing what Hampton tried to put up Mag's dress."

"Ooh," Magnolia squealed, as embarrassed as she was tickled. "Just what kinda girl do you think I am?"

"That's exactly what we's trying to uncover, deary, but you's too tight-lipped to tell. Hell, I might as well get on back to work. At least then, I won't be bored to death. Next time a tall, dark, handsome man comes along and swoops you up in his arms, either give him some and let us in on it or keep the entire arrangement to yourself. I'll tell you, youth is sure 'nuff wasted on the young." Lillie, an old thirty-six, smacked her lips then returned to her duties. Pearl Lee winked at Magnolia and smiled approvingly as the others gave in and followed suit.

Actually, there wasn't all that much more to tell, other than the promise Hampton made to cinch another date within the week. Magnolia found herself searching behind Pearl Lee's cottage every morning for a second invitation to appear. On Friday, that very thing happened.

It was in the last days of March when Hampton fell in love, real love. He wore a brand-new light-colored cotton suit with a white shirt to accent the sparkling smile he wore on his lips. Magnolia, too anxious to sit, stood on the other side of the door at Pearl

Lee's, waiting to be swept off her feet for the second time in a week. She felt like a princess in training when he flashed his brilliant smile with a humble bow. "Hey, y'all," he said respectfully, like a young man calling on a girl's biological family. "Pearl Lee," he nodded cautiously, still insecure about her feelings regarding him dating her pupil. "Toussaint, how you do?" Hampton added eventually, doling out a full stack of salutations.

Toussaint grunted sorely, having been given the task of feeding Odessa, their toddling daughter, while Pearl Lee fussed at him over the half-empty bottle of bourbon she'd found hidden in the pocket of his winter coat. "Turn around," he demanded. "Let me see what you look like thereabouts. Uh-huh, appears kinda shady to me." Try as she might, Pearl Lee couldn't contain the chuckles tumbling out of her mouth. What had begun as subdued giggles eventually came pouring out as riotous cackles.

"Sorry, Hampton, but you do fare remarkable as the young suitor," she admitted happily. "I hope y'all have a good time."

"Thanks, Pearl Lee. I was hoping you'd be all right with me calling on Magnolia, seeing as how you done put yourself in charge of her safekeeping." He peered down at his sweaty palms. Hampton wiped both hands against his trousers. "Toussaint, thank you, too," he added when the frown on his brother-in-law's face clung on for dear life.

"Don't keep her out too late," Toussaint snarled. He enjoyed feigning hostility toward Hampton while boiling underneath. He hadn't yet forgiven his wife for snuffing out his Friday night high. "Now git along before somebody catches wind of you prowling." That sounded like a great idea, so Hampton bit on it.

Finally taking time to notice Magnolia's ensemble, a navy pleated skirt falling just below her knees, a beige knit pullover, and brown leather slip-ons, Hampton blushed. "Magnolia, you look beautiful tonight. I hope you's hungry, too. We got reservations at the Caledonia Inn."

"You trying to feed me dinner at a hotel?" she asked, rather embarrassed those words really came out of her mouth so early in the evening.

Pearl Lee spoke up before her brother managed a reply. "Relax, girl. That's a swanky nightclub you's being hauled off to." There was a hint of jealousy in her voice. She didn't know he could be so revering. "Hampton must think a lot of you."

"I think a heap of him, too," answered Magnolia. When she batted her eyes at him, Pearl Lee smacked her lips.

"Ohhh, brother, I do believe it's more than a notion. Y'alls so sweet my teeth are starting to rot. Mama's gonna be sorry she missed this. I'll do my best to rehash it for her, stitch by stitch."

Hampton grinned awkwardly. "I stopped by there first. She wasn't in, though."

"She lit out an hour or so ago, up to the meeting hall for her regular quilting circle. Talk about serving in the big house never gets old, I reckon." The meeting hall was nothing more than an old schoolhouse that substituted for a church when there was a traveling priest assigned to the area. Otherwise it was a place to go when they wanted to get out of the house without getting dressed up to do it.

"I guess we'll be going now. Pearl Lee, Toussaint." Hampton took Magnolia by the elbow, handling her gently, like glass.

Toussaint glanced up to sprinkle his thoughts on the occasion. "Have enough fun for the both of us, Hampton. Lawd knows I ain't in for none. Keep a good lookout, and don't have her out too late."

When Hampton pulled Magnolia through that door, she felt her whole life change. She watched as he spied to the left then to the right before easing down the creaky wooden planks. His eyes were peeled as they crouched through the tall sugarcane fields toward the Delacroix boat dock. Magnolia wasn't bothered in the slightest by taking risks. Even the unnerving sound of dogs howling in the distance didn't affect her. With Hampton by her side, she felt completely safe. Hampton couldn't feel anything but adrenaline coursing furiously through his veins. He exhaled wearily as they made it to the clearing between the plantation and the wide Terrebonne Bayou. "Whew, we's home free," Hampton affirmed quickly. He led Magnolia to the gangway then helped her down into the boat. "You can relax now."

She gazed into his eyes with the aid of the amber moon shining overhead. "I thought you knew, I set my mind to relax the moment you pulled me through the door at your sister's." Magnolia possessed a certain calm, one of an old soul who didn't concern herself with anything outside the moment she breathed in. She was mature for eighteen and mentally sharper than most girls her age, Hampton gathered, but she was still younger than the women he typically associated with. Caught in the middle of taking it slow, like Pearl Lee suggested, and allowing himself to be led by his carnal desires, Hampton decided to take his cue from Magnolia. He settled in, rowed downstream, and enjoyed that moment in time. "You is something else, Magnolia. I mean, something else. For eighteen, you's some kind of special."

"Thank you, but I can't take all the credit. Pearl Lee's been tutoring me some. Not just in books but in life, too. She helped me to get ready for you," Magnolia said casually. "I was fussing and fretting that I wasn't pretty enough. Pearl Lee said beauty ain't, I meant to say isn't, a gift but an ongoing undertaking."

"She ought to know, been undertaking it since we was kids," Hampton jested. "Y'alls good for each other. I can see that."

"What about us, you and me? Are you playing me on the square or just playing me?"

Hampton smirked with disbelief. "Who taught you to talk like that? Pearl Lee's got to learn her limits."

"Wasn't nobody who taught me to speak up for myself. I'm just a tiny speck on this side of nineteen. Shoot, I'm old enough to vote for president."

"Maybe so, but you'd have a fight on your hands trying to cast a paper ballot in the state of Louisiana. Colored folks got no rights down here. Colored women's got less." Hampton realized how that comment sounded condescending, so he went after a way to mend it. "But Jim Crow laws don't have to stop you, not from dreaming. Maybe there will come a time when a man's skin won't factor into whether he's hired for work or whether he can sit at the front of the streetcar or not."

"That was nice, Hampton, you saying something hopeful to make me feel better. Yeah, I knew what you were up to. You so sweet to me. How long should I expect you to keep it up?"

Having been put on the spot, Hampton couldn't find a lie in his heart, not even if he had a million years to search for one. "As long as you allow me to be," he confided openly. "Maybe even after that if I ain't ready to stop." The twinkle in Magnolia's eye affirmed what she thought of that. Unexpectedly, the enchanted gleam vanished the second Hampton tied the boat rope around the wooden dock post at the crawfish farm.

A sunburned middle-aged white man stood behind Hampton on the gangway platform. He was silent and stern. His clothes looked dirty and worn. The long-barreled rifle lying across his arm was shiny and polished. Magnolia gasped. Her fearful expression sent a shock wave through Hampton. "What? What is it?" he asked before following her gaze to the man's weapon. "Whoa, mister! I didn't steal this boat," he explained, with his hands hoisted in the air. He purposely placed his body between Magnolia and the end of the rifle barrel to protect her.

"So says you," the white fellow growled. His tenor was frightfully menacing to Magnolia. "If you saw a man helping hisself to your property, wouldn't that bear a close similarity to stealing?"

Hampton shook his head slowly. "No, sir, not if that man was to have permission to use that property. Willie Pope told me it was all right to borrow it, long as I brought the boat back just as found. There ain't no damage come to it by me."

"Willie!" the man called out. "Get out here!"

Magnolia grabbed the hem of Hampton's sport coat. He whispered to her, explaining that everything would be okay, then he tried hard to believe it himself. There was a loud commotion in the bait and tackle shack situated just off the water. Eventually, a short black man pushed the door open and started toward them. He rubbed his eyes then yawned groggily.

"What the..." he said, when his eyes focused. "Mr. Voller, this is Hampton, a friend of mine. I give him the okay to take the boat," he yammered excitedly. "It was just sitting there, and Hampton give me five dollars to run it up the bayou a ways." Willie's eyes played back and forth like ping-pong balls. "Hell, maybe he got a thing for boats."

"It ain't your boat to loan out," the white fellow argued. "Now, I don't take kindly to thievery or to niggers fooling with my property without getting my word on it. I can see my way to forgiving this misunderstanding for, let's say, ten dollars." When Hampton heard the man's proposition, he lowered his arms. He recognized a shakedown when one slapped him in the face.

Hampton reached inside his trouser pocket slowly and deliberately. "Ten dollars? I done give Willie five already. Here's another five."

Mr. Voller shook his head the same way Hampton had earlier. "Uh-uh, ten dollars for me. It's my boat."

Hampton pulled a wad of money out of his pocket and flipped off another crisp bill. He helped Magnolia off the tiny watercraft onto the landing, then he paid the man his price. Willie shrugged his shoulders as the nervous couple marched past them. "Thanks, Willie, for nothing," spat Hampton. After escorting Magnolia to the car he'd parked along the road, he pulled off leisurely, staring in his rearview mirror. Hampton couldn't help but chuckle when he saw the white man hand Willie his piece of the catch. It wasn't a bad hustle, getting money on the front and back end of a deal. Hampton later told Magnolia all about it. Understandably, she didn't find it the least bit funny.

9

HUNGER

Hampton cruised down Canal Street in his secondhand heap like it was a limousine. He glided along the wide avenue with his arm draped on the front bench seat. He would rather it be cradling Magnolia's shoulder, but she was giving him a heavy dose of the silent treatment. "Come on, girl, ease on up out of that rut. I apologized for laughing at what Willie Pope and his pal put us through. Hell, I'd have done the same only charged more." Hampton puckered his full lips and then made annoying smacking noises. "I bet you'd liven up if I was to stop this car right here, pull you out, and kiss you up one side of that fine brown frame of yours and down the other." Magnolia's eyes flew wide open. She couldn't hide her amazement or pretend she wasn't stirred up by his threat to maul her passionately in the middle of New Orleans's busiest thoroughfare.

"You wouldn't do no such thing, Hampton Bynote," she hissed playfully. "I know you wouldn't." Magnolia screeched like a child on an amusement park ride when he slammed on the brakes, stifling heavy traffic behind him. "Hampton, you get this car going right now!" She cut her eyes at people gawking at them from the sidewalk while avoiding other motorists looking on when they passed on either side. Car horns blared loudly. The noise was deafening. Magnolia placed both hands over her ears, squeezed her eyes shut, then pleaded loudly, "Okay, okay, Hampton! Get 'er going! I'll liven up! Whatever you want, I'll do it. Just go." Hampton laughed, threw the car in gear, then proceeded normally as if nothing had happened. Magnolia kept her ears covered and eyes closed until they made a full block. "I thought you said you'd be sweet to me," she reminded him. "That didn't last nearly as long as I thought it would."

"Oh, you meant starting now?" he said, grinning back at her. "I was just funning, Magnolia. I wanted to show you a good time and some of the things tourists is supposed to see in Nawlins. I was thinking on some dinner, some dancing maybe, and then browsing on some of the sights we got." The fact that Hampton had put a lot of thought into his date with her caused her to gush all over.

"Boy, you're a swell fella at wooing a girl, mapping out the whole evening and such. What other plans you making for me?" she said, flirting with her eyes.

"If I was your keeper, I'd tell you. Since you's currently on loan, I'll keep it to myself."

"On loan from who?" she spat, brooding over what he said. "And what you mean by that, anyway?" Hampton waited until he parked in the lot behind the Caledonia Inn before answering. Magnolia was upset because of it. "And another thing, I can't stand that about you already."

"What?" Hampton yelled loudly. Magnolia had him on edge unlike any woman he'd taken out before. He wasn't sure how he felt about that. It did keep him on his toes, though. He realized that right off.

Magnolia hopped out of the car and slammed the door to give him a taste of his own medicine. "How you come out with answers when you get good and ready. That's just plain mean, Hampton, mean." He circled behind the car to set things straight. Magnolia pouted nonetheless, turning her back on him.

"Magnolia, I ain't used to being pushed into answering nobody on the quick. You got me going in all directions at once. I'm starting to feel like a long-tailed cat in a room of rocking chairs." He put both arms around her waist and held her tightly, just like she wanted him to. "Don't be so easy to rustle. Besides, the fun is just about to begin." Hampton released his warm embrace. He backed off when his penis began to stiffen. Magnolia spun on her heels. She glanced down at the bulging knot in his pants then smirked at it.

"Fun, huh? You're going to put that fun on hold until I've had dinner. Come on, handsome, I'm real hungry," she moaned seductively. Hampton's mouth watered. It hadn't occurred to him that he was real hungry, too.

The Caledonia Inn was a Negro-run spot on the corner of LaSalle Street and Tulane Avenue. The establishment prided itself on hot food and smoking music. It was rumored that Louis Armstrong once played there for twelve straight hours and as soon as he finished, his magical horn was sent directly to the Jazz Hall of Fame for mounting. Other stories, many more colorful, circulated about the famous jazz and blues dinner den and lured both tourists and locals toward the brick archway gracing the restaurant's entrance. Bones had an in with the manager. He assured Hampton a table for two. At eight-thirty on the nose, he and Magnolia strolled past a gathering of patrons outside, all hoping to get in before their appetites for jambalaya and jam forced them to seek Cajun cuisine and Crescent City concertos elsewhere.

"Don't study that line none," Hampton whispered. "We's got the inside dope." Magnolia held his hand tightly when she received evil stares. "Anyway, standing around is for suckers. A friend of mine done put a word in with the management."

"Sorry, man, we sold out," the doorman barked, like he had to all the others for the first fifteen minutes. "Unless you got a reservation, a real one, then get to the back of the line."

"Check that list of yours for Hampton Bynote, table for two at eight-thirty." He held his breath as the sharply dressed colored man ran his skinny finger down the page in a big black book.

"Oh, yes, sir. You're a very important guest," he acknowledged with a smile that came out of nowhere. "We're to hold your table all night, if need be. Sir, Miss, come right this way." The gate-keeper removed the chain to let them pass. Magnolia bubbled over with joy when the anxious group on the sidewalk groaned. "I said, we's sold out!" shouted the doorman again. "Ain't no more tables so y'all may as well come back tomorrow, with some reservations!"

On the inside, extravagantly attired couples mingled over candlelit dinners and peach champagne, a house specialty. The Bynote party of two was shown to a table near the bandstand with a placard that had RESERVED stenciled on it in fancy lettering. Once Magnolia sat down, she peered around the room. Mostly everyone appeared to be looking at them. "Ooh, Hampton, I don't know if I like all this attention. It feels like I'm trapped in a fishbowl." He felt the same way but dared not voice it. "Ahhh," she gasped, after perusing the menu. "Six dollars for a blackened catfish plate? How are you ever going to afford all this?" She flipped the menu over to read the other side. "How much they charge for unblackened?"

"Shush, Magnolia, don't make a stir. People is likely to get the wrong idea about us." He'd noticed couples from nearby tables smiling at them.

"What, the idea that we's fool enough to overpay for a plate of whisker fish? I wish they'd mind their own business."

Hampton was in a real pickle. Bones neglected to share the lofty entrée prices and costly cocktails. After he'd shelled out fifteen dollars to Willie and his friend, he had only twenty-five dollars left. That would have been plenty had they dined just about anywhere else. Hampton nudged a smile forward when a tuxedo-wearing waiter brought over an iced-down bottle of bubbly and a basket of hot rolls. *A whole bottle of champagne*, Hampton thought. He drew close to contemplating how foolish he'd look when the bill came and he couldn't square it; then out of the blue, a silver lining shone through the dark cloud hanging over the table. Bones signaled hello from the bar with a shot glass of gin nestled between his fingers. "Magnolia, I'll be back in a tick," Hampton said apologetically.

"Uh-uh, you ain't leaving me here. What if your feet get itchy and you run out on me?"

"That won't ever happen," he told her with great assurance. "Not now, not ever." He strode by smiling faces from all directions, all grinning in his. It was eerily disturbing. Hampton assumed they'd all either had too much to drink or somehow discovered just how little money he had on him and couldn't wait to see him grovel. Something was going on, something very peculiar. It should have been an easy guess Bones was behind it.

"How you like the setup, Swagger?" asked Bones, fitted in a brown pin-striped suit, Stetson hat, and alligator shoes. "I told you I'd look after you."

"You put me in it, all right. Bones, I can't come up with the grip to spring for this banquet. Have you seen the money they's asking for meals?" The white man opened his mouth, leaned his head back, then tossed the shot of gin down the back of his throat.

"That ain't no way for a professional baseball player to act. It's all been taken care of."

"Man, somebody had better tell me something. First, the waiter brung over expensive-ass peach-tasting champagne and hot rolls that ain't nobody asked for, then here you come with crazy talk about ball playin'."

"Guess I'd better clue you in. See, in order to guarantee you a seat with these other colored big shots, I had to fudge your credentials."

"What credentials?"

"Well, hell, I had to make up something when the manager asked me why he should hold a table for you when there's always a crowd fighting to get in. Shit, I told him you were the newest player for the Kansas City Monarchs just passing through town for the night." Bones downed another shot of gin while Hampton tried to make sense of it. "Don't get bent out of shape. It worked, didn't it? I mean, that was you sitting over at the last open table like you'd swallowed a frog? Oh, did I forget to tell you that I'm springing for the high cost of vittles in this palace?"

Hampton was relieved. "If you could swing it, sure would take a load off." Bones opened his wallet and slid a twenty-dollar bill into Hampton's palm on the sly.

"Don't mention it, Swagger. We're pals, I won't forget that." Bones patted him on the back then winked proudly. Hampton was gravely unaware that he'd dug himself a deeper hole to climb out of. Bones would see to that. "So, who's the schoolgirl?" he asked in a meddling tone.

"About the sweetest thing I know. Her name's Magnolia

Holiday, like that famous singer." Bones leaned forward to get a better look.

"I don't see one damned lick of resemblance," he said, chuckling heartily. "Does her mama know what you have in mind after fattening her up on dirty rice and French mouthwash?"

"Don't worry on her account. She's legal, damn near nineteen. Shoot, I ain't but twenty-two myself. I'm measuring my luck. Won't be long before I close the deal."

Bones suggested he get back to her before she came to her senses, chickened out, and headed for the door. "I'm out on the prowl for an easy rider who can go 'round the turn without stumbling, and you come out of the gate with Susie Q." Hampton glared at Bones then held his tongue. A few weeks ago Hampton felt the exact same way about Magnolia, plus he was holding Bones's money in his hand. That was twenty good reasons to keep his comments under wraps where they wouldn't humiliate him. "Get on back to her." Bones sighed reluctantly. "Enjoy yourselves. Come by the auto shop about one o'clock tomorrow. I'll be in the back. School ought to be out by then."

Yet again Hampton kept quiet in regard to Bones's assessment of Magnolia's youth. True enough, Hampton's usual cup of tea was somewhat more mature and substantially more full-bodied. He put any notions to rest about robbing the cradle after rejoining her at the table. When she asked where he'd been, Hampton answered, "Just talking to Ivory Arcineaux. Bones is what they call him. Me and him is in business," Hampton added, to make their affiliation sound more dignified. "He's the one who set all of this up."

"While you was off with the man who set all this up, I've been fighting off that waiter from bringing more bread by the table. I don't want to pay for it by the loaf." Hampton snapped his fingers to summon the waiter back. He winked at his date with a new resolve and another man's money propping up his self-esteem.

"Please get the lady whatever she wants. She's the first ever to work on keeping money in my pocket," he said jokingly, and the waiter dashed off for another hot bread basket.

Magnolia had a good laugh when she learned the reason everyone paid so much attention to them. "A ballplayer?" she cackled, three glasses of champagne into her meal. "Well, you got the frame for it. What else are you built for?" Hampton leered across the table in a calculating manner. He was having the damnedest time seeing the eighteen-year-old that Pearl Lee and Bones saw. Magnolia had stretched out his comfort zone, his imagination, and his pants. She talked the right game, even for an older woman. He couldn't have known she'd rehearsed those tawdry lines from romance novels she kept hidden in her suitcase. She couldn't have foreseen the predicament they'd cause once she'd actually used them.

After dessert, Hampton tipped the waiter generously. With Bones at his back and Magnolia on his arm, his evening had all but been designed by the stars. Magnolia asked if they could walk awhile before going back to his place. Hampton obliged. He ushered her to a tall brick fence surrounding the Feeble Minded Retreat, a well-known backdrop where young lovers declared their affections for each other by carving their names in the old brick. Hampton used the rim of a quarter to commemorate their relationship. With Magnolia watching intensely, he was certain not to expose the other ten such bricks bearing his name beside those of previous girlfriends he'd wooed as well. After the finishing touches were carved in, their courtship was truly set in stone. Magnolia moaned with wine on her breath as she pressed her lips against Hampton's.

"I don't want to go back tonight," she cooed. "Carry me to your room. I'll settle things with Pearl Lee tomorrow."

"If I take you there, I'm likely to be your keeper by tomorrow. Pearl Lee won't have no say-so over you then."

"Ooh, that's music to my ears, honey. Let's get alone so you can beat on that drum."

"You said a mouthful."

"As long as you don't scuff up my heart none, I'm in for the duration."

By the time Hampton had parked his car on the street and gotten her upstairs, Magnolia hinted on all sorts of sensual behavior from those books she'd read. No sooner had Hampton slipped off her skirt and her blouse than she slouched on the bed and started in immediately with a noisy chorus of snorts and snores. Magnolia slept like a newborn baby full of well-seasoned seafood and peach-flavored champagne. Hampton stared at supple breasts pushing against her bra, her warm skin and snugly fitting panties. He yearned to satisfy the lusty ideas he'd rehearsed in his head along with the ones she recited. When the reality of deferred satisfaction set in, he was surprised that it didn't bother him half as much as he anticipated it would have. Magnolia was in his grasp, in his bed, and in his arms.

10

FUN AND FUNERALS

The following morning, Hampton left a note next to a carton of orange juice and a bag of beignets. He didn't know if Magnolia wanted anything that reminded her of the fruity spirits after she'd wandered too far into the bottle the night before so he took a chance, but the bag of sugar-covered pastries couldn't miss. She needed something in her stomach to soak up the alcohol and smooth out her morning. Hampton's instructions were short and to the point. *Make yourself to home, enjoy the snack. I'll be right back. Signed, Hampton.* He kissed her on the forehead then pulled the bedsheet over her breasts on his way out.

Hampton hustled onto the Canal streetcar line toward the Mississippi River. Bones told him to visit his hangout, an auto repair shop off Decatur Street, which had served as the planning stage for most of their heists. Considering they were two men from different cultures, their paths intertwined without incident. Hampton was a one-trick pony, a second-story man with slick skills and catlike reflexes. Bones kept a number of tricks in his bag, not all of them good. However, he was digging down into that bag of his when Hampton strolled into the back of a huge building made entirely of galvanized sheet metal. The gray warehouse had the name LeFleur's Auto painted on it. It served as an additional source of income for Bones, a hideout and a place for his youthful street musicians to practice without being hassled.

When Hampton heard the four-piece brass band blowing hot enough to melt all of that iron, he searched for Bones in the back office. The small room at the rear of the building had a small steel safe mounted inside a makeshift closet that wasn't visible unless someone was told where to look. The safe was there but Bones wasn't. When the music stopped suddenly, Hampton slid a wooden partition aside then stepped through to another part of the building where cars were serviced on occasion. Sitting in a director's chair next to a 1949 Ford truck with a severely smashed front bumper was Bones. He was snapping the daily paper, pointing at it, and ranting on about injustices in life and death. Four colored boys dressed in tattered jeans and faded shirts, none older than twelve, listened intently while catching their breath.

"That's why you gotta get all you can in this life while you're alive!" shouted Bones. His voice rose like a Baptist preacher's seeking to save a large congregation of souls. "I didn't want to believe, but here it is in black and white how two city workers was killed during that steam-pipe explosion. Sure, it could have been an oversight not to mention the colored fella's name, but no! Some newspaper this is, reporting only half the news." Bones nodded hello to Hampton but he was seeing red, too much red to stifle his tirade. "I ought to do something about the way this thing went down. This poor man, what's his name?" he asked feverously.

"Uhh...uh, Pettiford Lafall," answered Louie, a stringy eleven-year-old named after Louis Armstrong.

"That's the one!" Bones howled, his arms outstretched toward the young boys. He went back to spouting off about the *Times-Picayune* with so much vigor that he almost fell off that tall canvas chair of his and into the hundred-gallon grease pit below. It was then Hampton realized his friend hadn't slept a wink. Bones had been up all night, probably with more than one woman, and was now running on fumes. He stood up finally and pointed his right index finger at his miniature quartet. Obviously, they had witnessed the erratic behavior before. None of them seemed disturbed by it. Hampton watched in admiration as Bones blasted the newspaper, a local social organization, and race relations in general. He described his distaste for all concerned, from beginning to end. True enough, there had been an underground explosion wherein two people died instantaneously, one colored and the other a white man named Carl Blake. Second, the newspaper's account of the tragedy was a touching story about the white worker's years of dedicated service, without so much as one mention of the black man's contributions. Third, word had gotten around that the Benevolent Order of Pipe Fitters, a white membership organization, had prepared a grand funeral march to honor their fallen comrade. Bones admitted to having been on the phone all morning, trying to get in touch with the group responsible for aiding the deceased colored man. After he found no suitable answers as to why the same honor wasn't to be bestowed on the memory of poor Pettiford Lafall, Bones decided to take a stand. He instructed the boys individually, handed them five dollars each, then dispatched them to do as they were told.

Hampton felt out of sorts. There was a plot to instill civil disobedience afoot and he didn't have a role to play. "Man, you's on fire. Where'd all that hot-damned heat come from?"

"Hey, Swagger, sorry you had to see that. I'm not set on

changing the world, but wrong is wrong. It ain't fair to leave off the death of a Negro in a news story just because he was one." It was no secret that big city periodicals often omitted stories of Negroes unless they involved criminal acts against white citizens. Then, a story was fodder for the front page. "Well, why are you still standing there? Don't you want in on this?"

"I was starting to feel a little left out," Hampton admitted. "What can I do?"

"You can run home, put on your churchgoing duds, and meet me with the others at St. Louis Cemetery on the Iberville side entrance." Bones shrugged when he noted Hampton hadn't moved an inch. "Well, what is it?"

"Can I bring a date?"

"Aha, you've picked up a full-sized woman already?" he asked, really wanting to know. When Hampton's head teetered forward in a semishameful manner, Bones ribbed him again. "Oh, I see, school's still in. Hey, do what you gotta." Bones reached into his pocket, then reeled off a spread of bills. "Here, take this. Dress up your gal, get her a permission slip, and bring her on with you then. See y'all there."

"Man, you don't have to do this," said Hampton while counting the money Bones had given him.

"Don't mention it. Just make sure she's properly attired for a great big party. It ought to be a kick."

Hampton ducked out of the auto repair shop the same way he entered it, through the back. Smiling as he hustled up Toulouse Street, he hit a left into the Quarter on Bourbon Street. Halfway down the block, he saw it. The seven-foot-long Lucky Dog wiener cart always enticed him like a fan dancer parading around a burlesque stage. Hampton ordered four hot dogs and two sausage links with onions. Wearing his widemouthed smile once again, he scoffed down a sausage link before catching the streetcar to collect Magnolia.

Nibbling on a piece of fried dough, she languished on the bed in that tiny rented room. Her head felt as if it was coming unfastened. She peered up sorely when Hampton came through the door on a cloud and slammed the door excitedly. "Ouch, that hurts, Hampton," Magnolia whispered, a grimace weighing heavily on her face.

"Sorry about that. I'm just excited is all." He sat down on the bed next to Magnolia then waved his greasy lunch sack in front of her nose. "These here are one-of-a-kind lucky dogs. You're gonna need to get something solid in you," he said after spilling over, teasing her about what didn't happen the night before.

"I feel just about as awful about that, Hampton, as I do about my head ringing. I'll make it up to you soon enough, don't fret."

"I ain't studyin' that right now," he said eagerly. "You've got to shake off that sad sack and pick yourself up, yeah." Hampton began to shuffle his feet to a calypso beat going on inside his head. "Come on, yeah," he sang, "we got a date and can't be late."

"Please, Hampton, slow down." Magnolia groaned. "I know we're set to see the animals today. I don't expect they'll run off before we get there."

"Uh-uh, baby, we's up against a change of plans."

"What, we're passing on the zoo?"

"Yep. I'm treating you to something more better, a funeral."

"Oh, no!" she whined.

"Oh, yeah, you'll need a new dress, too, and we's short on time." Hampton started reeling off money for Magnolia's new duds and tossing bills on the bed to prompt her response.

"A brand-new dress?" she asked anxiously, staring at more

cash than he'd spent on the expensive dinner. "Where'd you get all that?"

"I copped some from that friend of mine. We get into some sure things every now and again," he offered calmly. "I told you last night we was in business together. Knowing Bones is good as money in the bank." Hampton was referring to the locked money closet hidden in the back room of the auto shop.

"You don't have to pay this money back?" she asked pensively. When Hampton shook his head assertively, Magnolia hopped off the bed and into his arms. "Let me get myself together then. I'll be ready in no time. You know, there's a nice navy blue number I saw in a storefront window the last time I was here, and"—she muttered while gliding into the bathroom—"and I'll need a pair of new shoes to match that dress. You know I wasn't all that keen on seeing no stinky animals, anyway. Delacroix 'nem got plenty of those and I see 'em every day for free." She hummed from the other side of the slightly opened door. Magnolia flitted around in that bathroom on a natural high, bumping into things and knocking over others. Hampton laughed as he peered through the thin slit, seeing what he could without being disrespectful.

"Where's your teethpaste?" she called. "Never mind, I'll just gargle real good. Snatch up that money off the bed so we won't be late." Hampton was correct about Magnolia, she was some kind of special. She buzzed past him with a small handbag clutched in her mitts. Hampton purposely paused at the door before leaving the room.

"Don't you even care whose funeral we's shuffling off to?"

"Was he a good friend of yours?"

"Never met him," Hampton answered, his lips parting nicely to force a grin.

"Good, then he didn't die owing you no money," Magnolia reasoned with a straight face. "Well, let's go get my dress!"

Hampton darted out onto the sidewalk in front of Krauss Department Store after Magnolia asked to see every dress in size six. He was surprised to see Bones's Cadillac making a U-turn in the middle of the wide thoroughfare. When he parked next to the curb, Hampton stepped to the passenger-side window. "Hey, Bones, I see you got this fine machine primped and polished for the cemetery show."

"Yeah, I'm on my way over to the cemetery now. I sent word for the procession to get going early because the other funeral starts at two-thirty." There were many lines drawn in New Orleans, color lines, cultural lines, and bloodlines. Bones didn't want to risk crossing all three at once by parading in a potentially heated altercation. "I think it best I don't mix in, but believe you me, I'll be rooting from the fringe."

Hampton hung his head remorsefully. "I know you will at that, seeing as how this was your idea. Magnolia's inside getting fitted now. We'll be along directly. I can't wait to see the fireworks."

"The poor soul couldn't get no respect in the papers so we're going to telegraph the angels in heaven that Pettiford Lafall is coming in with a bang."

"That's a powerful notion," Hampton agreed. Then a renegade thought streamed through his mind. "What if Lafall happens to be booking a room in that other place?"

Bones chuckled at the question before answering it. "Either way, they's about to get put on notice with one hell of a wake-up call." He was still laughing when he guided his shiny car back onto the avenue.

Hampton rushed inside the store to hurry his funeral date along. After viewing a slew of dresses, Magnolia selected the first one she'd laid her eyes on, a fetching navy blue satin gown with a flip collar and three-quarter sleeves. She used some of the money she'd made toiling in the washhouse to purchase a sleek pair of satin flats to match. Hampton nearly fell over when Magnolia put on her new threads and strutted out of the back room like a sophisticated magazine model.

"Wow, Mag, you look too good to be second-lining." After Hampton explained that the term referred to the host of dancers following the initial coffin procession, Magnolia tossed her head back and laughed agreeably.

"That's true, baby, but I look too good not to be seen by everyone who will be. Let's get a move on. I've cost us enough time already." When Hampton hailed a taxi, Magnolia questioned him with a raised brow.

"With yams that nice, you deserve to ride in style." Magnolia agreed with that, too.

Over one hundred mourners and curiosity hounds assembled at the home going for the colored city worker who'd met his untimely demise. The young boys Bones had paid to get the word out prevailed in overwhelming fashion. They used rhetoric they heard in the dirty auto shop to stir up Negroes in their community. Magnolia was speechless when Hampton explained that his white business partner was behind the grand affair.

A colored minister preceding the horse-drawn coffin carriage wiped sweat from his brow for two reasons. One, he was compensated handsomely to rush through the burial ceremony, and the other was the high probability of a fight breaking out once they reached the entrance, for Carl Blake, the white pipe fitter, had been severely overshadowed at a neighboring cemetery. Bones had learned the route to be taken for Blake's procession and purposely negotiated a thundering exit after a heartrenching march into St. Louis Cemetery No. 2. As the crowd swelled at the gates of the cemetery, the old minister kept a keen eye on his pocket watch. After the pint-size quartet completed a slow sentimental tune, he offered condolences to Lafall's widow and small children. Attendees came to know Pettiford Lafall from what they heard about him on the streets, and they summoned up tears over the way he died and had almost been forgotten. Women were falling out, swooning and fussing over the man laid to rest inside a modest wooden box. Magnolia was simply glad to be in the presence of someone famous, dead or alive. She assumed the deceased craftsman had been one heck of a plumber to cause the wealth of wailing and carrying on. "Hampton, why are they putting that stone hutch over the casket?" asked Magnolia when it seemed a very odd thing to do. "They think somebody's gonna come around to steal him?"

"Naw, girl," he snickered quietly. "They can't bury him underground in Nawlins, too much water underneath. He's liable to pop up and flop out of that box if they did." Magnolia placed her arm around Hampton's waist when it occurred to her that none of the people buried in the cemetery were beneath the soil. That sent chills through her.

While Magnolia overanalyzed the practical tradition, she was floored by the pomp and circumstance that followed. The minister hurried through his patented send-off then led the gathering toward the St. Louis Street exit, where other would-be mourners had been instructed to congregate. The speedy burial service concluded what had begun with soul-stirring dirges and sad hymns by the miniature musicians in their Sunday-best suits. Now that the business end of Pettiford Lafall's send-off was complete, the minister struck up the band. The boys started in with long overplayed notes that sounded like a crowd of whining clowns before they quickened the pace and precision of their song. Forming what was commonly known as the first line, the minister and the family of the deceased kept in close step behind the band. They twirled umbrellas and decorative parasols overhead while clapping with the joyful beat. The second-liners of the parade, consisting of spectators and everyone else who followed the first line, danced wildly with handkerchiefs and hats waving in the air. It was a spectacle and the biggest send-off of the year to be sure. Magnolia couldn't believe it all happened down the middle of a main street. For three blocks the music blared. Dancers were grinding and gyrating in broad daylight. Eventually, Magnolia was coaxed by Hampton into provocative strutting and shimmying with the best of them.

When Hampton spotted Bones wearing a satisfied grin and sitting on the hood of his parked car, he whistled to get his friend's attention. "Hey, honey, there's Bones. See, right over there." Magnolia saw a fat man holding a poodle and mistook him for Bones. Apparently, he wasn't the sole white man transfixed by the outlandish activity passing by. Even so, the moment Bones caught a glimpse of Hampton, he hopped down off the car then leapt into a wickedly funny dance of jooks and spins to the rhythmic syncopation. Hampton didn't know the cost for such a celebration, but the ten minutes that ensued were priceless.

Just as anticipated, they ran into Carl Blake's minuscule delegation of friends and family at the corner of St. Louis and James streets. The priest assumed the accumulation of colored mourners would stop and allow the smaller group to pass. The adult musicians for the white man's funeral made valiant attempts at staying with the sorrowful songs they trumpeted but were eventually dismayed at the youngsters' persistence and audacity to keep the party going until the last second-liner had crossed through the intersection. "Finally!" Hampton laughed riotously. "White people getting to see what it's like waiting on coloreds. I wonder if they admire the view back there."

"I like it fine from where I stand," Magnolia giggled. "It feels real good."

11

The Living End

Folks in New Orleans find just about any reason to throw a party," Magnolia howled as she sat in Pearl Lee's kitchen reliving the jazz funeral from the day before. "I wouldn't mind being put to rest with horns blaring and dancing all around. Wow, it was something to see, I'll tell you."

Rayletta stood over the black cauldron-shaped pot, stirring the gumbo she'd been fussing over for hours. "Sounds like a sight to behold, women and men getting all beside themselves over a soul going home to glory. It was a grand time, yeah?"

Magnolia placed her hand over her heart then sighed. "That poor man's death was simply the living end." She laid the cotton canvas she'd been crafting on her lap and smiled brightly. "Hampton said his white friend, Bones, was to blame for all that fun and spoofing, but I know he had something to do with it. You should have seen the way those boys wailed on the instruments, with their chests stuck out all proud and proper. It was like somebody told them to make sure me and Hampton had a good old time." Magnolia carried on as if she were alone in a daydream. She hadn't noticed that Pearl Lee and Rayletta were both holding in their chuckles.

"Well, you'll have quite a few rumblings to speak of when you get back up north," Pearl Lee suggested. "Maybe if you ever get around to finishing that quilt you been doting over, you can show them that, too," she jeered playfully at the slow progress Magnolia had made with her first quilting pattern.

"Don't you worry about what I got in the works," Magnolia said flippantly. "I done started to figure out a couple of things on my own. There's more to being a grown woman than quilting." After placing both hands over her mouth she let out a wild squeal. "Ohhh, I didn't mean it to sound so nasty."

"But it did," said Rayletta, a faraway look in her eyes.

"Tell me about it, Mama. Hampton done got this girl's nose wide open," Pearl Lee thought out loud.

"Uhh-huh, now I'm concerned about what other things he's got wide open," Rayletta smarted. "Child, don't let no man and I mean *no man* get you into deviled straits. Life can get real unfriendly if that happen." It was obvious to Rayletta that Magnolia knew as little about deviled straits as she did about stitching a decent quilt together. "Listen to me good. A woman's got all her wits about her until a man puts a baby in her belly, then her mind gets as cloudy as this here roux." She didn't wait on a response before adding another nugget of wisdom along with a basket of crawfish to the chicken, sausage, and vegetables in the pot. "You just got to Newberry, Magnolia. Don't fool yourself into thinking you got Hampton or this place figured out yet. Either can do you something bad as sure as the wind blows."

"Mama!" Pearl Lee called out in a thunderous voice that shook Magnolia. "Somebody's at the door. It's Hampton, I'd bet." That was the only way she knew to convey that her mother had said enough without making a federal case about it. All of the women looked toward the door as the knob turned. When Hampton stepped through it, Magnolia's breath raced from her lungs.

"Hampton, it's not safe for you here," she whispered, rising to her feet. Rayletta squeezed out a labored exhale as she approached her son with both arms outstretched to greet him.

"Can't you see, Magnolia, this man's in love and don't care who sees him? His papa was the same, it's true." Rayletta threw her arms around Hampton and hugged him for the longest time. "I don't blame you, boy, some things is worth the trouble." Hampton was holding his mother but eyeing his woman the entire time.

"Yes, Mama, some things sure is," he agreed. "Hey, Magnolia, Pearl Lee. I could smell the gumbo rolling in that pot from down the way."

Magnolia put the quilt aside and brushed both of her sweaty palms against her blue jeans. "Hampton, you ought not have come during the daylight. What if the Mister or that Trotter seen you at the front door?" He laid a longing grin on her, hot enough to melt butter.

"If'n that be the case, I won't buckle. Everything I care about on God's green earth is right here in this house. My kin and my"—he chose his words carefully in his mother's presence—"everything else." Pearl Lee ran to the door and peeked out. She was concerned about Hampton losing his life over *everything else* in particular.

Pearl Lee returned with her palms moist now. "Okay then, let's try to keep quiet and enjoy a nice Sunday dinner 'cause you never know how long it'll last," she asserted as the front porch step creaked like it did when Hampton arrived. She forced down a swollen gulp. "Hampton," she whined quietly, "get out through the trapdoor." He didn't move an inch. "Please *get*," she whispered, her back pressed against the door. Three hard knocks pounded on the wood.

"Pearl Lee!" Trotter shouted. "I know you're in there. You and Toussaint might as well open up now. I heard Hampton's been seen on the grounds and I need to check it out."

Magnolia took her seat, laid the quilt over her lap, and then closed her eyes. Hampton scooted onto the floor reluctantly. His eyes questioned Toussaint's peculiar sleeping behavior. He hadn't seen a grown man huddled into a fetal position and sucking his thumb before. Rayletta used the sole of her shoe to shove Hampton out the trapdoor hidden beneath a throw rug near the wrought-iron bed frame. She shook her son-in-law to wake him. Toussaint stirred. He wiped at his mouth and sat up on the bed.

"What is it, Rayletta?" he asked as the pounding continued.

"Trotter's at the door and he's aiming to kick up a fuss. Maybe you can go and talk to him, peacify him some."

"Peacify him? For what?" he said, stumbling toward the door. "What the hell happened whilst I was sleeping?" Toussaint slid his right arm into the shoulder strap of his overalls before opening the door. Trotter stood on the other side when he did. He was with two other men, all of them carrying shotguns. Toussaint backed up nervously without realizing his nerve had already given in to retreat. "What's all this here about?" he said eventually. "A man can't have Sunday supper with his family in his own house no more?"

Trotter's jaw tightened as he spoke up. "We ain't seeking no disrespect, Pearl Lee," he answered, peering over Toussaint's shoulder as if Pearl Lee was the head of the household. "Me and my men just come by to make sure Hampton didn't come to join your supper is all."

"Ain't no call for all this," Toussaint told Trotter as he observed the fire power he'd assembled. "We haven't seen Hampton, and by the looks of things, you's scared as hell to run into him yourself."

Crouching under the house, Hampton searched desperately for a weapon to fight back with, assuming a melee was imminent. Tripping over a sharp object sticking out of the ground, he placed both hands around it and tugged with all his might. He gasped and lunged backward when the gnarled stump he'd yanked on was attached to a woman's arm. Hampton made a noisy thump while clawing at the dirt to get away from it.

Tension inside the old shack thickened. The white men pushed past Toussaint to investigate. "I guess you're gonna tell me you didn't hear that, either," Trotter hissed. "Fellas, check it out."

Rayletta sent up a silent prayer. Magnolia was afraid to make a peep as well. Pearl Lee gnashed her teeth. She rushed ahead of the white men stomping toward the lounging area in the rear of the house. "Hold on a minute!" she screamed. "My child is sleeping in there." Pearl Lee snatched Odessa up from the bed in one effortless swoop. She peered down between the dusty floorboards, pleading with a strained expression for her brother to remain still if he wanted to remain alive. Both men used their long gun barrels to riffle through the hanging clothes in a makeshift closet, then they poked under the bed and behind the curtains.

Hampton didn't move a muscle although his mind raced feverishly just beneath their boots. In an instant, he'd traveled back to a place tucked in the recesses of his childhood memories. He remembered chasing a baseball into the crawl space of his parents' house. As a small boy, it hadn't occurred to him when he heard lovemaking noises, groaning and grunts emanating from above, that his father was on a hunting trip, until his father's favorite song faintly tickled at his ear. Hampton also remembered raising his head, wondering who was making those sounds with his mother. He crept out of the darkened hideaway with his baseball in hand. His father called out to him from the foot of the grassy hill behind the row of former slave shanties. Hampton, no older than five at the time, turned toward the house then back to his father. He didn't understand what was going on then and didn't think of it again until that very moment. Rayletta was entertaining another man. He shut his eyes sorrowfully when it came to him that it was the Mister's boots hurrying down the front steps of his house that day. Delacroix had seen Hampton gawking at him like a ghost who'd materialized before his eyes. It took seventeen years for Hampton to recognize the guilt Mr. Delacroix wore on his face the day he fled. Hampton had worn it, too, when jumping out of a second-story window as he was fleeing a spiteful reprisal from Thelma's husband.

Hampton swung ferociously when someone nudged him with a broom handle through the open trapdoor. "Hey, man, keep it down," Toussaint scolded. "They's gone now, but you gotta keep quiet. They could circle back."

Hampton's eyes blinked rapidly. He was caught between the truth he'd realized regarding Rayletta and Mr. Delacroix and the story attached to the contorted hand reaching up through the ground. He'd rather have been shot by Trotter's men than face his mother with a damning memory from his youth. He tried to pull himself together while climbing out of the hole in the floor. How long had it been going on? And did the affair have anything to do with the accident his father incurred at the sugar mill, subsequently ending his life? So many questions swirled in Hampton's head. So many that he couldn't speak when Rayletta approached him.

"What's got you, son?" she asked, placing her trembling hands on his wrists. "Lawd, he's hardly breathing. Toussaint, go fetch Madame Baptiste. Hampton? Hampton, baby? Snap out of it. Tell Mama what's got you."

He slid her hands away from his as if she'd soiled his shirt cuffs, when it was his father's memory she'd sullied. "I just recollected something about you and the Mister," he answered sorely. "How could you do that to Papa?" he added, in pain. "I gotta leave now, and y'all don't have to worry about me coming back. I'm sorry for ruining supper, Toussaint, Pearl Lee. Magnolia, you don't belong here. I'll pay your bus fare home if you so inclined to go." Hampton peered around the room like a man in a foreign place. "Take care of baby Odessa, Pearl Lee. Toussaint, you need to take care of that dead girl rotting under your bedroom floor. Appears she wasn't all the way dead when you planted her. She reached out for life till the very end."

Without another utterance, Hampton opened the front door and walked out in the same manner he'd entered, leaving everyone except Pearl Lee stunned. She'd learned of Rayletta's tryst with Ransom Delacroix much in the way her brother had, purely by chance. She never did let on because it hurt too bad acknowledging what she'd heard from other young girls in school, scores of women in Newberry sharing the same secrets, white women as well as colored, each pretending the other wasn't privy to the troubles hidden away in their hearts. The moment Trotter announced his engagement to a local beauty queen three months ago, Pearl Lee felt the brunt firsthand. She became the next in a long line to carry another woman's burdens while sharing her man's embrace at the same time.

Rayletta was numb. She pondered what exactly had come over Hampton during his stint beneath the trapdoor. She doubted that he could ever make sense of it, so there was no use discussing a way of life she didn't fully comprehend herself. Rayletta was completely confident of one thing before wandering from her daughter's home that afternoon with a troubled spirit. She'd never see her son again. Rayletta broke him in two, without raising a hand; as only a mother could.

Family squabbles were as prevalent in Virginia as anywhere else, so Magnolia had witnessed her share of them. They typically ended with someone getting leveled with an angry fist. It was the first time she'd seen it play out this way, with calm words proving more effective. Magnolia stood on the wooden floor coddling her quilting essentials close to her chest. Unbeknownst to her, she had been sucked in to the prevailing winds of the farming community as she had been to the comprehensive quandaries plaguing Hampton's family: Rayletta's indiscretions exposed. Faith in what Hampton used to believe in severely shaken. Murder an irrefutable necessity. It occurred to Magnolia that there were two avenues available to her. One of them involved getting on the first thing smoking out of town. She chose the road less traveled, rolling up her sleeves to pitch in.

"Why don't I take Odessa home with me tonight?" she offered. "I'll take good care of her. You all need to sort out what to do about Sadie. Hampton told me darned near the whole state of Louisiana is sitting ten feet on top of water." When Pearl Lee failed to respond directly, Magnolia took it upon herself to act in their best interests. She found a pillowcase and gathered some of the baby's clothing and toys and put them inside it. Odessa was sound asleep when Magnolia packed her off that evening, but the sinful spirits affixed to the Bynote family had only begun to wake.

12

Bottoms Up

"What the hell is Sadie doing down there, sprouting up out of the ground?" Toussaint shouted once they were alone. His hands trembled as he raised them toward his ears. "Ahhh, my head feels like it's about to pop open, Pearl Lee. I need me a drink now." He'd experienced severe pains lately and a strange bout of unexplained behaviors. Since alcohol actually seemed to curb the torment rambling inside of him, Pearl Lee gave in. She raced to the cupboard and pushed aside a mason jar filled with sugar.

"Here, baby, take it. I'm sorry for bringing this on you," she whined repentantly. Pearl Lee wrung her hands, hanging her head as Toussaint guzzled whiskey in a blatant attempt to soothe his anguish. "That's it, go ahead and drink."

Toussaint finished the bottle and used his sleeve to wipe his mouth. He staggered to the kitchen table and plopped down in a chair. The weight on his shoulders was too great. "I asked you a question, woman, and I deserve an answer," he grunted, his eyes flaming red with resentment. "You planted that woman in the dirt, and I want to know if it had something to do with Trotter."

The distressed expression he wore frightened Pearl Lee. Her husband had always been a loving and forgiving man. Realizing he was up against a wall of uncertainty, she took a seat and joined him, hoping to ease the pain.

"Toussaint, you know I love you with all my heart and then some. Sadie, she came around sassing me and kicking up lies about you and another woman. She wouldn't say who," Pearl Lee lied. "I told that heifa to shut up about you but she wouldn't." The lies continued rolling off Pearl Lee's tongue once she started.

"See, we had words and then there was this struggle," she ranted sorrowfully. "Sadie tried to hide it, but she had designs on you, honey, and I wouldn't stand for it." Pearl Lee stared directly into her husband's tired eyes and hid the real reason for killing the other woman. During their quarrel, Sadie had threatened to expose the affair with Trotter if Pearl Lee refused to stop seeing him. Sadie's boasting hastened her murder. She bragged about being the only one Trotter really cared about. For admitting to being another of Trotter's conquests, Sadie got a carving knife plunged into her throat. It took Pearl Lee two hours of intensive scrubbing to wash the blood from her wood floor. Since the water ran beneath the house, softening the dirt, it was the perfect place to stash the corpse. "I am sorry, Toussaint, really I am. If I could take it all back I would," she offered falsely, bundled in a web of deceit. Pearl Lee's only true regret was bumping off Sadie before getting her to confess she was the person who tucked a chicken foot under their mattress with a lock of Toussaint's hair tied to it with a black satin ribbon. If she had it to do all over again, Pearl Lee would have coerced a declaration of guilt from Trotter's other squeeze and then cut a gash in Sadie's neck afterward.

Eventually, Toussaint brought both hands down from his

head and sighed. "So it all started from spiteful words between you and Sadie?" he asked quietly.

"Yeah, a quarrel over you is all, and then..." she said, her voice trailing off when she was all lied out.

"A goddamned quarrel? Huh, I guess I don't have to ask who come out on the wrong end. Didn't you know I could never see loving nobody but you? I might show my teeth to other women every now and again, but that's just for grins. I'm a one-woman man, Pearl Lee. Yours." He explained why he hadn't told her about Sadie's improper advances toward him over the years. He didn't see any good coming from it considering Pearl Lee's quick temper. Other women's innuendos didn't make a dent in his resolve despite how flattering they were. Toussaint was old-fashioned, he concluded honestly. It was too bad his wife couldn't truthfully say the same. While his eyes may have strayed plenty of times, his commitment to their marriage never did, not once.

There was silence in their home, a wicked, unnerving silence as they waited for the sun to fade over the horizon. It was half-past eight that evening when Toussaint grabbed a shovel from his back porch. Pearl Lee opened the hatch over the trapdoor to meet him there. When Toussaint circled to the side of the house nearest their bedroom, he was surprised to find his mother-in-law on her knees and up to her elbows in soil. She'd placed a lantern beside the grave to illuminate what should have been kept in the dark forever. "I was starting to think I'd be moving this gal all by myself," Rayletta huffed. "I ain't in no shape to be carrying on like this, and she already done begun to spoil." She fanned at her nose before turning her head away to draw in a fresh breath. "Whew, she's ripe."

Pearl Lee was also shocked to see her sickly mother in old overalls, toiling like a field hand. "Mama? What you doing out here?" she queried shamefully. "This has nothing to do with you. Me and Toussaint is gonna fix it."

"She's right, Rayletta," Toussaint agreed. "This is me and my wife's problem. We'll handle it."

Rayletta struggled to pitch out dirt with a tin plate after overlooking what they had to say. "Huh, appears to me y'all could use every bit of help you can get to make this ugly business go away. Pearl Lee, get in there and fetch me a rag to tie across my face. We got to move quick." Her daughter seemed confused. Rayletta appeared unreasonably calm during the dead woman's excavation.

"Mama, you ain't bothered none about doing this?"

Placing both hands on her thighs to rest, Rayletta prepared to divulge a secret she'd hoped her daughter would have no need of knowing. "What? You think Sadie is the first loudmouth to get herself anchored into the ground? Hurry now and help me to dig her up, then I'll show you where we put the others."

Pearl Lee backed away from the hole in her floor in total disbelief. She was too bewildered to inquire what others and how many others there might be. She thought she knew everything that went down on the Delacroix Plantation and just about everything that happened in Newberry, too. Pearl Lee hadn't come close to discovering the sagas surrounding her own family.

After they tied rope around the stiffened body and pulled it from beneath the cottage, Toussaint dumped the bloated corpse in a wheelbarrow. Rayletta instructed him which direction to strike out in. She and Pearl Lee lagged behind to talk privately among themselves. "Where is this place you speak of, Mama?" Pearl Lee asked in a way that suggested she was upset over hearing about it just now.

"Don't concern yourself with that just yet. You need to come out with what really brought this on." She pointed to the spoiled remains stretched out in the wheelbarrow like a decaying scarecrow. "Keep going dead ahead, Toussaint," she commanded, "and then push toward the boggy creek."

"What if he hears?" Pearl Lee uttered softly.

"He's got a chest full of doubt and liquor pouring from his sweat. He can't hear nothing but his own breath blowing in front of him."

Pearl Lee pursed her lips stubbornly before she openly revealed what she couldn't force herself to tell her husband. "Sadie was gonna tell Toussaint about me and Trotter. She said she never liked me, anyway, so it wouldn't bother her to ruin my life. I begged her not to break the agreement and then reminded her of the Glory Road killings. That fat cow laughed in my face, Mama. She said she didn't care what happened, just that I was to stop letting Trotter get behind me like the agreement say. Didn't matter if I turned him down, he didn't care for that big moose."

Rayletta paused. She looked her daughter over thoroughly just as she had years ago, when her child sprinkled the truth over with fiction then. "He, who?" Rayletta huffed suspiciously. "I see now. This ain't about your husband as much as it about Trotter, is it?" When Pearl Lee failed to meet her serious gaze, Rayletta had her answer. "This changes things. You was wrong to dash out Sadie's life and not be sure if there was a need for it. Jealousy guided your hand, child; nothing but raw jealousy. I remember when your pride was tied up in Toussaint's looks. You didn't fool me when you got hitched to him. Everybody can see he's a pretty man. I'm not one for bad-mouthing, but your husband should have figured out what was going on behind your back before some busybody was spouting off about telling him what was happening behind his. You know he tends to be simpleminded. Shoot, Toussaint is sometimes as thick as a brick when you get right down to it."

"That's part of it, too, Mama. That Sadie had a hex put on Toussaint. I found the charm betwixt my mattress and springs. She didn't come clean on it before I cut her up, but I know she's the one who did it."

"If that be so, there won't be no remedy to remove the evil charm. Things like this has got to be done in reverse and by the one who angled the spirits to upset things in the first place." Rayletta noticed tears streaming along Pearl Lee's cheeks. "Crying ain't gonna help you now. You got to do what you should have when this trouble first stuck its face in yours and made you act out so. After we put this soul to rest for good, you take Toussaint to his great-auntie to see if she can soften the hex somehow. Maybe she can take the charm Sadie left behind to loosen at least some of the demon spirits from it. I've seen it work before."

Rayletta yelled for Toussaint to stop at the enormous cypress tree and start digging to the left of it. "I'm not gonna be here too much longer, so I'll tell you something you can't open your mouth to nobody about, and I mean nobody." Pearl Lee nodded her head that she understood. What she was about to hear was deeper than life itself. "I cried every night when I carried Hampton. That day, before he was born, I passed out cold and landed on my belly. I must've fell on him. My knees buckled under me when somebody dropped a dead boy pup on my doorstep. The dog's eyes were matted closed. That pup came ahead of time, or maybe had been cut out just to haunt me. I expect it was the Mister's new bride who had it done. Lawd knows she didn't understand how things worked back then. After catching us together, she had the right to run out on him and bring harm to me." Pearl Lee watched pensively as her mother acknowledged what she'd discovered by mistake as a curious little girl wondering what business Mr. Delacroix had sneaking around when her daddy was in the fields. "I woke up with half the village standing over me, gaping and wailing," Rayletta continued. "They was praying to Jesus and gibbering in the old-world tongues, too. It felt like Hampton was doing flips in my womb. Then something went awry, because he stopped moving altogether. I didn't feel a peep out of him or nothing. That next morning, my water bag broke. It hurt so bad I wanted to die right then and there. I sent for the midwife. Your papa sent for Madame Baptiste. By the time either of them got there, I'd forced the baby out on my own. Hampton's eyes were shut tight like a mean fist, and he was dead as that pup I found dumped at my front door. The midwife went on about her way. Madame stayed behind. She watched all the praying and moaning for him to wake up until everybody done give in and quit. Somehow, Madame Baptiste conjured up some powerful medicine to make him stir."

"Black magic?" Pearl Lee uttered quietly.

"No such thing. Medicine, herbs, and roots is how she did it. Two days later, Hampton coughed up a ball of hair stuck in his throat. He was the only child I ever heard of trying to get up and walk before he got his first cry out good."

"I think the hole is deep enough," Toussaint huffed exhaustedly from nearly twenty feet away. "Can I toss her in yet?"

"Yeah, she's been ready to go home," Rayletta replied. They took turns shoveling the mound of dirt over the rotting corpse and praying for all of Sadie's sins to be forgiven. Then, as casually as you please, they returned from whence they came, bearing the full comprehension of what they'd done and the dues to be paid when their time came to meet the same fate.

13

Gone Fishing

Three days had passed since Hampton stomped away from Pearl Lee's home and from overwhelming heartache. Learning that his mother had been unfaithful to his father cut him deep. In his eyes, Rayletta ate, drank, and slept atop a pedestal. Now Hampton didn't know how to feel about her. She'd always done everything right. Sexual involvement with a white man, no matter how rich and well respected, couldn't have been seen as more wrong. Family miseries pulled at Hampton the way none of his own could. Troublesome feelings tore at his insides, churning angrily in the pit of his stomach. He holed up in his room, unsettled and languishing in a pool of pity. He felt alone and empty until that same annoying neighbor from down the hall came rapping on his door again, griping about "that damn telephone." Dressed in a sweaty undershirt and a wrinkled pair of slacks he'd slept in, Hampton growled irritably. He raced to the door and snatched it open. He was prepared to try his luck against the man with the big voice, which always seemed to materialize when he'd been terribly behind on sleep. To Hampton's dismay, the dark hallway was completely vacant. Frothy venom mounted in the corners of his mouth as he promised himself to learn which of the tenants was dead set on being a nuisance. He planned on busting that fellow's door and getting even. Hampton figured that anyone should have known better than to disturb a man when he wanted to be alone with his despair.

With no one to match blows, Hampton slinked over to the alcove to take the phone call he'd been summoned to in the first place. Bones was on the line complaining about having to hold the enterprise together all by his lonesome when the time had come to kick up their criminal activities a notch. "Swagger, I'm getting fed up with chasing you down. I thought we was going at this thing of ours all the way. You want to bow out or something, just say so!" Bones ranted on.

"I know I got the right to if I wanna," Hampton replied evenly. "And you ought to know that ain't my way. I'm direct when my mind is made."

"Yeah, that's what I was hoping. We've gotten by with the capers we've pulled, but I'm thinking on making a big splash. I really need you to strap up and throw in with me. I got a line of some easy pickings, a lot of loot," Bones said eagerly.

Hampton listened with a discerning ear. Something in Bones's voice was off a measure. He sounded as if he was making a pitch instead of merely bringing his partner up to speed on the status of their association. "I hear you squawking, Bones, but you ain't said nothing yet worth hashing out. What're you getting at, or is it something you ain't saying that I ought to be concerned about?"

There was an uneasy pause in the conversation. Bones was taking the time to choose his words carefully. "Don't go getting all punchy on me, Swagger. It's just that I've been doing some heavy thinking and came up with a way to go upstream to trap us some bigger fish. Maybe even catch us a gator or two."

"I don't like gators," Hampton answered quickly, clueless to Bones's jesting.

"Not real gators, man. What's going on with you? I'm talking about something to fetch us bunches of cash. Lots of these rich folks have famous paintings and statues and heirlooms and such. I aim to relieve them of a few pieces is all."

Hampton hemmed and hawed before agreeing to snap out of his funk. Making enough money to sit on sounded ideal, especially after he'd decided to turn his back on Newberry with its plantation problems and move up north where people were more civilized. The dead girl growing out of the ground beneath Pearl Lee's floorboards and his mother's treachery didn't sit too well with him. The more he thought about it, the better Bones's suggestion appealed to him. "Okay, I'll meet you at the auto garage. We'll have to talk about a different split on the take, though. Loose cash ain't gonna get it no more. I'm looking to bail out in a week or so. There's too much happening at home for me to stay put, and there's not a damn thing I'm interested in doing about it, either. Hell, yeah, I'll throw in with you. See you in a minute."

Bones had spent several weeks staking out potential victims in the French Quarter, all of whom were men with wealth he'd confirmed personally, gambling habits, and questionable sexual appetites he'd witnessed firsthand. Hampton didn't question Bones's decision to focus their attention on an area west of Dumaine all the way to Canal Street, which encompassed fifty-six square blocks of densely populated homes belonging to some of the wealthiest people in New Orleans.

Later that evening, Hampton hopped behind the wheel of his car with Bones at his side, multiplying visions of grandeur in his head. And if they managed to pull down the kind of money his friend had promised, Hampton's desire to start over up North wouldn't be too far off. That alone was good enough reason to follow Bones's lead down the dark narrow streets originally built hundreds of years earlier for horses and carriages.

The first mark on their list sat near the corner of St. Ann and Royal, where an oddly fascinating gate surrounded the house. Hampton crouched down beside the intricately designed fence, an iron masterpiece painted green with yellow patches, fashioned to resemble interwoven cornstalks. He grimaced at the thought of throwing away good money merely to entertain passersby. In Hampton's mind, there couldn't have been any other reason for the expensive gate. It wasn't constructed in a manner to keep men out who had a notion to climb over, nor would it contain a yard dog that felt the need to squeeze through gaps in the elaborate design. Any man foolish enough to blow a wad of cash on what had to be a whim, Hampton concluded, deserved to be unburdened from further foolhardy extravagance.

The three-story house, with huge bay windows overlooking a broad cobblestone walkway, rested on a plush green lawn. The wood trimmings had been painted a dusky shade of yellow to complement the metal corncobs fastened onto the gate out front. Bones surveyed the surrounding area patiently. He waited until a young couple passed along the sidewalk before waving Hampton over to join him in the tall shrubs near a side window on the first level of the mansion.

"Shhhh, quiet, Swagger," Bones whispered when Hampton accidentally stumbled over his toolbox. "You gonna wake the dead and everybody else trying to catch some winks in this town."

"Sorry, Bones. Just a little excited. This here is one giant-size house. I'll crack the window then open the back door." He'd learned that Bones wasn't very skillful at climbing. After he'd used his tools to unlock the window latch, Hampton raised the wooden frame and slipped in silently. Hardwood floors covered the first level decorated with antique furniture, brass collectibles, and crystal knickknacks. While slinking toward the rear of the house, he noticed sculptures of naked Negro men in stone and bronze proudly displayed. It seemed peculiar to him because colored men weren't permitted to purchase property within the Quarter limits. And Hampton couldn't imagine a white man showing off what he called "nigger trinkets" in his own home. Bones had run clean out of patience by the time Hampton finally made it to the back door to let him in.

"Swagger, what took you so long?" he snapped. "You gonna get us pinched."

"Quit your bellyaching," Hampton huffed in retaliation. "You is in, ain't you?"

Bones glared at him. "It took you long enough. I was starting to think you got lost in this palace."

"Stop hassling me, now. Something about this place puts me in a sentimental mood. The man what owns it must have a thing for colored men; there's naked carvings of them scattered all around."

"You planning to lift a few for yourself?" Bones asked with a disapproving sneer. "Good. Then let's bag up something we can hock." He shook his head then playfully shoved Hampton up the first set of stairs. "We'll start at the top and work our way back down. Keep some room in your sack in case we come across something interesting on our way out." Hampton nodded that he agreed with the idea. He'd been known to overvalue items that Bones demanded he leave behind in place of others worth fencing later on the black market.

When they reached the second-floor landing, Hampton tossed an empty canvas sack over his shoulder before ducking into a room to the left. Bones turned on his flashlight and headed in the opposite direction. Typically, very few people kept their expensive belongings on the third floor. The master bedroom made the most sense, so that's where he began his search. He often found a jewelry box or rolls of cash. "There is no need of being greedy," he'd say. "Jailhouses are stacked deep with greedy thieves, greedy and sorry for it."

Hampton kept that in mind as he placed a silver shaving set in his sack. Taking the commemorative world's fair china server from a dresser display occurred to him before remembering how easily china broke the last time he had the same inclination. He could stomach going to jail over greed, but not under the thumb of stupidity.

Bones found himself conflicted the very moment he entered the largest of six bedrooms. He couldn't believe his rotten luck when discovering an unexpected guest. The homeowner was fast asleep in his mahogany sleigh bed. Bones tiptoed closer to the old white man, who had quite a bit more hair in his ears than he did on his head. Bones picked up a half bottle of liquor from the nightstand next to the bed. Hampton stepped into the room just in time to witness Bones slowly raising the bottle with a determined expression.

Hampton waved his hands frantically, gesturing for Bones to lower the bottle. He'd decided to chalk the robbery up to a plan that didn't pan out. Hampton wanted to turn back and dash away before the man woke up to a diverse pair of burglars hovering over him, resulting in the last thing he ever saw. Hampton silently pleaded with Bones when he threatened to smother the elderly man with the pillow lying beside him. Eventually, Bones returned the pillow to the bed then wiggled five fingers close to the man's face. When the gentleman didn't awake, Bones shrugged his shoulders as if to insinuate his prey was just as good as dead already with a snoot full of whiskey. Hampton persuaded his companion to collect what he could and escape without adding assault to their plight. Finally, they gathered an assortment of valuables and two hundred and change in folding money and exited through the back door together. They couldn't help but chuckle at the way the old fellow slept soundly while having been fleeced of exquisite cuff links, necklaces, and diamond rings.

Hampton was still laughing until they arrived at Bones's hideaway and discovered that all of the jewelry they stole from the house was phony. There wasn't one genuine precious stone in the bunch. Bones got a kick out of being taken for a ride. Hampton found it only half as funny because he was counting on fast money. What happened next was a major catastrophe.

Bones told Hampton to keep an eye on the third house on St. Peter's while he stepped out of the car, hidden beneath a cluster of cypress trees. He opened the trunk and pulled out two well-worn coveralls with "Tandem Plumbers" embroidered on the back. After slipping into one and handing the other to Hampton, Bones leaned against the car and crossed his legs casually, as if he had all night to think about what had already been premeditated since he thought up the home invasion scheme with Hampton. "Hurry up, Swagger," he said, staring at their next target, a split-level house facing the dimly lit street.

"What is this for?" Hampton asked, curiously fingering the cotton jumpsuit sitting on his lap. "I don't expect to get dirty."

"It's just a precaution."

"A which?"

"A precaution, it's just in case somebody sees us, they'll think we're a couple of pipe fitters on the late shift. No one would be the wiser if they saw two crooks walking right out the front door." Once again Bones sounded plausible, so Hampton didn't doubt his reasoning. As soon as they were both similarly attired, Bones struck out toward the coral-colored house. He was sure of the owner's absence because he'd kept an eye on him for weeks. Every Thursday night the house was completely vacant for a time. Bones knew exactly when that would be. "Let's get to it," he asserted boldly, opening the chain-link fence.

As usual, Hampton tossed one item after the next into his canvas bag, but Bones wasn't moving with nearly the speed he was accustomed to. "What's the matter with you? We got four more to rummage through after we's done here. This fella must have a wife or lady friend 'cause there's two wardrobes in the other room, both stuffed with nice dresses and such. There's even a satin bathrobe. I'm taking it for Magnolia." When his mentioning of Magnolia didn't seem to affect Bones the way it had earlier, Hampton couldn't tell if his partner was listening. "Bones? Bones?" he called out. "What's got into you? I said I'm gonna do some shopping in the next room for Magnolia."

"Shhh, somebody's at the door." Both men collected their bags and tools then scurried for the closet in the master bedroom. "Nobody's supposed to be here for hours," he lied. "Hush up, so I can think."

Hampton peeked through the louvers in the closet door. He clutched the handle of a clawhammer when he heard a single set of footsteps approaching. The offbeat click-clacking of high heels drawing closer put a frown on his face. Remembering how his sister Pearl Lee meandered painstakingly in the same manner when she had her fill of cheap hooch, he could tell right off those weren't men's shoes shuffling slowly across the wood floors. A tall blonde with long thick hair staggered into the room and flicked on the light switch. Hampton watched as the inebriated party crasher, in an unflattering blue cocktail dress, failed to notice that two of the drawers in the armoire had been rifled through. "She's sauced," Hampton hissed quietly.

"Don't you think I can see that? Let's see what happens. Maybe she'll go into the bathroom, then we can scoot out." They observed what they could through the horizontal slits in the wood door. There was the sound of women's shoes plopping on the floor. Seconds later, a dress whizzed by their eyes.

Hampton felt out of sorts when he reconsidered how colored men had been hanged for looking at a white woman the wrong way. He was about to see one disrobe down to nothing. His chest tightened instantaneously. *Oh, Lawd, she done got undressed. I'll do hard time if she sees me in here*, he thought. Hampton's mind was scattered.

Bones was in complete control. He expected everything that had happened so far. He'd counted on it. "Well, looky there," he said, the impish grin spreading across his thin lips. "That ain't no lady."

When Hampton craned his neck to get a better vantage point, his eyes widened with astonishment. Standing in front of the mirror attached to the bureau was a cross-dresser in nothing but lacy lavender-hued panties with a pair of frilly hose to match. Hampton, realizing the person he'd been afraid to set his eyes on was a man in drag, was more than a trifle confused then. He was literally repulsed. "What the hell?" he mouthed, as if he didn't want to believe his eyes.

Bones continued to stand pat until he grew weary of waiting for the man to fall off to sleep. Without warning, he sprang from his hiding place. The thin man screamed like a woman, instinctively using his big hands to cover his flat chest when he saw intruders bolting toward him.

"Shut up, bitch!" yelled Bones, accompanied by a stiff right cross. He dropped the homeowner to his knees with one punch. "Don't make me have to tell you twice."

Hampton was halfway down the stairs when he heard the man begging Bones to let him go. "Please, just take what you want and leave," he whined. "I won't say a thing. Please, mister! Please don't hurt me."

"Swagger!" Bones called out. "Swagger, come in here." He instructed Hampton to tie the man to his vanity chair but Hampton hesitated, not wanting to touch what he didn't understand. "This ain't no time to be squeamish. Do what I tell you and everything will work out fine." Still Hampton refused to do as he was commanded. Bones recognized the dilemma he faced. Having been raised to protect females made it difficult for his accomplice to harm a man playing the role. Bones removed the obstacle embedded deep in Hampton's upbringing by ripping the yellow wig from his captive's head. "Now do what I told you!" Bones said forcefully. "He's a boy, Swagger. His wanting to be a girl don't make it so."

It didn't take a split second for Hampton to mull it over. A man wearing lipstick and a stocking cap over his short brown hair was a strange sight but one he could deal with. Bones wielded a long sickle-shaped knife while Hampton strong-armed the victim against his will. Amid grunts and gripes, he was securely anchored to the chair with a stretch of twine from the pocket of Bones's coverall.

"Nooo, nooo, no! Don't do this!" he cried. "I won't tell. I won't."

"What we gon' do now?" Hampton queried nervously. He didn't know what to do or how to feel about their dilemma. "Somebody's likely to hear him making such a fuss."

"I'll lull him a bit and find something to stuff his mouth so you can button it shut." Hampton looked on as Bones swung his fists. Sounds of bone mashing against bone reverberated off the walls in the delicately decorated room. Bones seemed to enjoy pummeling the defenseless man, bound and helpless. A rally of powerful blows snapped his head to and fro time and time again. "Now he's good and ready to oblige. Trust me, he won't give you no trouble."

Their prisoner began to squirm erratically, dodging and bucking wildly to escape the fate Bones had in store for him. Hampton couldn't have imagined the other man's destiny while fastening a long strip of masking tape over the cross-dresser's lips. If Hampton had known Bones better, there wouldn't have been any need to speculate how the ordeal had to play out. Between ferocious flurries, Bones casually collected valuables as the man mumbled through the tightly fitted gag, a fistful of panties cinched with a band of tape. Veins in his neck and forehead began to swell as he fought desperately to sustain consciousness. Streams of makeup-stained tears slid down his face after Bones whispered in his ear, informing him that it was no random break-in. It was an execution.

"Damn sissy is tougher than I thought," Bones said, delighted with himself. "He's more determined to live than I would have figured. Maybe we'd better skin out of here before another nance shows up. I'd hate to go diving back into his unmentionables drawer for another handful of silk panties." Bones recognized that Hampton was visibly shaken and equally perplexed by his actions. "Hey, Swagger, why don't you go on ahead? I'll be there in two shakes." Hampton stalled initially. Bones grew persistent. "Go on, scoot. I'll swoop up the other stuff and meet you at the car."

There was no way for Hampton to predict what would happen after being sent away to see if the coast was clear, or so he'd thought. From the porch, he peered down the avenue to the left and to the right. He was set to race back inside with a good report. Looking through a glint in the window shade, Hampton witnessed Bones violently plunging his long sickle-shaped knife into the stomach and chest of his captive. He wanted to look away but couldn't. Seeing Bones slice at the man's flesh threw him off balance. The haunting expression Bones wore when carving the man to pieces sent Hampton reeling. It was like looking at two people trapped in the same body, both strangers to each other.

Hampton's mouth fell open as blood squirted from the cross-dresser's wounds, splattering crimson throughout the room. Killing a man in self-defense or out of necessity had its place. However, gutting a man in cold blood didn't sit right with Hampton. Neither did the reality that Bones had dragged him into the middle of a murder. Even worse, the vicious slaying of an important white man.

14

Front-page News

Hampton spent a goodly part of the next day looking out his window. He didn't know what or who might be after him, but he couldn't rest for dreading reprisal over his connection to the white man's death. He replayed the gory scene of Bones slashing away with violent strokes and then blood spraying from the man's wounds. Those visions, running lose in his head, shook Hampton down to the soles of his feet.

When evening set on the city, he mustered the courage to leave his room. He sneaked down the back fire escape to the dirty alley below, all the time vigilantly surveying his surroundings. He didn't notice anything out of the ordinary once rounding the building on the corner of LaSalle and Poydras streets. There were always people pounding the sidewalks in the colored neighborhood, coming and going at all times, so nothing raised his suspicion. That didn't stop Hampton from keeping an eye out regardless. At the corner newsstand, he bought a paper and told the man to give him two candy bars as well. It hadn't occurred to him that he'd given a whole dollar for a thirty-cent purchase.

When the vendor turned to return his change, Hampton had disappeared.

With the daily newspaper folded under his arm and his sugary dinner shoved inside his pants pocket, Hampton climbed the fire escape, quickly ducked back in the window, then drew the shades. He scanned the front page for information concerning a murder in the Quarter, assuming it would have made headline news because it was a white man who'd been filleted like a catfish. He continued flipping through the pages, holding his breath each time his eyes drifted toward the next article. Perspiration continued to gather on Hampton's forehead despite seeing nothing written about the botched burglary that couldn't have ended worse than it did.

He paced the floor until someone from the apartment below banged irately on the ceiling with a broom handle and yelled for him to "sit his ass down." Hampton complied as best he could. He plopped on the bed and put his feet up on the railing. Since Bones had told him to cool his heels for a few days, that's what he tried to do. Never roaming any farther than the corner newsstand, Hampton stayed close to home and to the telephone. He'd grown antsy waiting for the darned thing to ring, for a loud, annoying voice to shout through the door that a white man was summoning him to take a call, or for a sign that everything would be all right. It was on the fourth day that Hampton got his hands on some news he could use. Unfortunately, it didn't pan out like he'd hoped.

Once again, he shimmied up the fire escape with a pocketful of candy and a folded *Times-Picayune* in his grasp. Had it not become a routine, he might have browsed the headlines like everyone else in the city had that day. On the top of page one, above the fold, were four of the most terrifying words he'd ever read: CITY COUNCILMAN BRUTALLY MURDERED. Hampton was afraid to read any further. It was as if the title had his and Bones's names secretly engraved within the bold type. After no mention of gruesome homicides for days, it had become common knowledge to everyone all at once that Councilman Huey Boyette was viciously stabbed to death during what appeared at the onset of police investigations to be a robbery. Next to a flattering photograph of the deceased, the story began with a portrait of gratifying words, painted to reflect the retouched picture that barely resembled the wig-wearing cross-dresser that Hampton had witnessed gasping for his last breath as he choked on his own blood.

Boyette was hailed as a confirmed bachelor who had worked his way up through the ranks of civil government. He had begun his career as a junior superintendent with the Orleans Parish juvenile detention commission. It was rumored that he had several district assemblymen in his hip pocket and a good chance for a mayoral bid had he not been murdered. There were many other rumors alluded to in the newspaper although none explored his lifestyle or the slew of allegations of misconduct leveled at him during his tenure on the juvenile board. Two reporters explored his wealthy family's ties to the current governor and a long line of state representatives. It was clear to see, even for a simple man like Hampton, that Huey Boyette had been bred to become a great man on the shoulders of his relatives. Neither his ancestors' powerful influence nor their abundant wealth could save him when he needed them most. Hampton wanted desperately to believe the deceased had merely been in the wrong place at the most inopportune time. Flashes of Bones plunging holes into Boyette's chest chased all of those silly notions away.

Word on the street quickly spread that the police were on the trail of a serial killer who targeted homosexual men. Boyette's family forced the local paper to omit his private life by threats of slander, but they couldn't stop the overflow of gossip circulating through every pool hall, tavern, and Sunday school in New Orleans. As it turned out, the councilman numbered fifth in a sordid line of murders previously thought to be unrelated. Despite adamant objections from the police department and the lead detective, Archie Mouton, a host of FBI agents arrived to help them sort out matters. That was Boyette's family's influence showing up days too late to help him and just in time to make the lives of Detective Mouton and some of his associates stickier than molasses. Mouton promised his superiors he'd bring about a conviction within the month. In twelve years of chasing criminals, he never once let the facts of a case get in the way of a big arrest.

Hampton repeatedly dialed the number he had for Bones over the next twenty-four hours. When numerous attempts to reach him by phone failed, Hampton had no choice. He showered, changed into casual clothes, and struck out to look for him. There weren't any signs of him anywhere. He assumed Bones was either in hiding or had bailed out of town for fear of capture. Hampton decided if he couldn't locate Bones fast, he'd do likewise and take his chances on the lam.

The city was caught in the throes of a royal fit. While cruising by watering holes he and Bones frequented together, Hampton heard choruses of police sirens blaring into the night air. Uniformed officers openly rousted gay lounges, interrogating patrons relentlessly, looking for potential suspects and chasing hosts of unsuccessful leads. Stories of federal agents crowding the New Orleans Police Department washed through the Grizzly Bear

Lounge. Rumors swelled by the second. Big-city reporters rented hotel rooms by the busload, thrill seekers and serial killer enthusiasts flooded in from all over the country. Hampton couldn't understand what produced such a frenzied interest in death all of a sudden when New Orleans, like other cities of similar size, accepted murder as a normal albeit appalling occurrence. One man thought to be responsible for a group of homicides didn't seem to make a bit of difference to Hampton. His main concern was finding Bones and getting a better grip on what had happened that night in Councilman Boyette's home, and why.

Outside the Moon Bar, an all-white establishment, Hampton loitered for three hours. If Bones was still in town, it was likely he'd show up there sooner or later. Around midnight, two men dressed in business suits stumbled out of the nightspot two sheets to the wind. Hampton dodged nimbly as one of the fellows staggered to the curb and hurled vomit into the gutter. When the middle-aged drunk peered up from his squat position, he cast an angry leer at Hampton.

"What urrr you looking at, spook?" he grunted.

"Yeah, help him up or beat the pavement," his wobbly friend hissed.

That was a sure sign Hampton had been hanging around the wrong area far too long. He sighed as if the white men were merely nuisances that didn't warrant a response. As Hampton smirked at their attempt at bullying him, Bones wheeled around the corner in his Cadillac.

"I said scat!" the larger of the white men barked, from his knees. "Damn nigger, what's wrong with you?"

As Bones parked his polished automobile across the street, Hampton shook his head thinking how he was in the right to pump two shots into the one with the foul mouth. Not the type of man to back down from a fight, Hampton winked at the nasty cuss then at the entire situation. "You better be glad you's too pitiful to whoop and he's too zooted to stand or else I'd get it in my head to clap the both of you right here, right now." He steadied himself for a showdown and whatever else followed until Bones hurried over with his hands raised. Hampton moved his thin jacket aside to reveal his black snub-nosed revolver. He'd been on the outside looking in on life for four days and it had begun to grate on him. Living on candy bars and newspapers had taken a toll. "Me and my friend here got business and it ain't with you unless you want to nudge me toward it," Hampton huffed at them.

"Hold on now, Swagger," said Bones with an excited sneer. "What's this you got going on?"

Hampton rested on Bones's question as he studied the other men's eyes. They were scared now and it showed. Eventually, the older one bent down to help his pal to his feet. "We were just yelping at the moon is all," said the steadier of the two. "We see you're a busy man, mister. Nothing's happened worth spilling blood over. Come on, Merle, let's make tracks."

"I don't care what that nig says, this is still America and jigaboos got no business talking to decent white men that way." The liquid courage he'd gulped down in the bar clouded his brain. Hampton sensed it, but he wouldn't let go despite the presence of other white men exiting the saloon.

"Unless you want those to be your last words, you will shut your fat trap and leave me to my business." Hampton purposely kept the collection of inebriated men in front of him. Bones tugged at his jacket as the loudmouth picked up and dusted himself off before heading in the other direction, with racist epithets on his breath.

"Come on, Swag. They don't want none of you." Bones was right, they didn't want their misconceptions about colored men's fears to get them crossways with breathing. Bones convinced Hampton to move along before someone sent the police by to investigate the cocky gun-toting Negro with a chip on his shoulder.

"Fine for you to do what the hell you want then yank on my coat when I get to acting out," Hampton barked when they blazed their own tracks down the narrow street in Bones's car.

"I was just saving you from some trouble you don't need."

"Listen at you, Bones. If I didn't see you slice that frilly boy up like a Safeway chicken, I might be inclined to let you tell me about sidestepping trouble."

Bones swerved to miss a parked car, then he slammed on the brakes in the middle of the avenue. "You want to spend the rest of your life in jail?" he argued assuredly. "You'd cash it all in over some drunken words that don't mean nothing? This is the state of Louisiana and you's a colored man, Swagger, two important things you need to remember before pulling something like that again." Bones snorted a nose full of disgust as he mashed his foot on the gas pedal. "I declare, I don't understand how you made it so far without me."

"I was doing just fine!" Hampton spat, too upset to look at Bones. "As a matter of fact, ever since you killed that councilman and hid out, I've been wondering what you been doing." He turned his head to see what kept Bones from addressing his question. "Yeah, I read it in the paper. I can read, you know."

"I ain't been hid from you," he replied sorely. "I needed time to think."

"What was you thinking when you took that fella's life?"

Initially, Bones didn't feel as though he had to answer to

Hampton or anyone, for that matter. Then he shifted uncomfortably on the leather bench seat before doing likewise with his mind-set. “Hell, I didn’t want to gut that queer. But I sure as hell didn’t want him running to the police soon after we lit out and identifying us. I’d heard about the other sissies getting done in, and it made sense to fix things so’s to throw the law off in another direction. They were already looking for a man who got it in for queens.”

“And that man ain’t you?” Hampton asked suspiciously. He hadn’t shared how much of the brutal attack he’d witnessed and the tormented expression he saw on Bones’s face at the time. It was deeper than any hateful sneer ever cast at Hampton by a white man who’d just as soon spit on him than share the same snack counter.

“You don’t really believe I’d go around carving up good ole boys in dresses just because I can’t stand the sight of them? Don’t forget, I saw the way he turned your stomach, too. You sure these others murders ain’t on your hands?” When Hampton remained silent, Bones knew he’d made his point loud and clear. “See, it’s not so easy standing accused. I had to kill that man, just him! Didn’t know he was a city official, though. The way I hear it, you might say I did the councilman a favor.”

“A favor? If that’s what you call it, don’t do me none.”

“I hear tell, men like him got a tough row to hoe. They say living with the shame from what they do is a heavy burden to carry. It is possible that Councilman Boyette is better off now that I got that big bitch off his back. If you ask me, he’s better off by a long shot.” Bones whipped out a thick cigar then parked it in the corner of his mouth like an after-dinner toothpick. He was actually satisfied with the flawed rationale he offered, as if it made perfect sense. “You know something, Swagger, I’m thinking you’d be better off laying low for a while. Why don't you go look in on your ma? I bet she'd like to have you around a spell. I'm not trying to tell you what to do, mind you. It's just a thought."

Hampton spent most of the night in Bones's shadow. They visited one late-night pawnshop and stolen goods fence after another. While business was conducted on the inside, Hampton sat in the car trying to figure out what his next move should be. There was too much heat on the French Quarter to chance picking up where they left off. Police squad cars cruised the historic neighborhood around the clock. It had become the safest district in the city. By morning, Bones had conducted business with five brokers, netting the duo over twelve hundred dollars. Hampton's cut totaled five of that. Because he hadn't had his hands on five hundred dollars at any given time, he thought it would last at least a year. He intended to stretch it out, let it ride. Unbeknownst to him, life had other plans for him and the money in his pocket.

15

Black Magic

Pearl Lee didn't sleep a wink the entire night, mostly due to Toussaint's snoring. After her third consecutive day without rest and what sounded like a battalion of drunken soldiers, her eyes puffed up something awful. She was afraid they'd actually swell shut. Maybe then she could find a way to close her mind long enough to relax.

"Take a load off, Pearl Lee," Rayletta suggested from the other side of a Saturday morning cup of coffee. "If you don't put your feet up you're liable to fall right out of those shoes." She playfully poked her finger in Odessa's tummy. "Ain't that right, babycakes?" The toddler giggled agreeably. "See, told you. I also done told you what you need to do about keeping your bed dry at night. It's a damn shame what's happening to Toussaint. He's slipping fast." Rayletta had stopped by to see about her daughter, who she knew had been wringing her hands over her husband's nasty mood swings and increasingly peculiar behavior. Pearl Lee reluctantly divulged how Toussaint had begun wetting the bed although she decided to conceal his inability to maintain an erection past the few seconds it took for her to climb on top of it.

"Mama, don't," she whispered, barely mustering the energy to argue.

"Don't what? You told me what's been going on with that man of yours. I hate seeing the devil pee on his head, and I know you's tired of Toussaint making water puddles in your bed."

"Mama, shush!" hissed Pearl Lee, to quiet her mother's voice. She cast her weary eyes toward Magnolia, who was pulling out her hair over a difficult math problem. Her head had been stuck so deep in that arithmetic book that every word tossed around the small quarters missed her by a mile.

"Don't be shushing me. It ain't like Magnolia don't know."

When she heard her name, Magnolia popped her head up like it sprang from a box. "Magnolia don't know what?" she asked, only half interested in hearing the answer. In the time it took to blink, she'd dived back into her quandary of the hour. "It's bad enough Johnny needs to catch the four-oh-nine train to Kansas City that leaves Albuquerque at three. They expect me to figure out how he can make the seven-twenty-one to Poughkeepsie by nine. There's too many numbers, and I don't even know where Poughkeepsie is, anyhow."

"Do like I showed you and cross out everything that don't directly go into solving the problem," Pearl Lee instructed. "That math book can get a little tricky at times, Mag."

Rayletta slapped her knee and let out a full-grown chuckle. "And so can life, Pearl Lee. You should do like I told you. Go down and see your auntie-in-law. She got tricks and trick stoppers by the jar full. See if she can't conjure up a spirit willing to help cross out what you sure as hell don't need."

Pearl Lee wrestled with the idea while staring out the side window near the kitchen. "No, ma'am," she refused. "Believe me, it's plenty hard admitting what I got to admit to myself, let alone Madame Baptiste. You know she never did think I was good enough for her kinfolk."

Magnolia raised her head again, only much slower this time. "You intend on letting that stop you from seeing to Toussaint's ails?" she asked soberly. "If I knew how to put a love spell on Hampton without the mumbo woman's help, I'd do it between heartbeats." Her serious expression conveyed what was in her heart, so neither of the women doubted her sincerity. "You already got hold of the fella you plan to raise grandchildren beside. That's got to be worth getting your feelings hurt over. Well, isn't it?"

Rayletta gushed like a proud parent after hearing Magnolia's assessment. She grinned wide and long when Pearl Lee untied her apron strings. "You might not know a thing about catching trains, Magnolia, but you's a quick study on affairs of the heart. Pearl Lee, let me get my work clothes off and I'll run down there to see the witch with you."

"Uh-uh, Mama, some things a woman got to go at alone. Truth be told, *that witch* ain't too keen on you, either. I'll take my chances by myself." She placed her hand on Magnolia's, then thanked her with a warm smile. "You mind watching Odessa while I go see about this?"

"It won't be any trouble, Pearl Lee. That'll grant me another spin at winning her over so she can put in a good word for me with that uncle of hers."

Pearl Lee headed for the door with her chin up and her hopes pushing her forward. "I don't know, Mag, Odessa just might throw you over to get at Hampton herself. Ooh, she loves that boy something terrible."

Rayletta sighed gleefully. "Oomph, that makes three of us."

* * *

A sultry spring breeze danced with Pearl Lee as she strolled past the plantation house toward the densely covered marshlands dubbed Silt Bottom Swamp. Since no one had ever claimed land title or ownership to it, the nearly uninhabitable stretch of soft and mossy earth defaulted to the local wildlife and the powerful medicine woman. Pearl Lee contemplated turning around when she met the rickety old footbridge separating Madame Baptiste's swamp lodge and the rest of civilization as she saw it. Waterfowl cawed and fluttered. An incredibly fat bullfrog sunbathed, displaying his concern about the latest visitor from an overgrown lily pad. He eased a webbed foot into the water to reposition his float. Pearl Lee sneered at the monstrous amphibian when it appeared he was more interested in her than he was in catching flies. She poked her tongue out in a teasing manner. "You'd best keep your distance," she warned lightheartedly. "I ain't had breakfast yet." She almost laughed when the darn thing croaked loudly in a tone that sounded very much like, "So?"

"Leave Too-Too be, now," said a voice with a heavy French accent, from just beyond the tall grass at the foot of the bridge. "He pompous always. I reckon he used to be an earl. Maybe even a duke."

What a ridiculously silly notion it was that a grubby old frog could have ever been anything other than a grubby younger one, Pearl Lee thought as she rounded the tall grass into the clearing where an old brown woman clad in modest rags cast handfuls of chicken feed in her dirt yard. A family of domesticated birds clucked eagerly at the Madame's bare crusty feet.

"Don't turn your nose up at somethin' you don't know, gal," the witch doctor warned without raising her head or eyes from her morning task. "In another life, you very likely been a bear or a bull."

"Don't take much guessing what you had to be, bitch," Pearl Lee said under her breath.

"That may very well be, seein' as how you think I'm a bitch now," the older woman hissed matter-of-factly.

"Good Lawd, you read my mind? I'm sorry, Madame Baptiste," Pearl Lee apologized emphatically. The crafty priestess had done no such thing. She'd read her visitor's eyes instead.

"Let that be a lesson to you, now. I read minds, signs, and times. Isn't that why you come here, for me to make sense of nonsense?" she asked, with full knowledge of the answer. "If you love Toussaint still, what took you so long, chile?"

That's a good question, Pearl Lee thought as she followed behind, fearing the tiny coffee-colored woman half her size. After climbing two wide wooden planks onto the broad and uneven porch, she felt it necessary to explain her tardiness. "Madame, I wanted to come before now, but—"

"Quiet, chile," the woman interrupted. "Not yet." Pearl Lee's mouth was still moving although her words fleeted when she stepped past the weathered screen door and into a vast rectangular house. The water lodge measured thirty feet long and only twelve feet wide, giving it the appearance of a freight car with a slanted tin roof. The collection of animal skulls hanging in the windows or on the shelves aligned with rows upon rows of animal parts floating in jars of formaldehyde didn't give Pearl Lee pause. However, two strangers sitting in the front room of that shoe box–shaped house did. It had taken every ounce of gall she could muster to show up unannounced. To make matters worse, she'd forgotten to bring a gift in exchange for the old woman's wisdom and foresight. Both women smirked at Pearl Lee's empty hands, which were quick to form angry fists. Feeling out of place, she begged pardon to be excused.

"I'm sorry, Madame. I should have prepared something, and you have guests waiting to see you already."

"And we been waitin' for a half hour, yeah!" exclaimed the one closest to the door, with a covered dish resting on her thick thighs.

Madame Baptiste cast a scowl at the woman who spoke out like she'd cast chicken feed in her yard. She sprinkled just enough to keep her on her hook. "And you'll keep waitin' until the spirits move on your behalf. Meanwhile, don't stir a bit. Don't want to stall your reading. Besides, I been waiting on this girl too long as it is."

Like a disobedient child who had received a stern parental reprimand, the grown woman sniffled, then lowered her eyes to comply with the doctor's orders. After all, she still needed what the witch had to offer. Herbs, roots, and incantations were on the menu, but peace of mind was the house specialty.

Somewhat reluctant, Pearl Lee stepped into a part of the house sectioned off by a thick curtain fastened to a semicircle-shaped rod dangling from the ceiling by fishing wire. Everything about the house was makeshift, it seemed, including the table where she was told to sit. It was nothing more than a swath cut out of a mighty oak tree. When Pearl Lee was a young girl, the hovel filled with bobbles and trinkets sat on the water's edge like a monument to black magic and spiritual healing. Now it was just plain eerie.

Madame Baptiste, a world-class reader of facial expressions, utterances, and gestures, placed her hands atop Pearl Lee's to ease her concerns. "Don't fret none no more. We'll talk now."

She lit a marble basin saturated with clove and ginger spices and placed it on the stumpy table. Madame began to explain behind the heavy drawn curtain that the other two women in the waiting area were sisters from the Essex Plantation down the bayou a few miles. Both women had continuously eaten from the same slice of grief, jealous of each other's possessions. One of them was barren and therefore childless, while the other had three children and was presently carrying the child of her sister's husband, without her knowledge or permission. The history of surrogate mothers traveled back to biblical times and continued to be an acceptable practice in such cases as this, although the agreement rarely ended as amicably as it began. "See, the sisters come here every week, each wanting to know why the other has what she don't. I'll tell them soon how envy and a good-lookin' man has them both underfoot. They'll not be eager to share his first son between them. There are things we all must endure. Some, we do to ourselves."

"I brought this to help tell you what's been done to me," Pearl Lee said, as she took from her pocket the chicken foot that she'd found under her mattress. Before she uttered a single syllable, Madame Baptiste started in where her thoughts on the matter began. Pearl Lee sat silent and still while paying close attention to the witch doctor's words as she breathed in thick white smoke emanating from the stone bowl.

"Don't have to mince words when the truth will do. I know why you come. I saw what happened, saw you plunge that knife into Sadie's neck. Appeared to me she got her due all the way around. I don't regret what's done in the past because I took part in it, while in my right mind." Pearl Lee was afraid to blink, for fear of missing something. "I took the crumbs from the devil's table and turned the spirits against Toussaint," Madame admitted shamefully. She peered down at the charm placed on the circular stump. "That there is my handiwork. I ain't proud of it, no, wasn't either the night Sadie come to me holdin' a lock of hair with her right hand and a heap of vengeance in the left. She wasn't born with the gift but worried me to no end to teach her spells. No strong medicine at first, just chants to ward off bad aches and lonely nights. Said she'd pay me good money for the learnin', too, money I know she didn't come by on her own. So I screeched at her to tarry from me. Never did like nobody crowdin' my steps. The gal was headstrong, I'll give her that. Still, I knew it was somebody what put her up to pittin' me against my own blood."

"Toussaint?" Pearl Lee said, wincing at the sound of her husband's name. "Who made you hurt Toussaint?" The conjurer stared into the rising smoke before answering. She knew the name sitting on her tongue would sting like hellfire.

"Trotter Delacroix was the one did it." She wasn't in the least bit surprised when Pearl Lee's face contorted painfully like she'd been kicked by a stubborn mule.

"For true, yeah?" she whispered sullenly.

"For true, chile, for true." Madame Baptiste watched the younger woman wring her hands in such a way that she expected to hear bones cracking under the grueling strain. "Y'all been at it awhile, you and that white boy. Toussaint don't know that Sadie learned of it. She hatched a plot to make a baby for Trotter then cash in on him breakin' that sinful agreement what's been kept from colored menfolk all these years. He caught her comin' out of his bedroom one mornin' with his hairbrush and a pair of socks that belonged to him. Trotter slapped Sadie in the mouth and pulled out of her what she was aiming to do with them. I stood out there with Too-Too watching him when he sent Sadie in here to do his biddin'." Madame Baptiste took a slow sip from a tin cup, allowing Pearl Lee to question or comment along the way if she felt the need. There wasn't anything she could say up until then. Distraught with a storm of emotion brewing inside her chest, Pearl Lee was paralyzed. She couldn't have spoken if she'd wanted to. "It's heavy, yeah, I know. The truth so often is. I refused the money at first, then Sadie come trouncin' back with that man's threats on her lips. Said Trotter was bent on burnin' down my home if I didn't throw in with them. Said he would get it done with me inside it, too."

"You believed he would do such a thing?" Pearl Lee whispered fearfully.

"Can't help but believe a white man what's desperate and evil. That devil is a might chock-full of both. You love him, so I reckon it to be a tough pill to take, don't deny. Like I say, there's things we all must endure. Some, we do. Some, others do to us." Pearl Lee was visibly upset; her bottom lip quivered. She couldn't refute what the woman had said about her and Trotter, not a hint of it.

"What can I do about the hex you worked on Toussaint? He pees the bed and it's getting worse all the time. He can't hardly remember nothing. It's like his mind is failing."

"That charm was meant for you. Sadie brought Toussaint's effects by mistake. It troubled me, but I stood quiet when I recognized the slipup. Sadie doubled-crossed Trotter, me, and herself in the end. She sent the demons to your door after I showed her how. Ain't no way to snatch it back now." A bloodcurdling scream shot from Pearl Lee's core when she realized there was no help for Toussaint because Sadie was dead and buried by her hands. When she regained consciousness, her husband was carrying her home on the back end of the mule he'd used to dig up tree stumps. Pearl Lee was so happy to see him, and sorry at the same time. She promised to love him as best she could all the days of her life. After what she'd done with Trotter and to Sadie, that was the least she could do, the very least.

Madame Baptiste stood in her front window gazing across the footbridge over Silt Bottom Swamp. Once again, she had managed to reveal things no one should have known with the precision of an authentic clairvoyant. Her magic act wasn't facilitated with smoke and mirrors alone. A great measure of it was pulled off with an attentive ear for details and a U.S. Army–issue pair of binoculars. True enough, she had a gift for speaking things into being through the power of persuasion. From time to time, miracles were known to happen after she'd been paid in advance. Concerning those odd occurrences, the crafty soothsayer possessed no earthly idea but claimed the credit nonetheless.

16

Steal Away

Saturday afternoon, Hampton hopped into the driver's side of his secondhand Chevy that was ratty and in desperate need of a new muffler. He drove for an hour before realizing he'd roamed halfway to Baton Rouge. The midday air had begun to thin out. Heat rose from the two-lane highway. Like a faithful hound that wandered too far from home, Hampton was overcome with an indescribable urge to turn around and go back the way he came. He pulled onto the shoulder of the highway then swung a wild U-turn in the other direction. Hampton did what he'd always done when he felt lost. He took the Newberry exit off the interstate, traveling along the familiar farm road he knew better than any other in Louisiana, heading toward the Delacroix Plantation.

Weekend traffic was sparse in the rural community. Not many of the sharecroppers owned automobiles. The landowners who needed an excursion to shake up the monotony of farm living had undoubtedly awoken with the chickens, gotten their shopping done in town, and returned home by then. Hampton flew by acres of sugarcane aligned in perfect rows, each seemingly waving hello as he glided past.

Once over the bayou bridge, he coasted beside the white fence surrounding the Delacroix estate. Buck Ravenell teetered on a riding lawn mower. Hampton climbed out of his car, resting on the grass opposite the plantation's fence line. He took a white handkerchief from the back pocket of his tan trousers and waved it overhead to get Buck's attention. After a few minutes of animated signaling, the older man tipped his hat to acknowledge he'd been summoned.

"Hey there, Hampton," he hailed, cutting the motor down to an idling purr.

"How you do, Mr. Ravenell?"

"Fair to middling, I expect. At least that's my game plan." The older man wiped at his forehead and neck with a red rag. "I thought that was you sitting out here. You ain't coming in?"

"Naw, I ain't allowed to. The Mister's got a burr under his saddle, and I'm the one put it there," Hampton answered honestly. "Old family business, you understand."

"No, can't say that I do, son. Y'all got some strange ways I don't claim to be particular to, either, but work is work."

"That why you's putting in extra time on that riding mow?" Hampton asked, knowing the answer. The sugarcane harvest was at least three weeks off, so money was tight on the plantation, on both sides of the color line. If there was extra money in the Mister's pocket, Trotter's extravagant taste for sports cars and the predilection for spending his inheritance was sure to siphon off that, too. Loans were due three times a year, on the heels of each harvest. The Delacroix had been fortunate with high-yielding crops and minimal pest infestation. Buck's chances to keep food on his table and decent clothes on his family's back without falling in debt to the Delacroix commissary weren't as substantial. "Well, I don't mean to hold you, Buck," Hampton said, using the man's common name to push aside their difference in age and circumstance. "I've been a field hand most of my life, and it never seems to pay what it ought to. I could spot you a few bills until you can make way with the harvest." Buck's eyes drifted toward his run-over boots, then back up at Hampton's soft smile.

"I can't accept no charity, Hampton. I've come too far to start begging now."

"You think I'm interested in *giving* you my hard-earned cash? I like you, Buck, but not that much. I'll loan it to you on what they call a revolver."

"A which?"

"A revolver. I'll give you what I can spare, and you'll pay me back when you can with a little extra on the tail end," Hampton explained politely. "If you can't stand up to the terms we agree on, I'll come back to collect *with my revolver.*" The tired family man raised his hand to shield his eyes from the sun. He assumed Hampton was still smiling. He wasn't.

"I knew I liked your style, Hampton. We'll get along just fine, although I won't make borrowing a habit. I'll be in the black soon enough. Two of my younguns is pret' near pulling a grown man's share of work." Buck's mouth watered as his benefactor reeled off thirty dollars. He quickly shoved it in his pocket and checked over his shoulder to see if anyone had witnessed his windfall. "I'm beholden to you, son. You're a good man."

"It's easy when friends is on good terms. Slip up and sit on my money too long, that high opinion you's holding for me is sure to buckle then." Hampton's countenance was relaxed, so there may have been some doubt in the veracity to get his money back. He hoped like hell it wouldn't come to that. "Hey, you mind doing me a favor before you set the mower down?"

"Whatever you want, just ask," Buck replied eagerly.

"Could you run by and tell Magnolia I'm down here holding out for her affection and about to bust because of it?"

Buck Ravenell climbed back atop that riding mower and released the parking brake. He promised to fetch Hampton's lady friend then threw the machine into high gear. Nearly thirty minutes later, Hampton noticed movement among the rolling hills. He sat up in the front seat and stuck his head out the car window. His heart dropped when he recognized Buck's straw hat bobbing effortlessly. He predicted bad news, or else it would have been Magnolia striking out toward him on foot. Maybe Hampton overshot his expectations. Maybe what he felt for her wasn't enough of a motivation to ditch whatever plans she had and run off with him on a whim. Hampton felt like a fool in love until that loud machine approached the white fence, making a wide turn to deliver the package as promised, valet style. Hampton shot out of his jalopy with reckless abandon. His car door stood open while his arms followed suit.

"Mr. Ravenell, I sho' do owe you," he crooned loudly. "Man, you did it." Hampton reached over the fence and offered his hand to Magnolia. She kissed her chauffeur on the cheek and jumped into Hampton's arms.

"Why didn't you let me know you was coming?" she squealed with delight. "I'd have bathed and everything." He hoisted a canvas traveling bag onto his shoulder and lifted Magnolia over the partition with ease before staring at her for the longest time. Her blue jeans and short-sleeved plaid blouse made him laugh. She made an irresistible tomboy.

"I didn't know until I was parked right over there, Magnolia.

Sorry to drop in unexpected, but I needed to see you," he told her with a nosy audience. Hampton tossed his eyes at Buck, who finally got the picture. He cranked up that relic and pushed off for the machine shed with new money in his pocket and rest on his mind.

"Well, you see me," Magnolia said, leering at him suggestively. "Now what you gonna do about it?"

"The last time I heard you talk like that, I had the privilege to watch you fall off to sleep folded over drunk," Hampton teased as he helped her into the car.

"The last time I talked like that, I was eighteen."

"What makes today any different?"

"Everything, I made nineteen this morning," she answered with a spirited cackle. "I'm a woman in every sense and can drink and gamble in any state in the union."

"Look at you, blushing like a spring flower. Where'd you learn all that, in them schoolbooks?"

"Uhn-uhnnn," she moaned, mistaking his query. "I came by it naturally, like everything else I got."

"We'll see about that," he said, grinning ear to ear. "I got me a birthday girl, with an overnight sack, too." He was ecstatic that she had the wherewithal to pack overnight clothing. "Happy nineteenth. I'll do my best to make it a day to remember."

"And I'll do my best to let you," she cooed, with her head lying on his shoulder. "My first birthday wish came true when you showed up. Thank you so much, Hampton."

Magnolia beamed all the way to New Orleans. She even found it possible when explaining how Toussaint had to carry Pearl Lee home after she'd passed out in Madame Baptiste's parlor with two other women gawking at her through the curtain she operated behind. Hampton confessed how he'd spent many Saturday mornings peeking through that old lady's dirty window shade. He laughed when remembering the time he'd gotten an eyeful with his friend Trotter Delacroix as a distraught young woman traveled forty miles to have the witch doctor smear salve over her third breast. "Yep, Madame Baptiste must have fondled that middle tit for damned near an hour. Me and Trotter stayed to watch the whole show, too. Didn't nothing work for the poor girl, but it did wonders for two hot and riled musty-butt boys. Man, those were the good old days," he chuckled. Hampton had also witnessed a late-term abortion, but he didn't mention that. It wouldn't have made for cheerful conversation on such a festive occasion. He couldn't see anything putting a damper on Magnolia's smile. It made him feel as though his future was just as promising as hers. It wouldn't be the last time his intuition turned on him like a rabid dog. Being right was its own reward. However, being wrong had a slew of consequences tied to it. Always did.

Standing in line for tickets at the zoo, Magnolia squeezed Hampton's hand tightly. "Ouch, woman," he grunted playfully. "I thought you was happy to see me."

"I'm just a bit skittish. I ain't, uh, haven't ever been to a real zoo before," she admitted quietly.

"Naw? Never?" Hampton threw his arm around Magnolia then kissed her forehead. "What other kind of zoo is there?"

"Well, there was this petting zoo back home for li'l children. Wasn't any wild animals, though, just farming beasts mostly. I think they had a peacock or two and a three-foot rat in a cage." Magnolia shuddered at the mere thought of animals much scarier than an overgrown rodent. "What if one of them gorillas was to break out?"

"Don't know if they got any gorillas to speak of. Maybe a chimpanzee and a couple of monkeys," he guessed, never having been there himself. "Don't worry, I'll save you if anything gets out of line, in or out of a cage."

"But what if there was two lions got after us?" she joked. Hampton considered his options then answered.

"Well, if they's two ferocious lions, you'd better have your shoes laced up tight, 'cause I'm willing to bet they like barbecue as much as people do," he joked. "If it comes down to it, the best you can do is to outrun the white meat."

Magnolia planted a kiss on Hampton's cheek. "Will you always know how to make me feel special?"

"I'm sure counting on it."

An afternoon at the zoo provided the budding couple an opportunity to stroll arm in arm and thoroughly be amazed. Magnolia gulped down one soda after the next and inhaled a full bag of cotton candy. When she began to feel queasy, Hampton suggested they hunt for real food.

"That's fine with me," Magnolia agreed. "Some of those big cats needed a good scrubbing, anyway. They smelled worse than I expected. Think they felt the same about us?"

"About you, maybe. I bathed."

Magnolia chased Hampton through the zoo exit with an armful of plastic souvenirs he'd sprung for. "Hampton, wait till I get my hands on you. You'll pay for that. Hampton!"

17

Dizzy

The evening sun set on Hampton's window after an hour of touch and tickle. While Magnolia anticipated a journey beyond heavy petting, he wasn't in any hurry. Instead Hampton convinced her to put on one of the outfits he'd bought at Maison Blanche Department Store and paint the town first. She adored the red cocktail dress the most, but a family of storm clouds hovered over the city. "I'd hate for you to get spots on that satin number and ruin it first night out," Hampton asserted. "I heard the weather guesser on the radio call for rain. While he gets paid even if he figures wrong, don't seem smart chancing it."

"See, that's why I'm hooked on you. Not too many men are thoughtful enough to look out for their good investment. I'll take your word for it. The dark blue getup does flatter me more in the waist. Give me a minute to freshen up." Magnolia waggled her tongue behind in his face. Hampton imagined her panties on the floor instead of riding up on her hips.

"Go on, now, before I change my mind," he teased with his eyes locked on her best asset until she disappeared behind the closed bathroom door. Hampton glanced down at his bulging boxers and frowned. "Sorry, but you gonna have to wait. I don't mean to stifle you, but I really like this girl. Make it up to you later tonight."

"Honey, did you say something?" Magnolia yelled from the washbasin.

"Nuh-uh," he answered, "nothing that bears repeating."

In a jiff, Hampton threw on a pair of black slacks and a brown short-sleeve pullover with four thin black strips running down the front. Hand in hand again, they strolled the sidewalk like brand-new lovers who couldn't get enough of each other. Magnolia flirted openly as Hampton's chest swelled with pride. He happened to be with the prettiest girl in town, as far as he was concerned, and that's all that mattered. Other men tipped their hats and smiled amicably at the young lady in the blue cotton dress fishtailing behind the knee. "See, I told you it was a looker," she jested.

"And like I told you, here comes the rain." Heavy water droplets fell from the sky just as the weather guesser had predicted. Hampton pulled his date farther beneath the record store awning to keep her new outfit dry. They held each other while scores of people darted out of the rain in a mad panic. "Look at 'em go," Hampton chuckled. "You'd think they was all made of sugar. We'll hole up here a spell then catch the streetcar to this li'l spot I know."

"We can't stand here all night, Hampton. The po'boy sandwich you had that woman make me wore off an hour ago," Magnolia heckled, watching the rain splatter against the pavement.

Once the rain subsided to mere sprinkles, they proceeded toward the streetcar stop. Hampton walked along the fringes of the awnings to shield Magnolia from remnants of the thunder shower. "Hey, there goes one now. Let's hop on and take a load off." Magnolia squealed as they raced for the crowded car. "Hold on to this leather strap, the ride tends to get bumpy." Magnolia eased her back against Hampton's chest until a seat became available two stops down the line. When he motioned for her to sit, she declined.

"I fancy the position I'm in now. I would sit on your knee, but we're not alone." An older woman sitting to the right of them snickered after overhearing Magnolia's risqué remark. "Besides, I'm tired of all the up and down you been putting me through today," Magnolia added. The nosy passenger's mouth fell open then, assuming the worst.

It wasn't too long after the rain stopped that the streets and sidewalks flooded with people looking to get out of the house. Stepping over puddles, Hampton stopped in front of Orville's, a quaint diner with cloth table covers and a seafood chef to beat the band. Bones had spoken of the restaurant, so it came highly recommended. Once Magnolia read the sign out front, she hesitated to go inside.

"What's the matter? They got the best crawfish in town," Hampton informed her.

"I hope they *got* other stuff on the menu, too," she objected. "Eating those things is too much work for beginners. I tried a mess of them at Pearl Lee's and all I ended up with was a mess and a gap in my stomach." She continued pouting until persuaded by a mouthful of soft kisses. Magnolia was embarrassed when it occurred to her that others weren't so keen on their public display of affection. She lowered her head and entered nonetheless.

The waiter was charming throughout the meal, gladly attending to each of Magnolia's whims. She asked for cleaner silverware and extra sauce on her entrée, a second helping of collard greens, and later, an additional beignet to take with her. Hampton felt sorry for the young man, who appeared willing to be ordered hither and thither by the attractive young woman with the big appetite. The waiter had the last laugh when the bill came. Then it was his turn to feel sorry for Hampton. Magnolia excused herself to the powder room to reapply her lipstick. She had sufficiently stuffed herself. An eight-dollar tab confirmed it.

"Eight dollars?" Hampton wheezed at the sight of it. He handed the waiter ten dollars to go away. "Oh, yeah, somebody's going all the way tonight."

Magnolia returned with her face made up to perfection. She found Hampton sitting where she'd left him, only now his hands were clasped together and resting on the table. "Thank you, Hampton. That was lovely," she sighed. "You pay the man?"

"Yep."

She scanned the table, wondering if she'd missed something. "Are we going to the movie now, or was there another type of entertainment you had in mind?"

"We'll catch a show then talk about what exactly that is. Oh, yeah, it'll be a long discussion."

"As long as I've been waiting, it had better be." Oddly enough, that comment wasn't ripped from the pages of any book. Magnolia felt it in her heart. Considering all she'd heard about sex, she was exploding with anticipation.

"I wonder if they got one of them special features at the picture show that run about three minutes?" he teased. Magnolia didn't find any humor in it. She turned her lips up and kept on walking. Hampton decided he'd continue picking at her to get another rise while strutting leisurely down Basin Street to St.

Peter Street. "You know, we could duck into that graveyard over there and skip the flick altogether."

"When it's your birthday, I'll let you choose... maybe," she joked.

"Maybe? Ahh, that ain't no kind of right," he replied as an eerie feeling washed over him. Hampton slowed his pace then casually looked back over his shoulder while purposely crossing to the other side of the street. No one seemed to be paying attention to them, although he was leery of something being amiss. "Uh-uh, that's not right," he repeated before yanking Magnolia into a narrow breezeway between two buildings. He'd noticed someone crossing over to the other side just moments after he did, in the same way he would have stalked his prey.

"What it is?" she hissed nervously. Her eyes were wide and worried.

"Hush a minute," he grunted. "Stay put, and I mean it."

"Hampton, you're scaring me."

"Shhh! You gonna get us clapped," he warned.

Hampton leaned against the brick wall near the walkway entrance. He held his hand up to his mouth to remind Magnolia to keep quiet. Her strained expression screamed out loud. Hampton inched closer to the slender opening when he heard a man's stride quicken. He squinted up at the muted streetlight while focusing on a plan of attack. With a split second to act, he had to make all the right moves or Magnolia might get caught in the middle of a bad situation. His blood raced through his veins as the shadowy figure passed the poorly lit walkway. Hampton jumped the man, who was wearing a cheap dark business suit. He slammed his tracker down on the sidewalk. Hampton rammed his fist into the man's ribs. He was sure of two things if nothing else. No white man in his right mind would have risked coming to that colored neighborhood to rob him. And the quickest way to take all the fight out of a foe was a sufficient amount of pain from the outset so he'd want it over as soon as possible. In short order, the stout stalker balled up to shield himself from another foray of stinging blows.

"That's more like it," Hampton spat, once the shadow had voluntarily given in. He began an interrogation with his bony knee pitted against a chunk of sternum and flesh. "What the hell kinda business you think you got with me?" he spat viciously.

"Hampton!" yelled Magnolia when she heard other men shouting down the street. "There's more coming."

"Not before I end this one," he threatened.

Upon hearing the death declaration, the white man's grimaces turned to grit. He shoved Hampton back and climbed to his knees before a stiff kick landed against his jaw. Like an overmatched prizefighter, the white shadow toppled over. He reached for his gun then stretched his arm toward Hampton, who swore he heard his last breath. He gasped when the hammer clicked, then nothing. The revolver misfired. Hampton turned on a dime before the assassin squeezed the trigger again.

"Hampton, let's go!" Magnolia clamored. "What was that man doing? Are you sure he was after us?" Until that very second, Hampton hadn't contemplated what he thought. There was a need to react and that's what he did.

"It don't much matter, but yeah, he didn't have no reason being down here after dark unless he was meaning to do some colored man harm. It wasn't gonna be me. Let's skin out." Hampton grabbed her hand and scurried down the block away from the voices Magnolia heard approaching. At the corner of St. Peter and James streets, a dark-color late model Plymouth wheeled toward them with lights flashing and police sirens blaring.

Magnolia held on to Hampton's hand for dear life. "That's the law. What do they think you did?"

"Nothing. I don't know," he answered in midstride. "I got to get you safe."

Magnolia kept up as best she could until the short heel on her shoe broke off. "Wait!" she wailed. Magnolia reached down and grabbed it while hopping on the other foot. Hampton tried to tow her along at a steady pace but she grew tired.

"Listen to me. I don't need them to catch you by my side. They do, ain't none of them gon' be in the mood to hear what you gotta say." He crouched down near a mountainous mausoleum at the mouth of St. Louis Cemetery No. 1, to stay out of sight. There was a chorus of police sirens now, all of them whining angrily, it seemed to him. As much as he resented splitting up, it was the only chance Magnolia had of escaping Hampton's fate. He was willing to spare his life for hers. "You got to run through the graveyard, and when you clear it on the other side, head straight for my place. Here's the key."

"I don't know if I can. I'm scared of what they might do to you. They're liable to kill you, Hampton, even if it's just for beating up their friend." Hampton knew her assertion was more than likely correct, but he couldn't let that stop him from doing the right thing.

"They's bound to find us if we stay out in the open like this." He took a deep breath, then pointed across the cemetery, lined with stone-covered coffins and raised monuments protecting the remains of lost loved ones. He hadn't thought about New Orleans graveyards in a long time, the need to place caskets on top of the ground because of the city's high water table. It could help

Magnolia's getaway if she did as he instructed immediately. "I don't want nothing to happen to you, Mag. I'll be fine if you get to going right now. Take that key, lock up, and wait. If I'm not there by morning, use the money in my top dresser draw' to catch a cab to Newberry. You got that?"

Sniveling uncontrollably, Magnolia nodded that she understood. It wasn't hard to comprehend a man walking into the lion's den for the greater good. But that didn't make it any easier for her to stumble through the haunted cemetery at night, all alone. "I love you, Hampton."

"I know, baby, I know," was his stoic reply. "Now git!"

As she trod over the hard concrete, zigzagging on a broken heel, Hampton shot out in the middle of James Street. He sprinted into the teeth of the dragnet, hoping to draw their attention away from Magnolia. He'd ducked into the rear of a massage parlor and back onto Basin Street when he heard a woman shriek, followed by three gunshots in a syncopated rhythm. He was about to give himself up, fearing Magnolia had been hurt. Suddenly, she screamed out his name.

"I'm coming, baby girl, I'm coming," he panted, returning to the graveyard at top speed. "Magnolia! Magnolia!" He chased through the stone maze, frantically searching for her.

"Hampton," she moaned softly, squatting against a statue of a man on a horse. She was ice-cold and shivering. Petrified to move, Magnolia had to be coerced.

"You want them to shoot me?" he growled. "Huh? You want them to string me up?"

"No, no, honey," she offered assuredly. "I want you home, with me, forever."

"Then get up and get yo' ass out of here."

She stared up into his dark eyes without blinking. "Okay, okay, but you'd better watch talking to me that way." She shoved him in the chest, then pushed past with a heavy resolve. Hampton almost smiled when she scooted off like he wanted. He promised himself then and there that he'd make her his wife if she'd let him. Conversely, he'd have one hell of a time making it through the night if the police caught up to him.

Dipping in and out of doorways from Basin to Tremé, he hit the slick back alley like a bear on roller skates. His arms flailed wildly to maintain his footing. Hampton's adrenaline surged as he raced top speed for blocks at a time. He doubled back to elude capture as several police sirens circled buildings he'd hidden in. Suddenly, they trailed off one at a time. When a dinner theater let out and it appeared the coast was clear, he strolled onto the sidewalk. He'd stayed on the move. A sense of false security set in as the streetcar rolled toward him on Canal. The conductor stopped to let passengers on. Hampton jogged up to it, a grin playing around the corners of his lips. All signs of security vanished as two police cars converged from the street behind him. A host of plainclothes detectives stepped down off the streetcar, guns drawn and steady.

"Yep, that's him," said the white man Hampton had beaten on earlier. He held a stained rag against his chin to soak up the blood pouring from his mouth. "That's the one we're after. He won't get away this time."

"No thanks to you, Cunningham," someone said from the passenger side of a parked car. "Well, let's see what's what."

Hampton was afraid to move a muscle. He hoisted both hands up and held his breath. White passengers gawked at him from the streetcar windows. It wasn't until he was handcuffed at the police headquarters that he knew why he'd been detained. By all rights, they could have shot him down like a dog as he ran for the streetcar. If these cops had been Newberry good ole boys tracking him, he'd have been dead already. These well-dressed city officers kept him alive because they wanted something from him, valuable information. Hampton prayed like hell that he'd have it to give them once the beating started.

18

Cracker-box Justice

During the five-block ride to the New Orleans police headquarters, Hampton kept an eye out for ambulances. He wasn't nearly as concerned for his own well-being as he was terrified for Magnolia's. A young colored woman was an easy mark for deviants looking to take advantage of a scared female hobbling on a busted shoe. When the unmarked car parked in front of the South Rampart station, Hampton knew it was time to start worrying about the next few hours of his life. There were several avenues to take when playing the shackled nigger role, he thought. True enough, the law had him by the short hairs, but it didn't necessarily have to stay that way. Dumb and dazed came to mind first. That was the "I don't know nothing so stop beating on me to tell you" route. Hampton suspected they were quite accustomed to seeing that one acted out to perfection. Then he pondered on all of the mischief he'd been involved in lately. Stealing cars, petty larceny, and forceful intrusion meant jail time, each carrying a hefty sentence for a colored man in the Deep South, especially since his victims were white as far as he knew. The last thing on his mind was the collection of murders he'd read about in the daily news and later questioned Bones about. Uniformed cops and jacketed detectives marched him through the front door like a lamb led to the slaughter, past hordes of officers all wearing the same hateful jeer those streetcar passengers flung at him. For the life of him, Hampton didn't understand their anger, not in the slightest.

"Yeah, we caught up to him," bragged the stumpy man Hampton had floored near the alley. "I had him going at first. Should have stomped his ass good when I had the chance."

A taller fellow in a blue sport coat frowned disapprovingly at the lie the other officer had told. "Cunningham, that'll be enough. You and Jamison get him inside squad room one and then get me some coffee. This might take all night."

Hampton felt a baton nudging at the base of his spine. He suddenly felt like a blue ribbon bull on the road to private auction. That tall drink of water with squared shoulders, mousy brown hair, and a smashed-in nose looked as if he'd been a football brute in another life. He was as tough as they came, there was no guessing about it. So far, he appeared to be in charge. Everyone was silently eyeing him and signaling their okay to beat the tar out of the colored man. Hampton paused when they wrestled him into that dinky little room across from the registration desk. He dug in his heels valiantly as the others watched him slide into his decidedly defiant mode of survival. More important, he stalled for time. Hampton needed to get his mind wrapped around Square Shoulders' temperament. If he was in fact the head man, his way of thinking dictated how his cohorts responded. In a fleeting glimpse, Hampton stared him down through the open door before someone slammed it shut from the outside. The large cop's narrowed eyes conveyed what he felt deep down. He didn't need Hampton, just somebody to spin his wheels on, a colored somebody to play a slick man's game of stall and brawl.

An hour passed in the musty box with faded walls, a three-by four-foot two-way mirror positioned near the door, and filthy floors. Hampton, left alone the entire time, allowed his head to nod, although sleep didn't appeal to him. He had grown tired of waiting. It was the same familiar tactic his father had utilized when he was a boy, and Hampton refused to stew in his own juices like they intended. He felt them gaping at him all the while, just as he'd done to animals at the zoo. Only he was on display now, nothing but a caged monkey to those white men on the other side of that glass.

Unbelievably relaxed when three of them finally entered the small dungeon where he'd been stashed away, Hampton sat up straight in the wooden chair at the sturdy table that took up one-fourth of the room. Cunningham, the stumpy cop still reeling from Hampton's stinging blows, entered first. He massaged the bruises on his face with his fingers, but when he realized how it looked to the prisoner he quickly jerked his hand away so as not to appear the chump that he most certainly was. The tall one Hampton had watched order coffee earlier was behind Cunningham. A third man trailed them both. His suit was more expensive than the coats worn by the first two. He stood a touch shorter than the brute in charge. His face was narrow and sunburned. Red. Irritated. It was hard to decipher whether he was highly pissed or working his way through an introduction to the southern climate. His hair was dark and neat, like the sailors Hampton had seen near the navy pier. He was not a regular New Orleans cop, maybe not a cop at all. A slight glance down at his shoes suggested he didn't walk on them any more than he had to. A man like that was either lazy or smart enough to get someone else to do his bidding for him. If it happened to be the latter, he was the most dangerous of the three. Men who didn't get their hands dirty lacked a sense of empathy. It was a lot easier to turn a blind eye than call off the dogs. When the door closed, Hampton wouldn't have to wait any longer. He'd discover in short order who was pulling all the strings and pulling no punches.

Cunningham slowly circled Hampton's chair twice in a menacing manner before taking his place at the front of the room. Then it was the brutish fellow's turn to rattle the monkey cage. "Do you know who I am?" he asked plainly. Hampton didn't reply. "Do you know why you're here?" Again, Hampton merely gazed up at him as if he were a bird on a wire. The cop didn't know it, but Hampton was watching his aim. "You must be guilty," he said assuredly. "See, in all my years of chasing and catching bad men, you are the very first to sit here all this time and not once ask why that is." When the prisoner's countenance didn't alter one iota, the cop eased off his sport coat then handed it to his lackey to hang on the hook. "I'm Detective Mouton and as I see it, that kind of behavior has guilty written all over it. Ain't that right, Cunningham?" When Mouton introduced himself by name, all dignified like it was supposed to mean something, Hampton remembered it from somewhere although he couldn't place it initially.

"He damn sure looks guilty to me," Cunningham cosigned, like a good little puppet. "Guilty as sin."

Mouton jingled coins in his pocket to distract Hampton from the lies he was certain the colored man had prepared for such an occasion. "What you got to say about that, boy?" To the detective's dismay, Hampton shrugged instead. "Oh, I get it. You're the strong, silent type. Detective Cunningham here says you were running off at the mouth when he... *had you going* in that alleyway," Mouton added sarcastically, to reprimand his underling's inability to apprehend the suspect.

"*He* wasn't one for explaining whilst my knee was planted in his chest," Hampton smarted, purposely hastening their inevitable attack. His patience had begun to thin out. Wondering what had happened to Magnolia persisted heavily. He needed to move them along and control as much of the interrogation as possible, even if it killed him. Cunningham drew in a deep breath then lunged at Hampton. The other men observed quietly as the cop lost his temper, smacking the colored prisoner on the side of his face. They seemed surprised when Hampton saw it coming but neglected to flinch. His head snapped back violently as Cunningham walloped him again.

"I'll bet you're in the mood for explaining now?" the stumpy officer hissed boldly.

Hampton withstood two of Cunningham's best punches while both hands were literally tied behind his back. He shook them off, spit blood on the floor, then shot a fierce scowl back at the officer. "Loose me from these irons, then me and you can talk about this some more." Cunningham postured like a schoolyard bully, but he reeked of false bravado and day-old funk. Mouton grabbed his subordinate by the arm to pull him away from Hampton. His next move was totally unexpected. Mouton reared back and floored Hampton with a stiff right hand, knocking him off his chair. The quiet man in the room was true to his nature. He stood silent with his head slightly rotated to the left. Had Mouton not snatched him up by the collar with his massive hands, Hampton would have laughed out loud for pegging the third man down to his slightly worn shoes.

Detective Mouton's face was less than an inch from Hampton's. His eyes glazed over completely. There wasn't an ounce of bigotry in them, not one. Hampton had seen his share of white-hot stares, boiling over with hate and fueled by something he'd never fully comprehend. Mouton was under complete control. Through clenched teeth, he whispered a memorandum that didn't add up when Hampton heard it. "Say nothing about Bones," he mumbled silently. "Nothing." Hampton landed back in the chair with the lead detective on top of him again. "That was your first warning, boy. I don't know who you think you are, but you will respect the badge my men carry, if not the person behind it!"

With a sharp pain knifing through his face, Hampton was seeing stars. "Oomph, maybe this is a good time to ask what you want with me," he groaned.

"The nigger's got a good head on him after all," Cunningham joked, until Mouton shut him down with a leveling smirk.

"Finally, we understand each other," he said to Hampton. "You, Hampton Bynote, are being questioned about the murders of seven men, all of whom were found dead in the Quarter." Suddenly, it was plain as day where Hampton had seen Mouton's name. He was the homicide detective investigating the deaths of those white men, the same one promising a fast arrest and a subsequent hanging in the newspaper.

"What! Murders! Who told y'all my name?" Hampton asked viciously. "Hell, naw! You ain't gonna put no murders on me and let somebody slip a noose around my neck. You can kiss my ass and beat on me till your arms wear out. I might have my hand in a few things from time to time, but I ain't made up to hurt nobody in the way them papers say. Uh-uh. No way. No how!"

Mouton sighed. "That fellow standing over there is Richard Cross, a real live FBI agent. He's smart, real smart, and he thinks you know something about those murders you ain't telling. I'm inclined to believe him, Hampton."

"You keep saying my name. Who the hell done sent y'all after me saying I'm the one to ask?" Hampton was staring at Mouton, who was sizing him up in return. The detective searched for signs of collapse. "Maybe the one who put you on to me is the one did it," Hampton said. "Seems kinda odd, *Detective Mouton*, how I'm the one getting interrogated in this goddamn box."

Mouton didn't like the answer. It sounded too accusatory for his taste. He lunged at Hampton again; this time the prisoner ducked. Mouton countered with a left hook and sent Hampton barreling down against the hard floor again. The FBI agent was very interested in the suspect's choice of words. Special Agent Cross had no choice. He was forced to step in or risk losing what possible leads Hampton could provide, overtly or otherwise. "Let me take a crack at this, Detective. Not all suspects are guilty until proven innocent, not even the colored ones. Help him up and remove the cuffs." Cunningham braced himself as he unlocked the steel clinching Hampton's wrists, then he backed away cautiously.

"He can find his own way to the chair," Cunningham brooded sorely.

Through a partially closed eyelid, Hampton saw Mouton fidgeting with his hands. That brief loss of composure relegated him to local-yokel status in the mind of his temporary overseer. Cross nodded for Mouton to help the colored man to his seat since he was the responsible party. When the detective hesitated, Agent Cross offered an ultimatum. "You can do as I ask or you can leave the room altogether. Honestly, I don't care either way. Your method of questioning has ended." Hampton, for one, was glad to hear that. He'd already experienced the bad cop, worse cop scenario. Someone had finally stepped in to play the good cop.

Eventually, Mouton acquiesced. He was concerned about losing his new pigeon and his spot in the limelight. Hampton thought it was the novelty of having his name on the front page that forced the detective to jump on the back burner as instructed. Mouton was severely committed beyond fleshing out this hot-box session, as they called it. He was playing both ends against the middle. In the world of glory hounds, it was dog eat dog. Hampton wasn't the reward, simply the rabbit.

Hampton grunted, feeling as though his face were coming unglued. Blood streamed from his lips and nostrils. Cross pulled out a cotton handkerchief and waved it in front of the suspect. "Here, clean yourself up. I believe a man should know why he's being held. You said you've read about the murders and you also said none of it has anything to do with you." Cross handed the hanky to Hampton after he exhibited steady signs of consciousness. "Tell me how it is that your car was seen near at least two of those homicides if you weren't involved?"

Two of them? Hampton thought. *Did me and Bones rob somebody near the same place and time other murders were going down?* "Mr. Cross, now I know y'all got the wrong man." Fearing he might say too much, Mouton went to get at Hampton a third time, but the agent halted him with a raised hand to desist. "It's possible to be mistook for another colored man. We do look alike to y'all. A man's automobile can't be that different from all the others, either. I ain't been near nobody getting themselves killed, least not while knowing about."

"That's not quite true. We had witnesses near the crime scenes to list all of the cars they remembered seeing on the streets, ones that didn't belong to their neighbors. Your Chevrolet was on two of those lists. A partial license plate put us on your trail. A few of the murder victims were found with human skin beneath their fingernails. We assume they fought back before being killed. Take off your shirt, Mr. Bynote," Cross demanded. "And drop your pants." Hampton eyed the agent suspiciously. He declined by shaking his head defiantly. "Detectives, remove Mr. Bynote's shirt and trousers, please."

"My pleasure," Mouton growled. Cunningham inched toward their captive. Hampton fought wildly once they cornered him. He kicked and struggled against their assault. Two additional cops flew into the tiny room to help subdue him. It took some doing, but they managed to wrestle Hampton's pants down around his ankles. He didn't have any fight left in him when Mouton ripped the shirt off his back. Amid clouds of contempt, a quiet storm rolled into the hot box. Lengthy scars maligned Hampton's back, crisscrossing from shoulder to waist. It was apparent that he had undergone a brutal beating some time ago, causing mutilated skin in the form of permanently raised snakelike welts. Special Agent Cross was especially regretful when no recent scars of any kind were discovered. He was sorry for humiliating his prisoner, the wrong man.

Mouton, now restored as the lead of the investigation, sent a uniformed officer to get a suitable shirt for Hampton. He'd seen a collection of mistreatment, torture, and neglect in his line of work. Never before had the old wounds of any man left him speechless.

After changing his clothes and later receiving treatment for injuries incurred during the interrogation, Hampton was fingerprinted and released. As a precaution, two patrol cars were dispatched to follow him and monitor his movements. He exited the station house, laboring north on St. Louis through the cemetery. Hampton doubled back over the path he thought Magnolia would have taken to reach his apartment. At daybreak, he rounded the corner in front of his apartment building. As he pulled open the glass entrance door, Magnolia sprinted toward him. She raced down the stairs at top speed, almost knocking him over. She had been huddled there all night, sitting, watching, and waiting.

"Oh, Hampton," she wailed, her eyes filling with tears. "I thought they might've killed you. Every time somebody passed by I hoped it was you." In the muted lighting, she hadn't noticed that his face was bruised and swollen in several places. When he opened his mouth to speak, a guttural groan slipped out instead. "Dear God, what'd they do to you?" Hampton smiled at her with his eyes as he nodded toward the stairs.

"Later, Mag. I need to lie down," was his painstaking reply.

19

Timeless Wounds

Hampton slept throughout most of the day. He moaned and cursed so much that Magnolia was terrified to wake him. She stepped next door to ask where a girl could get some decent food fast. A young woman suggested a small diner that delivered, then she explained how to make an order after staring at Magnolia's confused expression. The neighbor didn't ask about Hampton or his relationship to the unfamiliar girl babysitting his room. Magnolia was a woman in need, so the neighbor did what she could to help out. It was a random act of sisterhood, at a time of crisis.

Magnolia continued placing cool towels on Hampton's cheek and eyes even after the delivery boy had come and gone. Helplessness was the feeling that held her hostage while she vigilantly waited on a chance to break away clean. When Hampton awoke that evening, flailing and swinging his arms violently, Magnolia winced while dodging his furious blows. "Wait, Hampton! You're safe! You're safe," she asserted with soft palm strokes on his knotted head. "Shhhh, baby, you're all right now. I'm here. I'm right here." Hampton's eyes popped open wildly. His muscles seized.

When Hampton stopped breathing, his body hardened like a block of ice. Magnolia wrapped both arms around his neck, holding him close to her breast with all of her might until he began to gasp for air. "Ain't gonna let those men hurt you no more, uh-uh, no way. We're gonna run away from here, far, far away."

Hampton tried to speak. His words came out in dry, hushed whispers. "What—what happened?"

"It's all right, baby, don't worry about that. They beat on you is all, but you're still here." She wiped tears from her face before they fell from her chin. Magnolia didn't want Hampton to know how shaken she was.

"You really gon' stick to me after this?" he asked like a child who'd been stuck in a bad dream for too long.

Magnolia informed Hampton how he'd showed up with clear signs that the police wanted to make a point. He sat up in the bed, shook his head, then cringed when a throbbing pain reminded him how badly he'd been injured. His dark skin showed swollen purple marks where the detectives landed solid punches. Hampton turned to Magnolia. She was choking back on her strained sentiment. "Damn, I was hoping I didn't look as broke as I feel," he said jokingly. He told her about the hot-box interrogation and who did what when he popped off. Despite his explanation why the New Orleans PD hauled him in under intense scrutiny, then subsequently questioned him about murders, Magnolia appeared more interested in the jagged landscape on Hampton's back.

"Hampton, I'm sorry for what they put you through," she said, behind a heavy question begging to be addressed. "I'm even sorrier for what happened when you got those." He followed her eyes to the congregation of scars he'd purposely kept hidden from her.

"Oh, them? Ain't nothing but a boyhood memory I try to

forget. They's ugly, I know. Kinda look like a map scrawled onto me, I expect."

"There's nothing ugly about you," she corrected him, "nothing. I wondered why you'd rather stay hitched to an undershirt even when it gets hotter than a tin roof in here. The way you're so shamed of 'em makes it look like they still hurt, on the inside."

Hampton lowered his head. He mulled over what Magnolia said, knowing he couldn't deny how right she was. "Funny how my being black, blue, and scuffed made me recollect something my daddy used to say. It don't matter how bad you bruise or bleed. Being a Negro means the color of suffering is always white."

Hampton sighed miserably, turned toward Magnolia, and then told her how he and Trotter Delacroix were raised as closely as two boys could have been considering their differences. He reminisced how they learned to skip rocks on the bayou, being oblivious to how their lives would take two vastly conflicting paths. "Couldn't have been older than thirteen or so when things started changing around us," he said solemnly. "Trotter's ma would call him in hours earlier until I'd hardly see him at all. He had his lessons to get, play baseball over at the schoolhouse with other white boys, and such. You know, regular stuff they get to do. One day I looked up, we was years older but nothing alike. Trotter used to nose around our cabin at night. He'd sneak out his window and try to get a look-see at Pearl Lee in the buff whilst she was taking a bath or sitting on the slop jar in the outhouse." Hampton's teeth gnashed as that random memory came to mind, fresher than a spring breeze. "I told him to stay away from her and to run after some white girl he said he was sweet on. I picked at him until he had to fight me, then I beat him something awful that day. His ma, Mrs. Jennifer Ann, came tearing down to the village saying how I tried to kill her baby. Shoot, I just wanted to bust him up some. I just missed being around him, I guess. Once that fool was licked, I yelled for him to stay down. Trotter wouldn't, so I dropped him again with a knee in the gut, damned near caved in his ribs."

"If you whipped Trotter so, how'd that happen?" Magnolia asked softly, glancing at Hampton's scars again.

"The Mister," Hampton answered in the same subdued tone. "He chased me down on a horse when I ran. My daddy would have killed him dead for strapping me to that big oak tree, the one near the damn workday bell they keep out back. Too bad my daddy had passed on. Shoot, I would have likely gone to meet him, but Mama broke from the men holding her. She grabbed the bullwhip from the Mister's hand."

Magnolia nestled her head on Hampton's chest. "I didn't know," she whined. "How could you stay there after that?"

"Didn't. I stayed in the house for weeks, in a liniment wrap, to heal up some. Then one day, I climbed up from the floor and dusted myself off. I lit out, stayed gone for a couple of years, and made eighteen before going back to see my folks. Nothing had changed in all the time I was on my own. Change come slow if at all, they say. That's a truth so sharp it sting."

Hampton went on to confide in Magnolia that he'd gone to great lengths to conceal his seasoned wounds from other women, dressing in the dark and wearing undershirts during intimate interludes. Magnolia confessed she'd heard enough. She fed him two ham sandwiches with a side of potato salad, then she excused herself as Hampton guzzled a bottle of orange soda to wash it down. Now that Magnolia knew more about him than any of his previous romantic interests, Hampton figured she'd ask him to get her back to Newberry as soon as possible. Which road their relationship took from there wasn't his decision to make. The moment he heard the shower spray, Hampton assumed Magnolia's exit strategy had been set into motion. He couldn't blame her. His blacks and blues were numerous and scathing. After sharing two hardships from a full deck of tribulations, he figured Magnolia wasn't the type to stub her future on the likes of him.

Hampton stood up from his bed, scanning the small room for his car keys. If she asked to be taken to Newberry soon after she'd washed up, he was resolved to oblige her.

"I think we've talked enough for now," Magnolia said, ducking her head out of the bathroom. "I want you to show me everything you know about loving." Hampton pulled off all of his clothing, forced to rethink everything he knew about women. His chest heaved as he joined Magnolia behind the plastic shower curtain. She guided him to the head of the shower, unlike any of the characters in the romance novels she'd collected, then she began to wash his back and sooth his ills. Magnolia planted gentle kisses on each of the strikes the bullwhip had left behind. It was the first time Hampton allowed himself to shed a tear since the day he'd received the brutal beating as a boy. At that very moment, he was convinced Magnolia wasn't one to be underestimated. She was light in his darkened domicile, words to his muted soul.

Spending the remainder of the day in bed, Hampton listened to stories about her childhood. While none of them were half as colorful as his, they lent insight into the woman she had become and the woman he needed her to be. Magnolia's determination to catch up on her book studies and dreams of later owning a dress shop made Hampton proud to be the man she'd given herself to. Although she'd misled him about her sexual experience, he understood how enticing it was to grow up fast or at least give the impression she had. Men and women weren't that different in the end, each wanting to be something more than what life had mapped out for them. Hampton had little doubt that Magnolia would make a big splash in the world with her bright ideas and staunch fortitude. On the other hand, if he wanted a shot, a real one, at reaching out and grasping his dream of homeownership, he had to get a thing or two straight with Bones first.

The following morning, Hampton convinced Magnolia he needed to talk something over with his business partner, citing unfinished particulars to be hammered out. Although reluctant, Magnolia conceded. She kissed him again for the umpteenth time in as many days, then cast a labored smile. "If you get yourself killed behind what you and this fella Bones been up to, I won't find it in my heart to forgive you, Hampton. If we can't see eye to eye on that, then I'll let you take me home. If not, I'm staying put on this bed." She was dead serious. He understood just how emphatic she was and he appreciated her candor. Hampton, on the other hand, couldn't afford to be as up-front and honest.

A late model Ford four-door sedan tailed Hampton's car toward Newberry. He recognized the shadow he'd picked up before leaving the New Orleans city limits. He couldn't see maligning Magnolia with his lies and alibis, so he kept the sedan in his rearview mirror to himself.

After he said his good-byes near the main gate of the plantation, Hampton flew back to the city in his Chevy on a mission. He cranked the car windows down, felt thankful for the cool breeze, and then tried to find the right words to facilitate letting go of a severely wrong affiliation. His chances of keeping Magnolia with a friend like Bones in his life were virtually impossible. Ultimately, he'd be forced to choose between the two.

Hampton parked his car behind the auto body shop where he and Bones organized the burglaries. He touched the swollen contusion under his right cheek to remind himself how it came to be although he didn't need false adrenaline to initiate a showdown. Hampton secured his revolver in his back waistband as he pushed the large metal door aside. He invited himself into the storage room when he heard a gang of men cheering on a dice game played on a green-felt-covered pool table. Bones was hot on the dice and humming for a winning combination. He waved a fistful of sweaty bills in one hand, gambling feverishly with intentions of stuffing his pockets. Hampton stood a calculated distance from the excitement, five grown men and their money. He stared at Bones until acknowledged. Hampton received a slight grin before Bones went back to shaking the cubes of fortune in his tight grasp.

"Come on, girls," he yelled anxiously. "Get Daddy some more of that good stuff." Again, Hampton signaled for a private discussion. Bones continued his run of successful passes, collecting stacks of loose bills each time.

Hampton couldn't believe he'd been put off, considering he'd taken the violent thumping that rightfully should have been doled out to Bones. Bumped and bruised, Hampton stormed forward. With swiftness and utter disregard, he snatched the dice off the table. Now that he had everyone's undivided attention, there was no point in mincing words. "Excuse me, fellas, but y'alls gonna have to make tracks. This game's adjourned." In the midst of stern objections from the other men, cussing, and shoving, Bones stepped in.

"Not now, man, I'm hot in this hazard. Back up and let those tumblers roll."

Hampton punched the gambler who appeared the most reluctant to shut it down. He reached for a knife as his eye began to swell. "I'ma stick you for that!"

"What the hell you doing, man?" spat one of the bystanders.

"Crazy fool must be trying to get hisself shot," another of them concluded.

Unwavering, Hampton instinctively drew down on them with the gun from his waistband. "You ever have a day where you don't want to be bothered with standing for no bullshit?" He wagged his finger at Bones to solidify his meaning. "Well, this here is one of them days, so don't bother me with none of yours." The gamblers eyed one another peculiarly, contemplating what fate lay in store for them if they stayed.

"You's mighty sure of yourself agin' all of us, friend," growled the biggest of the lot.

"This is fixing to be a life-or-death situation. Anybody who wants in is welcome to hang around. Don't make me no nevermind either way." Hampton cocked the hammer on his pistol.

"Whoa!" the outspoken gambler shouted, both hands raised defensively. "We can see you have a lot on your mind that don't include us. We'll get our things and be out of here in a jiff."

Bones enjoyed watching Hampton's conviction at play. He couldn't help flashing an impish grin. After nodding so long to his gaming associates and good-bye to their money, he slammed his hand down on the pool table. "What's got you sideways, Swagger, rumbling up on me whilst spilling over with piss and vinegar? You scared my pigeons off, and before I could strip them clean. It's plain that you wanted my ear. All right, then, I'm listening. This had better be good, and her ass had better be fat." Bones huffed angrily when he remembered how well the dice game was tilting in his favor. "Damn. You know I hate leaving money on the table. Let me get my hat." Hampton followed closely as Bones jammed an unlit cigar in his mouth then shrugged into the back alley for some air.

"You ain't asked me once how I managed to collect the knuckle prints on my face," Hampton fussed irately.

"That's 'cause I already know. Everybody heard the police grabbed you up. The word is all over the streets how you clocked one before the net cinched, too." Bones snickered then, like he'd told a funny joke.

"Huh, I'll bet there's something you didn't know. They been following me, Bones. I ditched them in the same place we floated that stolen car. What's more, the law's been after me to tell what I know about the councilman's death. They got their sights on me, something called an accomplice charge. Said somebody told them my car was parked close to a couple of them sissy murders. This city detective, Archie Mouton, called your name, too. I believe he's playing the feds on this case, but they's all in the bed together."

Bones seemed disturbed then. "The feds were brought in on this?"

"Hell, yeah, one of them was in the room when they was trying to smack some answers out of me."

"What did you tell them?" Bones asked evenly.

"I told them the truth, that they didn't know what they were talking about. I didn't have nothing to do with no dead man. Then I told them how killing wasn't my bag and that I only boosted cars from time to time. I wasn't copping to nothing else."

Bones stared at the ground while he reasoned with Hampton's assessment of the interrogation. His eyes burned holes into Hampton when he felt some important aspects had been conveniently left out. "What happened then?"

"Nothing, they just tossed a trick at my feet but I sniffed it out.

They was asking if I knew somebody who might be the type to kill the way the councilman got his. Now, who would that be?"

"Well, you sell me out?"

"What you think? Hell, naw! I got one way to go and I'm sticking to it. After that, I told them to go fly a kite." Hampton understood how implicating Bones would have also put his head on the chopping block. Besides, he fought off the urge to believe the man he'd come to know could commit such a brutal crime more than once.

"You went down swinging for me, Swagger?" Bones asked, having had prior knowledge of what occurred in that small room even before Hampton's dangerous tirade.

"It's more like we'd both swing on the same pole if I didn't," he replied honestly. As quick as the news spread about Hampton's detainment, word traveled just as fast regarding his outright refusal to speak on what he did know. Bones had received a phone call shortly after Hampton's catch and release, rehashing the entire interrogation. Bones thought it sounded a lot better coming from his pal's mouth, though.

"Thank you, Swagger. I'm beholden to you. I don't have but one real friend, so you're in a pretty exclusive club. I'll see to it that everything is taken care of. I have somebody on the inside with the local police. Good thing, too. Guilt can get kind of ornery at times. You've got to lick it before it licks you. Git on home or else they might try to grab you up again and this time shake harder until something does rattle loose. Go on now, Swagger. Git!"

20

Burdens

That evening, Magnolia helped Pearl Lee with dinner and the dishes. They stood over a large oval-shaped galvanized tub filled with bubbles and dirty cookware. Pearl Lee had been uncharacteristically quiet while listening to Magnolia's account of Hampton's troubles with the law. "Ooh, this water's hot," the younger woman hissed, reaching into the tub with a dishcloth.

"Yeah, you gotta wait until it cools a bit. I just added some water from the kettle." Pearl Lee gestured to the black cauldron sitting on bricks in the lit fireplace, which was the only way to heat water in the cabin. "Wait a spell and let it soften the grit. Everything in its own time."

"I wish it was all that easy, you know, to reason with." Magnolia leaned against the counter with her arms folded. She peered out the back window, then she let her eyes wander up and down Pearl Lee's blank expression. "Have you heard a single word I said?" Silence lingered behind Pearl Lee's glassy gaze. "No, I guess you haven't at that," she concluded.

"Haven't what?"

"You haven't been listening is what. I know you got a lot

digging at your heart with Toussaint's mind dwindling and such. It's just that Hampton might be in a world of danger if those policemen get their hands on him again."

Suddenly, Pearl Lee's countenance changed dramatically. She furrowed her brow and blinked rapidly like she'd been trapped in a daydream. "Forgive me. Toussaint's wandering off at night is getting the best of me. What's this about Hampton and the police?"

"That's what I've been trying to tell you. Me and Hampton were on our way to the picture show when this stump of a white man came out of nowhere. Hampton shushed me then started whaling on him something terrible."

"On a white man?" Pearl Lee asked, more astonished than anything.

"On a white cop. It was frightful scary. Hampton must've heard him trying to sneak up on us so we hid in an alley. When the white man hurried by, Hampton jumped him. Had his hands around the policeman's neck. He wasn't meaning to kill him, just get to the reason why he was onto us." Magnolia expected Hampton's sister to worry so she didn't blink when Pearl Lee began wringing her hands in the same pulverizing manner she'd done before. Afraid the woman would crack a bone with her strong fingers, Magnolia placed both of her hands over them. "Uh-uh, it's all right, Pearl Lee. Calm down. It's all right. Hampton made sure I got to his rented room safe before they caught up to him. He told me there was about a dozen of them, all toting guns and dirty looks."

"I heard those Nawlins cops are some of the meanest bunch. They didn't try to half kill him for whooping on the stumpy one in that alley?"

"Uh-uh," she answered, glad they didn't. "They put a row

of knots on his head, though. Hampton said they took it easy because they wanted some information of some sort. He came stumbling in later, after they let him go." Pearl Lee listened as Magnolia replayed the story. "See what I mean about things being kinda difficult to reason with?"

"Yeah, I do now," Pearl Lee whispered. "That brother of mine was bound to get mixed up in a bad fix. Did Hampton say what the police expected him to tell? Are they gonna leave him alone now? Why the hell was they onto y'all in the first place?" Her questions shot out rapid-fire rat-a-tat style. "I thought I was going to lose it over Toussaint, now this." She began to mist up around the eyes. Magnolia marveled, unaccustomed to seeing Pearl Lee wither.

"Hampton said he can handle hisself. I got no choice but to believe him and neither do you. I'll help you keep an eye on Toussaint. Don't waste any pity on your brother. That's up to me. He's gonna be my husband one day. It's only right I bear his burden."

Pearl Lee's eyes were consumed with surprise. "What the hell else happened between dinner, the picture show, and Hampton getting clapped by them cops?"

Magnolia smiled brightly. "I got me something good for my birthday."

"Dayyyum, girl. It must've been, 'cause you ain't stop grinning yet."

"Don't plan to, neither."

When the sun fell over New Orleans, Hampton sat against the iron headboard in his room. He'd searched for his name in the newspaper and forced a tired yawn when it wasn't there. He folded the daily over his knee after having read two articles detailing Detective Archibald Mouton's taking heat over murder cases piling up in the Quarter. Mouton vowed to continue beating the bushes as the death toll climbed to seven under his watch. Tourists stayed away from the historic district. That meant lost revenue for the city. Powerful politicians criticized the police department's lack of success in bringing the serial killing spree to an end. That meant Detective Mouton would more than likely step up his regimen of beating more than bushes. Just as that disturbing thought zigzagged in Hampton's head, there was a hard rap on his door. Initially, he figured the worrisome neighbor with the big mouth was back again to annoy him about a call, but the phone across the way hadn't rung.

Hampton hurried to the bureau, pulled out the top drawer, then palmed his revolver. He eased up to the door quietly. "Yeah, who is it?"

"Detective Archie Mouton," a calm voice answered.

"What you want? I done told you all I had to say." Hampton leaned away from the door when he feared it might get busted in on top of him.

"Open up, Hampton. I'm alone and I don't mean you any harm today. This is a friendly call." Hampton considered the man's tone. It wasn't in the least bit strained. It played more like how-do-you-do casual, so he took him at his word.

After twisting the knob slowly, Hampton cracked the door so he could peep out before committing all the way. Steadily, he held his gun behind the door while staring through the gap in it. "You say you alone, but where is Cunningham? That was y'all following me until I ditched you at that bend in the bayou."

The tall cop removed his hat, fingered the brim, then grinned mildly. "Yep, that was some pretty nifty driving. Cunningham is still pissed about having to be towed out of the swamp. So, are we going to talk through the door and give the neighbors something to talk about, or do I get invited in? Like I said, this is a friendly visit." Mouton noticed Hampton was acting cagey, so he worked at defusing a potentially volatile situation. "Why don't you put that heater away so we can talk?"

"Give me a minute," Hampton grunted coolly. He closed the door cautiously then strutted toward the bureau. Hampton slid out the top dresser drawer and slammed it shut so that his unexpected guest would hear it. He returned to the door with his pistol hidden underneath a loosely fitted shirt. "All right, come on in. I had to tidy up some," he lied unsuccessfully.

"Good, can we talk now?" Mouton asked with a cord of uncertainty running through it. He entered, looked over the sparse belongings, and then searched for a place to sit. The only chair in the room was covered with dirty clothes until Hampton transferred them to a wicker basket near the bathroom door. "Thanks, I could use a cigarette. You smoke?"

Hampton took a seat on his unmade bed. He shrugged at the man's question, still on guard and analyzing every syllable laid at his feet. "Nah, I never fancied it," he responded eventually.

"Not even a cigar every now and then?"

Again, Hampton sifted through the detective's words, expecting to discover a sneaky trick at the bottom. "No, sir, especially not no cigars."

"That's interesting, because I know you were in the councilman's house, maybe not the night he died but you've been there. I got the fingerprints back and guess whose were among them?"

"Thought you said this was a friendly visit. You aiming to take me in all by yourself?" Hampton positioned his right hand on the bed for quicker access to his gun. He wasn't going to jail for murder, not even if they sent an army platoon up to his room. Dying in a shootout was more dignified than being sent to the death house over something he didn't do. "What gives, Detective? I read in the paper about the hot grease they keep dipping you in, fussing about you not doing enough to solve them murders."

"You've been checking up, huh? I've been doing some checking myself, Hampton. I came across some mighty interesting information, too. It's the main reason I didn't pick you and your girlfriend up this morning, why I decided against sending my men up here to break down the door and feed you to those federal boys. Yep, information is power. And it was mighty powerful information that nudged me toward switching your prints with a third-rate thief who died in jail of pneumonia last year." Mouton had sufficiently shifted momentum in his favor. He had Hampton off balance and teetering uncomfortably.

"Information?" Hampton queried suspiciously. He figured the detective intended on getting a leg up on him by using the nuggets he'd picked up while following a hunch that came to him during their hot-box chat. "What kind of information would make you go through all that fuss? I mean, switching prints and all that."

The clever detective was in total control now. He crossed his legs, leaned back, and placed the hat he'd been primping over his knee. This is exactly where he wanted Hampton, craving information himself. "I've met a lot of tough goons, Hampton. Some are born that way and others, well, let's just say are made over time. You're harder than most. Not much puts a scare into you, leastways not a couple of bare-knuckle cops. I had a gut feeling that a tough guy like you had done a stretch or two in jail. Nothing turned up in the state files, federal nor parish records, either. I was ready to believe I'd been wrong about you until I stopped by the Orleans Home for Wayward Boys." He watched Hampton's jawline constrict as he continued. "The warden explained how a certain Negro boy got himself pinched for stealing meat out of the locked freezer in back of the Piggly Wiggly. While that offense wasn't heinous itself, the young fella laid a solid beating on the store manager who caught him making off with a mess of steaks. The warden said that colored boy, who was brought in on a three-year bid, didn't say one single solitary word during the two years they had him locked up. The warden also said it was the damnedest thing when he received a report that the troubled mute disappeared one night. Poof, just like that." Detective Mouton nodded his head like he fully understood something he couldn't have. "Know something else, Hampton? That old warden had a pretty good memory. He told me that the fella who walked off into thin air didn't take no shit from nobody, not even when the older boys teased him about fresh bullwhip lashes on his hide."

The policeman saw Hampton's trigger finger getting itchy, but he had a ways to go before forcing the colored man's hand, which is why he spoke respectfully and arrived alone. "Relax, now. Nobody's taking you back. I just need some answers. See, what's more puzzling to me than anything else is the fact that my office received a call about Ivory 'Bones' Arcineaux being responsible for one of the killings. You know why that's got me so confused, Hampton? Huh? You and I both are well aware that a white boy, a juvenile detainee named Ivory Arcineaux, was savagely murdered at the Orleans youth home the day before you pulled your vanishing act. How or why you took off isn't important. The point is, that call I received about Bones's being responsible for the councilman's murder came from that telephone right out there in the hallway. Now tell me, how is that possible when Ivory Arcineaux is dead? And why did you make the call if you and whoever the man using a dead boy's name were in on it together?"

In what seemed like forever, Mouton bounced that hat of his off his knee and patiently waited on answers that were not forthcoming. Moments after Hampton failed to respond to the slick backhanded interrogation, the detective dangled a carrot to help move things around on the suspect's plate. "Tell you what, get in contact with this Bones friend of yours and make sure he meets me at pier sixteen, midnight. Tell him not to worry. There won't be any funny business, no tricks. I just want to talk to the man and close these cases. I'll come alone. For your sake, he'd better show."

Hampton stared out his window as Mouton settled into the passenger side of an unmarked police car. Hampton thought it odd that he felt even worse than the night when Mouton and Cunningham beat the tar out of him. The detective dredged up feelings Hampton had worked hard at forgetting and a slew of haunting memories about a barbaric place unfit for any young man to endure, criminally disposed or otherwise. There was only one way to get a handle on his current situation and keep his freedom. Drop everything, get on the horn, and dial up Bones.

At eleven-fifty, Mouton blew out a dense stream of cigarette smoke as he stared out over the Mississippi River. Several barges glided down the watery canal. Two prominent riverboats went past, upper and lower decks littered with passengers counting the stars among the money they'd lost gambling. The detective eyed his rectangular wristwatch, wondering if he'd wasted his time by asking Hampton to turn on his accomplice. There were so many holes in the evidence Mouton gathered. City politicians, federal agencies, and local departmental brass were climbing up his neck, all wanting the same thing, for the reign of terror to end.

After he'd smoked his third cigarette down to the nub,

Detective Mouton flicked it into the water. Before he decided to call it a night and head home for a decent block of much needed sleep, footsteps paced toward him in a slow, deliberate manner. "I was beginning to think you got a kick out of hiding in the shadows while I huffed through a pack of Chesterfields," Mouton said jokingly. "I hope you don't mind me turning around to see who's been keeping me up nights." He hesitated then drew in a heap of apprehension. "Should I be looking to catch a bullet when I do?"

"Not from me," Bones answered, sure and steady. He'd put on his best suit, a black houndstooth number with wide lapels, and shiny two-toned shoes. "I've seen you in the papers plenty, Archie, and I've been anxious to see how the real thing stacks up. You're quite a bit taller than I imagined." Bones held his pistol waist high, with the hammer back, and held a three- by four-inch wooden box while Mouton turned with both hands raised.

"I'd hate to have a misunderstanding," Mouton called out, loud enough to be heard clearly by the man behind him. His eyes narrowed as soon as he laid eyes on Bones, noting his natty attire and the fresh cigar wedged in the corner of his mouth. That was the clincher. A chewed cigar had been left at the scene of each homicide, like a calling card. "It's funny how I spent all day trying to get a line on if you'd actually show. Interesting thought, how you're more and less than I figured."

"Should I take offense, Detective? That didn't nearly resemble any compliment I ever heard." Bones kept his gun pointed, sizing up the detective and any ideas he may have been cooking up to take his prime suspect in, dead or alive. "You came alone. I checked when you got here. An honest man and a desperate man often wear the same clothes when their neck is on the line. Whichever you happen to be isn't of any consequence, unless of course you intend to use your desperation to snare me. Then, I'd just as soon blast you right here and sharpen my teeth for the goon they'll sit at your desk once you're in the ground."

Mouton was glad he'd decided to ride solo. Overzealous patrolmen with itchy trigger fingers had ruined more cases than he cared to remember. His career was at stake, and there was no way he'd let some jumpy flatfoot send it down the tubes. Playing his cards straight had always been his best bet so he went with it. "Okay, I'm here and you're here. What do we do now, talk about why you murdered those men and give you a few hours' head start before coming after you? I have three pawnshop owners at the ready. All of them nailed your description and agreed to point you out as the man who sold them a dead man's chest full of stolen goods. That's three honest men ready to strap you in the electric chair."

Bones aimed the gun barrel at the larger man and then waved it in wide looping circles like it helped him to think better. "Don't forget what I told you about honest and desperate men, Detective. No, that's not quite what I had in mind at all. See, first thing is, if you take me in now, there might be a problem making people believe I acted alone. Where's my motive? As far as you know, I have none. You don't think you can prove I bound, gagged, and gutted those queers by myself, do you? Hampton Bynote's a colored. He might get in the mix and throw off your sure thing if people believe he outsmarted Nawlin's top cop with the whole city watching. Yep, he could spell trouble for you and me. Juries like things tied up with a perfect bow." Bones was really feeling himself. Mouton was openly intrigued and nibbling around the hook. He couldn't avoid wearing a heavy dose of curiosity on his face as Bones continued. "The way I think this should play out leaves us both a lot of wiggle room and guarantees you make captain by the end of the week." There was a question on Mouton's lips, likely more than one, but he held his tongue and listened. "That's a good boy, Detective. Now I'll tell you exactly what you need to satisfy those federal agents you're babysitting and the mayor, who can't wait to hand you a shiny new key to the city. In this box, there's a note with instructions, among other things."

"Instructions?" echoed the police officer, as if the word had popped out of Bones's behind instead of his mouth.

"Oh, yeah, every detail about those sissy-boy murders, what was taken from the scenes, where you can find the remaining articles, and what to do about all the evidence your crackerjack investigating turns up. If you look over what I have to offer and find you don't particularly agree with my proposition, then you can send your men after me, loaded to the hilt. I'll even shoot it out with them so it'll make the national newscasts. I'll go out in a blaze of glory if you'd like, with a ton of news reporters bringing up your rear."

Detective Archibald Mouton was faced with three choices, two of which didn't necessitate getting shot at trying to apprehend the suspect. He could have played the curious cop, read the note, placed an all-points bulletin out for a man fitting Bones's description, and then hoped to arrest the criminal before losing his job. Mouton's second option was reading the note, evaluating the information, and then following the instructions if he agreed to partner up with the admitted serial killer. He couldn't make a rational decision until he got his hands on the note so he agreed, in principle, to go as far as his good conscience allowed him. "I'm running out of time, Bones," Mouton confessed, "and that goes double for you."

"I've only got one more nance to look in on, then I'm done for good. I'm just taking out the trash, a personal issue, you understand. In two days, you'll have that pretty little bow and all the king's men slapping you on the back." Bones studied his potential partner. Mouton didn't even blink when he heard that yet another man was due to be slaughtered. He had already begun to see his name on the front page with quotes and photos highlighting his successes.

"You can guarantee two days and this will all be over?"

"With a bow to boot," Bones answered assuredly. "There's one hitch. You've got to grab up Hampton and put him where the feds can't gnaw at him. He didn't know what I'd dragged him into until it was too late to do anything about it. You've seen him. Hampton's a tough old boy but he's tired. Read the note, it'll tell you how to handle him. He'll go along with it all the way. He's a colored man in the great state of Louisiana, Detective."

"I see your point. Hampton's got no choice."

"None but what I give him. Now, you wait awhile before picking up this box. You come after me tomorrow, I'll burn the evidence. If you pick up Hampton on a stolen auto charge, I'll know you're with me. Am I clear on everything so far, Detective?"

"Only in Nawlins would any of this make a lick of sense to anybody. Yeah, I hear you loud and clear."

Detective Mouton shook his head as Bones backed away into the darkness. The veteran policeman had seen a lot of strange occurrences he couldn't easily explain, but the stunt Bones pulled took the cake. He wanted to kick himself for seriously considering what the natty dresser proposed. After the detective opened the box and pulled the councilman's ring finger out of it, he cringed. After he'd read over the note for a third time, Mouton left the docks prepared to wager his career on a murderer using a dead man's name. He had two days to complete the bargain that required selling his soul. He couldn't wait to close the deal.

21

Doubled Down

Six police officers staked out Hampton's apartment building throughout the night. Five of them sat patiently in two unmarked cars. Detective Mouton glanced down at his watch every few seconds, it seemed. In order to solidify his deal with Bones, Hampton had to be arrested by morning. Growing more concerned by the minute, the detective cursed under his breath. He glared at Cunningham then shoved open the car door to get some air. Mouton paced beside the vehicle, eyeing his timepiece repeatedly. He whipped out a cigarette and sneered while holding a lit match to the end of it. The cigarette fell from his mouth when Hampton's old clunker eased around the corner. Each of the officers snapped to, after having slouched for hours. They weren't informed as to why so many of them had to be dispatched since the suspect had been booked and released earlier. "Well, I'll be," whispered Mouton, as the predawn sky began to fade from a dense indigo to light purple. "He's late as hell and just in time. Let's grab him up, but don't scuff him any."

Hampton stepped out of the car with his back facing the

officers. He stretched and yawned. Before he could get the door closed, the sound of click-clacking shoes startled him. He dove to the ground with his arms spread apart. "Don't shoot!" he shouted nervously. "I ain't done nothing. I'm innocent. Y'alls railroading me. I ain't done nothing!"

"That's twice tonight you've lied to me, Hampton," Detective Mouton challenged. "We've got you dead to rights, and this time, it'll stick." Cunningham grinned heartily as the officers wrestled handcuffs onto the colored man's wrists. "Good, now I can work on getting some sleep."

"So you really think he was in on it?" questioned Cunningham, glad to see Hampton's face pressed against the filthy pavement.

"Yeah, we got him all right. His fingerprints were found all over a stolen car we pulled out of the swamp. He'll cool his heels in the parish work camp."

Cunningham scratched his head. He didn't comprehend the rationale for bringing along extra muscle to apprehend a common car thief. "You mean to tell me I've spent all this time sitting on my nuts and aggravating my hemorrhoids to catch this spook on a drive and ditch?"

Mouton wasn't of a mind to explain why he'd requisitioned all of the additional witnesses of Hampton Bynote's arrest. Bones had suggested it in his note. Mouton carried it out to the letter. "This spook is our ticket to deep pockets, unless you want to pass it up." He saw the bulge in Cunningham's throat when he swallowed hard.

"You're the boss," he uttered. "In for a penny, in for a pound."

"Don't let me have to remind you of that again. This could get hairy." Mouton noticed one of the officers itching to take out his frustration on Hampton. "Whoa, I told you not to crack him.

Let's get on back to the precinct house, boys, and wrap this up. Hampton, I don't want to hear a peep out of you until I say so. Got that, tough guy?"

"Yeah, I got it," he replied, a chord of manufactured angst in his voicc. Hampton had received a visit from Bones, telling him to get a thick chunk of devilment out of his system and prepare himself for a short stay in the gray-bar hotel. Their conversation was short and to the point. Hampton was informed that the walls were closing in and that he needed to be home by morning to seal a deal Bones made with the police detective. It was a hard sell at the outset, but Bones had it all figured out, considering Hampton was a colored man in the great state of Louisiana. His choices were severely strapped between thin and none.

Hampton settled into the backseat of the police car, worrying that Bones's idea of setting things straight included handing him over to Mouton on a silver platter. Within the next twenty-four hours, he'd know the full extent of his worries and Bones's ability to make good on his promises.

For the second time in a week, Hampton was booked in the New Orleans police headquarters. However, there were no futile threats this go-round, no derogatory names spat at him or angry fists flying. Hampton lay in a bottom bunk, dressed in blue institution clothes with NOCD stenciled on the back for New Orleans Corrections Department. Detective Mouton assured him the fix was in, according to Bones, and he was looking at no more than three months in stir by pleading guilty to grand theft auto. Having to be separated from Magnolia for ninety days seemed like a cakewalk as opposed to being hit with a death sentence for seven homicides, despite his insignificant level of involvement. All Hampton had to do was bide his time and catch up to his life where he'd left it. Being on the inside again wasn't as bad as Hampton remembered from his previous run-in with the juvenile department. He had three meals a day and lots of books to read. The more he thought about it, the closer he came to making peace with his incarceration. That changed when he was plucked out of his cell at nightfall the next evening.

"Hey, where y'all taking me?" Hampton questioned when three men opened his gate and shackled him with arm and leg irons. "Hey, man, somebody tell me what I did wrong. Hey! Get Detective Mouton up here, we had a deal. Hey!" Other inmates on his cell block witnessed the abduction, but none of them made a sound on his behalf. Each was extremely relieved he wasn't being dragged down the long corridor for God knows what.

"What y'all aiming to do with me?" he asked when a neatly attired white man in a dashing pin-striped suit entered the holding room where he'd been made to roost. The dashing DA glared at the colored man with disgust in his eyes. Hampton glanced at him, his small hands, thin nose, and perfect haircut. He resembled the steely federal agent except for his top-shelf cologne and broken-in shoes.

"You're Hampton Bynote?" the district attorney sniped. Hampton nodded slowly although he'd have given anything to be anyone else. Chained to the floor and facing uncertain torment, he lowered his head to await his fate. "I'm District Attorney Willard Preston. It's nice to see the man who took off in my new car and sank it in four feet of godforsaken swampland." The DA's thin nostrils flared, putting Hampton in mind of an overgrown mouse in stylish duds. He almost laughed—almost. "Mr. Bynote, we don't look too kindly on men who take things that don't belong to them. That automobile was a gift from my father. You ruined it. The car is a total loss. The plea agreement you signed with Detective Mouton calls for three months of easy labor. I've spoken with the judge and he agrees with me that ninety days isn't sufficient punishment. Punishment should fit the crime, don't you concur?"

Hampton didn't have to know what concur meant to know he was about to be on the sticky end of a big mess. "Mr. Preston, I can't rightly say what would make you feel better about getting your car took. I'm sorry for wrecking your daddy's present. If mine had left me something nice and somebody come along and swiped it, I'd be sore, too; even if I was at Mr. Rudolph's illegal gambling house when it happened."

The DA smirked at Hampton, who appeared bent on placing some of the blame at the politician's feet. "You are a piece of work, I'll grant you that. The judge and I have decided that fourteen months is a much fairer sentence than three."

"Fairer for who?" Hampton heckled riotously. "Naw, man! I said I was sorry about your car, but this ain't right. Go talk to Detective Mouton. Get him down here and iron this out."

"Count your blessings that I couldn't talk the judge into an even fairer penalty. You could be staring at a five-year rap," he said smugly. "If Detective Mouton has anything to say about this, he can take it up with me tomorrow." He sneered at Hampton again before leveling another verbal blow. "And, oh, don't get too used to these outstanding accommodations. Where you're going won't be half as cozy."

"I heard tales about men getting bent over in places like this. I just didn't know it would be the DA getting in the first poke."

Hampton didn't sleep at all that night. The small cell he'd been assigned seemed more appropriate for a dog. It was humid and restrictive. His bunkmate's thunderous snores interrupted his thoughts continually. Hampton couldn't wait to see the sun rise. He actually thought there was a chance of getting his sentence reduced once Detective Archibald Mouton caught wind of his dilemma. Just as the morning roll call began, the brawny cop appeared with Cunningham on his heels and two detention officers leading the way. "Now we're getting someplace," Hampton gloated. "I was about to have them send for you. That DA Preston showed up last night talking about—" he ranted until Mouton doubled him over with a powerful sucker punch in the stomach.

"If I wanted your opinion, convict, I'd have given it to you," Mouton grunted. "Cuff this piece of shit. He pissed off the DA, and I'm stuck transporting him to the work camp. Where's the justice in that?" The sturdy cop appeared extremely annoyed with Hampton's total existence. "The next time you let a politician screw you over, at least get him to spring for breakfast afterward. It's too early to be here, too goddamn early." He pushed Hampton out of the cell and into Cunningham's mitts.

"I got a call an hour ago to come here and fetch you directly to the camp. If I wasn't so hungry, I'd beat the black off you right now." Hampton held his midsection with both hands, cringing over the solid blow he'd received unexpectedly. He cut his eyes at the city detectives, then at the jailhouse cops who were visibly indifferent about handing him over. The jailers signed him out like a library book. They were simply doing a job, regardless of Hampton's safety, nothing more and nothing less. He understood that. He didn't like it, but he understood.

Cuffed in the backseat, with Officer Cunningham riding shotgun, Hampton observed the peculiar glances he kept getting from Mouton's sidekick. Something underhanded was in the works. He couldn't tell what had the stubby cop so jumpy. "Isn't that it up there?" Cunningham asserted, pointing at a lone shack near the water's edge in the warehouse district. Hampton leaned forward and craned his neck to get a good look out the front car window. The antsy hitch in Cunningham's voice put him on notice to be very concerned.

"Hey, fellas, this ain't the work farm," Hampton heckled nervously. "Hey, man! Mouton, what you trying to pull?" Finally, the veteran officer placed his arm on the rise of the bench seat. He signaled slyly to his partner, then checked the bullets in his revolver.

"Relax, Hampton. I talked to Bones about this, and he said for us to meet him here. Said he'd finish it and make things right for all of us." Mouton holstered his weapon then stepped out of the car. He lit up a smoke and started the clock-watching routine he knew all too well. Within a few minutes, he reached inside his coat pocket. He sighed painstakingly as he pulled something out of it. When he tossed the police-issue service revolver onto the backseat between his wingman and Hampton it was difficult to determine who was more afraid of the other.

"Y-you sure about this, Archie?" Cunningham stammered. "I mean, if this goes wrong." Hampton was just as uncomfortable. He was in the dark, too, and uneasy about ending up in the morgue.

"It won't," Mouton assured him. "I'm the boss, remember. Don't get in the way. I'll be right back." He considered reprimanding Cunningham for shutting his eyes and mouthing a silent prayer. Suddenly, he heard someone whistling a jovial tune. Bones waved to Hampton and the fat officer in the backseat turning green.

Bones scouted the immediate area for witnesses while examining his gun. He also studied the shack while approaching the lead detective, standing near it. "Morning, Detective. I'm honestly glad to see you and Hampton, too. Well, ready? Let's get it done then." Without further warning, Bones stomped against the front door. It busted in like a thin sheet of drywall. Detective Mouton flanked his play through the doorway. A scrawny white man in his late twenties scrambled from his sparse bedroom wearing nothing but boxer shorts. He shot across the dingy shack, scampering for the side window. A deafening gunshot blast stopped him in his tracks.

"Okay, okay! Please don't kill me," he pleaded from a cowering position on the floor. "I don't have anything you want."

Bones stared down on the mousy-blond man with a tapered buzz cut who was understandably terrified by the early morning intrusion. "Yes, you do, Lenny, and I came to get it. You owe and I'm collecting in full." Leonard blinked rapidly as he raised his eyes to meet his attacker's claims.

"What? How do you... how do know my name?" he whined.

"You have a very short memory, Lenny. I haven't forgotten, not any of the sins you committed in the Boys' Home." The frightened man's eyes widened dramatically. Bones grinned when Leonard recognized his face. "Yeah, it's all coming back to you now. You pimped out over thirty boys to the guards and to those late-night stag parties for their rich friends."

"Hey, hey, that was a long time ago," Leonard sniffled. "Besides, the guards made me do it. They made me."

Detective Mouton observed the oddest of reunions as Bones tore into Leonard. "Eight years didn't erase what you did, leading boys who trusted you into dark cages with perverts. How much did they pay, Lenny? How much was ruining those boys worth to them?"

"I'm telling you, I didn't have a choice back then. You were there. You saw how it was. Bunchy and Turk had all the muscle. Huey Boyette gave them money, lots of it, for throwing meat to his friends." As he pleaded his case, Detective Mouton ran their names through his mind.

"Tom 'Bunchy' Hill, Turk Olms, and Councilman Huey Boyette?"

Bones nodded his head assuredly. "Yeah, Bunchy and Turk ran the prostitution ring for years, turning out scared little boys. Only, Boyette wasn't no councilman then. He was a snake who brought the customers in through an old abandoned water pump station that ran underneath the detention's laundry room. Leonard here was a full-time recruiter. He'd set his wolf pack on the lambs and offer protection in return for late-night party favors." Mouton's lips tightened after it had all been laid out for him. Leonard saw the contempt in his eyes mounting.

"Hold on, I told you I had no say in what went on," he complained. "I-I had to do it or be served up, too."

Bones didn't agree. He shook his head with his gun steadied. "Everybody's got a choice unless somebody else comes along, holds them down, and takes it away. You had plenty of say for what went on in the Orleans Parish home. Pitiful screams, broken bodies, and wasted lives all fell on you. Seven of the fellas you pimped took their own lives. We can't forget Ivory Arcineaux, can we?"

"Wait, you can't blame that on me. Turk and Bunchy didn't mean to kill him. They were just supposed to rough him up some. He slipped in the shower and hit his head. I wasn't even there."

"Everybody knows you sent them, Lenny. You killed him, just as much as they did. Only, Bones ain't dead. I picked up his name and his cause. You had all the say in that black hole they stacked us in, but I'm the one with the muscle now. And I say it's time you joined Wiley, Lamar, Colton, Measures, Bunchy, Turk, and Boyette." Bones listened to Leonard whimper like a sick puppy, the same way the others had before he snuffed out their lives. "Leonard Lafon, you have been charged with unspeakable crimes against children and you shall burn in hell!" Bones squeezed the trigger. He pumped two slugs into Leonard, leaving a pair of gaping holes in his bare chest. Leonard coughed and gasped for air as the pool of blood widened on the dirty cement floor.

"Whyyy?" he moaned. "All that's been finished."

Detective Mouton jeered at him, wishing he'd been the one to fire lead into Leonard. "Halt, don't move!" Mouton shouted sarcastically, once the former child molester was dead. "Leonard Lafon, you're under arrest." Mouton looked over at Bones then shrugged his shoulders. "I guess he didn't want to go quietly. It's a shame when that happens. It's so unnecessary."

Bones spat on the dead man's corpse. "Now it's finished." He handed the smoking gun to Detective Mouton before showing him where to find a compelling bag of evidence planted in the back of Leonard's sofa. "Here's everything you'll need to convict this faggot in the papers, where it counts. This case is over, and you're as good as promoted already. How's that for a neat little bow, *Captain* Mouton?"

"*Captain*, that does have a nice ring at that. What about Hampton? You think he'll keep his mouth shut?"

"I can guarantee it. He's protected now. If he gets into an accident while on the inside, it'll be your door getting kicked in," Bones threatened. "It'd be a bigger shame for a new police captain to end up like some other people I know." He leered at Leonard Lafon's motionless body until Mouton did likewise.

"All right, partner, all right. You don't have to tell me twice." Bones had murdered eight men in cold blood for what they'd done. Although the detective didn't fear him, he couldn't see any benefit in crossing a serial killer who'd helped close the most widely publicized murders in the city's history. Bones left Mouton in the ratty house, alone with his thoughts, his cigarettes, and the motive he needed to close the case.

22

Heartbroke

Hampton hadn't been in prison blues for a week before witnessing what the wrong bit of bad news could do to an inmate. A desperate man who learned his father had passed away tried to escape by scaling the fence. He was captured, beaten, and thrown into a tiny metal booth erroneously referred to as "the cooler." The temperature inside of it easily climbed over 110 degrees. Hampton watched helplessly as the goons responsible for maintaining order tossed the grief-stricken convict into what a guy in his barrack aptly called "the devil's ass." Two days later, another prisoner actually made it over the wall after hearing that his child had drowned in a swimming accident. The tower guards shot him down just beyond the barbed wire. Hampton decided then that he'd meet prison time head-on, no matter how it came at him. It appeared that dealing with unfortunate occurrences outside of steel bars was far more dangerous.

The food wasn't bad. Heaping tin plates consisting of tasteless starches, fried chicken, and bland vegetables rounded out one drab lunch and dinner after the next. Breakfast generally included sliced ham, grits, and eggs but nothing as exotic as oatmeal, French toast, or fruit medleys. Hampton didn't quibble about the menu, unlike many of his contemporaries. Certain that nothing could have been gained by comparing home-cooked meals to countless mass-produced buckets of routine chow, he didn't bother to get bent out of shape. When his housing unit ran out of toilet paper days before the commissary delivery truck arrived to restock the barracks, he dealt with it without making a peep. No soap, no problem. Counting the time he had yet to serve proved most effective. With each passing night, his end date grew that much closer.

Hampton asked for the toughest work detail available, although his accomplished reading skills qualified him for easier and less stressful duties. Hampton was initially relieved to be outside, busting rocks at the quarry and maneuvering filled wheelbarrows back and forth to the dump trucks idling at the edge of an enormous pit. At times, Hampton was too tired to eat. Some of the men on his chain stole grub from the dining hall on his behalf. They forced him to stomach what he could until becoming acclimated to performing backbreaking tasks without falling prey to exhaustion. Thankful for the helping hands, Hampton divvied up cookies and candy sent from home to those who looked out for him. Although he kept to himself mostly, he stayed close enough to experience life on the fringes of theirs, where it was easy to step back into the darkness whenever necessary.

Mail call meant so much to the men he came to know by listening to their colorful jokes, dreams, and regrets, observing their defeat conveyed in Dear John letters, and sharing in the torment that imprisoned each of them. Hampton stood near the back of the crowd, collecting letters from home while refusing to open a single one. He didn't want to read perfumed scented correspondence from Magnolia explaining how she couldn't wait for him any longer, albeit miserable about it and forced to console herself in the arms of another man. Blistered hands, throbbing muscles, and occasional heat rashes were a far better existence, he'd decided. In that opinion, he stood alone.

"That's him right there!" a prison guard hollered when a convoy of cargo trucks pulled into the unloading bay. The gruff edge in the lanky correction office's voice caused several inmates on Hampton's line to take notice, each hoping his boisterous yelp didn't pertain to them. As the work detail filed out of the large green truck like a herd of cattle, dusty and just as rank, the tall, wiry guard shot a squirt of brown chewing tobacco at Hampton's feet. "Bynote, the warden done sent for you," he said, wiping sweat from his sun-stained neck with a soiled rag. "Don't know what you did, but I expect you's about to pay for it. Get to the front of this line. Get showered. And get to it fast."

"Yessuh, I'll get to it, boss," he answered appropriately. The man standing behind Hampton on the chain gang nudged him on the arm.

"Me and the boys was wondering if we can divvy up the letters you don't see fit to open," he asked playfully. "I mean, if you wasn't to make it back from your private tea with the warden."

Hampton shuffled up the wooden ramp toward the prisoner intake dock where leg irons were unlocked and collected on the tail of every shift. "If I don't make it back I figure there won't be reason for me to care. Ain't that right, Pete?" Hampton smiled at the elder Negro trustee with the wide ring of shackle keys.

"I reckon you got a point at that," Pete answered somberly, his haggard gray beard anchoring a mouthful of brittle teeth. He unlocked Hampton, knowing what prompted a special meeting to the air-conditioned administration offices. He'd heard through the grapevine how someone had kicked up quite a fuss with the parish detention board. Hampton was a country boy with big-city dreams; Pete knew that, too. He couldn't understand for the life of him who wielded a big enough stick to have the warden double-checking the landscape in his own backyard.

There was an outside chance his sentence had been reduced, Hampton thought, considering how he'd already done the original three months agreed to in the deal Bones had worked out with Detective Mouton.

He showered, wondering what side of the coin his luck would fall on. Without the benefit of dinner, he sat on pins and needles in the warden's office wishing for a quick outcome either way and a plate of the fried chicken and grits he could smell cooking in the dinner hall on the way over. Suddenly, a man dressed in a clean khaki-colored uniform stuck his head in the door to address the prisoner.

"Bynote, Hampton?" he called out. "Number four nine zero two three?"

Acknowledging how official that sounded, Hampton gulped then nodded his head. "Yessuh, boss. I'm four nine zero two three." The clean-cut white man shook his head as if to disagree with the way Hampton answered.

"Save all that yessuh talk for the gun-toting goons, son. Sit still a minute until the warden gets back and don't touch nothing!" he added rudely.

Hampton frowned at the middle-aged man's attempt to come across tougher than he was. It reminded him of the way Detective Cunningham put on fronts. He'd concluded that this neatly pressed fellow was just as soft in the middle when it came right down to it. A false sense of power had that effect on some men. It made them bark the loudest when no one appeared to give a damn. The last time Hampton saw Cunningham, he was too scared to make a peep.

The thought of frightened cops made Hampton smile. It felt good all the way down to the comfortable polished chair he was told not to stray from. That smile of his vanished when Bones popped his head in the door.

"Swagger, they told me you'd been sent for," said Bones, looking his former partner in crime over. "I see they're feeding you good." He noted how Hampton's shoulders had broadened and his neck was a might thicker in the short time he'd been incarcerated. "Pep up. I came to see about you. We're friends. Don't let this setback change all that."

"Man, what you doing here? If the warden finds you, he's liable to piece some things together." Hampton tried to shoo his visitor away, without moving from the chair. "Uh-uh, you need to get gone. I've seen what your kind of friendship can do. I get a damn good look at it every day."

"Okay, I wasn't up-front with everything, Swagger, but I knew you wouldn't have thrown in with me if you knew the whole plan I'd put together."

"You mean the one that's got me dodging dynamite blasts and falling rocks?"

Bones shrugged glibly. "Guess I deserve that, and you deserve to know why things had to play out the way they did. I took a big chance driving way out here, but I got a few people who find it in themselves to look the other way in times such as this. This isn't easy for me, hasn't been from the outset, either." Bones laid his hat on the warden's desk, then he sat on the corner of it all casual-like. Hampton thought he'd seen it all then. He squirmed in the polished chair with his palms moistening profusely. "Get that worried look off your face," Bones suggested firmly. "The worst has already been done."

"The worst, like you killing them people?" Hampton replied in a clear tone. He wasn't taking any chances in the event the warden or that sneaky district attorney happened to be listening in. Bones's associations tended to have lasting repercussions.

"Yeah, that and this. You being cooped up is hard on me, too. Matters being what they are, it could have gotten out of hand. Don't tell me that flipping on me didn't cross your mind. Sure it did, and I can't say I blame you. That's why I called Mouton personally from the telephone in your hotel. I told him to leave you alone and to inquire about me."

"You the one who called him?" asked Hampton, marveling at the brilliant strategy. "Only a white man can call the law on hisself then work out a deal to burn a sucker on the back end."

"I didn't mean no harm to come your way. Please believe that. From the moment you drove that DA's car into the swamp, I knew our paths crossed for a reason. I remembered you from the Boys' Home. I couldn't let on, didn't want to really. I don't have to tell you what kinds of things went on there, vile things with the man you saw me run my knife through," Bones said, not wanting to say his name.

"Yeah, Councilman Boyette," Hampton answered for him.

"He was a regular at the late-night parties. He was one of the bad men, we called them. The fella I shot in that shack was Leonard Lafon. You probably don't much remember him?"

"I do, though more than I care to," Hampton admitted.

"Then you also remember that he was supposed to be responsible for the younger kids. Did you know he pimped them out to grown men after him and his cronies got through?"

"I heard tell of some things that kinda went like that," Hampton replied.

"So you can imagine how I felt when I saw Lenny Lafon stroll by outside a drugstore window. I couldn't believe my eyes. God knows how I wanted to clip him right then and there, but the streets were too busy to croak him, leastways in public. So I followed him. I wouldn't have imagined in a million years what it'd lead to when Lenny slipped into a side door just past the quarter. It was a miracle. All of the ones who paid Lenny, the ones I tried to fight off me while locked up at kiddy camp, lounged in this so-called social club that didn't have a name over the door. Guess that made it more exclusive or something." Bones named off the men he saw in that hidden-away club for homosexuals of the same ilk, those with a penchant for raping young boys who couldn't refuse them. "Swagger, I lost my breath when I laid eyes on them, one by one. I thought my heart was exploding through my chest I wanted them dead so bad. You understand, right? I had a chance to get even so I took it, eight times."

Hampton's eyes drifted toward the cold cement floor. He contemplated Bones's past, what he endured, and the rage he must have felt when exacting his revenge. With a sorrowful frown, he stared into Bones's eyes. "You had to do it, right? I mean, it is over, seeing as how you got what you wanted?"

Standing from the desk, Bones lifted his hat slowly then placed it over his stubborn red hair. "It's done, that's true, but you're only half right. I got what I *needed*."

"I understand that plenty," was Hampton's calm response. "I laugh to keep from cracking up sometimes at how Mouton ended up in the captain's chair and I landed here in this one. What about you, Bones? What you gonna do with yourself now?"

"I'm going to flirt with the warden's personal receptionist on my way out. You ought to see her legs, two of the nicest gams you'd ever want to part. After I try my luck with that, don't know. Maybe I'll lie low awhile and gamble some. There's a few ways to make a little money if you're careful. I am sorry they stretched your time from three months when they should have rung your freedom bell this morning." Bones offered his hand to Hampton. After holding it out longer than he expected, Bones grinned softly as if he understood a thing or two about Hampton's reluctance as well. "By the way, if you need something call on old Captain Mouton. He owes you more than you owe him. Don't you forget that."

"Bye, Bones." Hampton waved from the chair he'd begun to despise. "Thanks for coming up to see me."

"Couldn't have gotten my business straight without you, Swagger. I owe you, too. That's something I won't soon forget." Bones stepped through the doorway wearing a much softer expression than the one he initially brought with him. Hampton almost felt sorry for him. He couldn't see wasting pity on a free white man when so many colored fellows on his cell block needed it a lot more.

A woman's voice, strained and muffled behind the thick office door, caused Hampton to leap from the polished chair that had begun to annoy him. The prison warden pushed the door open, with the man dressed in khaki on his heels. He was flapping copies of legal documents with both hands, pursing his lips, and cawing at someone to calm down like an overgrown crow with ruffled feathers. "Now, that won't be necessary, ma'am. I assure you that will not be necessary," he debated.

"'Cause I got lots of them that I ain't even sent yet," Pearl Lee asserted from just outside the office. Hampton craned his neck to steal a peek at the waiting area. His eyes and ears were wide open, but he still couldn't believe any of it. "Where is he?" she panted, waving a handful of envelopes. "That parish judge gave me these papers. He said y'all got to let me see my brother."

Hampton shrugged when the warden glared at him from behind the desk. Upon removing his glasses, the warden sighed heavily. "Sturgeon, you heard the woman. She's got papers." The warden gestured for the visitor to enter. "Mrs. Baptiste, come on and say hello. While I don't typically hold family reunions in my private chambers, in honor of your efforts you more than deserve it."

Pearl Lee placed one foot in front of the other. She eased into the office, pensively afraid the letter-writing campaign she instituted would somehow fall short. One hundred and nineteen letters altogether, sent to politicians throughout the state, had finally brought her peace in knowing that Hampton was alive and well. "Hampton?" she said, surprised to find him not only faring well but impressively so. "I would ask how you do, but I can see that for myself," she huffed. A glint of resentment showed on her face.

Hampton moved toward her for a brotherly embrace until remembering where he was. He looked to Warden Tyner for his permission. "May I, sir?"

"Be my guest, and you'd better make it good," he said, hiding traces of a smile. "I can't stomach the thought of getting more of these." He pointed at a basket stacked with white envelopes forwarded to the prison by very important men, all passing the buck and pressuring him to arrange the meeting Pearl Lee had been clamoring about. "Matter of fact, take all the time you need," he added, glancing at his pocket watch. "I'm going to supper." He instructed his subordinate to wait outside the door so they could have a decent level of privacy.

Once alone, Hampton hugged her tight then pulled another chair onto the middle of the floor. Pearl Lee straightened her powder blue dress but refused the offer to sit. "You had Mama, me, and Magnolia worried sick over you. You up and got yourself jailed without so much as a phone call. I had to go to Nawlins and run down that policeman who busted you just to learn where you was."

"You went all the way into town to see Detective Mouton? For me?"

"He ain't no regular police no more, he's the big fish now. I hear you had something to do with it, too. He let on but wouldn't say how, just that you were put away in here and if I kicked up enough dust they'd tire out and let me see you." Pearl Lee circled Hampton, boiling with the intensity that had gotten her thus far. "When word reached Newberry how you'd been pinched for boosting a car, Magnolia put on a cry that lasted three whole days. Why didn't you answer any of the letters she sent? You could have let us know how you was, instead of letting us think the worst. Don't they give you the mail in here?" When Hampton turned his face from hers, she had her answer. "Well, I'll be a monkey's auntie. You've been ducking us, your own folk and the girl who loves you?"

"I'm proud of the trouble you went through to come up here, Pearl Lee, but you don't understand how things is. It pains too much to think how everything keeps on moving outside of here. Inside of these walls, living stops." Pearl Lee laid her purse on the warden's desk and placed her hands on Hampton's shoulders.

"So you don't know none of it, none of what's been happening?"

"What's there to know that I didn't when I landed on this rock pile?" It was obvious to Pearl Lee then that Hampton hadn't dared to consider anyone he couldn't do a thing about. It was simply easier to pretend they didn't exist.

"Not that you seem to care one way or another about what go on out there, but I'm happy to be the first to say you gonna be a daddy before long." A lively chuckle flopped out of her mouth when Hampton's knees buckled. He fell onto the chair he'd previously gotten for Pearl Lee. "Uh-huh, that's how me and Mama thought you'd take the news. Mag thought you throwed her out after you rocked her steady for her birthday. She ain't showing yet, but the bun is set to rise in due time, Papa."

Hampton's staunch approach to live only within the confines of what imprisoned him had begun to come apart at the seams. "Magnolia, how she feeling?" he asked somberly.

"Oh, she fine. Eating like a workhorse, though. Don't worry about her, she won't complain no more once I get home with a good report."

"And Mama? She think any less of me for carrying on with Magnolia?" He glanced at Pearl Lee, expecting to hear his mother's choice words for mounting one mistake on top of the other. "It's that bad, huh?"

"There's other reasons I been pushing so hard to speak with you, Hamp. Didn't know it would take so long, though. I wish all news was good news." She went to wringing her strong hands while formulating the hardest thing she'd ever had to say. "Mama, she wasn't in no place to talk about doing wrong. She laughed so hard when Magnolia started puking her guts every morning. In a way, it made her burden lighter. See, Mama was expecting a baby, too. That's why Mister Delacroix carried her over to the colored doctor, to remove it. It was the Mister's child." She cowered back when Hampton leapt to his feet.

"You lying, Pearl Lee! That's got to be a lie!"

"It's the truth, I swear!"

"Ahh, nawww!" Hampton moaned. "It can't be. It just can't be."

"I know, I know, but listen to me. Mister Delacroix loved Mama. You should have seen him. Mama couldn't eat nor sleep. She hurt so from the sickness that colored doctor found in her belly. The Mister was heartbroken when...she passed on a few weeks back!"

Three prison guards came crashing down on the reunion with the warden leading the charge. The moment he saw Hampton's expression, he demanded they step aside. He'd seen that look before, a grown man reduced to the child he was when first falling in love with his mother.

"I'm sorry, Mrs. Baptiste," Warden Tyner apologized. "You went to a great deal of trouble getting here and I applaud that, but I'm afraid you have to go." He asked his personal assistant to see that Pearl Lee got a cab ride to the bus line. Hampton was taken to a solitary cell where he was placed on a three-day suicide watch. He was right after all. Dealing with the tragedies that happened on the outside was the hardest thing an inmate did while serving time.

23

Unchained Melody

Hampton was spent. He'd been awake for the last three days of his fourteen-month incarceration. Several of the men on his cell block looked on with envy-filled eyes when he strolled down the long corridor toward the gated exit. Hampton's steps were slow but steady. Prison time was a tough bill to pay when the uncertainty of freedom overshadowed the luxury of obtaining it. Hampton's release papers were signed and stamped by the warden. Uncertainty was wrapped in the fear that accompanied being free. He had become a stranger unto himself. The simple life he knew too well had contorted into a series of frightening, complicated questions. With a parcel cradled in his arms, denim work clothes wrapped in brown butcher paper, Hampton sighed, nodded his good-byes, then followed the guard through a maze of hallways and quiet pathways. Hampton didn't have to voice his reservations concerning finding his place in the world again; the burly jailer sensed his reluctance as he shuffled through the sliding gate, glancing over his shoulder. "I can't believe it's over," Hampton whispered. He eyed the monument of concrete and steel.

"You'd better or else you'll be back fast enough to make your head spin," the guard assured him. "Go on, son. Concern yourself with clean, lawful living." Hampton lowered his head in deep contemplation. He mulled over the best advice he'd heard in a month of Sundays.

"Thanks, boss," he answered plainly. "I believe I will at that."

The guard watched as another ex-convict eased back into society with even odds of making good on a second chance. "On the gate!" he shouted loudly. The ominous sheet of metal slid between the two of them, separating both men in time and space.

Tired and hungry, Hampton fingered five crisp dollar bills and the paper bus pass handed to him with the change of clothes awarded an hour before. He grinned at the money in his strong, calloused hands, thinking how it wasn't much and at the same time all he owned in whole world. "Five dollars and a fresh start," he said, strolling down the dusty sidewalk toward the bus depot.

"That it?" he heard someone say from an open convertible Cadillac. "They don't spring for bus fare no more?" When Hampton recognized the voice, he stopped on a dime and then chuckled.

"Bones," he said, laughing heartily now. He turned to see if his ears had lied to him. Bones was leaning in the front seat of the shiniest black car he'd ever laid eyes on. "How'd you know I'd be walking out today?"

"Well, I got this friend who works in the warden's office. She's pretty good with getting me information and such from time to time."

Hampton snickered at the thought of Bones cozying up to the

warden's receptionist, like he said he would. "You don't say. Was everything you put into it worth all you got out of it?"

"It was a hard nut to crack at first," Bones answered. "But you know me. I can be quite persuasive behind a handful of lies and a bottle of cheap champagne."

Hampton stroked his cheek with the back of his hand. "Is that all it took?"

"Yep, that's when she got naked," he replied jovially, sharing a private joke with a friend.

Hampton shoved the bus note and all of his walking-around money in the front pocket of his trousers. "Uh-huh, I expect she did at that."

Bones reached across the front seat to open the door. He stared at Hampton, unsteady in his deliberation. "You can stay mad at me all you want, Swagger, just as long as we're still friends in the end." The motor purred while Hampton reasoned with himself, his past and future. Since his feet hurt and his stomach right along with it, the appeal of a comfortable ride in a new set of wheels engulfed him. He threw the parcel of clothing into the backseat then settled in on the passenger side.

"I want to thank you for sending money to Magnolia whilst I was locked away. You didn't have to do it."

"The hell I didn't. Captain Mouton made sure fifty dollars per month made it to your sister's house without fail. Everybody had to hold up their part of the bargain."

"Wasn't no bargain for me," Hampton groaned. He held out his hands, ashy and trembling.

Bones pulled onto the road, guiding that slick black automobile like a chariot. "I know, Swagger, I know. All that's about to change. Matter of fact, there ain't nothing but changes and of course lots of money to be made now that you're free as a hummingbird."

"Yeah, lots has changed at that. Namely me," Hampton informed him.

"I know you feel a tad nervous about breaking in a new proposition. Don't let what happened worry you. I'm a respectable businessman now, well, mostly respectable, and—" he started before Hampton angrily cut him off.

"Take me home, Bones."

"That's where we're headed. I found a nice place for you off Gerard Avenue."

"Un-uh, take me to Newberry. I need to see the daughter I ain't held in my arms and the place where they buried my mama." Bones turned the car around and headed northbound on the thoroughfare. Hampton refused to set his eyes on the prison when they zoomed past. He couldn't afford to be reminded of the backbreaking work, blistering days on the rock pile, and stone-cold memories. What lay ahead of him was exceedingly more daunting.

Hampton barely said two words during the twenty-five-minute ride to Newberry. Farm animals and field workers raised their heads when the Cadillac breezed along the river road toward the Delacroix Plantation.

Bones glanced over at his pal with a disapproving leer. Nothing about the county appealed to him, not one single thing. "Hey, Swag, is this really what you want? This is hardly even civilized. Slaving and lifting and whatnot, thought you'd gotten enough of this back at the prison camp." He waited on a reply that never came. Instead, Hampton instructed him to deviate off the main road onto a narrow driveway, scarcely wide enough for a wagon to pass. On either side of the unpaved path were rows upon rows of Negro graves. Bones stopped the car as if he knew the exact spot where Rayletta had been laid to rest. He nodded toward a hillside on the right. "I'm sorry, Swagger. Me and Mouton went in on a fine tombstone. We figured since you couldn't do it yourself..." His words trailed off when Hampton's chest swelled with remorse.

Hampton climbed out of the car and headed up the hill with slow, measured steps. Twelve rows back he kneeled down at an impressive concrete marker with RAYLETTA BYNOTE 1911–1957 carved into it. Hampton placed his hands on the stone, stroking it softly as if he were soothing his mother's woes. "Hi, Ma. I don't have the words. I did a lot of bad things, one of 'em they locked me up for. Ain't much else to be said I guess, excepting for I'm sorry I wasn't here for you in the last days. You with Pa now, so I'm sure you'll make out fine." Hampton peered at the wooden marker placed at the head of his father's grave, which paled in comparison to the one that Bones and Detective Mouton chipped in to buy. "Ma, Pa, don't seem to be no secrets left between none of us now. Wrong is wrong any which way you slice it. I got the chance to do right. The fast life ain't for me no more, no how. I'm aiming to take care of my baby girl and do right by Magnolia, if she'll have me. Y'all got each other, and that's the way it ought to be, together." Hampton wiped the tears from his face, stared at the clouds, and sighed. "I'll do better, y'all. That's my promise to you both."

Afterward, Bones avoided conversation as much as Hampton did. He chewed on a fresh cigar to pass the time. It was nearly six in the evening when the flashy automobile crossed over the wooden bridge at the mouth of the Delacroix Plantation. Hampton placed his hand on his chauffeur's arm. "This here is far enough, Bones. I'll go the rest alone."

"Nonsense. I can carry you all the way to the front door. You know, some of that curb service like the carhops do over at the diner."

Hampton squeezed with his powerful grasp to show that he meant what he said. "Uh-uh, this is far enough." He released his grip, then pursed his lips as if to apologize. "I'm much obliged, but how you think that man is gonna let me on if he sees me roll up in this chariot of yours? These is simple folk, Bones. Ain't no how they gon' understand us."

The deflated expression in Bones's face spoke volumes. He had plans, all of which included Hampton being by his side. "You ain't got to beg that redneck for crumbs, Hampton." Bones used his friend's given name. His words truly came from the depths of his heart. "I told you before but it appears I need to say it again, there's lots of loot with your name on it. I've been holding it for you in that safe of mine. It could be the start of something big."

"I ain't got no right to that money and you know it. Prowling with you is what got me pinched. Naw, I can't use it, not one cent." Hampton's determined scowl shut Bones down. He slapped the steering wheel then killed the motor.

"Mind if I sit here and watch my best friend volunteer to trade one prison for the next?"

"Suit yourself, but don't come no closer than this." Hampton held out his hand. Bones looked as if he wanted to spit in it, then his thin pink lips curved into a smile.

"On second thought, I think I'll pass. Some things a man's got to do on his own, don't matter if it's the right thing or not." Finally, he shook hands with Hampton although reluctantly since their good-bye was not on his terms. "I'll miss you, Swagger. You'll always have means and me to lean on if things don't work out."

"I won't have need for either."

Hampton was a proud man. Bones always admired that about him. "Things tend to change, so make sure you keep that in mind," he offered.

"That'll be easy," Hampton answered sadly. "Forgetting is the hard part." He picked up his package from the backseat, waved to Bones, and then strolled through the gate. He didn't look back when the Cadillac raced down the dirt road. The past had its place. Now Hampton needed to find his.

24

No Trouble, No How

The courtyard work bell rang three times, calling for the end of a workday as Hampton approached the large white two-story house. He noticed its magnificence, its azalea bushes and finely manicured landscape, the thick columns that seemed adequate enough to hold up the sky, the broad cement veranda skirting around the entire first floor, and the six windows on both sides of the house, built for cross ventilation on long hot summer days. The plantation house loomed larger than ever in the shadows of his despair.

The door opened slightly when Hampton reached the base of the front porch. Cautious, he kept his hands visible due to his forbidden return without notice to Mr. Delacroix. As he began to second-guess his decision to walk right up and plead for his old job back, the door swung opened. Mrs. Jennifer, the lady of the house, staggered out of the doorway, holding half a glass of mint julep and a loose grip on sobriety.

"What're you doing out here?" she asked sloppily, her head tilting forward like a lead weight. Hampton hoped she wouldn't fall over and him receive the blame. Suddenly, she snapped her head up like a jack-in-the-box toy. "Hampton, that you?"

He nodded assuredly and then wondered if it was smart to admit it. "Yes'm, it's me," he said unsteadily.

"It sure is," she giggled. "And all grown up, too. Mr. Delacroix would be so proud, I'll tell you. So proud." She sipped from her glass, eyeing him curiously over the top of it. If he didn't know better, she was flirting. Hampton was about as uncomfortable as could be so he put on a fake smile. Words built for that occasion weren't invented yet, and he didn't want to be the first to try out new ones. "Your mama, she would be proud, too. Funny how they both wished you were here in the end."

Hampton realized she meant the Mister was dead as well. He'd had no way of knowing. Neither could he have imagined delivering a canned speech to Trotter. Before he could offer his condolences for Mrs. Jennifer's loss or back out of his decision to grovel, Trotter walked out onto the veranda dressed in work boots and dirty clothes. He stared at Hampton like a man expecting to take advantage of a sensitive situation, then he pulled his mother by the arm.

"Come now, Mother," he whispered softly. "It's a mite cooler in the house. And I thought we agreed on only one drink before dinner." It was obvious she'd overshot her quota. Jennifer Delacroix wiggled her skinny fingers at Hampton while being steered away. He turned about-face, starting down the brick walkway when Trotter yelled after him. He was sitting on a metal rocking chair as if it were a royal throne and called out again when Hampton was slow to respond. "Hey, you came for something! You leave without it, don't come back." Trotter lit up a hand-rolled cigarette and waited.

The promise Hampton had been made moments before was a good one. He aimed to keep it. Although Trotter was looking down on Hampton, he could use a knowledgeable hand like Hampton to do the work of two men, work Trotter wouldn't have to do himself. Eventually, the ex-con made his way back to the base of the steps. He shifted his weight from side to side, trying to settle in on a direct statement.

"Well, speak up or be gone," Trotter hissed dismissively. He'd been groomed for the lord of the manor role and was playing it to the hilt.

Hampton cleared his throat. "You know I been . . . locked away. I also got my mind made up to stay out of trouble."

"And, go on," Trotter insisted, behind a cloud of smoke.

"And I'm letting you know I'm needing a legal way to keep clothes on my family's back and put food on the table. Since I got a youngun now I ain't in no position to bargain. You tell me I can come back and take up here, it'll be the way you say."

Trotter leaned forward with a steely gaze. "The way I say? All the way I say?"

Hampton pursed his lips then pushed out exactly what Trotter wanted to hear. "Yessuh, you got my word." He bit down on his bottom lip as the young white man stood from his perch.

"All right then, you can work for me as long as I say and as long as you do what I say." He didn't stand around to hear Hampton's answer. Trotter had what he always wanted, the upper hand. That was more valuable than any measure of respect.

As the wind stirred, Hampton noticed two women dressed in washhouse rags standing on the walkway that circled the manor. Pearl Lee's smile was brilliant despite wringing the tension from her hands constantly. The second woman reminded Hampton of

Magnolia although visibly wider in the hips and fuller across the chest. He raised a hand, shielding his eyes from the sun's glare. His heart rate quickened when he realized the other woman was in fact Magnolia, all grown up and beautiful. He bubbled over with heaps of emotions while jogging toward her. Magnolia leapt from the ground anxiously. When she landed in Hampton's arms, she clasped her wrists behind his neck, tighter than any of the shackles he'd worn during his jail term. Hampton was absolutely certain that her kind of restraint fit him perfectly.

"Oh, Hampton! You're home!" she squealed excitedly. "My man is home! We prayed for this day," she gushed. "We all missed you so much, so much."

"She's right, Hamp," Pearl Lee seconded. She looked on patiently while itching to join in. "Lots ain't like it was, but you back. Yeah, we're a real family again," she added, involving herself in the couple's embrace. Tears of joy flooded her eyes, making it easier to hide the pain in them.

"I'm here for good, too," Hampton reassured them. "Me and Trotter done worked it out. I was a fool to think I deserved better than this, better than slave wages and doing nigger work. This here is all I'm ever gon' be. I may as well accept it."

"Don't say that," Magnolia asserted, kissing Hampton's neck. "You're a good man, a darn good one. The right time will come, yours and mine. This'll do until then, Hampton, until then. God will make a way, He always does. He's got to. You're home, and that makes for a nice enough beginning."

"Sure do," said Pearl Lee. "Look at my baby brother, built up like an oak tree. You'd better not act up, Mag, I can't push him around like I used to."

"I'll take care of the pulling myself. This strapping fella's got a lot of pushing to make up for." Magnolia stared into his eyes again with disbelief. "I'm scared to look away now that you're here. Christmas came early this year, for all of us." She kissed Hampton on the mouth, in broad daylight.

Pearl Lee snickered. "Uh-huh, that reminds me. There's a darling li'l girl you must be dying to meet."

"Joyce," Hampton answered in a subdued tone. "Yeah, I'd be mighty pleased to meet my daughter. It only seems fitting."

"It'd better happen quick or Odessa's likely to have another playmate," Pearl Lee suggested.

Hampton lowered Magnolia onto the ground. "You think that baby girl of ours might be inclined to take in a 'mergency wedding?" he asked, dropping down onto one knee at Magnolia's feet.

Magnolia's lips quivered. "Oh, my...you only just got home."

"Don't matter, Magnolia." Hampton sighed. "I've been waiting better than a year to come to you with this. Now it don't seem like I'm worthy of asking it. You got to know why I didn't write you."

"No need to go into that," she answered, embarrassed by his sincerity. "Pearl Lee already cleared that up."

"It needs to be said by me. I couldn't stand to be apart from you and be reminded of it whilst denying it to myself. Marking words down on paper...well, I couldn't."

Magnolia threw both hands on her hips. "All I needs to know today is, are you gon' ask to wed me or not?"

"Guess it didn't come out right, but that's exactly what I'm asking. I'd be proud to take your hand, if you'll have me."

"Yes, I'd love to be your wife, Hampton," she said, cradling his head against her. "I've been waiting better than a year for you to ask me. We got a bright future, me and you, together."

Hampton rose to his feet and kissed Magnolia hard and long. Pearl Lee felt like a third wheel so she slipped off quietly. Other sharecroppers, sauntering in from the fields, took in a sight not often seen on the plantation. A colored man displaying his love for his woman so close to the main house was a rarity if not a first. Each of them tipped their hats, grinning at what they considered a grand spectacle. When Hampton pulled his lips from Magnolia's, she caught her breath. "Whew, I feel a might woozy," she cooed gleefully.

Startled when over twenty men, women, and children applauded Hampton's return and the hottest kiss they'd ever seen executed in public, Magnolia blushed.

"Oh, hey, y'all," Hampton hailed. "Hiya, Mr. Ravenell. Ladies. Fellas. How y'all do?"

"Not half as good as you," Buck Ravenell heckled. "Welcome home, Hampton. Welcome home."

"And y'all are all invited to my wedding," Magnolia howled ebulliently, her face flushed with unbridled excitement. Magnolia stood by Hampton's side as the multitude of colored men congratulated him with encouraging words. Women from the washhouse wrestled Magnolia away, cackling about wedding dresses and how much Hampton had physically matured. One of the women went as far as to say how prison seemed to agree with him. Magnolia wouldn't concede that, although she couldn't wait to see what else had grown. In the midst of pomp and circumstance, no one noticed Trotter Delacroix observing the entire ceremony from an upstairs window. Hampton didn't have to catch him spying to know he was. Jealousy still had a firm hold on him. Neither prison bars nor upper hands could change that.

25

Bitter Tears

Fifteen years later

Despair swept through the room. Odessa writhed bitterly with her nightgown gathered around her narrow hips. Pain poured from her lap. Rain seeped from the ceiling, splashing against the wooden floorboards. Water overflowed from buckets placed throughout the tiny bedroom. Magnolia, watching pensively, swayed back and forth by the bedside. There were several comforting words she wanted to say, although nothing would have eased Pearl Lee's sorrows. She'd blamed herself when Odessa's stomach began to poke out like a ripe melon several months ago. She tried to beat the truth out of her stubborn sixteen-year-old to no avail, then she attempted knocking the baby loose from the womb after Odessa adamantly refused to confess which man played a major part in her current catastrophe.

Where had all the time gone, Pearl Lee pondered as she paced the room with balled fists at her side. With a bastard grandchild minutes from entering this world, Pearl Lee was forced to admit she'd failed as a parent. She had seen other young colored girls become teenage brides with husbands barely old enough to pee off themselves. Odessa was going to be different, Pearl Lee had promised herself too many times to count. She believed that a strict diet of Sunday church service, schoolwork, and looking after her mindless father, Toussaint, would keep Odessa busy enough to steer clear of harm's way. Three days into 1971, the world outside of Newberry was firing at a hellish pace. Dramatic changes sprang up everywhere. Young Negro men returned from Vietnam with wild afros and even wilder stories of gore and death. Young colored girls were experiencing life faster than seemed possible. Their white contemporaries were equally promiscuous, although remedied unwanted pregnancies with a hefty check to the local doctor or tried their luck with a back-alley quack. However, neither of those outcomes was slated for Odessa. She was a good student and a dutiful daughter despite the sometimes headstrong ways that she inherited from her mother. Since Odessa wasn't courting seriously nor drawn to any particular boy, a teenage pregnancy didn't make sense whatsoever. With no one else to shoulder the shame, it toppled down on Pearl Lee. And she was beside herself.

Lightning ripped across the darkened sky again. Odessa's mouth flew open but nary a sound came from it. Aching from an intensity she couldn't comprehend, the young girl clutched her stomach and groaned. "Goddammit, Odessa!" shouted Pearl Lee. "You knew this day was coming so ain't no need in crying about it now." She twisted her lips in disgust as her only child anguished in pain. "Hold her down and sooth her belly some, Magnolia."

"I'm trying, but she won't hold still," Magnolia fussed. "Besides, where is Madame Baptiste? I expected her to beat me here."

Pearl Lee tilted her head in direct opposition to hearing the old woman's name. "Madame said she won't come near this house long as my child is holding. Old witch must be losing her starch. She said this baby won't ever meet the man whose seed he sprouted from. That old fool," added Pearl Lee, hoping deep down inside the voodoo doctor was wrong.

The young girl grunted profusely, managing to keep lips fastened as best she could and all the time staring at her mother's mean scowl. "Odessa, you need to relax now. That baby wants to come tonight, so you have to let it." Odessa slammed her eyes shut. Pearl Lee conceded. She cringed when another thunderbolt clamored loudly just above her head, sounding close enough to tear through the tin roof. Afraid the electrical storm was God's way of complaining about her conception, Odessa held her tongue all the more. Magnolia did what she could to quiet her niece's nerves. She brushed aside Odessa's thick soft mane with one hand while dabbing a cool towel on the girl's moist forehead with the other. Odessa, the color of ginger peach, was beautiful. She was blessed with her mother's handsome features and her father's Creole complexion. Though only a child herself, it was easy to understand why boys her age buzzed around her at school and grown men stumbled over themselves when she came around. Regardless, no one claimed the child she bore.

"It's getting closer, Odessa." Magnolia sighed. "Won't be long now."

Rustling pots and pans in the kitchen, Pearl Lee peered through the window. She found darkness and Toussaint. He sat on the back porch in a rocking chair, his mind half gone. *I ain't cut out to be no nana at this age*, Pearl Lee thought. *And poor Toussaint, he don't know he's about to be a grandpapa. It's probably better this way. God bless the weary and the weak.* Pearl Lee shook her head wearily then lifted one of the pots off the floor. She quickly dumped the water into a larger metal tub, heated by firewood. She cast a fleeting glance at Odessa, who was coming unglued due to something that couldn't be undone. Pearl Lee contemplated her daughter nearing motherhood, then she took stock of her own life, gazing at her reflection in the windowpane. She'd seen other thirty-nine-year-old grandmothers, all aging too fast after the realization set in that their roads had taken a wrong turn someplace in the past. Pearl Lee brushed a lock of hair away from her face, noting how she and Odessa were so much alike, concealing truths and hiding lies; innocence lost on one account and sins exchanged on the other. Pearl Lee determined that the best part of her life was behind her now. Once she contemplated the men in her past and their contribution to the strain she endured, Pearl Lee couldn't help wondering who Odessa's child was likely to resemble. Suddenly, she felt anger creep inside of her all over again.

"Dessa, get out of those panties and slide these towels under yourself," Pearl Lee hissed. "And be quick about it." Odessa cowered against the iron headboard, shielding her face with a pillow and shaking her head vehemently. "You gonna do what I say, girl," Pearl Lee barked. "You didn't get like that with panties on, and that babe can't get here that way, either, so hand 'em over." Still, the frightened girl objected. Pearl Lee raced to the bed, tore the pillow from her daughter's hands, then snatched her underwear off violently. "And you gonna tell me who the daddy is!" she ranted, whacking Odessa with a hairbrush repeatedly.

"Uh-uh, Pearl," argued Magnolia, coming to the girl's defense. "You know that ain't the way."

"Then tell me what is," she fussed, slapping at her daughter's face. "Move back, Mag, so I can get at her. She laid up with some no-account boy and won't speak up against him." Pearl Lee lunged at Odessa thoughtlessly. Rage propelled her. "Tell me who did it!" Whack! "I said to spill it!" Whack, whack!

"Nooo!" Odessa screamed. "Mama, I can't!" She covered her pubis while fighting off her attacker.

"You can and you will. I'll be damned if you gonna be tramping around here making babies and keeping quiet about it. You gonna answer to me about who did this or so help me I'll choke the life out of you myself."

Magnolia shoved at her sister-in-law as Odessa wailed miserably. "Pearl Lee, settle yourself before you kill this baby. I know you're upset but this . . . ain't . . . right." She struggled mightily to force Pearl Lee's grasp from Odessa's throat.

When Pearl Lee came to her senses, she blinked her eyelids rapidly as if awakening from a trance. She gasped for air. Her chest heaved desperately when Toussaint's face startled her. It was pressed against the window. He'd witnessed her assault on his child. If not for the storm raging outside, Pearl Lee would have sworn he was crying. She backed away from Odessa, gawking at her hands as she wiped them on her soiled apron.

"I'm sorry, Mama," Odessa whined sadly. "I'm so sorry."

Pearl Lee watched Toussaint stroll away from the old cottage in the midst of a downpour, hoisting a bottle of whiskey and dragging a shovel behind him. "I'm sorry, too, sugar, real sorry." Pearl Lee didn't have any idea what caused Toussaint's odd behavior or what it would lead to. Furthermore, she was clueless about the lengths Odessa would have traveled to keep the details of her unholy conception and the name of her rapist secret.

26

Tossed and Turned

Magnolia tussled mightily to get in her front door. Heavy rain often caused it to swell and made it difficult to pry open. She threw her weight against it then barreled inside her cottage, screaming, "Hampton! Get your boots!" She flicked on the lights, dashing toward the bedroom. Hampton stirred in his nightclothes.

"What's the matter, Magnolia?" he asked, rubbing his eyes. "Odessa's baby come yet?"

"Yeah, a minute ago, and it sent Pearl Lee after Trotter," she howled anxiously. "She's off to the main house and hell-bent on murder."

Hampton grumbled. His eyes turned bloodred. Much like a full moon caused people to howl at it, stormy nights typically brought out the worst of bad situations. Hampton slipped on his pants and shirt then stumbled into his boots. Magnolia's bottom lip quivered as she handed over Hampton's loaded revolver. He squinted at it before tucking the gun inside his waistband.

"Good thinking," he said, heading for the door with a rain poncho thrown over his shoulders. "Joyce, you and Janeen stay put in the bed," he ordered sternly. Joyce held her younger sister close and nodded slowly.

Magnolia stood in the doorway, afraid of what she'd seen when the baby was born and baffled at how Madame Baptiste knew trouble would result because of it. Additionally, Magnolia was concerned over what was likely to happen when Hampton followed Pearl Lee's steps to the main house. "What are you gonna do, Hamp?" she shouted after him. "What are you gonna do?"

"Save my sister from herself if I can," he shouted back, "and kill a man if I got to."

The plantation house was lit up like a ballpark. It appeared that every possible light had been put on inside. Pearl Lee chased Trotter around his bedroom, swinging a butcher's knife wildly. Trotter, actively dodging his lover's spiteful attempt to fillet him, knocked over a tray of water glasses and a crystal keepsake. His wife screeched angrily for Pearl Lee to leave her bedroom. Their small sons, held closely by a middle-aged nanny, wailed from a room across the hall. Meanwhile, Trotter's mother sat ever so still in her bedroom at the end of the hall. Listening attentively, she calmly poured herself another stiff measure of brandy. The house was in utter disarray. Mayhem blared at a feverish pitch.

Hampton felt anger throughout himself as he climbed the staircase. He reached the second level, veered to either side, and then darted right toward the heated commotion spewing riotously into the hallway. When he heard his sister's voice rising beyond sanity, Hampton pulled his gun and cocked the hammer. He rushed through the doorway of the master bedroom with its fine antiques, frazzled nerves, and bewitching spirits. His eyes widened as Pearl Lee sliced thin air in half with violent swats. "Whoa! Whoa, Pearl Lee!" he fussed.

"Get her out of here!" the white woman screeched irately. "She don't belong in my house."

"She's gone crazy! Tell her to settle down," Trotter insisted, his hands raised defensively. Somewhat relieved help had arrived, he was still extremely concerned about his wife learning more than he ever intended from the babblings of his grief-stricken colored mistress. He used Hampton's arrival as a diversion to reach for a shotgun behind his headboard.

"Pearl Lee, you got to cool out now," said Hampton as firmly as he knew how without further provoking her. "Whatever the problem, we can talk it out." He moved closer to his sister, merely an arm's length from Trotter's wife, who was crouching on the bed in hysterics. Hampton followed Pearl Lee's hateful glare. Trotter was backed into a corner, with a weapon trained on the intruder. Screams multiplied.

Fury dripped from Pearl Lee's lips. "That yellow-headed bastard baby," she muttered. "Odessa squeezed out a yellow-headed bastard! You ain't got no rights bringing that mulatto child into my life." Trotter's eyes narrowed when he heard her accusations. The barrel of his gun dipped momentarily. He tried to fathom Pearl Lee's rationale.

"What's going on, Trotter?" his bewildered wife asked.

"Nothing, Mary-Beth," he answered quickly. "Keep quiet while I sort this out."

Hampton eyed Pearl Lee just as Trotter had, with a confused expression. "All I know is you got that scattergun aimed at my sister. She might be wrong for coming here, but that don't matter now." He leveled his pistol at Trotter's head. "I'd advise you to put that thing down before somebody gets real hurt, real bad."

"No, no, Pearl Lee's got to get out of here first," argued Trotter.

"What's she doing here?" Mary-Beth raged incoherently. "Tell me, Trotter."

"Told you to shut up, Mary-Beth," he spat back, growing more irritated by the second.

Pearl Lee wiped tears from her cheek, waggling the blade again only slower now. "Go on and spill it, Trotter. Tell her what's been going on down at the cottages, and around my *back door* in particular. Don't leave out nothing about that agreement white men and colored women been keeping hush-hush all these years." What sounded like gibberish to Hampton played even stranger to Mary-Beth. Despite Trotter's mouth moving, nothing came out. Hampton had seen a desperate man's indecision turn on him. The result always left somebody dead.

"Uh-uh, Hampton," warned Magnolia from the doorway. "This has gone too far already. Nothing else needs be said about it."

"He's gonna drop that thing and speak up or I'm gonna drop him," Hampton answered. He tossed a heavy dose of resolve at Trotter, in the same manner that got him beaten to within an inch of his life by Mr. Delacroix. It was impossible to tell what would happen next with Trotter caught in his own web, unable to spin out of it and unwilling to discuss his scandalous ways in the presence of his wife.

Lightning struck outside the big window at the end of the hall. Thunder roared. Both men prepared to fire when the sound of shattering glass took center stage. Magnolia craned her neck, peering into the hallway. What she saw took her breath away. Mrs. Jennifer, still the lady of the manor, stumbled down the hall with both hands covered in blood.

"Enough of this!" she muttered eerily. "Enough! I'll not live with it anymore."

Trotter heard something alarming in his mother's voice. He nodded for Mary-Beth to go out and see about her. The moment she did, he tossed the shotgun aside.

Mary-Beth scooted past Pearl Lee to reach the corridor. "Mother Delacroix," she called out, just as Mrs. Jennifer's knees buckled. She yelled for the nanny to come quick with towels and water.

With a temporary reprieve at hand, Magnolia sought to make the most of it. She couldn't chance what Hampton might have done if he'd learned about the gentleman's agreement while holding a loaded weapon. "Come on, Hampton, we need to go. Get Pearl outta here. Get her safe," she added, to remind him of his previous pledge.

Trotter held his hands up in a pleading manner. He lowered his head and then swallowed hard. "You can't believe I had anything to do with Odessa's baby," he offered solemnly, speaking to everyone in general and specifically to his longtime lover. "I care about her like she was my own daughter. Think about what you're saying, Pearl Lee."

"I'm asking you the same question, Trotter," grunted Hampton. "What are you saying exactly?"

Magnolia stood between them now. "I believe him, Hampton. Come on, Pearl Lee, Trotter couldn't have done this." She cut her eyes at him curtly. "He loves that girl, you know it." Magnolia had witnessed Trotter playing with Odessa on several occasions, specifically when Toussaint experienced episodes of feeblemindedness and disappeared into the woods for days at a time. Hampton was even more confused than before. He had no choice other than to take his wife at her word. "Come on, let's go," Magnolia insisted, helping Pearl Lee to gather herself. "We'll let this pass for now and get on back to living peaceful."

The three of them crept down the back staircase and out the

servants' door, leaving the house in utter disorder and Mrs. Jennifer mumbling in the background. "Can't live with no more lies," she cried. "I'm so tired. No more lies."

Once they reached Pearl Lee's cottage, Magnolia clutched Hampton's arm. She sent her sister-in-law inside then advised her husband what needed to happen next. "Honey, I got Patricia Ravenell in there to look after Odessa and that little boy of hers. She ain't but half Pearl Lee's size so I'll stay here in case she flies off the handle again tonight. I'll look in on Joyce 'nem after things get numb in there." Her eyes roamed at Pearl Lee's home. "I don't know how I'd take it if one of my girls was to end up like Odessa. I do know it touched Toussaint something awful. Why don't you see if you can find him before he hurts himself or worse."

"How much you been keeping from me, woman?"

"Only what I needed to, no more than that," she replied assuredly. Hampton must have agreed because he didn't push the issue. He realized women had their reasons for withholding information. Men found reasons to justify their secrets just the same.

"You don't expect Toussaint knows about Trotter and Pearl Lee's carrying on?" Hampton asked finally.

"I expect he knows a lot more than that."

Hampton glanced toward the sky as a light drizzle fell like sifted flour. He struck out after Toussaint with a lantern and a rifle. Wild predators were the least of his worries. While treading toward the wooded area east of the plantation boundary he considered the two-legged kind and the opposition they offered. He encountered a family of raccoons and a wandering opossum, which he snagged and bagged for dinner, but no Toussaint. Then he heard what sounded like laughter, down by the swamp's edge. Hampton held his lantern high to brighten the path. Just on the other side of the rise, he discovered a large mound of dirt. He remembered what Magnolia said about Toussaint heading off with his hands full. Hampton nearly stumbled over the shovel and into a vast and deep hole. He placed the lantern and rifle on the ground when his eyes found an empty bottle lying next to Toussaint, who was floating facedown in the grave he'd dug for himself.

Hampton slid into the pit. He yanked on Toussaint's jacket to turn him over. He flinched when a crawfish scampered out of the dead man's mouth. "Why'd you do this, Toussaint?" Hampton groaned. "You didn't have to. . . ." He hissed sorrowfully. "Damn fool. You didn't have to do this." Swept up in the present circumstances and the remnants of a man who had battled his demons and lost, Hampton stood in the puddle and held his friend for the longest time. He understood what it meant to be in love without the means of cultivating the relationship. He couldn't lie to himself about knowing the pain Toussaint must have endured when the realization set in that he'd shared his woman's love with one man and was unsuccessful at protecting his child from yet another. Together, they managed to grind down on Toussaint's will to live until there was nothing left.

27

Mama's Baby, Daddy's Maybe

Morning rolled in quietly. No one rang the massive courtyard bell that signaled the beginning of the workday. Many of the colored sharecroppers stepped out onto their cottage porches wondering why they'd been given a day off. Heavy rains from the night before were thought to be the cause until word spread quickly of Toussaint's suicide, late-night drama with Hampton's family at the mansion, and the birth of Odessa's son with a suspicious complexion and hair color. The scuttlebutt continued when Trotter parked his new truck outside of Hampton's front door and leaned against it.

Joyce, Hampton's fourteen-year-old daughter, looked out front when she heard a car door close. Pecan brown and the spitting image of Magnolia, Joyce was as pretty as a picture. She thought a lot of herself and of her keen features and smooth skin. She believed in towing the line but often found it hard to keep from daydreaming about life outside the plantation. Infrequent trips to New Orleans, on special occasions, opened her mind to all sorts of things including the idea of black people going into business for themselves, which Hampton tried to quash against

Magnolia's wishes. Joyce wasn't sure why excursions into the city caused spats between her parents, but she and Janeen giggled about it nonetheless.

Joyce's brow creased when she saw a look on Trotter's face she didn't recognize. "Daddy!" she whispered insistently. "Daddy, Trotter Delacroix is out front."

Hampton raised his head from his third cup of coffee to address her. "Well, what's he doing out there?"

"Nothing yet," she answered as best she could. "He's leaning mostly."

"Hmm, I don't reckon he'd waste his precious time coming down here just to lean." Hampton smiled at his elder child as he got up from the table. "Stay inside and out of sight. It's disrespectful to look in on grown folks' discussions."

"Yes, sir," she replied, put out by his strict edict. Joyce watched as Hampton nestled a pistol down the back of his pants. She couldn't hear what all of the crying and yelling was about when her folks returned home in the middle of the night, but she assumed that it hadn't been settled by the time she climbed out of bed for breakfast.

Joyce watched Hampton ease out onto the front porch. Magnolia and Janeen entered through the back door, carrying clothes donated for Toussaint's funeral.

"Where's Daddy going?" asked Janeen, the thirteen-year-old who favored Rayletta more than anyone thought possible. She twisted her ponytails then blew a bubble to amuse herself.

"Shush," Joyce replied irritably. "He's going out to square off with Mr. Trotter Delacroix. I'll bet he shoots that white man dead if he has to." She was merely repeating what she'd overheard him saying as he stormed into the night after Pearl Lee.

"What white man?" Magnolia asked, with her brow noticeably

raised. She folded a man's suit coat over her arm then leaned in closer to her daughter, awaiting a response. When it took Joyce too long to answer, she tossed the garment aside, then she wandered onto the porch to take a look-see for herself. Hampton sat on the arm of an old love seat with his thumbs pushed down in the front of his pants near the belt loops. Magnolia spotted the handle grip of the revolver poking out. She nodded good morning to their visitor while placing her hand on Hampton's shoulder just as she had a few hours ago in Trotter's bedroom. That was her way of reminding him there was a lot to consider, especially all he stood to lose if he pulled that trigger unnecessarily.

"Honey, *Mr.* Delacroix was just stopping by to say how sorry he was," said Hampton. He glanced at the shovel resting against the wood shingles near the door. It was the one that Toussaint had used to dig a grave for himself. Hampton swallowed hard when he remembered his friend's body floating in a deep puddle, wondering if Trotter was the cause of it. Magnolia read his mind. She smiled awkwardly and grabbed the shovel by the handle.

"What's this thing doing here? I'll take this out back and leave so y'all can talk." She nodded again to Trotter while allowing her free hand to brush along the ridge of Hampton's neck ever so casually. He almost chuckled at her constant reminders.

"So?" Hampton said, now digging at mud from the bottom of his best work boots with a sharp stick.

"So, it's like I was saying. I didn't have anything to do with Odessa's baby, and I promise that if any of my men did I'll do to him what I know the law won't. It's hard to say how much I feel for Pearl Lee. Don't expect you to understand it, I can't figure it out myself at times." His head fell forward when the shame of their affair became too heavy to bear. "I don't know what to say about Toussaint, either. He will get a decent burial. I'll see to that." His offer to pay for Toussaint's services came from the same place as the surprise visit: his guilty conscience.

"No need," said Hampton, his eyes trained on the chunks of dirt falling from his boots. "I'm already looking after it. For now, he's put away in the icehouse cooler until I can muster up some extra money." Trotter felt the strain in Hampton's voice and his duty-bound responsibility to take care of his own. Although it was no secret how strapped for cash Hampton was so close to harvest time, he couldn't argue against it so he didn't bother. "Don't concern yourself with it," Hampton contended eventually. "I'll have my brother-in-law out of your icehouse and in the ground by tomorrow night." Hampton's eyes floated to rest on Trotter when he failed to leave.

"How's, uh... how's Pearl Lee making out? If you don't mind me asking." Magnolia, listening from the cracked window, cringed. Three seconds passed before she heard him speak up.

"For a woman whose child just birthed a baby of her own and her man drowned hisself in sorrow because of the pain that come from it, she's about what you'd expect. A might pissed off at the whole world."

Magnolia blew out a dense stream of relief. At least he didn't start blasting.

"That wife of yours, Mary-Beth, how she *making out*?"

"A might pissed off as well," Trotter answered, as if he'd have to deal with her salty disposition for quite some time.

"I imagine she is at that," Hampton agreed. For the first time, he contemplated the fallout on Trotter's end. It couldn't have been easy to calm Mary-Beth's concerns and keep his mother out of the bottle and blabbing about what other lies she'd grown tired of carrying around. "Anything else?" Hampton said with a good deal of empathy in his voice.

"I hate to say it, but with all the rain hereabouts lately, the harvest is gonna be delayed a few weeks." Trotter's information did not come as news. It was his way of reminding Hampton that his portion of money from sugarcane sells would also be delayed.

"With all what's been happening around here, going on in private and whatnot, a harvest delay is about the only thing I seen coming." His eyes smiled at Trotter when his lips refused to. It took a lot for the white landowner to stop by and pay homage to Hampton's family in broad daylight, regardless of what anyone else thought. For once, he saw how fire burned tragically on both sides of the color line.

"I'm thankful to you, Hampton," he said resolutely. Trotter tipped his hat, jumped into his truck, and puttered up the road slowly. With muddy fields to contend with, no work on the schedule, and no place to be in particular, he wasn't in a rush to hurry home.

"I'm so glad that ended nice and easy," said Magnolia from the doorway. "He's hurting, Hampton, for too many reasons to explain."

"I know, Mag, I know."

Hampton rummaged through his toolbox in the bottom of the closet. He collected a well-worn wrench set and a pair of scarcely used vise grips. Magnolia watched with a heavy heart. She'd seen him out of sorts once before and prayed that would be the last time. When he heard the jewelry box playing from the bureau, he paused. "You'd better not be doing what I think you're doing."

"I've told you before to watch how you talk to me, Hampton Julian Bynote," answered Magnolia, who was fishing around in it for the only diamond ring she owned, one that Hampton saved up five years to purchase. "If you can part with your tools, I can spare to hock this ring. You'll get it back in due time, I trust in that." Magnolia heard Hampton's outright refusal to take Trotter's money and that decision, however difficult, put his back against the wall. Pawning her diamond was a small price to pay if it meant a decent burial for Toussaint amid the misery Pearl Lee had to endure.

Hampton threw his tools into a cloth sack then held his wife against his chest. "I wish you wouldn't, Magnolia. Times is hard, but..." he started to say. He couldn't bring himself to admit how much he needed the diamond ring.

"Times are what they are, no more, no less. Man, you should talk to Pearl Lee before you leave. She could use some propping up. Besides, you ought to meet your nephew." Magnolia fingered the pear-cut stone and handed it to Hampton. "I'll see what can be done to this coat I got from the church this morning. Father O'Leary was kind enough to let me rummage in the clothing bin. With a bit of stitching, this will do fine for Toussaint's funeral." Magnolia turned her face away when she felt a knot thickening in the base of her throat. "Go on now. I got to see the girls off to school and you have lots to do yourself."

When Hampton walked through Pearl Lee's front door, she was standing over the sink and staring out into the sugarcane fields just beyond the common area behind her cottage. She'd done it thousands of times, waiting for Toussaint to come strolling home or Trotter to sneak up for a quick rendezvous. She was certain that neither of those would ever happen again.

Hampton waved hello to Odessa, who was breast-feeding on the bed. "Hey, Uncle," Odessa sang, like a kid with a brand-new toy.

"How you do this morning?" he asked. The salutation was meant for both Pearl Lee and Odessa. Pearl Lee turned toward him. Dark circles surrounded her eyes. It was apparent she hadn't slept a wink. "I came to meet the birthday boy, but he appears to be having his breakfast now."

"He's almost done, Uncle. A greedy one he is at that. Ain't that right, Eric?" she cooed.

"Eric? What kind of name is that?" asked Hampton.

Pearl Lee grinned unexpectedly. "She said she read in a book someplace that name means 'top ruler' or some such. I'm partial to the name Elroy, but Odessa says it sounds old."

"Eric," Hampton said, trying the name on for size. "It'll be kind of nice to have a top ruler in the family for a change."

The labored smile on Pearl Lee's face put Hampton in mind of his mother's when troubles had dug in real deep and she did her best to shrug them off. "Trotter stopped by this morning," said Hampton, segueing into the real reason he came calling. "He wanted to let you know how sorry he is, about everything."

"I'll bet he is sorry at that. Should've seen Mary-Beth's mouth pop wide open when I come busting that bedroom door in." Pearl Lee got a kick out of replaying it in her head. "Doubt she'll ever speak to me again."

Hampton chuckled. "Would you blame her?" Pearl Lee ignored the comment. She went to cleaning up the breakfast dishes in the sink instead of addressing it. That wasn't the response Hampton intended on getting in return for his off-color wisecrack. "Well, anyhow, I'm going into Nawlins to see about a couple of things."

"What time you coming back? I got to make plans for Toussaint. I would say I can't believe he's gone, but the truth is he left a long time ago. May he rest in peace," she added, suspecting he wouldn't. Catholics didn't believe in suicide, and even though her husband's death could just as easily have been accidental, she knew better.

"I done carried him over to the icehouse. He'll keep good until

I get some money for a becoming send-off. Plan on starting services tomorrow afternoon. I ought to have things set by then." Hampton did an about-face and headed for the door. Odessa covered herself then climbed off the bed with her son in her arms.

"Here you go, Unc," she announced, holding the infant out like a prize ham. "Ten fingers, ten toes, and one cute little button nose." Those were the words Hampton had amused Odessa with until she turned nine and immediately informed him she was way too old for that.

Hampton felt obligated to hold the child he'd heard about in the throes of calamity. While holding the baby, who was no bigger than a loaf of bread, he shot a glance at Pearl Lee as if to ask what to do next.

"Well, don't you want to see what a top ruler looks like?" she said, answering his silent query. He pulled the soft blanket back and drew in a deep breath, hoping he wouldn't see a resemblance to any man he knew, white or otherwise. Hampton almost laughed when he saw a helpless newborn with a head full of curly blond hair, squirming to get comfortable in a stranger's arms. Hampton grinned proudly then returned the baby.

"He's a fine boy, Odessa. You did good." It was Hampton's turn to hide the emotion on his face the way Magnolia had. "I'll check with you when I get back, Pearl Lee. Don't fret. I'll handle things as best I can." Hampton jumped in his old Chevy, which sat inoperable more than it actually ran, and then he headed along the bayou toward the city. "Troubles come in bunches when you don't have use for none at all," his father used to say. Hampton nodded his head in agreement all the way out of Newberry.

28

Easy to Remember

The first pawnshop Hampton visited had a chain on the door. The sign read SOLD TO NEW OWNER. He didn't have any better luck with the next two places, where white men stared at him harder than they did at his prized possession. One of them even accused him of stealing the ring. Hampton was beginning to feel like his old self when the shopkeeper told him to get out or he'd call the cops. Trying to soak Magnolia's ring was harder than he thought and much tougher than it had been previously. Next on his list was an off-the-beaten-path jewelry broker who'd fenced stolen goods for Bones. Hampton figured on an easy transaction with a shifty precious gems man from his past. He strolled inside, past an armed security guard posted on a wooden stool near the front door.

"Hey, Fletch," he said, hoping the thick-gutted white man would remember just enough about him to make a decent offer. When he reached in his pocket, Fletcher eased his right hand beneath the counter. "Whoa!" Hampton grunted, praying the fat mule didn't buck. "Ain't no need for that. I guess you don't recall all the business you did for a friend of mine a while back. Bones Arcineaux and me brought a lot of stones here." Once again, Hampton found himself face-to-face with a distrustful expression.

"Yeah, I recall just dandy and that's the reason I'm throwing you out before you bring the law down on me again." He traded glances with the security officer, standing behind the counter. "As I recollect, you had some problems with the chief of police and a whole string of dead men you didn't mind slicing up."

"That wasn't none of me. I did time for car stealing and that's it. I done steered clear of trouble and don't plan on seeing the inside of prison again," Hampton ranted. "I fell on hard times is all. This here is my wife's ring and I swear befo' God all I want is a fair soak for about a month." Eventually, Fletcher's hand came out from under that counter empty.

"Well, stands to reason you didn't off all those fellas or they'd have fried your butt years ago. Sorry, but I didn't like detectives going through my inventory with a fine-tooth comb. Hell, I had to give over most of the stuff you and Bones boosted as evidence so's they wouldn't lock me up." Fletcher still wasn't sure if he wanted to do business with Hampton until he recognized the sincerity on the colored man's face. "Let me take a look at that," he said, gazing at the stone with a jeweler's glass. "Uh-huh, you say this is your wife's? What'd you spend on it?" He knew what it was worth and wanted to see if Hampton did as well.

"Bought it at Maison Blanche for a hundred and seventy, on sale in the display."

Fletcher moved the glass from his eye so he could shine it on Hampton. The shopkeeper took in Hampton's broken-in boots, well-worn jeans, and unkempt hair. "I would ask where a farm-hand got that kind of money, but I don't really want to know."

"Don't worry, it's legal," Hampton replied glibly. He reached for the ring to call off negotiations but Fletcher closed it in his meaty paw.

"I believe you, and I'll give you forty dollars to hold it for a month. If you don't come back, I'll sell it."

"Forty dollars?" Hampton was insulted. "I thought you said you believed me."

"I do, and that's why I'm willing to put up forty bucks."

"Eighty. I'll take eighty for it," Hampton countered. "It's worth twice that."

"Yep, down at the department store, but I couldn't move it for any more than seventy."

"Okay, I'll take seventy then," said Hampton, proud that he'd nudged up the price.

Fletcher, unscrupulous as ever, opened the cash register and tossed three twenty-dollar bills onto the countertop. "Sixty and you got yourself a deal, but let me tell you. It'll cost you seventy when you come back for it." He knew how to discourage desperate men from returning for quality goods.

Hampton took the money, sneered at the armed guard, and then slammed the door on his way out. Sixty dollars wasn't half of what he needed for the mortician to work on Toussaint. The going rate was one hundred for a low-budget embalming and makeup session. He could pay off the cheap casket once the harvest came in. "Sixty rotten dollars," he spat while cruising the streets of New Orleans with a bad taste in his mouth. He'd driven several blocks when a strange notion came to mind. Hampton took the next left turn then smiled. There it was. The auto body shop where he used to hold heist meetings with Bones was still there, unlike some of the old haunts he once frequented.

Climbing out of the car, Hampton remembered some of the

good and bad times that took place inside the large metal building. He wandered in expecting to find rows of dented automobiles and perhaps a friend or two. Instead, he found a barren warehouse with rusted car parts thrown here and there. He was also surprised to find a colored man serenading the scene with a brass trumpet. Hampton kept his distance while listening to the sweetest music he'd heard in years. It took him back to another time, one springing full of hope and happiness.

"Sorry, didn't see you there," said the man, wearing a compacted afro and a black turtleneck sweater. "So you came back to say good-bye, too."

Hampton studied the fellow, who appeared to be in his mid-twenties, but failed to put his face with a name. "Come again?"

"You don't remember me, huh? Name's Louie, Louie Grange." The smooth-talking hipster said his name like it was supposed to mean something. "I'm on a lot of records now, but I got my chops right here in this garage, Mr. Hampton." He licked his lips then tooted on the horn again, this time a much sadder song than before.

"Louie?" uttered Hampton. "That little kid who used to hang around here blowing with his band? That was you?" Louie played on a minute, smiling all the while as if it meant a great deal to be remembered for his youth.

"Yes, sir, and the birthplace of my prosperity is going to be torn down three weeks from now. It's gonna be a parking lot for the city, they say. I figure that's why you came back, too." Louie eyed Hampton suspiciously when there wasn't any evidence that he knew about the impending demolition, then he pulled out a rag to wipe down his horn.

"I kinda came to see about some business. Times ain't what they used to be, you know." Hampton excused himself then wandered into the office. It was empty, oily, and just the way Hampton had hoped. The safe where Bones had hid money and trinkets they'd stolen was still there. It had taken a beating where someone tried to pry it open. Hampton chuckled at himself for thinking there could be anything of value inside after more than fourteen years. He took one step toward the doorway then turned on a dime and scratched his head. "What the hell?" He sighed while kneeling down to fiddle with the battered lock. Hampton played with the combination just for grins. He nearly fell over when it opened on his third try. He pulled on the steel door, excited about achieving what others had tried and failed to do with force. His neck craned when he stumbled over something on the top shelf. There was a strap of bills tied by a purple ribbon, which he could tell had at one time been blue. Hampton peeked over his shoulder then lifted the money out. A note was fastened to the stash in a handwriting he recognized. *Swagger, if you came looking for help, you must really need it. Spend it in good health. Signed, Bones. P.S. If you ain't Swagger and broke in to steal his loot, rot in hell.*

Hampton laughed out loud at his old pal's humor, then he caught ahold of himself. He flipped through the stack, counting one hundred and seventy-eight dollars total. Figuring it must have been a sign, he shoved the currency into his pocket on his way out. Hearing taps, reserved for a military burial, Hampton stopped in the vast garage to hear it play out.

"So there was something in that raggedy safe to be had after all," said Louie as he put his horn aside. "Lawd knows me and the boys tried like the devil to bust off the hinges once you stopped coming around. You was good to us, kept a little change in our pockets, and even talked old man Williamsburg into letting us practice here when he wasn't banging on them hot cars you brought him." Louie noted Hampton's expression as he polished his horn. "Yep, we knew them cars were stolen. Didn't make no never-mind to us. We was kids and happy to be just that." He placed the trumpet in a black leather case, smiling as if it were yesterday all over again.

"Hey, Louie, you recall playing this pipe fitter's funeral for a man named Bones?"

"Bones? That's that friend of yours? Yeah, sure do. Me and the boys get together and talk about it sometimes. Heck, because of that stunt Bones told us to pull we got hired out to perform at all sorts of private parties and such. Most of us play professional now. We joke on how that jazz funeral was our first paid gig. You tell Bones I said hey and thanks, if you see him," Louie whispered, as if there was something about Bones and Hampton's relationship that shouldn't have been spoken of too loudly. "If there's ever anything I can do for either of y'all to show my gratitude, just holler."

Hampton thanked the man, said his good-byes, then made two stops before he dashed off toward Newberry. With so much on his plate and no time to waste, he pulled into the service station where Buck Ravenell caught on as a part-time attendant to make ends meet. Hampton asked if he could employ the older man's sons to help him move the body. He'd have gone it alone but feared breaking off one of Toussaint's frozen limbs like a Popsicle stick.

Later that day, Hampton announced throughout the village that his brother-in-law was going home in style and his family would greatly appreciate everyone's presence. Pearl Lee was pleased he'd taken it upon himself to make the necessary arrangements, considering her hands were full and money was tight all around.

On Saturday morning, Hampton met with a parish priest

in his church office. He thanked the clergyman for agreeing to his terms for Toussaint's funeral services. Father O'Leary, a redheaded thirty-two-year-old, was seven years younger than Hampton but his responsibilities were immense. Most of the white priests in Broussard Parish floated through on twelve-month pastorships before being reassigned. Many of them detested straying from normal Catholic traditions pertaining to worship, but it was in order to sustain Negro membership in the rural churches. Oftentimes, uncommon requests such as Hampton's were greeted with objections. After listening to the reasoning behind Hampton's plea, Father O'Leary eventually agreed to partake in it.

The mortician delivered a casket to the back stables of the Delacroix Plantation at noon. Hampton harnessed the coffin onto a wagon decorated with dozens of carnations. Precisely at one o'clock, Father O'Leary arrived at the main gate. He was cloaked in piety and a white robe with green trim surrounding the collar. Hampton, in his best suit, exited his cottage ahead of his family. Others on the plantation followed closely. The wagon pulled in behind as they headed up the road toward the colored cemetery. Two altar boys preceded Father O'Leary, swinging incense lanterns while keeping in perfect step. It was a humid day for early January although no one bothered to complain. Hampton appeared concerned. He scouted the landscape continuously.

"What's the matter, honey?" Magnolia whispered. "It is warmish for this time of year." Before he could render an explanation, a soulful trumpet serenade began just over the ridge. Hampton smiled knowingly while the massive gathering looked to one another for answers. Although no one could see the mysterious trumpeter yet, the priest instructed the young boys to continue the march.

Once the procession ascended to the top of the hill, they were saluted by a jazz quartet and an array of female singers who'd moments before stepped off a band-tour bus. Louie's group played beautifully, to the amazement of onlookers. Magnolia grinned at Hampton then, thinking back on her last jazz funeral and the excitement that ensued. Pearl Lee was saddened by the spectacle. She was sorry that Toussaint wasn't able to witness his friends paying respects to the sounds of mesmerizing music. He loved to see colored people gather without bearing the brunt of work tools and canvas sacks. No doubt, Toussaint would have approved.

Father O'Leary steadied himself at the burial site. Pearl Lee stood closest to him with Odessa on her opposite side doting over the baby. Pleasant words were tossed in along with dirt over the casket. Tears streamed and cries erupted near the end, when the realization of finality crept into the crowd. Odessa was given an opportunity for the last word. She shook her head, shot a questioning glare toward Father O'Leary, and then brushed a thick lock of hair away from her eye. "Good-bye, Daddy. I'll miss you," was her subtle salutation to the only man she'd ever loved. Ashes to ashes, dust to dust, amen.

The audience milled about, showering Pearl Lee and Odessa with warm hugs and well wishes until that same trumpet's song drew them from the cemetery and out onto the road. Louie played the pied piper. His mates continued the sorrowful dirge for an eighth of a mile before dispensing with funeral hymns altogether. Joyce's younger sister, Janeen, wrapped her arm in Hampton's when the band struck up a tune so loud that it startled her. Shouts of hallelujah and glad times emanated from everywhere at once. Janeen, frail as a sack of bones, peeked to see what was happening. The women who accompanied the musicians hoisted yellow umbrellas into the air. They paraded seductively, twirling umbrellas like spinning tops. Father O'Leary stood out of the way and watched. It was sacrilegious in his eyes, women kicking their legs up, juking erratically at a time of mourning. He had heard of wild goings-on, but it was much worse than he imagined. Magnolia strutted as well, though quite a bit more modestly than she did premotherhood. Odessa skipped and spun with a newborn in her arms, celebrating her father's life and the memories he left in her heart. Pearl Lee was too embarrassed to exhibit joy outwardly along the dusty and unpaved road, although her spirits were genuinely lifted.

"Y'all really gave 'em something to talk about," Hampton chuckled as he shook hands with Louie at the tour bus steps. "I'm much obliged to you, Louie."

"Don't mention it, Hampton," the trumpeter replied gleefully. "Truth is, we got some new members from up around Chicago and they ain't never seen nothing like this. Besides, we could use a warm-up session before hitting the club circuit. Glad to repay the favor, friend." They shook hands again, smiled, and parted ways. Hampton envied the younger man, who had the world to see and nothing to keep him from it. Conversely, Louie stared out the back window for the longest time at the man partially responsible for his promising future.

29

Hard to Forget

Hampton forked another helping of pecan pie into his mouth later that night. Pearl Lee doted on him. She saw to it that his glass of milk was sufficiently cooled while he finished the dessert she'd brought over as a small token of her appreciation. "There, there, now," she hummed delightfully, buzzing around Magnolia's kitchen. "Hampton just loves my pe-can pie, always did. Ain't that so, Hampton?" Joyce and Janeen peeked over the sofa back to catch an odd occurrence in their home. Pearl Lee danced around as if her feet didn't touch the ground at all. Hampton wasn't sure what to make of it, either. He'd seen a few women take their husband's deaths in peculiar fashions, but this was off the charts. Magnolia understood what her best friend was going through, overcompensating for the numbness boring down deep inside while feeling an intense desire to be needed, useful. "After dessert, I can make coffee and then maybe help you darn some of Hampton's socks and the girls' stockings and... and..."

"And that'll be all for tonight, Pearl Lee," Magnolia answered politely. "Hampton's got a wife, and the girls don't need but one mama. Why don't I come over to visit you, Odessa, and the baby?" She cut her eyes at her daughters, instructing them to make haste. Joyce and Janeen tore out of the living room area immediately, then peeped through an opening in the sheets serving as a partition between the den and bedroom. They didn't know whether to giggle or pray for their aunt, in obvious dire straits. After watching Magnolia toss her arm around Pearl Lee's neck to wrestle her out the front door, Joyce and Janeen giggled first then prayed afterward.

Hampton heard them laughing and carrying on. He grinned heartily until Odessa's plight came to mind. She was a breath older than his girls. Then, in a blink of an eye, she was a young woman with a mouth to feed and a new set of rules to live by. Hampton stood up from the small table to put away a saucer and drinking glass. He fought off the sadness, remembering a universal truth he'd learned the hard way, while in his youth. *You ain't never too young to start paying the dues of life*, he thought. *When the time comes, we all got to pay.*

"Girls, tell your mama I'm going into Nawlins to look for some extra money," he said casually. Hampton continued to pick out his fresh haircut until he realized no one had responded. "Hey, y'all heard me?"

"Uhh-huh," answered Janeen. Joyce neglected to answer. She simply rolled her eyes instead, in the same manner she'd witnessed Magnolia object to Hampton stepping out of the house on a Saturday night.

"Where should we say you're off to?" Joyce asked irritably. She lay flat on her back, pulling a string of yarn from the ball she'd wound tightly. Hampton didn't like her tone. His lengthy bout of silence transmitted that loud and clear. "Yes, sir. I'll just give her the message, Daddy."

"That's more like it. You girls need to get this kitchen cleaned up before going off to bed." Hampton hid a smile as he grunted further instructions. "And don't go causing your ma no trouble now. She's tired." Hampton found himself awaiting yet another response. "Girls?"

"'Night, Daddy," they replied in tandem, neglecting to stand firm in a commitment likely to be broken. To misbehave was one thing. To misbehave after promising they wouldn't was out of the question.

Hampton threw on his best polyester blazer before he hit the door. He packed a sandwich and a revolver, figuring to be in for a long night. One of the stops he'd made earlier in the day was the barbershop. The other was a quick stop at the fairgrounds. Hampton had wagered on three horses after listening in on conversations for tips inside the men's restroom. He even handed towels to two gentlemen whose information sounded the most credible. Hampton hadn't seen a horse race, much less bet on one, but each of his three picks finished in the money. Hampton smiled, counted his mounting nest egg, and thought how easy handicapping racehorses was. He didn't think his luck could hold forever, but he was willing to ride it a few more times around the track.

Hampton's idea to hang around the men's room didn't fly so well during the night races. Two other black men hustled towels, cigarettes, and breath mints as a vocation. When Hampton languished too long without tipping them, the attendants gawked at him insistently. Forced to rely on luck rather than the inside dope, Hampton studied the racing form on his way to the betting windows. "Bagpipe don't sound like a fast horse," he muttered softly. "Rajun Cajun, now that appears to be a stag with some giddyap. I'll pick him in the second and U Next Sugar in the third. Yeah, that sounds like it might work." Hampton circled his choices while the line inched forward.

"Well, now, as I live and breathe," a familiar voice said from a nearby beer and peanut stand. Hampton's mouth dried out in a split second. He folded the racing form he'd been drawing on then slipped it into his back pocket. Hampton didn't see the sport in wagering on horse races. He'd shared many times how he viewed the track as a place where some desperate people went to scream their lungs out next to other desperate people doing the same, and all of whom appeared to be short on luck and long on stupidity. Fearing he'd have to eat those words, Hampton turned slowly to greet an old friend. "Swagger, how you been?" asked Bones. He pinched the brim of his white fedora with a black hatband. Hampton nodded respectfully after noting Bones's stylish wide lapels, spotless leisure suit, and shiny leather shoes. "Don't be that way, come and spend a minute with your old pal. It's been what, fifteen years?"

Hampton glanced behind him, his feet still anchored to the exact same spot as before although the line surged forward. Several gamblers, all very anxious to place their bets, wondered if they should go around him or if he'd move ahead. Pressured by an old friend and his own indecision, Hampton vacated his place in line. "Hiya, Bones," he said, feeling underdressed in his old companion's company. Faded denim and twice-broke shoes couldn't measure up to a fine wardrobe. Even more, he felt like an underling who'd poorly mismanaged his luck as well.

"Look at you, Swagger," cheered Bones with a firm handshake. "You look swell. I'll be damned if you don't. How's life down on the farm?" Hampton couldn't tell if he was being made fun of or if Bones had something up his sleeve.

"Can't complain," Hampton said, eyeing the betting window intermittently. He'd made it to the races with time to spare and was itching to get in on it. "Hey, Bones, it's good seeing you, but the man is about to close those shutters on me and I expect to put some money down."

"Go on then, blow your grip on a bunch of slow glue buckets. What's Magnolia gonna say when you turn up busted with your pockets blew out? She ought to be good and grown by now and likely to be the fighting kind at that." Hampton wanted to slap Bones across the mouth until he realized there was a point to be made, if he hadn't already.

"What you sayin'?"

"Just offering to personally take your bets. If you win, I'll pay up. If you lose, we go into business like before, like I wanted to when you lit out of jail and then turned your back on me." Bones pulled a cigar from a silver case and pushed the end of it into the corner of his mouth. "You got less than a minute before finding out if running into me was an accident." Hampton's eyes danced to the man behind the betting window and the man behind his previous incarceration.

"You'll pay a hundred percent of my winnings? No bluff?"

"I'm insulted. When have you known me to crawfish on a deal? Matter of fact, I left you a parcel of money in a safe once and that was just in case you needed it." Bones already knew Hampton had taken the loot he'd put in the safe over ten years ago. Hampton was sorry for asking what turned out to be a ridiculous question.

"I didn't mean it the way it came out, Bones," he apologized.

"All bets!" shouted the money collectors.

Hampton scratched his head, then he agreed to Bones's offer. He watched the races, quietly wishing his horses to nudge their way across the finish line first. Hampton should have recognized a sucker when he looked in the mirror. Each of the nags he picked came in dead last. Running into Bones saved every penny he had to his name. Three hundred and twenty-nine dollars was more than enough to provide food and a bundle of clothes for his wife and daughters. However, making a way to include Pearl Lee's household plagued Hampton. He frowned then threw his racing forms in the trash can, next to the promise he'd made at Rayletta's graveside. "Two things first: How long you known I got that knot you left me outta the safe? And second, what kind of business is *we* into now?" Bones's grin spread across his face the same way it had when he laid eyes on Hampton minutes before.

"Some things, my friend, is meant to be a mystery," he answered, skillfully killing both birds with one stone.

Hampton listened to Bones's propositions all the way to the parking lot. He explained many viable options, complicated schemes, and outright devious undertakings. Hampton passed on stealing then reminded him how it didn't pan out so well the last time. Bones laughed. "Yeah, Swagger, you got me there. There's this other thing I have a line on. It pays ten percent." He made the proposition in a way that piqued Hampton's interest. Bones chewed on his stogie while Hampton did likewise to the potential moneymaking enterprise.

Hampton stared at the dirt beneath his worn shoes. He kicked at a rock or two before taking the bait. "Ten percent of what?" he asked finally.

"Glad you asked." Bones explained the job in great detail, making Hampton fully aware of his expectations and the aptitude necessary to perform the task. He figured the type of man willing to put every penny he owned down on a horse's nose was open to being ridden like a mule if the price was right.

"So that's it? I get to keep ten percent of what I bring in? What if it don't come off like you say?" Hampton asked, playing the devil's advocate.

"You get paid to make it come off just so or you can march right back up to that betting window and toss your money in like you was about to when I stopped you." Bones's eyes dimmed in an ominous manner that almost sent Hampton reaching for his gun. "It's been a while, Swagger, but we're still friends, you and me."

"Yeah, guess there ain't no changing that."

"Why would you want to?" Bones smiled softly when his old pal made his way in the opposite direction.

Hampton strolled into the tavern just off the fairgrounds proper. Cigarette smoke filled the busy room, which had been quite a bit calmer when Hampton stopped in for a beer earlier in the day. He took a seat at the bar and waited on the fellow Bones said was his inside man. When the fellow fitting Bones's description sauntered in like he owned the place, Hampton observed him from the fringes. The bartender noticed his watchful eye.

"If you got any ideas to rob Riley Dobbs, forget about it," the server offered.

"Who said I was in the takedown business?" Hampton smarted without blinking.

"Well, now, if you're thinking on taking out a loan, I can help you with that." He poured Hampton a swig of whiskey to grease the skids. Hampton tossed the shot back then slammed the tiny glass down on the bar.

"That's mighty hospitable of you, but I got half a mind to strike up a deal I can live with." Hampton made a beeline across the tavern. As he approached the colored gangster decked out in crushed velvet and platform shoes, a larger man appeared out of nowhere to wedge himself between them. He held his meaty hand inches from Hampton's face as a warning.

"You got a problem, fool?" the behemoth grunted.

"I need to meet the man. We got business." Hampton locked eyes with the sturdy bodyguard so he could use his hands without being detected. "I don't want no trouble, just a few words."

"I don't like the way you look, and I don't like—" he started to say before he felt the barrel of Hampton's gun poking his rib cage.

"Told you, I just wanted to talk to Riley. All this could have been avoided." Hampton eased his revolver down by his side so that no one would be the wiser. He didn't want another overzealous henchman to get the wrong idea and shoot up the place. Leaning against the bar, calm and collected, Hampton felt a gnat buzzing around his ear. It was the bartender, playing his position too close to the base.

"Smooth move, but I had the drop on you all along," he whispered spitefully. "And you stiffed me on that drink."

When Riley Dobbs heard what had happened, he took a long gaze at Hampton then sent word to invite him over. "Like I said, I'm about to strike up a deal," Hampton said dismissively. "Put that drink on my tab. Looks like I'll be around some." The bartender smacked his lips as Hampton blew him off for the second time.

"It takes a pair of giant nuts to roll in here alone, demanding sit-downs and whatnot," Riley said before giving his blessings to be joined at the reserved table. "You think doing time on my block gets you special privileges?"

"I don't think, I—" Hampton answered, struggling to recognize the man he once knew well. "Ten of Twelve?" he said as it came back to him crystal clear.

"Ten of Twelve," Riley repeated with his hand extended. "You ain't changed at all, Hampton." Serving on the same chain gang, they were accustomed to calling out their number on the line when linked together for transport. One or two men with the inclination to flee was an everyday occurrence. However, convincing an entire row of prisoners to make a break for it never happened, not once.

"Man, you changed a lot," Hampton admitted. "Money sho' do agree with you."

"Yeah, but this gut I'm building on don't." He slapped at his belly then laughed as it jiggled. "Good living is gonna kill me if I let it. Hey, I heard what you pulled on Stubby," Riley said, sneering at his oversize security.

"Stubby?" Hampton repeated, taking note of the man's nickname. "I see you ain't lost your sense of humor."

"Some things a man needs to hold close to his vest." His comment implied the time had come for Hampton to speak his reason for the interruption, considering how he hadn't recognized Riley Dobbs beforehand.

"Bones told me to come in and find you. He said you'd have some work for me."

Riley stroked at his thick goatee. "You ain't in no trouble, is you?" Bones was trouble, and Riley remembered Hampton's cursing him in his nightmares.

"Not any trouble I know of," answered Hampton. "If you got a problem with Bones, it don't have to concern me. I need the work." Riley picked up a pack of cigarettes. He eased one out then placed it between his thick dark lips. The gangster struck a match. He let it burn before speaking his mind. "I ain't got no gruff with Bones. The question is, do you?" He held the match to the unfiltered end then drew in a measured breath. "That Bones get you jammed up again, it better not rub off onto me," he declared somberly. "I always liked you, Hampton, but I'd hate to smoke you like this Pall Mall."

Hampton found himself caught between two very dangerous men. Riley Dobbs didn't elaborate on whether he merely distrusted Bones or hated him altogether. It was obvious he reserved harsh feelings for Hampton's longtime pal. "Hey, look, we ain't got to discuss any of that. Just tell me what you want done and I'll see that it gets did," Hampton asserted. Before hearing what Riley Dobbs had in store, he had already begun to wonder if losing all of his money on the ponies would have actually meant breaking even.

30

Late Nights and Liquor

At two a.m. Hampton dragged through his front door with the smell of liquor on his breath and an undeniable hitch in his step. Magnolia sat on the divan in a faded floral housecoat with her arms folded. She was half asleep and completely perturbed. When she yawned, Hampton saw an opportunity to plead his case.

"I'm running late but some work got in the way."

"Work? Smells like you found time to mix in a little fun while you were at it." She studied Hampton's face for signs of culpability, the kind most likely associated with the female persuasion.

"Wasn't nothing like that, Magnolia," he answered, knowing what she meant. Hampton remained near the door as if he anticipated someone coming through it behind him. Collecting on bets for Riley Dobbs made for a host of enemies. Shoving his gun in their faces when they refused made it harder to punch the clock and let down his guard when the job was done.

"You alone?" she asked, gathering her housecoat at the chest.

"Yeah. It was a long night," was his quiet reply.

"It have anything to do with Bones?" Magnolia's words dripped from her lips slowly, like a broken faucet. Surprisingly, her question eased his mind.

Hampton took a seat next to his wife, leaned back, then placed his hand on her thigh. "How'd you know?"

"The only time you ever have a loss for words is after running the streets with *him*." The way she said those words almost made Hampton cringe. "Thought you were finished with that sort of business and through with Bones altogether. You got a family now and two girls depending on you to stay out of trouble!" Magnolia covered her mouth when her voice raised three octaves.

"I know how it sounds, honey, I do, but this is different. When I ran into Bones, it was the best thing could happen," Hampton explained. "I was about to make a big mistake, a big one. It's a lot weighing on me with the harvest rolling late and with all that Pearl Lee's got going on. Now, I don't expect you to understand."

"I understand you went and got yourself hooked up with the man who took more than a year from your life and stole more than that from me," she interrupted sharply. "I don't want to go through that again. Besides," she said, glancing at the hanging bedsheet that partitioned the girls' sleeping quarters, "they need a good example more than anything so they'll know what it looks like up close."

Hampton nestled the back of his head against the sofa cushion. "They already got what they need in you. What I need is some sleep." That was his way of shutting down the conversation once and for all. Magnolia conceded for the time being. She needed time to think.

* * *

Rays of bright yellow screamed loudly through the front room windows. Hampton's face contorted miserably as he shielded his eyes with a throw pillow. "Who let the sun in?"

"The Lawd, thank goodness," said Magnolia, with a stern look on her face. Hampton wiped at his mouth then twisted his lips disapprovingly.

"Well, tell Him to put it back."

"You can have a talk with Him yourself when we get to church," she smarted adamantly. "Joyce, Janeen, it's time to wake now. Church service ought to be good today. Father O'Leary's been heating it up lately. Something must've lit a fire beneath that robe of his."

Janeen pushed the covers off and sat up wearily. Joyce pouted. "Mama, I don't want to go. I want to stay home with Daddy." Magnolia fired up the stove, neglecting to offer a response initially.

"Uh-uh, he's got a few things to say to the Lawd firsthand. There's no better way to do that than in the Man's house. Get on up, everybody. We're likely to be calling on God a lot, and I'd rather He recognize us when we do." Hampton knew it was futile to debate the point. Magnolia was right about keeping a closer walk with the Almighty, bearing in mind the kind of troubles he was likely to encounter on his night job, but then she was usually right about everything. Hampton almost smiled when that occurred to him. Almost.

The small shack had undergone a few modern upgrades over the years, including a smattering of electrical appliances and a makeshift shower. Hampton soaked his head while his family dressed and pressed. He heard Janeen's excruciating shout when Magnolia nipped her ear with the hot straightening comb. That also meant breakfast was finished because there were only two eyes on the stovetop and only one of them worked. Hampton dried off in record time to avoid another of his wife's evil leers. "Can't a man get a biscuit in *my* own house?" he yelled, partly making fun of Magnolia's previous comment.

"Your plate is warming in the oven," she yelled back, noticeably sweeter than before. "Hurry up now or we'll be late, and I'm tired of sitting in that back pew. It squeaks something awful."

Hampton darted out of the cottage, nibbling on a sausage biscuit, and he was still sucking between his teeth when he pulled onto the grassy lot on the side of the white wood-framed church building. Magnolia blushed with pride as always. There was something irresistible about getting dressed up in her Sunday-go-to-meeting best, even if her clothes weren't much to brag about. Family meant the world to her. A godly family was the most a poor black woman in rural Louisiana could hope for. When Hampton escorted her past the squeaky pew, all was well with her soul.

During the church service, Magnolia sang to her heart's content. She swayed joyously with the organ music, praising her good fortune, two healthy children, and enough food in the cupboard to throw together a decent dinner. Other families weren't so lucky. Magnolia pitched in to help them out whenever possible. Lately, she found herself scratching to do the same herself. She was prayerful for high prices in the sugarcane market and fair wages for work the colored sharecroppers had done during the last season. Any more than that was foolish, she'd determined years ago. Magnolia prayed because it just didn't pay to dream.

Hampton worked diligently to stay awake. When he did nod off, he was greeted with a pointed jab in the ribs. His daughters giggled each time he endured a stiff needling because his head would snap upright, then he'd apologize to Magnolia with eyes pleading for forgiveness. Throughout the service, he received a goodly number of sharp elbows along with a message from the Good Book, and each time he repented.

Afterward, Hampton stretched and yawned, much to Magnolia's dismay. "You can't still be sleepy after calling the hogs and interrupting the father's sermon?" she whispered curtly. Hampton shrugged his shoulders instead of answering, knowing there was no appropriate answer. "You ought to be ashamed," she added, seeing to it that he was. Hampton manufactured a pitiful face to insinuate as much. His long frown was so pathetic Magnolia chuckled as they proceeded toward the exit with other members of the congregation. "Father, that was a touching message today," she said, shaking hands with the spiritual leader.

"Thank you, Magnolia, I do try to impart what the Lord puts on my heart to share," he said, smiling brightly. "And what did you think of it, Hampton?"

"Of what? Oh, the sermon? Fine, it was fine, Father. Good sermon. I know God must've been proud," he answered, moving along like his shoes were on fire.

"Well, at least He had something to be proud of," Magnolia teased, once they spilled out onto the cement porch. "*Fine, fine*," she joked, imitating Hampton's voice. "You didn't hear two words that man said all morning."

"I did, too. A-men."

"That's shameful and one word. See if you can round up the girls. I need to see if the meeting room is going to be available for a quilting bee next week. It wouldn't hurt to rustle up some extra money. Joyce's school shoes need resoling, and Janeen's getting so big she can't hardly take her sister's hand-me-downs anymore. They're nearing the same size."

"I'm working on it," was all he could say. The expression she dropped at Hampton's feet suggested his new employment paid more than yawns. Trotter was forced to cease offering credit at the plantation commissary. It was the first time since his father died that he'd secretly borrowed against the farm in addition to the upcoming crops. Times weren't merely changing; they had turned into something different altogether.

31

School Daze

Monday afternoon, Janeen sat in the sixth-grade social studies class daydreaming. Carrying the family banner proudly, perfect attendance, and even better grades had their drawbacks. Boredom was one of them. Magnolia was a stickler for knowing the answers before the teachers asked the questions. She preached from day one to grab education and hold on to it like a grudge. Joyce set the standard with straight A's, year after year. Janeen wasn't about to drop the torch and disappoint her mother irrecoverably. So she threw her hand up nonchalantly each time the class was stumped by a difficult state capital. "Butte. The capital of Montana is Butte," she replied plainly, to the chagrin of one student in particular, although she doubted she'd ever set foot outside Louisiana. Billy Earl Cartwright, a mischievous twelve-year-old and small for his age, shot a spitball at Janeen's head. When she turned to answer fire with a mean-spirited sneer, he flipped his eyelids inside out and stuck two fingers in his nose to further annoy her. Janeen couldn't help snickering at the prankster's antics. A split second later, the teacher asked if she thought there was anything funny about other students slacking in their responsibilities. Of course she shook her head regrettably. Billy Earl eased out a sigh of relief when she didn't rat on him. He shouldn't have been surprised. Janeen passed up several opportunities to subject him to the teacher's leather whipping strap. He'd managed that enough on his own.

After school, Janeen waited outside the eight-room building by the flagpole. Once Joyce arrived with her girlfriends, they started for home. "I heard you got a stern glare from Mrs. Wilson," said Joyce. "I'll bet it was that nasty li'l cuss Bill' Earl picking at you again. Huh, I'd turn him in if I were you. Might teach him a lesson at that."

Janeen shrugged. "He doesn't mean any harm, and he makes me laugh. Mama says laughing is good for the soul."

"Mama also said she'd tan your backside if the teacher sends another note home," Joyce argued. "A girl's got enough troubles in life without letting some filthy boy cause more of it." That was straight from Magnolia's mouth. She'd taught her daughter well.

"Speaking of boys," said Carolyn as she nudged Joyce.

"Oh, yeah. Janeen, Carolyn and I have to talk. Go on ahead ten paces so's you won't try to listen in."

"I knew this was coming," Janeen grunted, quickening her step. "I don't want to hear some old stupid talk about who you think is cuter out of Thomas Green and Lawrence Filby. You ask me, both of them look like cavemen."

Joyce stuck out her tongue. "Good thing nobody's asking you. Now git!" She didn't have to say it twice. Janeen skirted along, books under her arm and her knee-length dress blowing in the wind. She had grown accustomed to the older girls discussing anatomy, chemistry, and oftentimes misconceptions regarding biology.

"So, who do you think is the finest, Thomas or Lawrence?" Carolyn asked with a naughty leer.

"Well, Thomas's gray eyes are just dreamy. Lawrence has the biggest muscles. I guess it all depends on what makes you swoon the most. Me, I'm gonna marry a man with muscles," Joyce cooed. Suddenly, her smile dissipated. "Carolyn, what do you think about my cousin Odessa and her baby?"

"What do you mean? Do I think she got that baby on her account, or if she was held down and took?"

"Yeah, that's exactly what I mean," replied Joyce, staring down at the road. She remembered being awakened by the commotion following Odessa's delivery and how the lid was almost blown off the Delacroix mansion. Children with fair complexions weren't a complete rarity due to generations of French and Anglo blood mixed with that of slave descendants. However, Odessa's son, Eric, exhibited few characteristics of his African heritage. Joyce decided to let the discussion fade. She dared not share what she really thought about Odessa with Carolyn, a well-known blabbermouth in her own right. "It's just a shame that it happened either way," she'd concluded.

"Odessa should have been standing when she did it," Carolyn added as an afterthought.

"What's that got to do with anything?"

"A girl can't get pregnant if she does it with a boy while standing up. Everybody knows that." Carolyn raised her eyebrows as if she'd revealed one of the keys to the universe. Joyce reasoned with her newfound misinformation then stopped suddenly in the middle of the road.

"Standing up? Is that even possible?"

Farther up the way, Janeen ran into Billy Earl Cartwright. He appeared to be waving a broken tree limb at something near the edge of the pond. "What you poking that stick at, Bill' Earl," she asked, stretching her neck to get a closer look. Just as she leaned forward, he lifted the limb out of the water with a snapping turtle attached.

"Yo' boyfriend!" he yelled, holding it near her face. Billy Earl chased her with it until he was out of breath.

"Quit, Bill' Earl!"

"Gimme a kiss first," he bargained.

"No way. You put that snapper down. It ain't funny."

"Yes, it is, too, but I'll quit. I'm tired as hell," he cursed. "I got to stay out of my papa's tobacco. Shoot, it done took my wind away."

"You smoke?" she asked, more surprised than concerned.

"Hell, yeah, and drink, too, when I can poach a nip without getting caught." He tossed the turtle into the pond then dusted off his clothes. "So where's my sugar, sugar?" The boy stood on the tips of his toes and puckered his crusty lips. Janeen crinkled her nose, staring at the diminutive boy with a gigantic ego. She was utterly repulsed.

"I'll peck you on the cheek, but that's as far as this goes, you understand?" She didn't trust him or his busy hands. "Now, close your eyes and put your hands behind your back." When he obliged, she moved in to plant one on his jaw, but he turned his head at the last moment. Their lips met. He howled. Janeen spat.

"Oomph, that's some mighty sweet stuff," he heckled, humping the air victoriously.

"That was gross. You're gross, and so is what you tried to do with your tongue." She shuddered when thinking about his cheap maneuver.

"Relax, sweetie, I could teach you a whole lot of grown-up stuff. I seen my uncle and his big fat wife belly rubbing in the barn last Saturday night. They was mostly hugging and squeezing until she let out a mile long fuss-and-cuss when he stuck his thang in her."

"Oomph, stop talking to me about that," Janeen objected.

"What's the matter, you only talk about the loosey-goosey with that boyfriend of yours? I bet you like that white reverend. Maybe it's him you're saving all of your humping for. I know about some of the other gals he likes to kiss on."

"His name is Father O'Leary. He's a priest. That's better than some old reverend," she asserted. "For your information, a priest is the closest thing to God on this here green earth."

"For your information, that fancy reverend of yours buys his liquor from the store where my sister Birdie sweeps up. He don't wear his preaching clothes when he's in there, but I seen him."

"So what, a spiritual man is likely to stray from the straight and narrow from time to time, but that doesn't make him out to be a letch."

Billy Earl frowned when he felt the need to prove his point. "Okay then, I'll bet he puts his moves on you in due time."

"That's disrespectful and improper to speak of a righteous man in such a common way. God's gonna get you for that, Bill' Earl, just you watch."

"I got a quarter in my pocket says that cracker preacher gets you first."

Janeen didn't waste the mental energy speculating on Father O'Leary's private life. She'd heard his name whispered here and there, but Magnolia said it was pure foolishness and that the priest was an upstanding man, which is why she allowed Joyce and Janeen to earn a few nickels cleaning up the church kitchenette and mopping the floor every so often. The terrible things being said about the father were immediately dismissed as ludicrous in the Bynote household. That's all there was to it.

With dinner on the stove and two unusually quiet girls on her hands, Magnolia suggested they get out of the house. "You know, Odessa could probably use some company. I think Pearl Lee could, too." Reluctantly, her daughters slid into their shoes and headed out the door. They passed one of Magnolia's clients standing on the porch with her snooty fourteen-year-old daughter, Nancy, who rolled her eyes and pinched her nose shut. Odor from a nearby pig farm was overwhelming at times, even to those who had grown accustomed to the stench. "Afternoon, Joyce, Janeen," the stoutly built women saluted kindly.

"Afternoon, Mrs. Johnson," Janeen said amicably. Joyce reserved her words, glaring stubbornly at her schoolmate Nancy, who dressed nicer than most of the girls in her grade, largely because of the dresses Magnolia made for her.

"What you looking at?" asked Nancy while continually holding her nose.

"It's another word for mule. Look it up," Joyce muttered as she passed by.

"Ooh, Mama, did you hear what Joyce called me? I can't help it. This place stinks like a hog pen."

Mrs. Johnson scolded her daughter silently before tearing into her. "Shut your mouth, Nancy, disrespect ain't acceptable no matter how far down somebody is in life. The Bynotes are good people. Mind your manners or you won't be getting that chiffon dress you asked for. Sorry, Magnolia, you know how these youngins can test your nerves."

Magnolia accepted the backhanded apology on behalf of the child. She overlooked the comment about scraping the bottom in life. Nonetheless, Mrs. Johnson entered to sort through dress patterns despite what she thought of the Bynotes' humble abode.

Magnolia had become a talented seamstress, and there was no substitute for quality on the cheap.

Over at Pearl Lee's, Janeen bounced the baby on her knee. In total bliss, she didn't think about Billy Earl's wicked rants regarding Farther O'Leary or rumors of his impropriety with young girls. Janeen could think of nothing but how precious that baby boy was when Odessa taught her to change his diaper.

"You feel different now?" Joyce asked her when they were in private.

"About as different as a sixteen-year-old mama who was told not to come back to school for the rest of the year. Seeing as how I'm the scourge of the tenth grade, I'm not feeling tip-top, as you can imagine." Odessa peered into her first cousin's eyes, where she saw a buffet of warnings, but only one made it past her lips. "Look, don't you let any man lie to you and then get away with it. I promised something I shouldn't have. Don't end up like me if you can help it. That's all I can say." Odessa's words insinuated she couldn't help her situation or at least didn't think she could have at the time it happened. "I love you so much, Joyce." She hugged Joyce's neck for the longest time.

"I can't breathe, Dessa," Joyce huffed.

"Sorry, just that things will never be the same between us now. I already miss walking to school together and talking about boys and such. Mama says I got to get a job on the plantation to earn a keep for me and Eric. I'll see you around, though, cousin." Odessa's smile returned as if it had never waned. Joyce couldn't comprehend how she managed to find joy with her childhood snatched away too soon. She put it in the same boat with having sex while standing up. Some things were simply beyond her grasp.

32

Yesterday's News

Hampton was making good money. Working for Riley Dobbs had allowed him to stash away two hundred dollars over the past two weeks. He kept his money in the safe at the auto body shop, waiting on Bones to show up so he could hand over the ten percent he owed. Bones was right about making things pay off in one way or another. Whether Hampton's gruff words, mean-spirited threats, or acts of bodily harm convinced Riley's clients to settle, everyone paid in the end. Earning a reputation for strong-arm tactics, Hampton kept his eye on the prize: looking out for his own. Before he knew it, a once-forgotten dream had reemerged. He was actually thinking about moving his family into the city. Sharecropping never paid enough to get ahead. It wasn't set up to do anything but keep the impoverished broken and busted. Hampton's audacity of hope allowed him to see a lighted path at the end of the tunnel that had caved in on his ancestors.

In the office at the rear of the tavern, Riley counted stacks of money. "Now see here, Hampton," he said, proud of himself and his newest bad-debt collector. "Because you done went and made a name for yourself, folks don't think twice about paying what rightfully belongs to me." With his tongue, he played with the toothpick wedged in the corner of his mouth. "Yeah, man, you stay with me and you'll do all right for yourself." Hampton couldn't argue with that, but another glance at Riley's bundles of money gave him the distinct feeling that the gangster was doing a great deal better since he came aboard. Hampton's second thought took off like a shot when someone knocked on the closed office door. Riley furrowed his brow because of the unfamiliar raps. The secret code was three knocks, followed by two more and then a single one. Hampton watched Riley's eyes as they questioned the unusual interruption. "See about it," he whispered while sliding the money off the desk into a metal drawer.

"Yeah," Hampton grunted. His fingers gripped the pistol handle beneath his synthetic jacket.

"It's the man," a voice replied calmly.

Hampton was puzzled. He shrugged at the peculiar response. Riley knew all too well what it meant. His jaws clenched. "Go on and open up." When he saw Hampton still poised to strike if necessary, his boss shook his head. "No need for that. Play it cool." Hampton concealed his gun then opened the door. When his eyes landed on the older white man, neatly dressed like a businessman, the desire to strike again washed over him. He fought it off like a bad cold.

"Riley Dobbs," the white man said, grinning. He sized up Hampton like a man used to handling himself on the streets. "This is new, I take it." He was referring to Riley's enforcer.

"You didn't come down here to inspect the help," answered Riley. He opened the cash drawer, eased his hand in, then came out with an envelope. He slid it across the desk with a solemn nod. Hampton wasn't sure if Riley was working for the sturdy visitor or if they were in business together. Before Hampton could lend it any more thought, he had his answer.

"Very nice doing business with you," the white man said. He eased the thick envelope into his breast pocket. "This payment satisfies your commitment to the police retirement fund."

"Yours especially, huh, Chief Mouton?" That was Riley's way of impressing Hampton. Being in cahoots with the New Orleans chief of police had its privileges. Monthly payoffs ensured zero interference from local cops.

Mouton? Hampton thought. He'd recognized the man's voice, but that was as far as it went. Mouton's gray hair and sagging shoulders suggested the cost of corruption may have been more than he'd assumed. Hampton's eyes widened. He remembered what Mouton had done for Pearl Lee, the sentence recommendation made on his behalf, and the murder rap he and Bones put on the pedophile they murdered. It was difficult for Hampton to stand there feeling like a sixth toe and trying not to get noticed.

"I don't plan on quitting because you got a cushy job with the governor's office," Riley told his partner in crime. "Yep, I heard all about it. Don't let the doorknob hit you where the good Lawd split you, on your way out."

"You think of that all by yourself? Nah, I doubt it. Don't take any wooden nickels, Riley. I'd hate to read about something happening to you." The chief tipped his hand to Riley then saddled Hampton with an irritated frown. "I thought I'd heard wrong about you, Hampton. I see it and I still can't believe you're hustling for this fancy thug. You should watch the company you keep." Hampton's eyes fell to the floor.

"Detective, I—" he offered before further words eluded him.

Mouton cast a nasty leer at Riley then placed a kind hand on Hampton's back. "Why don't we talk a little bit on the way to the car? The air in here is kind of rank." Riley knew the game Mouton played. It was his turn to impress Hampton at the fancy thug's expense. Hampton followed the subtle demand for his presence with a sorrowful glance at his employer. Alone now, Riley slammed the drawer shut and wiped the bile gathering in the corners of his mouth with a silk handkerchief.

When exiting the watering hole, Hampton braced himself on the sidewalk. He expected to see Detective Cunningham behind the wheel. Instead, there was a much younger man who reminded him of Mouton in his muscular, head-thumping days. "I been meaning to look you up to thank you for doing right by my sister, Pearl Lee, when I was on the work farm," Hampton said apologetically. "Never did seem to get around to it, though."

"That's old news, Hampton. You lived up to your part of the agreement. Even when the DA pulled a fast one over his car you drowned, still you kept your word. Jail time couldn't have been easy. You need to remember that, too, when chasing people down behind Riley Dobbs's money." Hampton stared at the bulge in the chief's breast pocket then, questioning the money he'd made behind Riley Dobbs. "You've kept your nose clean for a long time, Hampton. I've kept tabs to make sure you didn't go astray. After not so much as a parking citation, was it Bones who got you mixed up in this?"

"Uh-uh, ain't seen him since parish prison days," he lied, waiting to see if it was successful.

"Hmm, that's good to hear. You'd do well to keep him at a distance." Mouton sighed as if he didn't believe a word of it. "All friends ain't real friends, Hampton. As for Riley Dobbs, he's bound to upset the wrong applecart and take a nasty fall now that I'm moving on. Do yourself a favor and follow suit before you get trampled when it all comes tumbling down. And it will.

Good seeing you again. Real good." Hampton froze on the dirty sidewalk as Chief Mouton's chauffeur glided the dark-colored sedan into traffic. He'd told several lies to police when cornered. Mouton was the most exclusive of them all. Hampton didn't feel so good about deceiving the man who'd helped him when he needed it most. He'd have felt a million times worse knowing Mouton wasn't fooled once.

On the edge of Newberry in a rented hotel room, Father Ellis O'Leary sat on a bed with a telephone receiver pressed against his ear. He sipped from a half-pint of whiskey then smiled to himself before chuckling into the telephone. "You wouldn't believe the funeral service I was paid to officiate." He laughed so hard he almost spilled his drink. "Okay, here it is and I'm not kidding. I couldn't make this stuff up if I tried." He gulped another swig of whiskey before continuing. "While I was rearranging my rectory, there was a tap at the door. One of my parishioners was huffing and puffing about a dead man he said was stuck in an icehouse. Well, I didn't know what to say and didn't know what to do when he waved five dollars in my face to preside over the service. Heck, I thought maybe he wanted me to pray for the ice to melt so they could shake the poor soul loose and thaw him out." He heckled riotously then slapped his knee. "Yeah, I know. Simple folk, simple remedies," he asserted sarcastically. "Get the white man to pray everything away." O'Leary listened on the line for a minute then shook his head. "That's what I thought he meant, too, but no. He actually wanted me lead a band of musicians into the cemetery and then dance a jig on the way out. What do you mean, what'd I do? Heck, I took the five bucks up front then charged another ten after the show."

O'Leary remembered how the women danced and twirled on the second line as Louie's band trumpeted the occasion with lively renditions of old funeral standards. "Va-va-va-voom," he added. "They may as well been naked. I'm talking really hot stuff. Well, sure, I heard about this sort of stuff before leaving Jersey, but come on. You should have seen me trying to keep my pecker from raising my robe. You know there's nothing sweeter than tender dark meat. Good thing there's absolution for the holy, because there's a lot of temptation to go around. What? No, I use the same method as before. The godly pact angle still works, and you know me, Phil, I don't look to fix what isn't broken."

The young priest gulped another swig of liquor then laughed at a joke being told on the other end. "Hey, that reminds me. I'll share this, then let you go. There's this cutest little peach I wouldn't mind plucking myself. It could get risky, though. Her sister is around a lot. Boy oh boy, I want her so bad it's killing me. Just last week, she was bent over gathering her schoolbooks and looking ripe. I thought I'd blow the wad and soil my shorts. Yep, I remember that time you did lose your cool. What? No, that's not the way it went. As I recall, I'm up six to five, and I'm about to close in on that lucky number seven. She's thirteen and ready. Oh, yeah, I'll be gentle. Okay then, I'll keep in touch."

When the phone call ended, Father O'Leary was determined to deflower another of the girls entrusted to his spiritual leadership. The mere image of his white, pale skin pressed against the rich complexion of a child aroused him. He'd spoken to a friend of the cloth who also believed he'd be forgiven and exonerated of any wrongdoing if ever brought up on sexual misconduct charges. Although it had never been proven, Father O'Leary was sent south from New Jersey after several of the girls in his neighborhood began to gossip about his come-on lines that could have easily been explained as harmless, if challenged. After being banished to the swamp, as he put it when complaining of his new assignment a year ago, he'd made the best of a sticky situation. Now, relishing his post in Newberry, Louisiana, Father Ellis O'Leary couldn't wait to bag his next unsuspecting victim.

33

Deep Seeded

Pearl Lee lifted a load of linens from the industrial-size dryer in the converted washhouse. What was once a timber shack with highly flammable materials stored near open fires had undergone several renovations. After numerous blazes and subsequent repairs, brick and mortar was added along with electrical machinery. Unfortunately, modern appliances didn't do much to lessen the strain. Working tirelessly in the poorly ventilated building was still as much a living hell as it ever was. "Whew, if it don't cool off soon, we're gonna pop like a firecracker," joked Pearl Lee as she stepped out onto the back porch to open another box of starch. "Here, Magnolia, hold this so I can cut it open." She reached into an apron pocket for her pocketknife. She wiped beads of sweat from her forehead with the sleeve of her shirt. "Just when I thought it was gonna slow up, here come another five bags to put in. You'd think those Delacroix was sleeping on different sheets every night." Magnolia assumed Pearl Lee had caught wind of Trotter's baby-making escapades. His wife, Mary-Beth, wanted to be pregnant, quick and in a hurry. Fearing that Trotter might have had something to do with Odessa's child after all, she wanted to keep him at home and doting over her.

"Well, I expect you'd rinse yours, too, after scuffing them up like they're doing." She chuckled into silence. Pearl Lee twisted her face like it hurt.

"What you trying to say? Since I locked the back door on him, he's breaking bedsprings at home now?"

"Hey, if you don't know I can't tell you," Magnolia replied sharply. "Now put that knife away before you go getting ideas." Pearl Lee followed Magnolia's eyes to her hand, firmly clutching the pocketknife. "Plus ain't nothing you can do about that now. If a married woman wants to trap a man she's already got ball-and-chained, then who's to stop her? You've got a fair share of admirers to sort out as it is."

"These broke scabs who come every year for the harvest? Don't make me laugh. Most of them only got half their teeth, and the others have less money than they got sense." Pearl Lee snickered after Magnolia burst out laughing. "See, ain't too much to sort out now, is there?" She continued in her amusement until Magnolia's eyes gazed into the distance. "What?"

"Over there. Trotter and Hampton," she answered, a faint smile dancing on her lips. They watched the men strolling near the sugarcane fields, not like men who worked together for necessity's sake but rather as friends passing the time.

"That's one thing I never thought I'd see again, getting along like they did when they were rusty-butt boys without a care in the world between them. It would warm Daddy's heart. Mama's, too."

Magnolia nodded her agreement as they disappeared into the fields. "What you think they're talking about?"

"I don't know. Bet it ain't about us. Let's get this last batch in the wash so I can help Odessa. She's getting pretty good with needle and thread. You've taught her real good, Mag." Pearl Lee's warm smile was thanks enough for teaching her daughter a trade. While hiring out for patchwork didn't pay well, dimes and quarters helped out considerably.

Trotter stood just inside the field, damp ground aligned with countless rows of eight-foot stalks. He stared at the dark soil beneath his feet. Sugarcane needed rich earth to thrive. The buff-colored dirt that covered the rest of Newberry wasn't fit to grow a turnip. "Mary-Beth doesn't like it here anymore." Trotter sighed. "I can't say that I blame her, though. She's tried to get acclimated, but she's a city girl, Hampton." He squatted down to grab a handful of soil then rose with it in his palm. Hampton saw that Trotter was getting at something. He had been for days. It started out with small talk, then jokes, and now this one-on-one discussion he'd planned on including Hampton in eventually. "You know my mother's gonna drown in a bottle before long," he added, shaking his loose fist to let the soil fall from it. "Life ain't what it used to be, I'll tell you that."

"What else you trying to tell me?" Hampton asked curiously while his friend fished for unfamiliar words.

"It's hard as hell admitting failure. Old ways are dying off like a big herd of wounded elephants. I'm thinking of selling the plantation. I might not have a choice when you get right down to it. Slow crops, red rot disease, cane beetles, droughts, floods, freezes," he said sorrowfully, "and those are just the things I couldn't do anything about. God knows I've done my share of dumb stuff, blown money, wasted time. When I should have been taking things more seriously, learning how to raise cane, all I did was run to town every chance I got and raised cain." He turned toward Hampton, expecting a reaction. He was surprised to see Hampton's straight face looking back at him. "Ain't you gonna say something?"

"What I've learned is to stand back out of the way and listen to a man when he decides to search his soul. Prison camp taught me that." Hampton shoved his thumbs into the front belt loops of his jeans. "We've had our differences, Trotter. Times I hated you then loved you till it pained me deep. I respect what you've tried to do here. Most other farms sold out or blew away years ago. I don't think your daddy would care one bit if you had a mind to chase your own dreams instead of his."

Trotter looked at Hampton peculiarly then took off his cowboy hat to let his head breathe. "Damn, man, that's got to be the most pro-found thing I've ever heard. Prison camp teach you that, too?"

"Uh-uh. Watching life go by on this plantation gave me that one," Hampton assured him. "When is this decision gonna get made, or has it already been hatched?"

"Can't say either way. My heart is here, where both our families live and die. A big company wants to make this a central sugar refinery for farms up and down the Terrebonne all the way to Monroe. They want to knock down the cottages and bring in heavy machines that'll double the fields and rake in a lot of money." Trotter's eyes nearly watered. It was one thing to miss the mark as a businessman and another to turn his back on all he knew, including his friends. "You know I'll make a way for you and Pearl Lee if I sell out. Not any of this sharecropping stuff, either, I mean real jobs."

"Looks like a baby chick to me," Hampton teased. "You do right by yours and I'll do likewise by mine."

"Now that you mention it, I noticed you hightailing it away

from here at night. Does doing right by yours figure into that city cop who stopped me in town to ask about you? Captain Cunningham, I believe it was. I don't think he likes you much. Said something about you and him going back aways." Again, he waited for a reaction.

Hampton wondered how long Cunningham had been following him and why Chief Mouton waited before he showed up at Riley's. "Well, it's like you said, he don't like me much." Hampton had to take his warning from Mouton more seriously now. If Cunningham was next in line for his position, there was no guarantee he'd allow Riley's free enterprise to continue, although there'd be dividends for him on the back end, too. Hampton had to watch his back or take a chance on serving prison time again.

Farther on up the road, Joyce opened the church door and followed Janeen inside. "I'll take the schoolbooks while you get out the dust mop and aprons," she told her younger sister. Janeen agreed.

"Okay, but if we get some extra money, I want a pack of gum this time."

"Uh-uh. Mama says to bring home every cent," Joyce insisted. "Besides, the father might be low on money this week. It's not polite to beg."

Janeen skipped off toward the rear of the church. She opened the storage closet, unaware that she'd been observed from the moment she entered. Father O'Leary stepped out of his hiding place in the confessional when she bent over to screw the mop handle onto the duster. "Hiya, Janeen," he said casually, with a soft smile. His hands were clasped together in front, to conceal his erection.

"Father O'Leary, I didn't see you there," she answered with a startled expression. "I'm fine, sir." Janeen hurried back to work, gathering rags to clean the auditorium.

"Fine is good, real good."

Janeen, a shy thirteen-year-old, missed the sensual overtone in his voice. "Well, excuse me, Father, Joyce is waiting and she's raring to go." She dashed off to get started.

Raring to go, huh? he thought. *By all means, let's get her moving then.*

Father O'Leary sauntered to the head of the small auditorium, past fifteen pews on either side. Joyce was dusting the wooden benches nearest the exit while humming a spiritual hymn. "Now, that's a beautiful sound, Joyce," he said piously.

"Thank you, Father. My mama calls humming a joyful noise. Sorry, I didn't know I was loud enough to bother you." Joyce avoided making eye contact when the white man came closer. She continued to dust and wipe, comforted by the fact that her younger sister was nearby.

"Listen, Joyce, I don't think there's enough work for two very capable young ladies. I'd like to pay you for your efforts, though." He held out a worn dollar bill.

"Father O'Leary, I couldn't take that after only cleaning two pews. I'll finish up first, then me and Janeen can get on home."

"Well, I'd like to show how thankful I am for helping me to keep the Lord's house tidy week after week. Cleanliness is next to godliness." O'Leary was growing impatient. He wanted to order Joyce out of the building but that would raise her suspicions, so he took a more subversive route. "You know what else is next to godliness, giving from one's heart." Joyce's eyes floated up to rest on his. She didn't catch his meaning. "Here, take this and get yourselves some snacks from the corner store. The sugarcane harvest is late, so I expect money is scarce at home."

"Yes, sir, it is," she said, visually locked on the dollar he dangled like bait. "This is always the toughest time of the year."

O'Leary withheld his grin when Joyce untied her apron. "Go on then, and make sure you get something for Janeen, too," he said in a comforting manner. A sinister leer shrouded his face once alone with his prey. With no time to waste, the priest pretended to review Janeen's work. "Ah, very nice job. You're such a diligent young lady." Janeen wasn't exactly sure what that word meant, but it sounded like a compliment so she took it as one.

"Thank you, Father."

"Hey, I have an idea. Why don't you take a break?"

"But I only just started. I'd rather keep at it until my sister gets back, then she can help me finish."

"It'll be all right. I've been meaning to speak with you about a grave matter anyway. This is the perfect time to get it off my chest. Leave those rags and come with me." Janeen wasn't concerned in the least. Because of Hampton's standing in the community, no adult male had ever dared speak out of turn toward his children. Unknowingly, she followed Father O'Leary into his rectory like a lamb to the slaughter. "You believe in God, Janeen, I mean really believe?"

"Yes, Father," she asserted, her demeanor changing to fit the question.

"You believe in heaven? You want to go to heaven, my child?"

"Sure do, Father. Is this what you've been meaning to ask me about? I could have told you as much while I kept working."

"No, I'm afraid it goes much deeper. Much, much deeper. You're special, so special. Just as I have been chosen as the voice of the Almighty on earth, you've been chosen by God to be cleansed of your sins entirely like a heavenly angel. Not only yours but Joyce's and your parents' sins as well. Don't you want a guarantee into heaven's gates? Or would you be the kind to throw this divine blessing in the Lord's face?"

Her eyes widened frantically. "No, sir, I'd do anything to get my family inside those pearly gates."

That was the sign of commitment he'd been aiming for. "Now, there's only one way to make that happen and only if you're pure. You are a virgin, aren't you?"

She nodded again, only slower now. "Yes, sir."

"Splendid." Father O'Leary began to inch toward her in a methodical manner. "The only way to be sure of your passage into heaven is to come through me." He stroked her small face with his hands, kissed her on the cheek and then on the lips. "Remember, this is not only for you but for Joyce and your mama and papa, too. Most of all, don't disappoint God by saying no to salvation." Janeen's shoulders were as tense as her lips. Eventually, she gave in, praying silently that God would accept her obedience and one day deliver her entire family despite the wrongs they may have been guilty of.

Joyce giggled when she heard herself humming. She perused the candy shelf for her sister's favorite, a pack of coconut-flavored taffy. "A beautiful sound, he says. That's what I'll tell Mama when she starts in with her joyful noise business," Joyce heard herself say as if Janeen were there to listen. When she discovered the brand of candy her sister loved the most, she smiled. *I have to thank the father again. He could have made us both stay behind and clean instead of letting me leave*, she thought while pacing toward the store counter. When the clerk asked if there was anything else, it seemed as if a switch went off in Joyce's head. "Janeen!"

she screamed, bolting for the door. The soda pop bottles she carried smashed against the floor. Joyce ran at top speed. Her penny loafers slapped against the sidewalk. "Janeen! I'm coming, Janeen!"

The auditorium was empty when Joyce reached the church entrance. She balled her fists when she saw the cleaning products Janeen left behind resting on the floor. She tried to imagine Janeen and O'Leary having tea or sharing a sandwich, refusing to envision anything other than the priest on his holiest behavior. When Joyce peeked through the crack in the rectory door, the picture she saw caused her knees to buckle. Father O'Leary's pants were gathered around his ankles. He held Janeen down on a folding table with her legs spread apart while he pumped furiously between them. Her body jerked tensely. Tears ran from her eyes as she glared into space, ceasing to see, hear, or feel. Joyce placed both hands over her face, hiding from the shame of leaving her best friend and sibling to be tortured by that beast. She wrapped her arms around her shoulders and rocked continually until she overheard the same declaration O'Leary dumped on her after he pillaged her body the first time.

"If you ever tell a soul what we did, the pact with God will be broken. You tell, you and your family will be cast into hell forever. Don't disappoint God."

Joyce sat on the back pew when Janeen stumbled from the priest's private room. She was bent over, bewildered, and wounded. Joyce held their schoolbooks in her arms, urging Janeen to hurry outside. "Come on, Neen, I'll get you home. Come on. Come on. You've got to tell me what happened back there," she muttered, as if she hadn't seen and experienced it for herself.

"I can't tell," she answered quietly. "I won't tell. Just keep walking. I'm so cold."

Joyce peered up at the warm sun then gawked at Janeen strangely. "Don't worry. God is watching over us. He'll make it right. Trust in that." Joyce marched alongside her shoulder to shoulder, hoping Father O'Leary's promise of redemption was worth what they both had endured in the name of salvation.

34

Devils and Details

"You were in private with the father? Why so long?" asked Joyce, hoping her younger sister was fortified with the courage to speak of O'Leary's travesty against God, when she wasn't. As far as Joyce was concerned, Hampton could pummel the priest to death with his bare hands and still be assured a place in heaven. Unfortunately, she couldn't confide in Janeen regarding her special time with the father without risking damnation. "Janeen, whatever happened back there, you got to tell."

"Can't do nothing about it now," the girl whined, wiping tears from her face at the plantation gate. "You won't understand, anyway. I was chosen, I had to, and that's it."

Joyce's narrow chest heaved as she gasped for breath. She did understand, too well in fact, considering the mind games played at their expense.

"Hold up," Joyce said, pulling on Janeen's skinny arm. "We got to hide your underwear until time comes to burn the trash. Then we'll throw it on the burning heap." Janeen hadn't thought of that, but it made sense. She didn't want to guess what would happen if Magnolia found bloodstained panties and then questioned her about it.

"Okay, Joyce, okay," she acquiesced. "I don't feel so good. I want to lie down."

No one was home when the girls pushed through the front door. Joyce tossed their books on the floor and rushed Janeen into their area of the small house. She pulled the partition across the open area to hide their shameful activity in the event someone arrived unexpectedly. "Now, take those off and hand them to me," Joyce demanded.

"Uh-uh, you got to turn around first. I don't want you to see." Janeen held fast until Joyce did an about-face. Sliding her underwear down with the tips of her fingers, Janeen wished she didn't have to touch them at all. She wished none of it had happened. Magnolia preached living right and seeking an eternal home with Jesus, so her children took it to heart. "Here," she said, passing them timidly. "Hide them good, Joyce. I don't want to mess this up."

Joyce nodded assertively. Laundry day for her family wasn't for another week. She lifted up the corner of the mattress then shoved the wadded evidence underneath it, positive she'd retrieve it before Magnolia switched the linen. Thinking fast, she raced to the kitchen. Fiddling around for a clean bowl and dishrag, Joyce pushed back the painful cries begging to get out. She shook her head to ward them off while running water into the small metal bowl. *I should have been there*, she thought. *I should have protected Janeen. She didn't have to do this. She didn't.* Joyce returned quickly to find Janeen standing in the middle of the room staring into space like she had moments after her assault took place. "We've got to get you cleaned up," she said in a kind whisper. "I know you don't want to, but..." Janeen objected but eventually complied.

Joyce was careful not to scrape the bruises on her sister's thighs and pubic area. Suddenly reminded of swabbing her own misery and the tears associated with it, she handed the damp towel to Janeen and turned her face away again.

Reluctantly, the necessary steps were taken to obscure the truth. Janeen eased on fresh panties afterward, very slowly, as if every part of her hurt. She pulled her wrinkled dress over her knees, caressing the soft fabric with her fingertips. "I'm gonna lie down now," she sighed, balling up into the fetal position. "I'm so tired."

For several days, Janeen tried to go about business as usual, but her countenance was far different than before. She was noticeably quiet around the house, and her participation during class was nonexistent. Billy Earl teased her relentlessly when she didn't readily answer every question as if she'd written the book herself. He fired spitballs, made disgusting gestures with his hands, and even pulled on her ponytail during recess. Despite his efforts to antagonize Janeen, she refused to acknowledge his playful antics.

On Friday afternoon, Billy Earl opened his desktop for a sharpened pencil. He was surprised to discover a shiny new quarter on top of his pencil box. Excitement filled his eyes initially. Then they fell dim when he realized who had left it for him. Janeen tossed a pitiful glance over her left shoulder when she heard his desktop slam. The young boy's head hung low just as Janeen's had since losing the bet. As soon as classes adjourned for the weekend, Billy Earl scurried around the school yard to bait her. The hand he'd held the quarter tightly inside ached because he'd squeezed it the entire time, pretending it was the priest's neck gripped by his tiny fingers. "We got to get his cracker ass for this," he cursed viciously. "I got a bat and a hammer. Just tell me which one you want to swing and I'll smash him with the other."

"That's just foolishness, Bill' Earl. Besides, I never *told* you it happened," Janeen muttered cautiously, not wanting to break the pact. The boy opened his fist finally. His palm was marked, the skin broken in several places.

"You didn't have to say it. Guess I knew by the way you been acting lately." They walked for half a mile before the precocious youngster mustered up the nerve to speak on the anxiety buzzing through him. "So when was it that sneaky reverend hunched on you?"

Janeen stopped in the middle of the road. She sneered at him begrudgingly. "I don't want to talk about it. And you can't go around talking about it, either, not to anyone. You hear me, Bill' Earl? You do and I'll never speak to you again." She pointed her thin finger so close to the boy's nose, it caused his eyes to cross.

"All right! Shoot, I won't tell, but I should have showed you how to stomp on his nuts when he came at you," he said. Billy Earl kicked a can with his angry shoe heel. "See, next time—"

"There won't be any next time!" she yelled spitefully. Janeen snatched a handful of the boy's shirt, shaking him mightily. Billy Earl was shocked by her rage. His eyes flew opened wider.

"I believe you! I believe you! Now let me go. Wasn't me who did you dirty," he grunted. He glared angrily as Janeen loosened her grip. "I believe you." He did believe her and subsequently vowed never to tell a soul, even if they offered to bribe him with a whole pack of cigarettes.

Late Saturday night, Magnolia was awakened by a nightmare. It was Janeen's. The girl tussled with the covers, huffing for air but blocked by Joyce's hand. "You got to hush, Janeen. Please... just hush."

Magnolia pulled back on the bedsheet then stepped into the girls' room. She was appalled. Joyce struggled to cover her sister's mouth with both hands. "Stop that!" Magnolia spat. "What the devil is going on in here?" She wrestled Joyce's hands away then pushed her aside. "Janeen! Janeen! Wake up, darling." Magnolia shook her child violently when she didn't respond. "What'd you do to her, Joyce? What did you do?"

"Nothing, Mama. I was just trying to keep her quiet so as not to wake you," she said, speaking in partial truths. Joyce leaned in when it appeared Janeen was regaining consciousness. She was afraid of what would follow from her sister's bad dream and pop out of her mouth unwittingly. "Neen, it's me *and Mama*!" she shouted.

Magnolia stared at Joyce's strange behavior, failing to make heads or tails of it. "Get back, Joyce. Go on and rustle up a damp towel. This girl is cold as ice." She held Janeen close to her chest, attempting to transfer heat from her body to her daughter's. "Hurry up, Joyce!" Magnolia searched for signs of fever but found none. As a precaution, she gave Janeen two aspirins and a glass of milk. "That's better, baby, that's better. It was just a terrible dream," she cooed, "just an ugly old dream chasing you." Magnolia caught a glimpse of Joyce, biting on her bottom lip and wincing at Janeen.

"Mama's right," she said finally. "Just a dream." Having been raped by a grown man sworn to be her spiritual leader was anything but. It was as real as the bond shared by the Bynotes. Joyce understood fully then that their secret must be guarded from exposure. All hell would break loose if anyone told.

Hampton came home an hour later. He undressed, placed his car keys on the worn bureau, then climbed into bed. "You're late again," Magnolia said. Her words were tender and void of resentment.

"Why you wide awake?"

"Janeen had a rough go with a nightmare. I should have expected it. Something's going on with her. She's been daydreaming a lot, and I can't get her to eat much of nothing."

"She won't eat?" he asked, falling off to sleep.

"She says she's not hungry."

"Wait till she gets hungry enough, she'll put on the feed bag then."

Magnolia, knowing it was something more than a simple loss of appetite, smiled at his uncomplicated response. She was troubled and needed to get it off her back with a mother-to-daughter discussion. Magnolia almost chuckled at Hampton's naïveté about young girls. The scuffs she felt on his knuckles chased the laughter from her chest. "Honey? Tell me the truth about something. The truth," she insisted. "Did you hurt anybody tonight?"

Hampton thought before answering. His words were cool and firm. "Not nobody who didn't deserve it." Magnolia didn't get another wink of sleep that night. Her daughters were keeping secrets for the first time that she knew of, and her husband seemed determined to get himself into some severe trouble. If only he'd found honest work in New Orleans like she'd suggested a hundred times. Hampton had inquired about several jobs. Because of his arrest record, doors were slammed in his face time and time again. Through a few old connections, he was offered a job on the city's sanitation crew. The pay was awful and duties considerably worse. Conversely, dumping other people's trash didn't appeal to a man who had exceeding amounts of his own garbage to dispose of.

During the next church service, Magnolia listened attentively to Father O'Leary's sermon. He preached a soul-stirring message of salvation, his third in the same month. Getting into heaven, walking streets paved with gold, and eternal life without a care to call her own meant the world to Magnolia, since life on earth offered difficult decisions on a daily basis and less than enough money to go around. Exhausted from working two jobs, Hampton fought to stay awake as usual. Magnolia felt sorry for him so she let him nod off without her customary jabs in his ribs. Church was the one place she thought God overlooked a man's struggles, as long as he tried to overcome them. She firmly believed that Hampton would someday gain lawful employment then stay awake long enough to take something from the worship service other than a chance to rest his eyes.

Bracketed between Magnolia and Hampton, Joyce and Janeen sat calmly in identical yellow sundresses handmade by their mother. The girls clasped their hands together tightly while listening to the hypocritical priest's fiery anecdotes concerning the Almighty's wrath on the ungodly and their place in the land or torment where hell's hounds nipped at burning flesh throughout everlasting ages. Joyce was glad when the sermon concluded. Janeen's fingernails were dug into her flesh the entire time.

Afterward, Father O'Leary instructed the altar boys to set up the Communion table so he could bless the congregation. Suddenly, the back door of the church flew open and slammed loudly against the wall. Several people jumped, unnerved by the startling boom. Janeen was one of them. Her eyes widened when a dark-skinned mountain of a woman stomped through the doorway like a 240-pound rhino cutting a path through the Kalahari.

The woman's pale-colored housedress was thin and worn. It waved back and forth as her stride lengthened. She approached the pulpit with one fist balled like a meaty ham and a girl child dressed in faded jeans and a dirty striped pullover in tow. The small girl looked to be around ten years old. With long pigtails cascading from her head, she shared her mother's sturdy build.

There was also an unmistakable resemblance although she kept her head lowered in a childish, remorseful manner.

Father O'Leary couldn't help but stammer when the woman took her stand a few feet from the pulpit. Despite her untimely interruption, the priest continued with the Communion service he'd initiated as if nothing out of the ordinary had occurred. He held the golden wine chalice steady as he peered past her, toward the congregation. Everyone looked on with stark anticipation.

"The shame you should feel right now ain't nothin' compared to the devil I'm gonna beat outta you for doing harm to my Billie Jean!" shouted the angry woman. "Look at her! Take a good look, 'cause where you's going, ain't nothin' this sweet gonna be 'round you for miles! You stole my baby from me. You took her innocence like it was nothin' and threw it away. As the Lawd is my witness, He saw for Hisself what you did!"

The young girl peeked at Father O'Leary from behind her mother's broad hip. His hands were shaking now. Subtle murmurs spread throughout the congregation. "All right, Sister Ora," he stuttered.

"Uh-uh, I ain't no sister of your'n, and you damn sure ain't no father of mine," she spat. Several members of the audience groaned at her utter disrespect. Hampton was wide awake then. He shot a questioning glance at Magnolia. She held his arm tightly. Janeen closed her eyes. Joyce was amazed and grinning impishly.

"You—you just can't come into the Lord's house and disrupt His service like this," O'Leary warned, pointing a judgmental finger at her. "Uh, this—this isn't the place to voice any concerns you might have about..." he stuttered nervously. "I'll be happy to meet with you later to discuss this in my office." He tried to put the woman at ease but his words didn't come out the way he'd hoped. She turned them on him immediately.

"What you mean, this ain't the place? This here is where you took her womanhood! Now the doctor says her womb is spoiled. No babies, not ever!"

Father O'Leary's hands trembled uncontrollably then. Wine began dancing over the chalice rim. Red liquid dripped from the embroidered cuffs of his brightly colored robe. Still the priest refused to lower the goblet. Faced with the demons he'd spawned, he turned ghostly white when his accuser forced her child down onto her knees then did likewise herself.

"Lawd Jesus, send Your angels down on this here earth and smite the devil standin' befo' me right now. He done ruined my baby girl, and I swear befo' all these people that I'll kill him myself if'n You don't. I'm prayin' that You release the arcangel to strike him down! Strike him down! Ohhh... make him bear the brunt of his unpardonable sins against me and mines. *Hemessa hemessa muertes abonimi! Abomini!*"

When Janeen's eyelids fluttered opened, she saw O'Leary's face. He was terrified, the same way she had been while trapped beneath his clutches. The large woman's unbridled emotion and panicked cries of innocence lost traveled through Janeen, yielding a sense of calm and resolution. All the pain she felt inside vanished. Father O'Leary, silenced by the awesome spectacle, collapsed on a bench behind the wooden table as five men from the congregation gathered the distraught woman from the floor. They wrestled her out the back door, kicking and screaming hysterically about vengeance being the Lord's. Her daughter, Billie Jean, followed behind them quietly with her head solemnly bowed, refusing to exhibit her aching heart or the tears resulting from breaking the pact she believed would doom her to hell forever.

Two factions developed after the church service ended abruptly, those who wanted the priest investigated and others who wouldn't allow themselves to consider the charges made. Magnolia sided with the latter. She wanted, needed, to believe in the sanctity of religion and all that Father O'Leary stood for. Hampton had seen his share of men, even good men, overcome by devils within to do unspeakable things. By the time he arrived home, his decision was sure. "I don't care what the 'vestigation turns up. Joyce nor Janeen won't be doing no more cleaning in that church unless you go along with 'em."

"Don't tell me you bought into what Ora Kremley put on the father? It don't make no sense that a fine preacher like him would have anything to do with hurting a little girl."

"Seems the older I get, the less things tend to add up all around," argued Hampton. "I done spoke on it, and that's that."

Magnolia placed her hands on her hips in opposition. "So what I think doesn't matter?"

Hampton took note of his daughters' interest in the adult conversation. "I done spoke on it, Magnolia," was his stern reply, "and I'm hungry for my supper." Both girls hoped their mother would let it go at that. There was no swaying Hampton after his mind was made up. For once they applauded his stubbornness.

Wisely, Magnolia neglected to challenge her husband's decision, but it didn't stop her from fuming over it.

35

Audacity of Pope

Magnolia wrestled with Hampton's decision regarding the girls working at the church. Two days later, she brought it up when Pearl Lee closed down the washhouse. "You got any red beans to spare?" she asked Pearl Lee. "I have some rice and a leg of sausage. We can make something out of it until Hampton gets home."

"Yeah, let me get this lock on and we'll see what's what. Odessa's starting to eat like a grown man. She don't do nothing but lay around the house unless I make her pitch in to help. It's like the life is being sucked out of her day by day." Pearl Lee secured the latch then pulled the tattered scarf off her head. "I thought Hampton was picking up work in Nawlins. Can't remember the last time I seen him after sundown."

Magnolia lowered her head wearily. "He's out a lot and I can't say exactly what he's doing. He's laid some extra cash on me but that's about it. I was counting on the change Father O'Leary gives the girls for cleaning out the church, but after Ora Kremley went and busted in with that godforsaken scene, Hampton won't let neither of them near it."

"I haven't been in the mood for spirituals lately, but I heard about it. Whew, wished I'd have dragged my butt out of bed for that one." Pearl Lee smiled, thinking about the mayhem she'd missed until a thought came to mind and flipped that grin of hers. "It's a shame what happened to Ora. She was headstrong but she didn't deserve that."

"Deserve what? You said Ora *was* headstrong." Magnolia's puzzled expression concerned her sister-in-law.

"Oh, you haven't heard. They found her yesterday, hanging in old man Roulade's smokehouse like a pissed-off side of beef."

Magnolia's jaw dropped. "What? Dead?"

"Deader than a doornail. They said the rope near about took her head off because she was so heavy. Three men had to cut her down. Damn shame it was. Let's see if I can scrounge up those beans."

News of the distraught woman's death had a grave effect on Magnolia when Pearl Lee seemed to chalk it up as a trivial fact. Mere days ago, Ora Kremley was a brooding and vibrant soul trying to right a wrong, whether in her own mind or not. Magnolia wasn't sure either way. However, there was no doubting that she was gone. Questions zigzagged through Magnolia's head all afternoon. None of it made sense to her. Accusations of a rogue priest molesting a child and a healthy woman taking her own life, if that was the case, were too much to reason with, so she pushed them into the recesses of her mind. Contemplating Ora's grief-stricken suicide was bad enough. Allowing herself to believe it could have been the result of murder made Magnolia feel sick. "On second thought, Pearl Lee, I'll make do with what's in the pantry. Feel free to come and dip in if you like."

Pearl Lee wrinkled her nose over Magnolia's shift in demeanor. "Okay. Was it something I said?"

"Don't be silly. I'm just tired is all, just tired." Once she was alone, Magnolia let all of the odd occurrences play a mean game of hopscotch in her head until it rang like a bell. Hampton was hardly at home, and when he was, he wasn't often awake for long. Janeen couldn't seem to hold down a meal when she did attempt to eat anything. Joyce doted on her sister as if she were an infant, not allowing her to do a thing for herself. Ora's hanging meant that something sent death after her. The sugarcane crop had been shopped and hauled to the mill, and for the first time since she could remember there was no harvest party to commemorate it. It was as if the earth had tilted on its axis, throwing everything off-kilter that she previously knew to be true. *What in the world is going on?* she thought, anxiously pacing the floor. *If it's the devil's hand, I'll slap it away from my family as best I can. As best I can.*

Hampton tossed a honey-bun wrapper out the window when he pulled his car against the curb in front a modest home in the ninth ward. Riley offered to pay a premium if he managed to a squeeze a collection out of a hard-to-catch debtor who had successfully eluded his other retrievers. When he stepped out of his car, Hampton kept thinking about Trotter's decision to sell the plantation. He peered up and down the street as most of the working-class black families settled in for the evening. Before he knocked on the door, a little boy opened it and rolled a scooter out onto the porch. Hampton hoped there was still a chance he'd made a mistake about the address. Strong-arming a man in front of his son wasn't part of the deal. "Hey, there," he said, smiling politely, "is your daddy home?" The boy nodded then pushed past him. Hampton watched the scooter glide down the sidewalk.

"Bryan, I done told you to close that door," a man's voice yelled from inside. Hampton slipped on a set of brass knuckles and stood to the right side of the door frame when the voice drew nearer. "Bryan!"

Hampton threw his forearm against the door when someone attempted to close it. "Agggh," he charged, barreling on top of the man inside the house. "Riley Dobbs wants his money, punk!" Hampton grunted after he'd scraped his knee on an impressive glass coffee table. The chubby black man gawked at the metal contraption gripped in Hampton's fist. He took two short steps back then darted through a sliding glass door. "Hey, don't you run from me!" Hampton hobbled after him, wincing and cussing through the sliding door.

"Run, Willie! Run!" a woman's voice screeched from an upstairs window as he dashed through the backyard and over a neighbor's fence.

Man, I hate it when they run, Hampton thought, giving chase. "Get back here, fool!" he scolded. He was surprised how agile the squatly built man was as he leapt over the third fence in a row. *That fool is really moving. No wonder ain't nobody caught him yet*. Hampton continued his pursuit. He laughed inside when the stubby fellow ripped his pants while dodging a German shepherd four houses down the block. "That's what yo' ass gets." Suddenly, Hampton's prey slowed to a complete stop. He bent over, fell onto his knees, then coughed and sputtered. "Don't play that heart attack game with me, pal. I done seen that one before." When Hampton reached him, the man was still convulsing in a pool of vomit. "Man, that's just nasty," he scoffed. "You should've just paid up."

"You—you wouldn't have caught up to me if'n I hadn't just ate," he argued pitifully.

Standing over him, Hampton chuckled. "Okay, I'll give you that, but I'll take what you owe Riley, with interest." The man upchucked again, shaking his head. "Ahhhg! Is that chitlins? Ah, damn. That is chitlins. Come on, man, and get up from there before you make me sick."

"What happened, Papa?" the man's son asked from his speedy scooter. He looked on, casting an evil eye on Hampton.

"Nothing, Bry, Papa just got a little dizzy, and my friend here is gonna make sure I get home all right." He glanced at his assailant with sad, trusting eyes. "Ain't that so, Hampton?"

Staring at the stumpy man peculiarly, Hampton's mouth opened wide. It was the first time he'd actually put a face with the name Riley Dobbs sent him after. "Willie. *Willie* Pope?"

"In all my glory. You mind giving me a hand up?" With his assailant's help, Willie climbed to his feet. He wiped his mouth with the back of his hand then took off running again, only much slower now. Hampton reared back and laughed. He had to respect Willie's gall although he beat the man to his back door. Willie wasn't done; he sneaked in the front.

The lady of the house refused to let him enter their neatly furnished house smelling like a pigpen. Hampton laughed all over again when the poor man's desperate rants went unanswered. Dressed in tight polyester slacks and a halter top meant to be worn by a smaller woman, she pushed him out the sliding glass door then shook her head insistently.

"Uh-uh, you stink!" she sneered. "Get Hampton to wash you off first."

Hampton tilted his head to get a better look at her. "Marie Joliet?" he said, as if his yesterdays had played a ridiculous joke on him. His childhood friend and his old flame were married with a child and an extremely impressive home.

"That's Marie Joliet Pope," Willie snarled, both hands parked on his knees. He cut his eyes at Hampton shrewdly then he glared at Marie, who was spending an inordinate amount of time looking over Riley's dangerous thug. "Go on, woman. Put some food on for my friend and cover yourself up. Can't you see we got company?" Marie backed away, stealing another glance at Hampton. Willie turned on the water spigot then handed the hose to Hampton. "Well, you heard her. Don't just stand there. The least you could do is rinse me off."

Considering how strange this business call had gone thus far, Hampton agreed to squirt the hose at him. "How'd you get yourself into this?"

"What, me and Marie? You the one who introduced us. Took me two years to hook her and been reeling her in ever since."

"Nah, man, I mean the debt to Riley Dobbs. He's a bone breaker, Willie."

"Ooh, that's cold," he said, fighting off the frigid water spouting from the hose. "I heard you was running with Dobbs 'nem and that you was his main head thump'." Willie dabbed his clothes with a towel Marie had tossed outside. "Honestly, I was hoping they'd send you. Maybe I could talk my way into some more time to pay up." His cut his eyes at Hampton again, contemplating yet another escape route.

"Not if you run off again. Look, I can't do nothing about the money you owe. Maybe if you stop gambling, I can work something out." Hampton laid the water hose aside to keep his hands free.

"Naw, you got it all wrong. I don't play the horses, cards, or shoot dice. Marie is the reason I'm up to my eyeballs in hock. Everything that woman sees, she wants. Dinettes, doodads, trinkets, jewels, you name it. You tried to warn me but I didn't listen. What can I say?"

"You got me in a predicament, Willie."

"What the hell do you think I'm in?"

"Damn you."

"Does that mean you're letting me go? I mean, you could tell him I outlasted you. You see I still got some moves."

Hampton stroked his chin to draw on an answer. "Yeah, but then he'd offer my premium to somebody else, somebody who wouldn't mind busting up all that nice stuff Marie talked you into getting for her. Besides, my family's got to eat, too."

Willie sat down on a metal chair. The cuffs of his pants dripped. "I got a big contract with the city about to come through. Ask Dobbs if he can give me a week. I'll make good on it, all of it."

"You gon' get your hands on eight hundred dollars? All at once?" Hampton was interested. Very interested.

"Maybe, you don't know. But they's about to build this big-ass football stadium. They say it's gonna be the biggest in the world."

"Keep talking."

"Well, I'm into construction and in good with some of the white boys on the planning commission. Lots of black families are getting thrown out onto the streets over this coliseum. Oh, yeah, there's been protests and picketing by folks who's getting the boot."

"They can do that, make folk leave their own homes?"

"Been doin' it for months already, one block at a time. They even got a fancy name for it, something called urban renewal."

Hampton smirked at the idea of displacing thousands of working-class citizens in order for fat cats to stuff their pockets. "Wow, that don't sound no kinda right. How'd you get in on it?"

"Told you, that commission they put over the thing says they got to have so many black folk making a little money on it, too. Those white pals of mine told me how to bid and what to do with the paperwork. Just like that, I'm in like Flynn."

"Damned if you ain't. Is it too late for me to get in on it?" Hampton asked, merely as an afterthought.

Willie leaned back in the chair like a big-time businessman. "You know, that's not a bad idea. You're a hard worker, no doubtin' that. There will be some heavy liftin' and haulin' off once they blast a great big hole to lay the foundation. Seein' as how you did some time in the parish work camp, you know your way around blastin' caps."

"And I've busted my share of rocks while I was at it, too," Hampton asserted jokingly. He could see the wheels turning in Willie's head. "Come on, Willie, Trotter Delacroix is liable to sell the plantation in a month or so anyway, and my wife's been after me to go legit. This could be my ship coming in right alongside of yours."

"It is kinda your fault I'm in this jam with Dobbs. It might give me the chance to get back at you some. Yeah, I'ma work your ass like a Hebrew slave."

Hampton's chest swelled. "You mean I got the job?"

"You gonna let me slide on the beatin' you came to give me?"

"Man, you ain't got to worry about nothing. I'll fix it with Riley Dobbs. You'll get the space you need. Just don't forget me when time comes to start handing out picks and shovels. Ahh, man, I really need this." He shook Willie's hand until it was wrestled away from him. "I don't know what to say."

"How about good-bye," Willie grunted, waving him off like a bothersome fly.

"I owe you, Willie Pope. I owe you, man. I owe you."

Willie pushed out a hearty sigh of relief. “Keep Dobbs’s goons off my ass and call it even.” Hampton eased down the street nice and slow. He was stuffed full of pride. Magnolia’s prayers were answered, and it felt so good making the best out of a bad debt.

36

Hell-bound Bang

Magnolia couldn't stop thinking about Ora Kremley and her child's fate. Seeing Billie Jean's frightened face exhibiting the humiliation Father O'Leary inflicted cast an indelible shadow over her. Troubled, Magnolia was forced to concede that something had happened. There was no conceivable rationale for that kind of untoward behavior. A rapist priest was simply unthinkable previous to the incident at the church. Now it stared her in the face. Magnolia could hardly stomach the sight of it.

To busy herself, she began to scrub her floors until her hands ached. Despite how diligently she scoured, images of debauchery on the lowest scale continued to appear. Too upset to go on, she kicked the wash bucket aside and entered her daughters' room. Magnolia decided to wash all the clothes Father O'Leary may have touched. She intended on doing the same to the girls when they arrived home from a school pageant planning session. Hurling dresses and pants onto the damp floor, she felt her chest tighten. She had unknowingly sent her pride and joy into the devil's den. Magnolia trembled at the thought of allowing a child molester unfettered access to her children. Fearing what might have happened made her flesh crawl. Realizing how easily it could have been her busting into that church and lashing out with hateful and painstaking rants sent a chill down her spine. *How could I?* Magnolia groaned. *How could I have left that man alone with my babies, breathe on them, and God knows what else he wanted to do with them?* Magnolia found herself raving like a lunatic, dripping with animosity. *Hampton even knew better than to trust him. How could I have been so blind? Lawd, please help me if he laid a hand on my children.* After every stitch of the girls' clothing lay sprawled on the middle of the floor, she grabbed at the bedsheets, violently yanking them from the worn, soft mattress. "I got to get this clean," she spat. "All of it. All of it!" A bundle of frayed nerves, Magnolia fell to her knees. Balled in her fist were the panties Joyce had hidden on Janeen's behalf. Breathless and seething, Magnolia peered around the cottage oddly. She felt woozy, dazed. She shook her head vigorously to snap out of it.

Suddenly, she gazed at the wad of cotton trapped in her hand. She squinted at the dried bloodstains while loosening her grasp. A stickler for cleanliness, Magnolia instructed her daughters to manage their underwear particularly well during their menstruations. Without fail, any and all accidents were handled immediately by rinsing undergarments with cold water. There was only one explanation as far as Magnolia could see. Joyce had been fooling around with boys and keeping secret about it. What else had gotten past Magnolia, she wondered, and how many lies were used to cover them up? It was difficult to imagine Joyce as a sexually active teenager, but then she'd been wrong about Father O'Leary. Magnolia climbed to her feet feeling regretful, the poorest judge of character, a failure to her children.

Fifteen minutes passed before Magnolia heard voices

approaching the front door. Joyce chatted endlessly. She was obviously very excited about something, just what Magnolia couldn't tell exactly. Regardless, all of that giddy exuberance was about to run headlong into the train wreck that would become their lives. "And then, David Baxter says, 'Oh Joyce, I'd love to be your escort if you'll let me,'" Joyce chided from the front porch. "I thought I was going to die right there on the gymnasium floor. You know, I always did think he was the cutest of all his friends." She turned the doorknob, overflowing with glee. "He's the smartest boy in the class, too. Just like I—" she started to say until her eyes told her mouth to close in a big hurry. The house was ransacked, dresser drawers were open, their belongings were piled high as if trampled on. "Mama?" Joyce called out. Janeen was afraid to speak.

Magnolia sauntered out of her bedroom, calm as a gentle breeze, with the incriminating panties dangling from her fingers. She locked eyes with Joyce as if she'd come in without her younger sister. "Joyce, you'd want to explain this, and I mean right now."

"Mama, we—" uttered Janeen.

"We nothing," Magnolia interrupted. "This is between me and her. You should run on over to Pearl Lee's and see if you can help with Eric." When Janeen didn't move quickly enough to satisfy her mother, Magnolia shot a stinging glare her way. In the blink of an eye, the youngest daughter was gone. She puttered on the porch nervously. Janeen was scared what might happen to Joyce for something she'd done so she hung by the front window. She squatted down and peeked through the curtains to watch her best friend in time of crisis.

Magnolia insisted that Joyce come right out with it. Joyce chewed on her bottom lip while gathering herself. "Well, I don't, I mean, I can't say anything about it, Mama. I promised I wouldn't."

"Promised who?" Magnolia barked, with her temper rising.

"Mama, I can't say that, either," Joyce whined defensively. Magnolia charged with her hand raised. "I'm sorry, Mama. I'm real sorry." She dodged her mother's right hand but neglected to clear Magnolia's backhand. Joyce crumbled onto the floor, wincing apologies. "Please believe me. I promised not to say." Magnolia came at Joyce again, this time with her hands balled mightily. Janeen skirted through the door then threw her frail body on top of Joyce's to shield her.

"She didn't do nothing, Mama!" Janeen cried. "Don't hurt her!"

"Move back, girl, so I can get to the bottom of this." Magnolia snatched Janeen by the heels and jerked until she let go of Joyce's dress. She went after Joyce for a third time. "Is it that David Baxter you protecting?" Whack! "I didn't raise you to be no tramp!" Whack, whack! "I'll teach you to go sneaking around boys and then lying to my face about it!"

"Stop, Mama! Stop!" Janeen wailed. "She's not lying."

Magnolia was relentless. Even though Joyce huddled against the floorboards as best she could, furious licks grazed off her shoulders and head. "Shut up, Janeen. Stay out of it."

Janeen gulped. "I wish I could, but those aren't Joyce's panties, they're mine." Magnolia froze when Joyce uncovered her eyes. The way she pleaded silently with Janeen substantiated that the girls were telling the truth. Magnolia was speechless for the longest time. "I had to, Mama. I had to," Janeen admittedly quietly.

"Don't blame her, she had no choice," Joyce cosigned.

"You, Janeen?" Magnolia whispered pensively. "No, baby, no. When? Who?"

A foul hush settled into the room. No one was prepared to venture further into the abyss that had engulfed them. Pearl

Lee appeared in the doorway, behind Odessa. They'd heard the screams and what transpired subsequently. "It was Eric's daddy," Odessa submitted. "Wasn't it, Janeen?" Her face was taut and shrouded with an unyielding resolve. "It happened in his room." Janeen shook her head slowly, but she couldn't form the words to deny it. Magnolia flopped onto her behind when it occurred to her who had been with Odessa.

"That bastard priest?" Pearl Lee hissed. "You knew that bastard was messing 'round with other girls, Odessa, and didn't warn us about him?" Pearl Lee struck her daughter across the face. Venom collected in the corners of her mouth. "You let this happen to your cousin, and who knows how many others? Shame on you, Odessa. Shame."

Swelling closed Odessa's left eye. Still she gathered the strength to explain how Father O'Leary convinced her to obey his will. Pearl Lee couldn't believe anyone would have been so gullible. Magnolia fully understood. Their daughters were raised to believe in God's word and in the men who did His bidding. She couldn't have known what would become of their exceeding obedience. Father O'Leary and his contemporaries counted on it.

Magnolia was beside herself. She sent everyone to Pearl Lee's, Janeen with fear and trembling, Joyce with misguided bruises, and Odessa with her pitiful omission. Magnolia wandered from the village on foot, without as much as a single word as to where she was headed or when to expect her return.

More than two miles down the road, Magnolia trod past the general store that also served as the local bus station. She saw Billie Jean being ushered onto the Greyhound bound for Mississippi with a child-size suitcase tucked securely under her arm. Magnolia was drawn to the small child's haunting expression.

She hadn't ever seen anyone look so lost and alone. *May the Lawd be with you*, she thought, trudging along the dusty pathway dressed in faded jeans, Hampton's navy-colored sweatshirt, and run-down house shoes.

Magnolia shook on the church door latch, unclear about what she'd do if it were unlocked or what she'd say if someone happened to show up while she waited. Father O'Leary was the last person she anticipated to see packing his personal items into a station wagon at the rear of the building.

"Father?" she uttered. "I need to speak with you."

He flinched when he realized she was standing just behind his car. "Can't talk now, Magnolia," he grunted dismissively. "I've got to be in Mobile by tomorrow."

"I don't think you're gonna make it," she said, fidgeting with her hands. "See, you've got a lot of people to answer to. Me being one of them."

"Sorry, but I don't have the time." He brushed sweat from his face with a white handkerchief then went back to loading his car with boxes.

"You raped my daughter. You ought to at least render me the respect of hearing me out." Despite her insistence, he continued on with business as usual. "I said you raped my child, *Mistah* O'Leary."

"Joyce is a liar if she told you that's what happened."

Magnolia nearly stumbled then. *Joyce, too*, she thought miserably.

"The jezebels of this parish have already cost me my post and a stern, undeserved warning. Now I've been reassigned because of their nasty insinuations."

"The diocese knew what you've done and all you got was a warning. Uh-uh, that ain't hardly enough for what you did."

"Sorry, but you're wasting my time. I've paid my penance and there's nothing you or your brazen brats can say or do about it." The priest hastily pushed past Magnolia to retrieve the last boxes stacked inside.

"That's where you're wrong," Magnolia told him as she blocked the door.

Sneering, Father O'Leary attempted to force his way by her with a box of sermon notes. "What do you think you're doing?"

Magnolia pulled a black revolver from underneath her sweatshirt. "Making you pay for the sins you committed." She wielded the gun toward him. O'Leary tripped over a box as he fled. Magnolia inched closer.

"This is all a big mistake," he whimpered pathetically. "This—this is the Lord's house."

"Good, then He can watch."

"Don't do this," he begged. His mouth was frothy with desperation as tears ran from his eyes. "Please stop!"

"Is that what all of the girls said when you had your way with them? Is that what Odessa cried before you put that baby in her stomach?"

"No. No. I'm not even supposed to be here."

Magnolia lowered the gun barrel into his mouth then cocked the hammer. "That's why I'm sending you straight to hell."

Bang!

37

Ransacked Rendezvous

Hampton leapt from the driver's side of his rattletrap, an ancient Buick with three bald tires. Humming all the way to his front door, he slapped his thigh eagerly thinking how life had finally thrown a fastball he could hit. Willie Pope's job offer couldn't have come at a better time. With Chief Mouton stepping down and Cunningham, that stooge of his, nosing around about Hampton's affairs, it was going to be a pleasure breaking the good news to Magnolia. She would be so happy to hear their luck had turned for the better, which was long overdue. Before turning the doorknob, Hampton had it all figured out. It wouldn't take two seconds to discover just how wrong he was, about everything.

Clothes were balled up in a jumbled pile in the corner. Dresser drawers had been pulled out and overturned on the floor. Hampton's smile vanished when his eyes found his daughters huddled together on the divan. They were unmistakably scared. Of what, Hampton couldn't have guessed. His eyes wandered throughout the shack, searching for his wife. After he was sure she wasn't there, he studied the two frightened girls, who'd been crying.

"What's all this?" he asked softly. "Where's your ma?" Neither of the girls answered. Instead their eyes fell to the floor as if ordered to do so. "So nobody's gonna say, huh?" Before they mustered an explanation, Pearl Lee came barreling through the door.

"Hamp, you gotta come quick!" she gasped. Her dreadful expression sent a cold chill through him.

"Magnolia?" he uttered, concerned she'd been hurt.

Pearl Lee nodded timidly. "She needs you now."

"Stay here," he demanded of the girls, with a solemn glare. There was no doubting they had some idea what had happened to her, hence the quiet tearstained faces and the visible bruises on Joyce's forehead and neck. There were so many questions that no one appeared willing to address. Hampton took a deep breath after following his sister's steps to her door. He was afraid of what he might find on the other side.

"It's gonna be all right now," Pearl Lee whispered when she pushed it opened. "I got Hampton with me. It's gonna be all right."

Magnolia's face was vastly different from what he anticipated. There wasn't a scratch on it. Also void of expression whatsoever, she stood in the center of Pearl Lee's front room listless and dazed. A quick glance at Odessa's swollen black eye confused him all the more. Assured that he could hash out any disagreement Odessa had with his children or the effect it may have had on his wife, Hampton glided toward Magnolia with his arms outstretched. "Heyyy, don't fret none. Girls will be girls, but they family," he said, wrapping his arms around her shoulders. "We'll straighten it out, baby. Ain't nothing we can't fix," he added as something poked him. Hampton peered down at her oversize sweatshirt. Magnolia flinched as he lifted it to take a peek underneath. The sight of his revolver tucked in the waistband of her pants floored him. Hampton pursed his lips sorrowfully then eased the weapon out. He held it to his nose and sniffed the barrel to surmise if it had been fired recently. The smell of gunpowder nearly flattened him.

"She had to, Hampton," Pearl Lee insisted. "Weren't no way around it."

Trying to comprehend Magnolia putting a gun on someone was difficult enough; how she managed the nerve to pull the trigger was unfathomable. Hampton wanted to know the hows and whys, but there was one issue more pressing. "Who was it?" he said, holding the gun by his side.

Magnolia's gaze went through him as she parted her dry lips to speak. "Father O'Leary."

"The father?" he repeated. "You killed him?" She turned her eyes on Hampton, then sneered the way he had after being asked about roughing up Riley Dobbs's delinquent clients.

"Yeah, he wasn't nobody who didn't deserve it."

"Good Lawd, Magnolia. You clapped a priest?" Hampton stomped around in circles, biting his bottom lip and grimacing painfully. "Dammit, woman! This is bad. Real bad." The world started to spin in that wooden cottage. There wasn't any reason to belabor the point, no reason to discuss how her decision to plug a white man in southern Louisiana endangered their lives currently and in the hereafter. Hampton grunted angrily. "Tell me what made you act out like this? Lawd, please try to forgive my wife," Hampton prayed grievously. "She's sorry for shooting him. She's awful sorry."

"Stop it!" Magnolia hissed. "I am not sorry, not one single bit sorry. He had it coming!" Hate dripping from her mouth gave Hampton pause. "God, what did Father O'Leary do?" he asked finally.

Pearl Lee trounced up behind him. "I told you wasn't no way around it," she argued. "I'd have done it myself had I known what he was up to." She took a moment to collect herself then tore a hole into the lies Father O'Leary baited his hook with to snag young unsuspecting girls. Pearl Lee laid it all out for him to consume. Hampton couldn't believe what he heard. After Odessa's name rolled off his sister's tongue behind Joyce and Janeen's, he almost wished he hadn't.

Hampton's eyes exhibited the sadness he felt down to his core. He chased the visions of his daughters enduring the tragedy of rape from his mind then gnashed his teeth angrily. Pain shot through his heart like a deadening bolt. He wanted to reach out to Odessa, who sat on her bed holding the consequence of the assault in her arms. Wishing he could have been there for her was useless. However, there was so much to be done now. "Did anybody see you, Mag?" he asked, once Pearl Lee had spoken up on her behalf. "You sure *he* was all the way dead?" Magnolia didn't know which question to respond to first, although she was certain that O'Leary couldn't survive with the back of his head blown off.

"Wasn't no one at the church but us," she replied plainly. "Can't say if anybody saw me leave, though. And as for him being dead, yeah, I finished him all the way."

Hampton sighed hard. His mind was running at top speed and then some. He had to get Magnolia and his children far away from the parish sheriff's reach. He needed time and money, neither of which he had at his disposal. "Snatch Joyce and Janeen and pack up two or three pillowcases, just clothes, nothing else," he commanded Magnolia. "You did what you had to. Now I got to step up." He left additional instructions then drove his heap directly to the front of the plantation house.

Trotter Delacroix appeared with a dinner napkin in his hands after Hampton banged on the front door relentlessly. "Hampton," he said, questioning his abrupt and peculiar arrival. The only other time he dared to grace the white man's porch, he was in dire straits to do right by his family. Trotter had the distinct feeling Hampton was facing the flip side of the same coin.

"I didn't mean to interrupt your supper, Trotter, but this is important," Hampton said, his head bobbing nervously.

"Yeah, I can see that." He closed the door behind him and stepped out onto the veranda.

"I got to get away, fast and far."

Trotter nodded that he understood even though he couldn't have. "Is this tied to that Cunningham fella who asked me about you in Nawlins?"

"Naw, this is something altogether different. I got to put my hands on some money, tonight." Hampton hoped his boss would dispense with the questions because he didn't want to end their relationship on the heels of a lie.

Trotter must have read his mind. He let up on the quiz. "I got a couple of hundred to spare, but I can do a lot better when the wire hits the bank in a day or two. I got a good price on the crop this time." Trotter wouldn't have typically shared financial information with the help. However, Hampton was more in line with business partner than a hired hand.

"Thanks, but that won't get us far."

"Us? Who you plan on taking with you?"

"Don't worry, Pearl Lee's staying behind," Hampton answered, after reading Trotter's mind clear as day.

"Wish I could do more," Trotter apologized with a firm handshake.

"One more thing, you don't know nothing if somebody was to come around asking."

"You can count on it," Trotter replied honestly. He choked back on the sentiment pushing up his throat as Hampton burned rubber on his cement driveway. It would be the last time he'd see his oldest friend. That feeling of loss touched him in a way he'd never forget.

Hampton drove along the Terrebonne Bayou for miles. He fought the temptation to hold on to the persuader Magnolia used to blast O'Leary. Contemplating what he'd learned about being caught with incriminating evidence, he was forced to rid himself of the revolver. He stopped over a desolate bridge, shook his head, then flung the gun as far as he could. Unless there was an eyewitness, there wouldn't ever be much of a chance to convict Magnolia.

With a great deal of regret, he motored into New Orleans. It was almost eight o'clock when he turned onto Decatur Street. His bald tires screeched when he slammed on the brakes. The gray auto garage had been demolished sooner than he expected. There was nothing but sheets of metal, thrown about by a bulldozer. Hampton's heart raced as he flew from his automobile toward the pile of rubble. He climbed over the top of busted plaster, Sheetrock, and bent steel, clawing at the wreckage. Using a long rod, Hampton pried several heavy layers off one another. Fraught with concern and sweating profusely, he heaved against the rod to leverage the biggest barrier. He grunted and cussed while moving it aside. *It's got to be here*, he thought. *Please be here.* Try as he may, the safe was nowhere to be found. It had likely been discovered during the destruction, hauled off, and broken opened. Feeling no better than a whipped dog, Hampton had nowhere to run. Low on money and short on time, he paced erratically on the broad slab of concrete.

"Something wrong, Swagger?" a gruff voice asked from the

shadows. Hampton stumbled over a wooden two-by-four when he turned around. He wiped at his mouth then shrugged his shoulders as if to say if it weren't for bad luck, he'd have no luck at all.

"How you do, Bones?" he greeted uneasily. When Bones, dressed in a fancy blue suit, didn't respond, Hampton tried to get a read on him. "Funny meeting you here."

"Hand over the money you owe me and we'll both have a big laugh." Bones made a joke, only no one was laughing. "You've been holding out on me, Swagger. Where's my share?" He kept one hand in his jacket pocket while Hampton stalled.

"I ain't held out, Bones. I've been holding on to it, every penny. It's just that I ain't seen you in a while."

"I'm here now, so let's have at it. I know for a fact Riley's had you plenty busy. My cut should come close to ninety dollars. While it's not a lot to get excited about, it does belong to me." Hampton's reluctance put a disapproving frown on Bones's lips. "You do have my cut?" Again, Hampton stood pat. "You remember that night we threw in together, that night on the swamp road south of Rudolph's gambling house? I told you then it'd get gritty if you crawfished on a deal on me." Hampton remembered just as well as Bones did. Unfortunately, he was the one who happened to land on the wrong side of their agreement.

"Yeah, I was there and I recall just fine. There's no other way to spin it. Man, I'm sorry, but I don't have what I owe you." Hampton looked over his shoulder at the spot he dug in earlier. "I kept it in the safe. You can see they done tore down the garage. Somebody must've seen it and carried it off. There's nothing I can do about that."

Bones spat on the ground then pulled a cigar from his inside breast pocket. "If you can't come up with what's mine, you'd better get to doing something about it." He bit the tip off and spat it out like he'd done to the bad taste Hampton's story left in his mouth.

"This is a bad time for me, Bones. You got to know I'm good for the money."

"Nah, I don't think your word is good enough anymore. See, I knew a man like you once, a banjo plucker with a crippled hand. When it came down to it, all he needed was one good thumb. What I'm saying is there's something that'll square us, something to help you get by, too." Hampton peeped at his secondhand wristwatch. He didn't have time to debate, so he gestured for Bones to come out with it. "I've had an eye or two on the streets," Bones said slyly, "and I think the time has come to take over Riley Dobbs' territory, without any feuding to arouse the cops, you understand. I'd be obliged and just might cut you in if you croaked him, real quietlike, nice and neat."

Hampton stumbled back a step. Bones was talking cold-blooded murder, of a gangster, no less. "Whoa, hold up a minute. I know there ain't no love lost between you and Riley, and I ain't one to care why, but leave me out of it. I'll get you your money and set things right between me and you."

"Look who's telling who what he ain't gonna do. I ought to pump a bullet into your skull for jumping bad like this," Bones threatened. "I saved you, looked out for you and yours, too, now you're trying to double-talk me."

Hampton reached behind his back for a gun that rested at the bottom of the bayou. He threw his hands into the air to show they were empty. "Okay, I didn't mean to sound ungrateful. There—there's got to be another way out of this shy of murder."

"Uh-huh, do to Riley what I should have done to you for reaching on me. He's a snake and can't be trusted. Plus, from what

I hear, you're doing all of his heavy lifting and sticking your neck out for him while he plays the big shot. Don't be a fool, Swagger. There will be one boss in this town, and it's not that spook you're betting on. Do right by me. Make that accident happen to Riley Dobbs like I said or expect to meet one yourself."

There was a time Hampton would have shared what happened to his daughters with Bones and what Magnolia felt she had to do because of it. Not long ago, he could have turned to Bones for help, money, and a place to hide. That space in time had packed up and gone.

38

Nothing but Regrets

Hampton drove away. Bones stood in the middle of the street, wearing a menacing scowl. Hampton tried to shake the haunting image he saw in his rearview mirror. Full of regret, he made two laps around the same block before pulling his car against the curb. He regretted not having enough time between what Magnolia had done and receiving his share from the sugarcane crops to outrun it. Hampton also regretted going into Riley's tavern unsure and unarmed.

It was almost eight-thirty when he entered the smoke-filled den. The busy crowd watched a color television placed near the front of the pub. There was a basketball game on and it must have been a good one because everyone appeared to be glued to it. Hampton sneered at the bartender who hadn't grown on him yet, then made his way to the business office at the back of the building. The gargantuan bodyguard sat perched atop a wooden three-legged stool that creaked when he shifted his weight. He wore the ugliest multicolored polyester shirt. The pattern was dizzying and stretched across the man's broad chest like a road map. "How you do, Stubby?" said Hampton as casually as he could. Keeping the big ape at ease could come in handy had he the need to make a run for it.

"Same shit, different day," answered Stubby, glancing up from a wrinkled newspaper. "Go on in, the boss was asking about you an hour ago."

"Is that right?"

"Hell, yeah, I just said it was."

Hampton tapped on the door then reached for the knob. "See, I wasn't gonna ask who puked up on your shirt, but you had to get froggy." He hurried into the office and locked the door when Stubby folded his paper irritably.

"Why do you always go to picking at Stubby like that?" asked Riley.

"Because he don't like me and he don't try to hide it."

Riley sat behind his desk, chewing on a toothpick. He was dapper in a suit that looked as if it had been stitched together by a blind tailor. It was psychedelic and loud. Hampton squinted to cope with the strain. "So you like this suit, too?" Riley chuckled. "Everybody stares at me when I'm in it. Hell, that's what I paid the outfitter a mint for. Fine vines don't come cheap."

"Yeah, I imagine they don't," Hampton groaned, wiping his eyes. "That grizzly bear out in the hall said you was asking about me." Hampton thought he'd pitch small talk to help himself figure out a strategy.

"Oh, yeah" was Riley's sharp response. His demeanor changed in the blink of an eye. That bothered Hampton. "I didn't think I'd ever be having this conversation with you seeing as how you're my number one go-getter. Nobody stiffs me, not even you."

"What you mean, stiffed you?" Hampton barked.

"Man, sit your narrow ass down and be still when you do. I sent you after Willie Pope to collect my ends. I done already had to dispatch somebody else just to shut him up. He's bragging about cutting a side deal with you but wouldn't say what." Riley peered angrily over his desk at Hampton, then he poured himself a shot of sipping whiskey. He eyed his visitor while sampling the dash of liquor. "Got nothing to say for yourself?"

Hampton chose his words carefully. He wasn't one to pull a double cross and didn't want to get shot for something he didn't do. "Nothing that'll hold, Mr. Dobbs," he offered eventually. "Just so you know, I wasn't out for myself when I called on Willie. I didn't even know who stayed at the address you wrote down until I was after him on foot." Riley listened attentively to see if Hampton's version was different from the one his thugs beat out of Willie.

"Go on," he grunted solemnly, his hand cradling the pistol on his lap.

"I caught up to him, he puked his guts out, then called me by name. That's when I recognized him. We come up together on the Delacroix Plantation, and..."

"And you didn't have the heart to break his nose," Riley concluded on his own. "I know about country boys, shucking cane, and running along the bayou. Willie's like kin to you?"

"You can say that," Hampton agreed, hoping that was all he had to say.

"I figured as much. You don't strike me as the type to get snubbed out over a double deal. When was you gonna tell me about letting him go?"

"I wasn't," Hampton answered quickly, too fast in fact to edit his answer.

"Man, you is either the bravest or stupidest man there ever was." Riley began to snicker as he took another nip from his glass. "What *was* you planning on doing, then?"

"Pay you with my own money if I had to." Hampton hadn't thought of the snappy option before that very moment. It sounded good in his head so he went with it.

"Keeping friends must have some kind of a hold on you."

Hampton considered Bones and his deadly proposition. Then he measured how far Riley's neck was from the blade he'd shoved into his jacket pocket. "Good friends is worth a whole lot more than money, unless you ain't got none." Riley laughed then placed the .38 special in his top drawer. If he had designs on hurting Hampton, something changed his mind. "That's why I stopped by, Mr. Dobbs."

"Oh, again with the Mr. Dobbs. You're outta the doghouse, Hampton. Lighten up."

"Wish I could. The fact is, I been keeping the money you paid me, all of it. Somebody went along and snatched what I've been saving. Now I'm tangled in a heap of thorns. Trouble knows my name, and I always took my lumps like a man. This is different. I need a break, Mr. Dobbs." It pained Hampton to beg. Riley refused to let him when he saw it coming.

"Ahh, don't say nothing else." He respected the man in his office, so much so that he didn't want it to fade. Riley drank the rest of his hooch then poured one for Hampton. "Here, hit this good then spit out what's got you twisted into knots." Hampton accepted his hospitality as he glanced at his watch. He spent the better part of five minutes hashing out the entire sordid story about Magnolia, Father O'Leary, the girls, Odessa, and her son. By the time he finished, Riley had unwittingly removed his gun from the drawer. He stared at the metal lying on his desk with sad, dim eyes. "I've heard a lot of hard-luck stories. Believe me, you got 'em all beat by a mile. Take this," he moaned. Riley slid three hundred dollars to Hampton across the desktop. "And this, too." He scribbled some words and numbers down on a sheet of scratch paper. "The last time I sent you with a note you stayed true to your heart. Don't be the same fool twice." Hampton thanked him for the money and the advice. He stood to leave, hat in hand and somewhat puzzled.

"You don't like my friend Bones. What did he put you up against?"

"I never met the man and I hope I never do. Make no mistake, Hampton, he's no friend to you. I know that because you screamed his name in your sleep when we was locked up. He's the one who put you in that hole, that's why I hate him." Riley shook hands with Hampton for the first time, then told him to follow his direction to the letter. They parted ways as friends.

Hampton sat in his car with the motor running. He read Riley's note. Above the name and address of a Houston associate were the words: *What you know will get you by.* Hampton read over the message several times, all the more perplexed by what he viewed as a riddle. He couldn't concentrate on the conundrum because of breaking the deal he'd made with Bones to act as an assassin. Riley's comment about him not being a friend was vexing as well. Sitting alone, Hampton fingered the money he'd been given along with the note. Neither seemed sufficient to secure a safe harbor for his family. A new beginning required finances. He was poor and soon to be a fugitive on the lam. If only he'd gotten to the money kept in the safe on time. Nearly a thousand dollars would have served as a decent nest egg while he looked for work on the other side of his misery. *If only he had access to the money Trotter owed him for sharecropping*, he thought. *If only.*

While leaving the city, Hampton saw a billboard congratulating the New Orleans Saints football organization on breaking ground for their state-of-the-art stadium. Hampton huffed when he remembered the black residents who had to vacate their homes so that a bunch of athletes could play their games under a domed ceiling. He felt it was just as well he didn't get the construction job with Willie Pope's company. He'd worked hard to keep food on the table while stuffing money in Trotter's pockets. Willie was merely doing the same thing for other white men, he thought. Digging holes, busting rocks, and blasting earth sounded too much like prison work, anyway. Scornful memories of heavy lifting, dynamite blasts, and dangerous labor made Hampton angry. The thought of it actually benefiting his plight urged him to whip a U-turn at the next block.

Hampton circled around to the back of the billboard that was erected adjacent to the construction site for the Superdome. There was a tall chain-link fence and an armed security guard patrolling the perimeter. Willie told him there had been protests, speeches, and trouble. Hampton wondered how many other guards were likely to be on the night shift. Considering his dilemma, none of that mattered. He needed to get his hands on the tools they built the fence around.

After Hampton scouted the area hidden in the billboard's shadow, he decided it was the best place to shimmy over the metal barrier without being detected. He crouched down to duck out of sight as a car passed by on the side street. He stayed there a few minutes, watching and waiting. Another guard stepped out of a small trailer to stretch his legs. He shouted jokingly to his partner about a nagging wife and quickly returned to his post. Hampton had to move fast.

He scaled the fence like he'd wished to do on many nights while at prison farm. Fifteen years later, what he wanted was still on the other side of one. He continued climbing, swung his legs over, then dropped to his feet. He lifted a lead pipe from the ground and skulked deeper into the work site. An army of bulldozers and cranes made for perfect cover. Hampton surveyed the small wooden storage facilities, trying to determine which to break open first and knowing he might not have a lot of chances before the guard who'd grumbled about his bride made another appearance. Hampton had to guess where the explosives were kept. After busting the locks on three storage units, he found coils of copper and enormous spools of insulated electrical cables. Fearing that too much time had been wasted, Hampton inched closer toward the security trailer. He raised his leg to climb atop a rectangular-shaped metal bin clamped shut with a sturdy padlock. Three letters caught his attention: TNT. Finally, he'd stumbled onto the golden goose.

Using the pipe to bust the lock, Hampton strained mightily but it didn't budge. When he repositioned the shaft against the storage bin, the latch that held the padlock gave way. The security clamp fell to the ground intact. In the dead of night, the moon had begun to shine. Hampton opened the lid slowly, reached inside, and pulled out four sticks of dynamite, several feet of fuse, and two blast caps. Then he disappeared quickly into the shadows.

The car stereo whined as he started up the engine. Hampton adjusted the knobs when the New Orleans radio station he was listening to went off the air for the night. He shut off the stereo to collect his thoughts while rolling across the Broussard Parish line. At 9:17, Hampton realized he actually had the stones to do it. He was going to rob the Newberry State Bank.

Free of all inhibition and indecision, Hampton parked his car down the block, just behind the service station where Buck Ravenell worked as a part-time attendant. He cased the area like he'd done when pulling heists with Bones. As soon as the streets were vacant, Hampton crept to the side of the buff-colored brick building. Disabling the security system by cutting the wire was for professionals, men who cherished the art of coming and going without being detected. That would have taken planning and patience. Hampton had a pocketful of explosives.

He knew where the three-ton safe was housed within the structure. He knew the safe door was likely reinforced with steel bars. Hampton prayed that no one anticipated it being blown up from the side. Calmly, he measured off several feet of fuse before securing it to the blasting caps. Next, he fastened them to the dynamite sticks. Hampton ran for cover after lighting the fuse.

Within seconds, his body shook and his ears rang. The explosive charge was deafening. Hampton pulled a mask over his face although he didn't see a soul when stepping into the canyon-size hole in the brick and mortar. Just as he suspected, the safe door had been armored, but no one thought to spend the money on reinforcing its walls.

Nervously stuffing stacks of bills into his pockets, Hampton quickly gathered the money owed to him by Trotter, more than enough to get away clean and hide out for months. He was crawling back through the opening he'd created when it occurred to him: in for a penny, in for a pound. Hampton took what was rightly his, then he loaded up as many bags as he could carry at once. When all was said and done, he made it to the Delacroix Plantation with more than $150,000 bundled in the trunk of a car that was barely worth the full tank of gas he'd pumped in it.

39

Disappearing Act

Pearl Lee stood next to the door, peeping through the slight gap in the curtains. Hampton had taken off some time ago. For two excruciatingly long hours, Pearl kept vigilant watch for his return. After Magnolia stuffed three pillowcases with necessities and small keepsakes that meant a lot to her, she sat quietly on the worn love seat summing up her total existence. At age thirty-four, three sacks of clothes was all that belonged to Magnolia, but they didn't define her. Family meant the world, and she wouldn't trade all the riches in it for the man she loved and the children she'd killed for. Joyce and Janeen waited impatiently, fearfully, on either side of Magnolia. Both girls wanted desperately to know what would happen when their father returned but neither made a peep. Keeping in mind the tragedy they'd experienced in Newberry, contemplating moving on to God knows where was just as terrifying.

When automobile brakes squealed in front of the cottage, Magnolia threw both arms around her children to gather them in closer. Pearl Lee leaned toward the window. She held her hands up cautiously while spying into the darkness. "It's okay. It's Hampton and he's alone."

"What do you think he's gonna say, Pearl?" Magnolia asked for everyone in the room.

"Don't rightly know," she said, frowning sorrowfully, "though I expect we'll all find out directly." Pearl Lee went to unlock the door. Hampton lunged in, looking over his shoulder then out the window just as his sister had. "We all been waiting here, going crazy, too. Where you been?"

He rushed to comfort his family before answering. "Sorry it took so long. I've been putting some things together. Anybody come around asking about O'Leary?" Magnolia squeezed her daughters then shook her head.

"Nobody's moved, come or gone since you told us to wait here."

"Good, good. Then that's it. Come on, y'all. Let's go." He hoisted the pillowcases off the floor then turned toward the door. "Pearl Lee, I'll let you know where we settle, and I'll send you some money from time to time."

"How long you think y'all gon' be away?" she asked when the sadness of their departure finally set in. Hampton's eyes narrowed. He thought it was understood what had to be done and the difficulties that persisted with going on the run.

"We can't come back here, not ever. Magnolia killed a white man, a priest, and no matter how right she was to end him, this is still the state of Louisiana. I don't intend on letting them strap my wife to no electric chair. We got to disappear."

The gravity of Hampton's decision brought tears to Odessa's eyes first. She put Eric on the bed and raced to her cousins.

"I'm gonna miss y'all," she cried. "I'm gonna miss y'all so much.

I'm sorry for everything. Everything! Please don't hold it against me. I didn't mean to get nobody else hurt." Joyce hugged Odessa as tightly as she could.

"It wasn't your fault what happened to Janeen," she offered, still discounting the atrocity she suffered at the hands of a rapist. Janeen kept her eyes trained on Eric, a beautiful bastard child born to a young girl and a murdered man. He deserved his predicament least of all.

Magnolia clung to Pearl Lee near the door. "Pearl, this is bad. So bad. I wish we could stay. I know, I know. You and Dessa and the baby can come with us," she ranted. The grievous tone in her voice stabbed at Hampton as he looked on. "Yeah, we'll stay together and wherever we land will be home. Family and home." Her eyes begged Pearl Lee to go along. "They can come, too. Isn't that right, Hampton?" Magnolia asked, grasping at the fringes of normalcy.

Pearl Lee loosened her embrace then. She pursed her lips and backed away. "No, this here is home for me, always was and always will be. Moving around like a gypsy won't change that. Y'all best get going," she asserted as a final ruling. "Magnolia, you take good care of my brother, now." Pearl Lee rubbed her cheek against Janeen's then did likewise to Joyce. "You're good girls, but don't forget to look after your mama."

"Yes, ma'am."

"We won't, Auntie Pearl."

Magnolia sent her children out to the car. Hampton breathed in real deep when his sister buried her face in his chest. He wanted to remember everything he could about that moment to capture it. "Pearl Lee, you can come with us. I got a bit more money than I went after."

She chuckled awkwardly. "What's Trotter gonna do without me? Huh? Mrs. Mary-Beth won't let him touch her now. Yep, somebody went and left a tattletale note under her pillow blabbing on about us." Pearl Lee blushed. "What's between me and Trotter can't be explained."

"Then why you wasting words trying to?" Hampton joked. "You don't owe me answers to questions I won't ask. That white boy nearly shit a brick when I told him I was leaving, only because he thought that stood for you, too. Look, we'll stay in touch, but you got to keep it secret when the letters and money come. Folks might be after us for a long while. Ain't no time limit for what they can charge on murder."

"I understand. Just make sure you don't forget us, Papa, Mama, and Toussaint."

"I won't. I promise I won't." Hampton hurried to the car and started it up. He stared at the shack he was raised in, the same one his daughters called home, dreading what had to happen now. Hampton realized as much before taking off for New Orleans earlier that night. Nonetheless, it didn't lessen the soreness in his heart. There was no remedy for that.

As the jalopy hurled through the back roads of Newberry, Janeen caught a glimpse of a small boy sitting on a fence post and puffing on a cigarette. It was Billy Earl, enjoying himself with the pack of smokes he'd pinched from a drunken relative. He recognized the car then quickly began waving hello to his friend Janeen. She pressed her thin fingers against the back window, wishing she could reach out and touch him. As her family surged forward on the dusty trail, she said so long to Billy Earl, Broussard Parish, and everything else she was forced to leave behind, including her innocence.

* * *

Hampton drove for five hours before pulling over for restrooms and food. He bought sodas, honey buns, and cold sandwiches at a roadside diner off the interstate. They ate, drank, and slept in the car parked behind a big-rig filling station. When the sun came up, a state trooper rapped on the driver's-side window with his knuckles. He told Hampton it was illegal to tramp along the Texas highways and instructed him to find another place to be. With a stern warning in his back pocket and thousands of dollars in the trunk, Hampton was highly agreeable to getting on.

Once the car zoomed west on I-10, Joyce rubbed her eyes and yawned. She shielded her eyes from the sun to get a clearer look at the tall buildings in the distance. "Wow, Papa, what is that?" she asked, nudging Janeen to wake up. Not having stepped foot out of southern Louisiana, she was amazed by the metropolitan appeal of the giant city.

"That there is Houston," he replied with a calming voice. He imagined it would be very easy to disappear in a city with over a million people.

"Houston," Janeen said groggily. "Houston, Texas?" She sat up straight in the backseat to admire the grand spectacle. "Wow, look at all those tall buildings. Looks like they might fall over and crush everything."

"We read about stuff like that in schoolbooks," Joyce added. "Said people call them skyscratchers or scrapers, I forget which exactly, but they sure do brush against the clouds all right."

Janeen peered out of the smudged side window. Cars and trucks raced past, changing lanes at breakneck speed it seemed to her. "Where could all these people be going so early in the morning?"

Hampton took an educated guess. "Most likely to work in some of these skyscratchers, I suppose. Magnolia, how you think this suits you, tall buildings, miles of concrete below your feet, and people running around like ants?"

She turned toward him slowly so as not to miss the intriguing sights. "Don't know yet about the people, but I haven't a fondness for ants." She gawked at a diesel eighteen-wheeler as it sailed past in the next lane. "That truck has a produce sign painted on it. Maybe we should follow it to the market. I don't see a farm anywhere, and all these ants got to eat something."

The note Riley Dobbs gave Hampton was itching at him from inside his pocket. Hampton reached in and pulled it out. "There's a man I need to see. He ought to be able to tell us where to shop and flop."

"Flop?" Magnolia quipped. "Don't you have to dig up a job first?" Hampton smiled. He hadn't told her about the bank robbery yet. Once they got settled, he'd let her in on it then map out the rest of their lives.

"We'll talk about it in a while. Don't worry about eating. I got that covered." After Hampton stopped to gas up, he went into a phone booth to search the directory. There wasn't any match for the name Riley had written so he bought a map. Sure enough, he found Scott Street and the fastest way to get there. When they exited the freeway, tired and hungry, Hampton marveled at the vast number of black men and women who lived in the neighborhood. They were at bus stops, on bicycles, driving fancy cars, and dressed like they owned something. "Yeah, this looks to be the place," he uttered, thinking it appeared to be as good as any in which to vanish.

He parked in front of a blue two-story house on the end of the broad street, knocked on the door, and went inside. Seconds later he marched a path right back to the car. Hampton huffed as he jumped into the driver's seat without as much as a good-bye to the fat man standing on the porch with two half-dressed women at his side.

"Hampton, what happened?" Magnolia whispered, ogling the threesome. "Was that the man?"

"Yep, that was him."

"We just got here. Why we leaving?"

"That's a cathouse, and that fat mule is the wrangler," he barked, furious at Riley for sending his family to a brothel. Magnolia shot a stinging glare at the big blue house.

"Wrangler, you mean a pimp? What kind of friend would do that? Did he expect you'd be agreeable with holing up in a cathouse with your wife and children?" Now she was very upset, wondering what kind of business Hampton was involved with and the kinds of women it attracted. "Well?" she snarled.

"This ain't the time, honey," he said through clenched teeth. Hampton chose Houston because Riley said he'd help to get him established, find work, and assimilate. He didn't say anything about running women or bunking in a house where they were hired out by the hour.

Eventually, Hampton cooled down. He found a reasonable hotel off I-45 and checked into a room with fresh linen and double beds. For three months, they hid in the shadows, going to the grocery store at night and getting heavy doses of television during the day. Magnolia stopped asking where Hampton was getting money for the room when she opened his toolbox and found neat stacks of bills, arranged from largest to smallest. It was unmistakable that he'd taken it from someone. She prayed that no one was hurt when he did.

One Friday morning, Hampton dashed into the hotel room shouting for everyone to get up. Magnolia wrestled on her housecoat. "What now?" she yelled.

"We'll talk about it in the car." Hampton had seen a familiar face at the waffle house near the hotel. It spooked him. As it turned out, Houston was still too close to his past. "Don't take anything but the clothes on your back." He checked the window, grabbed his toolbox, and struck out for the parking lot. When Joyce and Janeen hustled toward their old car to get in, Hampton waved her over to another one. "Uh-uh, we're leaving that." The Buick was more suitable for the scrap heap than making a second getaway. In addition, the Louisiana plates were a cause for concern. He opened the door to a mint green Mercury Cougar. "Hurry up and get in."

Magnolia gathered her housecoat at the chest, doing as she was told. Hampton blazed from the hotel parking lot into abating traffic. Not another word was uttered for hours. Pearl Lee was correct in her assumption. They were bouncing around like gypsies, pulling up stakes at a moment's notice and leaving all of their belongings behind. "If you know where we're going," Magnolia sighed as they passed yet another cotton field heading north up I-45, "mind filling me in?"

Hampton glanced at the rearview mirror then exhaled. "I figure we'll ride this road until it runs out."

40

Long Way Home

After being on the highway just short of three hundred miles, Magnolia had time to think and make her petitions known. She stopped Hampton before he exited the car to pump gas at a service station just within the Dallas County line. "What makes you think this city is gonna be any different than the one we left back there?" she asked, still dressed in a housecoat.

"It's different because ain't no FBI men or Louisiana law dogs here looking for us."

"What you mean?"

"Back there, in Houston, I saw some white boys and Detective Cunningham stirring around the waffle house over by the hotel. Wasn't gonna be long before they talked to somebody who seen us."

"Cunningham? That's the stumpy little fella who had it in for you, the one you jumped in that alley all those years ago?"

"Yeah, none other. I seen him plain as day. He had some federal boys escorting him, too. That's why we had to pull up and blow." Hampton wanted to apologize for dragging his family through Texas. Words of repentance didn't come easy. Ducking and hiding didn't agree with him. He was growing increasingly agitated, like a wild animal in a cage.

While studying her daughters, asleep in the backseat of a nice, slightly used sedan, Magnolia took a deep breath then held her husband's hand. "Being on the run like this reminds me of the time you ran into that big detective who made chief of police. He had it in for you after you went and beat on Cunningham. You came home black-and-blue, busted up some, too." Magnolia caressed his shoulder lovingly. "You will get us through this, only there's something we got to do different. I can't remember the last time I put dinner on the table and the girls are tired of eating from a carryout box. I need—we need—a place to stretch out and relax and move around in. Hampton, we've been tucked away going on nearly four months. Joyce is cranky, Janeen is getting bigger than a house, and we got enough money to go looking for one. I mean a real home." She saw the wheels turning in that mixed-up head of his. Magnolia raised her brow when Hampton's taut expression relaxed into a warm smile.

"I guess there ain't much use in having this money if it's got to stay buried."

"Not all of it. Maybe there's a place we can rent that won't cost so much until we decide what to do next."

Hampton agreed it was definitely worth a look. He filled the gas tank then wandered inside the station to pay. There was a slight colored man on the inside. He appeared to be around Hampton's age when he glanced up at his customer and folded his newspaper in half. "That'll be seven dollars and thirteen cents, if that's all you need," he added, as if it was the millionth time he'd uttered those same words.

"Say, fella, I'm just getting into town and was kinda wondering if there was some nice places to rent, big enough for me, the wife, and two girls."

The cashier looked at Hampton's automobile with a discerning eye through the plate-glass window. "There are some real nice and some not so nice. With two daughters you'd want to go with the nice enough route. Here, take this paper and seek through the want ads."

"The which?"

"Man, where you roll in from, Mars? The want ads is this section of the paper right here." He jabbed at it with his oil-stained finger. "You can find most everything you'd need in it. I found this job in it three years ago and been searching for a better one ever since." The cashier chuckled when he told the joke and didn't care if Hampton failed to find the humor in it.

"I'll take a paper, then, and a street map, too. And thanks for the hospitality."

Hampton completed his transaction and returned to the car. Joyce and Janeen had awakened. Janeen complained of stomach cramps. Joyce complained of everything else. All and all, it wasn't a bad start to a new beginning.

At Magnolia's suggestion, Hampton found a two-bedroom, one-and-a-half bath wood frame home in a quiet neighborhood. Children roller-skated down the sidewalks. Most of the families went to church every Sunday morning. Hampton taught Magnolia to drive. Both girls sat out the remainder of the school year although they were given daily writing and math assignments from a textbook Magnolia picked up from a nearby library.

Hampton played it safe. He cut a hole in the floor of the bedroom directly underneath the bed. He stored money there and hoped to one day buy a safe to lower down into it. Magnolia cooked dinner every day. She hummed and doted over Janeen while rearranging the cupboards. Joyce grumbled about not being allowed to make new friends or to leave the front porch for any reason. Still, it was a far better house than the one they left behind in Newberry. This one had electrical plugs that were not connected to the lightbulb fixture, two toilets, two sinks, and one tub big enough to fall asleep in. Janeen had twice already. Despite unforeseen consequences, the Bynote household had begun to feel at home.

Initially, Hampton fought to keep out of sight during the daytime. He looked for work in nightclubs, beer parlors, and pool halls. Assimilating into metropolitan society was an eye-opening experience. Military men were coming home from Vietnam by the busloads. Some of them had physical infirmities; all of them were mentally damaged. Police stared at black men, for no apparent reason. Hampton quickly discovered they didn't need one. Madness, anger, and despair were eagerly overtaking kindness and hope. Dirty cops and illegal drugs were tag-teaming their way up the social ladder, slapping down everyone who stood in their way.

Hampton wanted to be his own man, invest in something, own something. After nearly nine months in Dallas, his longtime dream of home ownership had come back around to drop in on him. It was a surprise visit but welcome just the same. One glaring roadblock stood in his way. Any sizable bills of sale would have to include his name and identification. Hampton Julian Bynote was on the run, from what exactly didn't matter. Trouble was waiting for that man, he was certain of it.

Rooster Lewis owned a nightspot five blocks from the house

Hampton rented on 2nd Avenue. He'd purposely stayed away since the club owner had his hands in a few shady enterprises. The arrangement he had with Riley Dobbs warned him to keep his distance from bad men, but he needed something the local thug had in abundance: information. On the heels of desperation, Hampton parked his car on the street and stepped inside to see the man.

Standing behind the bar was an extremely tall, high-yellow black man with a bushy brown goatee circling his thick pink lips. He was covered in a wardrobe made from yards of red satin, with crimson boots and a hat to match. His outfit was fetching to say the least. However, in the middle of the day, the Rooster looked overdone to Hampton.

"Hey, Mistah Lewis," he hailed politely.

"Mr. Lewis is my old man. Friends call me Rooster," he said, sizing up Hampton as friend or foe.

"Okay, Rooster, I like that. Say, I'm renting a place not far from here and was thinking to buy." Hampton didn't want to divulge too much so he tiptoed around the question he was getting at.

"Good for you. Do I own it?"

"Naw, but the fella who do is thinking on giving it to me at a real fair price." Again Hampton left the conversation teetering. Rooster was beginning to get annoyed.

"Man, you been breathing up my air-conditioning and ain't said yet what's this got to do with me." He leered at Hampton peculiarly. "Come on and stop riddling me or I'm liable to get real pissed and real quick."

"Okay, damn. I need to get me some new identification. Not just for me, either, for my family to boot." Hampton lowered his head remorsefully. He didn't know Rooster or if he'd help out. That left Hampton on uneasy footing.

"Hot IDs, huh?" Roosted grunted lightly. "You don't look to be the dodging an ex-wife type so it must be the law that's got you trying to bury a life you don't want no mo'." He poured himself a drink then one for the guest whose name he hadn't yet learned. Hampton grinned when he remembered Riley liked talking over business with a glass in his hand. It seemed that gangsters hated drinking alone. "You say there's a family with you. How many people?"

"Me, the wife, and two girls," he answered as if placing an order.

"Do you want used handles or brand-spanking-new ones?" Hampton shrugged. He didn't understand the difference. "Shit. Used handles come from folk who died and sure as hell won't be needing 'em. New ones are really real and a lot more expensive."

"How expensive?"

"Let's just say I got a white boy down at the Social Security office who can make you and your family born again. That'll cost seven hundred."

"That's a lot of money," Hampton spat.

"You can't put a price on freedom, my man."

"Throw in one for a brand-new baby and I'll come up with the money."

"If I do this and you flip on me, I'll stomp a mud puddle in yo' ass."

"Ain't gon' be no problems on my end. I really need this to be on the level, Rooster," Hampton warned him. The darkness in his eyes suggested there was another side to this stranger looking for help. Rooster figured it was one that needed burying.

Hampton was itching to race home, pull up the floorboards beneath his bed, and reel off seven one-hundred dollar bills, but he had to play it cool. Instead he lowered his head and exited Rooster's establishment as if he'd have to beg, borrow, and steal to scrape it together. Men like Rooster were predators. He would blackmail Hampton until he bled him dry if knowledge of the bank heist got out.

Two weeks later, Hampton sat at the kitchen table with Magnolia, who was wringing her hands the way Pearl Lee had when she was troubled. "Do you think this man might turn us in?" she asked wearily.

"Naw, Rooster's a crook. He wouldn't bring the law around."

"Not this Rooster fella," said Magnolia. "I mean the other one, that white man downtown you supposed to go see."

Hampton shook his head. "That'd mean sending Rooster up, too, and I can't see him giving in so easy. You can always trust people who do illegal things to hold up their end just as long as they come out on top. You should have seen the sad sack I put on when taking the money to Rooster. It took him five minutes to count the wrinkled dollars, quarters, and dimes I poured out on his bar. He thought to turn me around but it occurred to him I might have started bawling right there on the spot. Oh, yeah, I'd have pitched a fit, too." Magnolia laughed until her sides ached. The mental picture of her husband wailing and crying about his family's well-being was a hoot. "You know that's the first time you laughed like that since leaving Newberry," Hampton told her. He was so glad to see it.

Magnolia rubbed her hand on the head of the infant sleeping across her lap. "I haven't had too much to laugh about, though I'm bound to get accustomed to this before long." She tried to smile about the newest addition to their family, a beautiful girl with fine curly hair and a light complexion, but she couldn't manage to force one on her lips. "If you feel it's safe, I'm with you. Lawd knows the girls missed too much school as it is, and this baby has to see a doctor for shots and such."

Hampton pulled a cap over his head and started out. He followed Rooster's directions to a place downtown. It felt like a boulder was sitting in the pit of his stomach when he realized the white fellow he was to see worked in the Federal Building. Pushing all fears to the back of his mind, Hampton caught the elevator to the fifth floor. He asked the receptionist for the Social Security office then went in the way she pointed, without so much as an utterance. At the end of the hall was a row of high-walled cubicles. Hampton located the nameplate he was looking for. It rested atop the last desk in the back.

"Can I help you?" asked a middle-aged white man. Hampton gave him a quick once-over, noting his nice leather shoes, wide necktie, and starched short-sleeve shirt.

"Yeah, uh, yes. I'm here to see Mr. Ernie Phillips."

"I'm Ernie Phillips."

"I'm—I was sent by Rooster," answered Hampton. He suddenly felt foolish for coming into this white man's workplace and rambling about some Negro named Rooster sending him. "I'm sorry, I don't know what I was thinking."

"Change your mind about the package you came for?" Mr. Phillips asked with a knowing wink. "You're late, but Rooster told me you'd be coming today. Have a seat." They sat across from each other while Phillips played around with a stack of index filing cards to waste time. As soon as the coworker in the next cube stepped away from his desk, Phillips pulled out his bottom drawer and laid an envelope that he'd kept hidden on his desk. "This is all you'll need, four untraceable Social Security cards and five birth certificates from a friend at the registrar's office. Parkland is the county hospital where your entire family was born. Rooster said there was an infant. She has to get her government card the old-fashioned way. In about a month or so, take the certificate of birth and stand in line downstairs. If you can make it out, fill in the necessary forms then send them in." Hampton overlooked the slighting remark concerning his ability to read and write. He nodded that he followed just fine. "One more thing, you've never met me. If you rat, I'll say you stole the information and help them send you to prison. Do I make myself clear?"

"As a liberty bell," Hampton answered.

"See that your family understands. They'll have to get used to their new names." Mr. Phillips started shuffling papers on his desk. He glanced up at Hampton with an annoyed expression.

"Oh, oh, thank you. I'll be going now."

"Good day," Phillips responded dismissively.

"Yeah, it's a very good day." Hampton walked out of the Federal Building as stiff as a board. His concerns about being a wanted man were unnerving. It seemed that every white man in a business suit was casing him. By the time he reached the parking lot, he was a tense bundle of anxiety. He opened his car door and placed the package on the driver's seat. When his stomach convulsed, Hampton lunged forward. He vomited on the ground, coughing violently until there was nothing but dry, excruciating heaves. Afterward, he climbed into his car and wiped his mouth. The priceless information he'd paid seven hundred dollars to obtain was burning a hole in the envelope. He sorted through the papers one at a time. New identities didn't come cheap but were worth every penny. He grinned at a Social Security card with the name Julian Hampton stenciled on it and a corresponding birth certificate stating that he was a year younger. His daughters also took his first name as their last. He didn't think it could have been so easy to say so long to the Bynote family moniker. Pulling out of the parking lot, he spat out the remnants of fear from his mouth and the name his father passed along to him right along with it.

41

A Grave Proposition

Hampton sang all the way home. His car stereo blared as he chimed in with New Orleans piano great Professor Longhair. "Tell me, baby, who's been fooling you?" Hampton snapped his fingers, thinking the eight-track tape player was the greatest invention of all time. Magnolia had grown tired of listening to the same songs, but the girls enjoyed watching their father howl over the music from the backseat. Now that he'd secured new futures with authentic papers to prove it, Hampton planned on taking them shopping to a downtown department store. There had to be at least one satin housecoat special enough for Magnolia. He'd decided before going to jail that she was the kind of woman who deserved one. Now she just might get two of them.

Whistling along with another track, Hampton nodded his head to the calypso beats that reminded him of home, Mardi Gras, and the Funky Butt Dance Hall where he fell in love with Magnolia. The perfect pitch his life had suddenly become fell flat when he rounded the next corner. Hampton saw a dark-colored sedan parked in front of his house. He'd seen that same car near the hotel in Houston. He had to make a quick decision, drive past with this head down or stop and risk getting hauled off for the rest of his life. A knot swelled in his chest. Magnolia and the girls were home alone. He couldn't live with himself if the people who'd caught up to them interrogated her. Magnolia would confess to save her family. She would lie to save her man.

Hampton eased down on the brake as he steered his car to the curb. He parked behind the sedan and got out slowly when he noticed the driver was still behind the wheel. There was no way to guess how many other men were inside grilling his wife for information. He jogged toward the house, thundering with each step. "Hampton Bynote!" someone yelled from the open car window. "Hampton!" the man hollered again when he didn't stop. "Don't make me put my gun on you!" Hampton froze on the emerald lawn. He raised his hands and turned to face the charges. Getting cut down by a hail of bullets was a vicious alternative. Staring into the setting sun obstructed his vision. He couldn't make out who had threatened him until the stranger strolled closer. It was a white man, short and squat in build, wearing an impressive wrinkled suit that smelled of sweat.

"Captain Cunningham," Hampton said, acknowledging his tracker.

"If you don't have anything up your sleeve, you can put your hands down." With mixed emotions, Hampton lowered them. To ensure his family wouldn't have to watch him die from gunshot wounds in the front yard, he was resolved to play it straight down the middle.

"You come a long way, Detective," Hampton said. He glanced at the house several times. "How many of them boys you bring with you?"

"None, I came alone this time. When we didn't pinch you in Houston, the feds decided to go in another direction."

"Another direction? Why y'all spending government money tailing my steps, anyhow?" he asked, trying to sound dignified and innocent.

"You're wanted for questioning in Louisiana. There's an open case where a naughty priest went and got his head shot off. Uh-huh, and that ain't all. The Newberry police are having the damnedest time figuring out a bank robbery that happened on the same evening."

Cunningham rested his hands on his sides then winced when the sunlight hit his eyes. He had an idea the acts were related. He told the New Orleans FBI division chief as much, then took it upon himself to prove it.

"See, the federal boys think a white man robbed the bank and that Father O'Leary, he was a victim of circumstance. Maybe he saw something he wasn't supposed to, or hell, maybe he just got in the way." Cunningham observed Hampton's demeanor. It hadn't changed since learning the detective came after him alone. "Me, I've got another theory. I don't know where you got your hands on the dynamite, but I do know you offed that dirty priest. What you got to say about that, Hampton?" Hampton hunched his shoulders, playing the dumb Negro the detective thought he was. "The man raped your niece, Odessa. Yep, I did some asking around back home. It turned out the good father wasn't so good after all." Again, he waited for Hampton to exhibit some signs of weakening. "Chief Mouton said you'd gone straight. I told him there was no such thing," Cunningham added to get a rise out of him. Hampton remained silent and unchanged. "Then you went and shot a white priest. That means I got the last laugh." He removed a pair of shiny handcuffs from his service belt. Now he was looking at Hampton for another reason, to see if he was willing to go peacefully or if there would be a struggle. Cunningham was older and slower than he was when Hampton whipped him in the New Orleans alley. He wouldn't hesitate to forgo the trouble of wrestling on the cuffs. Shooting first and then proving his theory later worked just as well as far as the aging cop was concerned. "How long have you been here, all respectable like this?"

Hampton smirked uncomfortably then considered Cunningham's question before answering. "What do you mean, respectable? I spend every day looking over my shoulder. Ain't nothing respectable when you're a man on the run." Hampton took a deep breath and placed his hands behind his back. "You know, it feels like a lifetime since I lit out of Newberry. And after spending eight months in a rented house that I intended on someday buying, I almost fooled myself into thinking I could put Newberry behind me." Cunningham reserved his philosophy on turning over new leaves when the front door opened. Magnolia stepped out onto the porch.

"Is everything all right?" she asked, fearing that it wasn't. Janeen appeared behind her, holding her child three shades lighter than herself. The baby, barely two months old, was swaddled in a pink blanket.

"Go on back in the house. Me and my old pal's just catching up is all." When Magnolia stalled, Hampton insisted she oblige his wishes. "Go on now. This is man talk. Take Janeen and the baby back inside." Magnolia frowned. Her worried eyes conveyed what she couldn't say aloud. Hampton was in it, deep. Nonetheless, she ushered her daughter and grandchild back into the house.

Hampton was surprised to find a twisted frown on Cunningham's face. He slid both of his thick hands down into his front pockets, then he swayed back on his legs. That scene on the porch, Janeen holding a two-month-old infant, reminded him of the time he called on Pearl Lee and was met by Odessa holding Eric in the same way. The detective appeared discouraged. He shook his head while staring at the sidewalk as if all the answers he'd chased over the past ten months sprang right up out of the ground. "Cute family," Cunningham offered uneasily. "Hampton, would you lie to my face if I asked who the mother of that baby was in your daughter's arms?"

"Would you blast a man who corrupted your child?" Hampton asked in return.

"Hell, yeah, I would, even if he was a man of the goddamned cloth." Captain Cunningham holstered his handcuffs. He looked over the neatly cut green lawn and then took in the fresh coat of white paint on the house. "This is very nice, very respectable, indeed. Looks like I've had my sights on the wrong man after all. I figure those federal boys were right. Guess they'll have to keep hunting for white bank robbers who croaked a wayward preacher for getting in the way. You're in the clear, but it's probably not a good idea to come around my neck of the woods." Cunningham tilted his hat back and headed toward his car.

"Cunningham. You're a good man, and don't you let nobody tell you different."

"Opinions vary, Hampton, opinions vary. I'll be sure to tell Archie Mouton you said hey. He'll like knowing you kept your end of the deal. Take care of your family. So long now."

"So long."

Hampton retrieved the forged documents from his car after Detective Cunningham made his way out of his life for good. He explained to Magnolia what happened and how it was all over. There would be no more looking behind them in grocery stores or using hand signals before getting into the car to indicate whether she was being followed or not. It was a load off the entire family. Joyce had a new last name and the proper documentation to begin her freshman year of high school. Janeen was fearful of the other junior high school kids teasing her about having a child. Hampton read over the birth certificate, which named him as the father of Janeen's baby, whom they called Sissy, and it listed Magnolia as the mother. Furthermore, he explained that no one must ever know any different in order to dissolve the link between their bright future and sullied past. Silence was the key to locking the door on family history, put away but not soon forgotten.

Later that same evening, Hampton handed Magnolia a crisp hundred-dollar bill. He sent her and his daughters to the market with one demand: not to bring home a single nickel in change. He tried to feel good about the narrow escape his life had become and the pain that riffed through the lives of people he cared for. It was very tempting to sit back and laugh it all away, like he'd done many times as a younger man hustling and having nothing to show for it afterward but a mean hangover. Hampton assumed it would take a number of years to come to grips with decisions he'd made and the chances taken, each leading him to the point of no return. He peeled back the tab on a can of beer, thinking how good it felt to relax for a change with the idea of moving forward finally on the horizon.

Hampton opened the daily newspaper and spread it across the kitchen table. When there was a knock at the door, Hampton assumed it was his family returning from the market with armfuls of bags and giggles to match. He rushed over to open it. In less than the time it took to blink, his yesterdays came crashing in again.

"Well, look at that. You are a sight for sore eyes. What's the matter, Swagger, aren't you gonna invite in an old pal?"

"Sure, Bones. Come on in," Hampton answered soberly. His labored grin wore on him like a toothache. "How you been?" he added, careful not to disrespect the gun in Bones's waistband.

"Been tired, Swagger, tired of looking for you." Bones wiped his feet politely then glided into the modest wood-frame house. He gave the den a once-over and stared at the open can of beer resting on the kitchen table. "Almost caught up to you in Houston, but the feds scared you off before I could stop in and say hello. I kept on their heels expecting them to show me where you went. Riley Dobbs sold you out the first time he got his hand slapped by the new chief. I told you he wasn't no friend to you. A bunch of special agents knowing just where to locate you in south Texas proved me right. Me, I like Houston. It reminds me of home. This house and this city are both a bit too slow and predictable for me." Bones stuck a fresh cigar in his mouth and proceeded to chew on it. He made a broad gesture for Hampton to crack open another beer at the kitchen table. "Man, this is nice, I'll grant you that. This ain't no slave shack," he added, in an insensitive tone. "I see why you was in such a hurry to run off." Bones rambled on about old haunts, new beginnings, and a man keeping his word or else.

Hampton listened attentively, wishing he'd never met Bones. Eventually, he voiced the question burning a hole in his throat. "How'd you find me after them government boys gave up looking?"

Shifting his weight at the table, Bones leaned back in order to access his pistol a lot faster if the need arose. "Remember the night we met on the bayou road? We agreed on one thing that night. Remember? Remember the promise we made about crawfishing on a deal?"

"Yeah." Hampton sighed reluctantly. "We said it'd get gritty if one of us backed out or sidestepped on making good."

"So you didn't forget?"

"Naw, and I got the money I shorted you." Hampton reached into his pocket for his billfold. "What is it, about seventy... eighty?"

Bones slammed his fist against the kitchen table spilling the can of beer. "You think I'd come all this way over a few bucks? Huh? After all we've been through together, I thought you knew me better than that. Maybe this new outlook you got or this dandy house must've fogged up your brain." He sneered at Hampton, daring him to say otherwise. "You promised me blood. You said you'd get Riley Dobbs but you didn't. That greedy toad is still breathing, and there's not a scratch on him. You can make this right. You can run on back home with me, pop Riley's fat ass, sit down to some blackened swordfish and étouffée at Galatoire's, then still be home in time for Santa Claus to coming sliding down the chimney."

Hampton eyed the stream of beer that had begun to puddle on the floor. He stroked his chin with the back of his hand, hoping Magnolia didn't return home before he'd had the chance to tidy up. "I appreciate the things you did for me, the help you gave, but this is where our association ends, Bones. I'm done doing wrong."

"Oh, no, that's a fine how do you do! I was there when you didn't have the gall to get away from the law at Rudolph's gaming house. I convinced you to get in the car and tear ass down that back road. That other time, you was a sniveling bitch, hiding in Councilman Boyette's closet that night he came home dressed like a beauty queen. You wanted to gut him, I saw it in your eyes, but it was me who geared up the nerve to slice and dice him for all he'd done back at the Boys' Home. Don't fool yourself, pal, without me, you're half the man you think you are. That's some gratitude. Don't forget I made you." Bones stood up and pointed at Hampton in a crazed, hysterical manner. "If it wasn't for me working deals with Mouton, your wife and sister would have starved while they had you locked up. Mouton was thinking of hanging all of those murders around your neck until he met me. Oh, yeah, you're either all the way in or you're all the way dead."

"Let me clean up this mess before," Hampton mumbled nervously. He turned toward a row of drawers, opening each one and fumbling through it. In the back of the last one, he found what he'd been searching for. Hampton whirled around to face Bones with a black .38 special gripped tightly in his palm. Bones was waiting. He steadied his pistol with an assuring smile.

"So this is how it goes down," said Bones. "I put a good proposition on the table and you pull a piece on me. Not such a good way to treat a visitor." He licked his dry lips then inched away from the table, all the while keeping a bead on Hampton. "I can't say I'm surprised you have to be convinced again. You shoot me then I pop you, who's gonna spend all that money you took from the Newberry cracker box bank? Yeah, I know about the money you made off with. Blasting rocks at that prison camp was good for something after all."

Hampton watched Bones carefully. For the first time, he seemed to lack the iron determination he'd always exhibited before. Hampton was stocked full of resolve. The time had come to guide his own path for a change, on his terms, even if it meant grave consequences. "I played the fool for you long enough. I helped you kill them men who raped and beat your little brother to death. Yeah, we all got secrets. Ivory told me about you, his hero. He knew I could talk when we was locked up, but he never once tried to make me. Maybe he just wanted somebody to listen to him. He was scared all the time, you know, and he hated the night more than anything because that's when they took him from his cell and did very bad things to him. He told me how he wished you'd make them fellas pay for hurting him. I figured that's why you took his name after he died. I missed him, too. Far as I can tell, you and me both have seen more than our share of pain."

"That's the way you see it?" Bones chuckled. He clicked the hammer back on his gun. "You prepared to die for a debt? Blood for blood?"

Hampton flashed a sorrowful grin at the man he'd called friend and swallowed hard. "I've been beat by the police, thrown into jail because of you. I've been hunted like a mad dog. My youngest daughter's saddled with a bastard child, the seed planted in God's house. Yeah, the way I see it, my debt's been paid and then some." Hampton's gaze drifted toward the floor as if weighted down by misery. "This is such a mess."

Besieged by second thoughts, Bones lowered his gun. "I didn't think what you owed me was worth dying for."

Hampton's eyes floated up to find Bones vulnerable, hesitant. He blinked twice, each time blasting Bones in the chest. Exploding muzzle flashes added fiery exclamations to the end of his life. Hampton exhaled matter-of-factly then fell to his knees. Writhing in anguish on the floor, Bones grimaced. He grunted three words and passed away silently with his mouth cocked opened. "Yes, Bones," Hampton replied evenly. "Blood for blood. Yours over mine."

42

Now What?

Later that night, Magnolia pushed the door open when her knocks went unanswered. She noticed a faint odor that reminded her of something she'd rather forget. Magnolia made a valiant attempt at ignoring the hint of gunpowder resonating in her nostrils. She threw a load of bags on the kitchen counter then shouted Hampton's name. Her daughters looked on pensively as she eyed a fancy felt hat resting on the countertop next to the open drawer that Hampton used to hide one of many guns placed around the house. Suddenly, Magnolia raced through the house. She searched each room praying she wouldn't find her husband's body slumped over like Father O'Leary's after she killed him. The smell of gunpowder was eerily ominous.

After hearing a rustling sound behind the house, Magnolia flicked the light switch and wandered cautiously onto the back porch. She gasped when her eyes found Hampton kneeling on the ground and covered in blood. She ran to his defense. "Baby, you all right?"

Hampton winced as he wiped his sweaty forehead with the back of his soiled sleeve. "Hey, keep it low. I'm fine. Don't fret all this," he asserted, speaking of his ghastly appearance. "This blood ain't none of mine."

Taken aback by the gory scene, a plastic blue tarp covering the freshly dug mound of dirt, Magnolia gestured for the girls to get back in the house and close the door. "He's all right, just cut himself a little. Go on and put the bags away. Be there in a minute." Both girls did as they were told after similar prodding from Hampton.

"Your mama's right. I'm okay. Can't wait to see what y'all bought at the market. Go on now."

As soon as they closed the door, Magnolia peered to both sides then threw her hands up. "You had me terrified that something bad happened to you," she ranted. "There's a fancy hat on the kitchen counter and there's a new Cadillac pulled into the garage. What you been up to?"

After wiping his brow again, Hampton glanced at the tarp stretched across a patch of troubled earth. "Been saying good-bye to an old friend. Bones drove all this way to look me up. He had it in his mind to put me to work again." Hampton shushed his wife when her lips parted to comment. "Uhhh, don't bother. He said some things. I said some things. This here," he remarked softly while knocking dirt from the shovel, "is how the discussion ended."

"I'm sick of the blood and the moving around, all the time afraid somebody's gonna find us," said Magnolia, a single tear streaming down her cheek.

"Everybody who's had a notion to look already has. I expect we're in the clear now. Hopefully, that'll be the case for good." Hampton tried to put on a steady smile, but it fell flat under the strain of circumstances.

"So what happens now?" she asked, somewhat relieved.

"Don't really know. But for the first time in my life, I get to take as long as I want to decide."

Magnolia Hampton
4512 Lamar Ave.
Dallas, TX 75237

December 21, 1971
Magnolia,

I'm so glad y'all made it to somewhere safe. Is Texas really as big as they say? You'll have to write me back real soon and tell me all about it. Newberry is never going to be the same since y'all left. Sheriff Killeen came by the next morning after y'all skinned out. He was asking all kinds of questions then kicked in your cottage door. They spent a lot of time looking for something. The next day, the newspaper said the state bank was robbed of $150,000 and they had some idea of who took it. After about two weeks or so they stopped talking about it altogether like it never happened. A runt-built white cop came from New Orleans and wanted to know more than what he'd already heard about Father O'Leary messing with little girls. He took one look at Odessa's boy then I didn't have to say another word to him. He scooted off like a child on a tricycle. I ain't seen him after that.

I'm glad you changed your names, in case they come around looking for Hampton, I mean Julian. The colored girls, here in town, are safer now. In all, more than twenty of them had been tricked by the priests, who told the police they were in on it together. Strange, how it still makes no sense to me. Thank you from the bottom of all our hearts for sending that dog back where he came from, to hell on a bullet. I never said it because I ain't one for getting mushy but I love you like a sister, Magnolia, always did. Please take care of you and yours. Odessa is a handful and Eric is getting so big. He's walking now and everything.

Well, this is where I get off as they say. Let's keep in touch like we promised. I'll be looking for your next letter. Kiss the girls for me.

Signed,

Pearl Lee Baptiste

Reading Group Guide

1. What did you enjoy/despise about Ivory "Bones" Arcineaux's character?
2. Did Hampton become a better man because of his relationship with Bones? Why or why not?
3. Which secret in the story was the most compelling? Why?
4. How did you feel about Pearl Lee Baptiste and her long-term affair with Trotter Delacroix?
5. Do you think Trotter was responsible for killing Toussaint Baptiste?
6. Was Mr. Ransom Delacroix responsible for the death of Hampton's father?
7. Was Magnolia justified in killing the priest, Father O'Leary? Why or why not?
8. What did you think of plantation justice after learning about Sadie's body planted underneath Pearl Lee's floor?
9. Did Pearl Lee treasure her love for Trotter more than the opportunity to start over with Hampton and Magnolia?
10. What did you think of Bones's plan to murder several men, implicate Hampton, then get Detective Mouton to help carry it out?

11. Why do you think Odessa, Janeen, and Joyce all kept quiet about the priest?
12. Should Hampton have taken Magnolia away from the plantation after his release from prison?
13. Do you believe that Bones had to die in order for Hampton's family to survive?
14. What was behind Detective Cunningham's decision to let Hampton go?
15. Is protecting some secrets worth dying for? Are any worth killing to keep?
16. If you were filming this movie, who would you cast as Hampton, Magnolia, Bones, Pearl Lee, Toussaint, Detective Mouton, and Trotter?

About the Author

Essence bestselling author VICTOR MCGLOTHIN is a former bank vice president who nearly forfeited an athletic scholarship due to poor reading skills. Ultimately, he overcame that obstacle and later completed a master's degree in human relations and business. Victor is also an online columnist of Victor Said?, a real brotha-to-sistah look at relationships.

Victor lives in Dallas with his wife and two sons.